THE FALLEN ARCHITECT

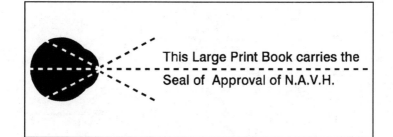

This Large Print Book carries the
Seal of Approval of N.A.V.H.

THE FALLEN ARCHITECT

CHARLES BELFOURE

WHEELER PUBLISHING
A part of Gale, a Cengage Company

GALE
A Cengage Company

Farmington Hills, Mich • San Francisco • New York • Waterville, Maine
Meriden, Conn • Mason, Ohio • Chicago

Copyright © 2018 by Charles Belfoure.
Wheeler Publishing, a part of Gale, a Cengage Company.

Wheeler Publishing Large Print Hardcover.
The text of this Large Print edition is unabridged.
Other aspects of the book may vary from the original edition.
Set in 16 pt. Plantin.

**LIBRARY OF CONGRESS CIP DATA ON FILE.
CATALOGUING IN PUBLICATION FOR THIS BOOK
IS AVAILABLE FROM THE LIBRARY OF CONGRESS**

ISBN-13: 978-1-4328-5876-6 (hardcover)

Published in 2018 by arrangement with Sourcebooks, Inc.

Printed in Mexico
1 2 3 4 5 6 7 23 22 21 20 19 18

The Britannia Fatalities

Denys Blair, 78
Ronald Cass, 52
James Croyden, 37
Robert Davidson, 12
Shirley Finney, 19
Daphne Foster, 46
Ted Hardy, 44
John Mapes, 41
Isabel Massey, 14
Hugh Rice, 53
Sir John Richardson, 54
Jocelyn Shipway, 31
Trevor Stanton, 42
Sibyl Treadwell, 36

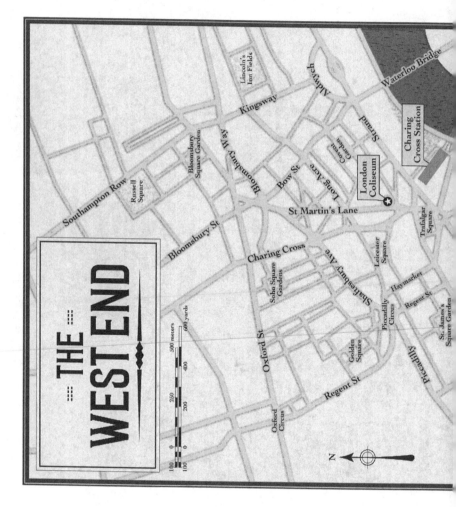

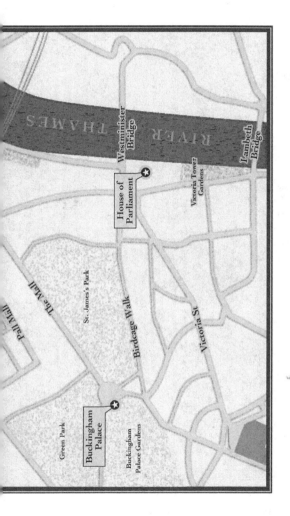

PROLOGUE

England, 1905

"I didn't kill all those people . . . *It wasn't me.*"

Tears welling up in his eyes, Layton pointed the electric torch at the thin, gold wedding band in the palm of his hand.

He smiled and placed the ring in his pocket, then shone the light again on the skeleton from whose finger he had taken the ring.

"I don't know why you did this to me, Peter. But thank you for giving me back my life."

1

"I was outside a lunatic asylum one day,
      busy picking up stones
When along came a lunatic and said to me,
      'Good morning, Mr. Jones;
Oh, how much a week do you get for doing
      that?'
'Thirty bob,' I cried."

"There ain't no finer music hall star than Jimmy Doyle, lads, not in the whole bleedin' world," Jim Sheffield yelled.

His two boys didn't hear their father. They were too caught up in Jimmy's performance, playing out on the brightly lit stage below. Like every member of the audience, the boys were stomping and singing along to his famous rendition of "Come Inside, You Silly Bugger."

It delighted Jim to see Clive and Edward enjoying themselves so much. Wasn't that what being a father was all about, bringing joy to your children? And they wouldn't be boys for long. Soon, they'd have to deal with all the harsh shite that came with being grown-up. So what was the harm in it, taking them to a brand-new London music hall on its opening night? It was something they'd never ever forget.

To hell with his wife, complaining about the one-quid admission for the dress circle. The fancy first-balcony level was worth every penny. Jim remembered his granny, who could scarcely afford it, taking him weekly to the Norwich Hippodrome. Two hours with amazing people who could make you laugh till you cried — she'd always believed that was worth missing a meal or a pint.

And what a place! The new Britannia Empire was beautiful, Jim thought, looking up at the huge domed ceiling. Real electric lights twinkled above him like stars in the night sky. The elegant white plasterwork on the face of the horseshoe-tier balconies that wrapped around the theatre reminded him of crème frosting on a wedding cake. Plush, red velvet, soft as a kitten, covered the seats. When the audience had filed in, they'd been so taken with the beauty of the interior that *they'd actually cheered and applauded the theatre itself.* The Britannia was bloody magical.

> "He looked at me and shook his head,
> And this is what he cried,
> 'What, thirty bob a week, with a wife and
>   kids to keep?
> Come inside, you silly bugger, come
>   inside.' "

Jimmy, who wore baggy checked trousers, a red derby, and a long, blue satin frock coat, started kicking out his gangly legs, dancing back and forth across the stage. The orchestra picked up on the excitement and played louder and faster, delighting the crowd, which sang louder and stamped their feet harder and faster. Jimmy, the music hall legend, had that special skill to make the audience feel like they were part of what was going on onstage. He had the house in the palm of his hand, and he loved it.

Jim playfully slapped Clive's back, and the boy beamed at his father.

> " 'Come inside, you silly bugger, come
>   inside.
> You ought to have a bit more sense.
> Working for a living? Take my tip;
> Act a little screwy and become a lunatic.

Oh, you get your meals regular, and a
      brand-new suit besides.
Thirty bob a week, no wife and kids to
      keep.
Come inside, you silly bugger, come
      inside.' "

The orchestra played even louder, the brass section pounding away furiously. To keep the momentum going, they launched into another chorus.

That's when Jim felt a slight vibration in the bottoms of his shoes. It traveled through the heavy leather soles into his feet like an electrical current. He looked about and saw other patrons staring down in bewilderment. Clive and Edward were doing the same, with puzzled looks on their faces. And all the while, the orchestra and Doyle played on.

An ear-splitting crack sounded, as though someone had crashed cymbals next to Jim's ears. The house lights flickered, and the high-pitched screech of bending steel filled the air, adding to the terrible cacophony. Just as Jim's panic-stricken eyes met his sons', the floor collapsed beneath him. He dropped like a rock, Clive and Edward plummeting alongside, their arms flailing above their shoulders.

Now, instead of a happy, raucous song, nonstop screaming filled the theatre.

A half hour later, Douglas Layton stood across Shaftesbury Avenue. Feeling as though he were trapped in an unending nightmare, he watched the police carry body after body out of the Britannia Empire Theatre — the music hall he had designed.

2

"One brown tweed suit with waistcoat, white shirt, collar, tie, one pair of brown Dunham shoes with black socks — all of which you're wearing now. One gold watch and fob, one house key, one man's comb, one silk handkerchief, one photo in a silver frame, one gold cigarette case, fifty-eight pounds in notes, and five bob in coins. Sign here that these items have been returned to your person."

Douglas Layton stared at the pen the prison officer had just dipped in the inkwell. Slowly, he reached across the battered wooden counter, took it in hand, and scratched his name across the form.

"That'll do ya, mate. Proceed out that door to the right. The alley'll lead you to the public thoroughfare — and mind you don't leave England."

Layton turned and shuffled toward the plate iron door. A blast of cold drizzle hit him in the face. Pausing, he gathered his jacket collar up around his neck. Staring down at the gray granite paving blocks, he began walking.

After twenty yards, the alley intersected a deserted road. He stopped and looked to his right, then his left. In both directions, brown gravel stretched through wet, green countryside to the horizon. It didn't matter which turn he took, he thought. Either way led to a frightening and terrible future.

Before he made up his mind, Douglas Layton turned to face the place that had been his home for the last five years. Mulcaster Prison. He had never looked closely at its exterior. The day he had arrived in the fall of 1900, his head had hung low in shame. Now he saw — with an architect's eye — that the place was well designed, all imposing stone walls topped with crenellations and punctuated with towers. A Crusader castle adapted for penal servitude. It gave the public reassurance that the felons inside could never get out and kill them in their sleep. Its design did its job beautifully, making the inmates feel less than human, as if they deserved to be there.

Prisons, Layton thought grimly, were designed by people who had never been in one. He must drop a line to the architect,

Sir Laurence Chance, a former colleague in the Royal Institute of British Architects, to tell him how magnificent his design was. He could imagine Chance's expression: he'd drop the note in disgust, as if a dead rat had been placed in his hand.

Layton had known when he'd opened the door of the prison that there would be no one waiting for him. His wife, Edwina, had filed for divorce and left with their four-year-old son, Ronald, just six months after he entered Mulcaster. He knew everyone else would shun him too, even his closest friends and colleagues. Neither they nor his wife had ever come to visit him. But he couldn't blame them; British society had ironclad rules, and one was this: don't associate with an outcast. Layton had become a social leper. To avoid him infecting all he knew, years of friendship and family were thrown to the winds, as if he'd never existed.

Without thinking about it, Layton jammed his hands in his pockets and turned left. England's high-security prisons were always built in the countryside. Mulcaster stood in the middle of Lincolnshire in the East Midlands, which meant a long hike to a village or any other semblance of civilization. It was just ten in the morning; there was plenty of daylight left. With no future ahead,

Layton saw no reason to hurry. He slowed his pace — and felt a hard blow on the top of his head.

Another missile flew past his ear. He ducked instinctively, touched his hair to see if there was blood.

"I've been waitin' for this day, you murderin' bastard. I swore to Christ I'd be here!"

Layton whirled and saw the woman, standing just five yards away. She was in her forties, had hair tied in a bun and a dark frock under a black coat. His first thought was that she was drunk or mad, but as he took in her stern expression, Layton realized he was mistaken. He watched, bewildered, as she picked up another rock and cocked her arm to throw.

"You bloody bastard!" she cried. "You killed me daughter. Twelve was all she was. Me only child. Crushed to death by you, you goddamn monster!"

The woman hurled the stone, which sailed over Layton's head.

"I was supposed to go that night!" she screamed. "Did you know that? But I got the woman cramps, so I gave the ticket to me sister to take Isabelle. She'd bin lookin' forward to it for so long. I dinna want to disappoint her. And now she's dead."

19

The woman fell to her knees in the road and doubled over, shrieking as though she'd been stabbed in the stomach.

"I ain't got nobody now . . . Nobody!"

Layton cringed and ran like a beaten dog with his tail between his legs, the woman's screams ringing in his ears.

"Murderer! They shoulda hanged ya. You don't deserve to live, you miserable bag of shite!"

3

In prison, Layton had been surprised to discover that no one asked about the crimes an inmate had committed. It was a man's own business. If he wanted to talk about it, that was fine, but a person was never asked. This came as a great relief to him, as he'd been convicted of killing fourteen people and injuring scores more.

He was scared to death in his first days, sure he'd be beaten or killed. But nothing happened. Murderers, rapists, thieves, extortionists, pedophiles — in Mulcaster, no one seemed to care. It wasn't as if his fellow inmates didn't know who he was. His name and photograph had run in newspapers around the globe for months, beneath lurid headlines about the Britannia Empire Theatre disaster. It was all people talked about. But to the other prisoners, it wasn't a "regular" murder. Not like knifing a fellow in a pub fight or shooting your wife and her lover in bed. This had just been an accident. Most of the men with whom he'd served his time didn't understand why he'd been convicted.

But Layton did. Day after day in courtroom five of the Old Bailey, the prosecution had accused him of being an incompetent architect, of incorrectly designing the steel trusses that had supported the Britannia's balconies. Through his carelessness, those fourteen people, including two children, had been crushed to death. Among the many injured, twelve had lost arms or legs. One man's skull was so fractured that he never recovered; the accident left him with the mind of a five-year-old. The severity of their injuries meant many could no longer earn a living.

Sir John Chichester, the chief prosecutor, described every injury in gruesome detail, showing photos of bodies so mangled that some jury members were sickened; one actually fled the courtroom to throw up. Witness after witness described that terrible night, the joy of experiencing opening night at the theatre turned in a millisecond to tragedy. Some wore stoic expressions. Some cried when they described the feeling of falling, of smashing into the floor and screaming desperately for help.

A man named Sheffield broke down when he described his son, Clive, a talented footballer who'd lost his leg. Jimmy Doyle, the music hall star, took the box and, with tears in his eyes, described the carnage he'd seen from the stage.

Layton's barrister withered under the assault. By the second day, he'd all but given up. On the witness stand, Layton tried to tell the court that the cantilevered balcony trusses had been designed correctly, with a safety factor two and a half times stronger than what was needed. As an architect, he explained passionately, safety was an essential feature of his designs. The Victoria Hall disaster in 1883, where 183 panicked children were trampled to death while trying to get down to the stage for free toys given out after the performance, had shocked the British public. In its wake, the London County Council enacted strict new building codes. Layton made the Britannia's hallways and stairs wider than required, allowing the audience at every level to exit in a speedy, orderly manner at the first sign of danger. He used a newly invented "panic door," which couldn't be locked from the inside. Mindful of the horrible fire at the Exeter Theatre Royal — 186 people dead in 1887 — he used newly available asbestos fabric to fireproof the great theatre curtain.

No one believed him. He couldn't prove that Shaw Construction Ltd., the general contractor, had erected the steelwork incorrectly; upon examination, the surviving trusses passed muster, and the steel fabricator swore that everything had been manufactured to exact specifications. Layton was vilified in the press, called the greatest murderer in British history. *The Butcher of the West End.* The newspapers made it seem as if the entire horseshoe-shaped first balcony had collapsed when, in reality, only a front section fifteen feet in width had failed.

The architect passed the ten-day trial in a dazed, dreamlike state. By the end, he believed himself guilty. Somehow, *he* was responsible for the death and destruction that night. He, and no one else. One of England's best architects had become a mass murderer.

Like the woman on the road, many Britons were outraged when Layton received only five years' hard labor. A man stealing sixpence from a tobacconist shop got put away for five years too. The papers howled for weeks. It was because Layton was a *gentleman* with friends in high places, they claimed. He should have been hanged.

But they didn't understand. The punishment wasn't just five years. It was daily torment for the rest of Layton's life. A day didn't pass when thoughts of the Britannia didn't crush him to earth, like a huge boulder dropping out of the sky. Visions of the two dead children were an especial torment; again and again, he saw their smashed bodies being carried out of the theatre. He agreed with the woman on the road. If only they had hanged him!

The day before his transfer from London to Mulcaster, Layton had tried to kill himself. In his cell, he cut strips of cloth from the underside of his musty mattress and formed them into a noose. Only the thought of his wife, Edwina, and his son, Ronald, stayed his hand. When they vanished from his life after only six months, the thoughts of suicide returned. But each time Layton was on the verge of carrying it out, he couldn't bring himself to do it. As far-fetched as it seemed, he believed it was still possible to hold his son in his arms again. Losing his wife, whom he loved with all his heart, was a terrible blow, but the loss of Ronald was almost as crushing as the guilt over the disaster. He thought of him constantly, but the one unforgettable memory of his son was seeing him run through a field of red poppies one summer at their home in Surrey. Barely taller than the flowers, Ronald crashed through them with joy. Layton ran that one image through his mind thousands of times in prison. It never failed to bring a smile to his face, maybe the only time he did manage a smile in Mulcaster. He knew he was probably fooling himself about seeing his son again, but that was what they called hope, and it had prevented him from killing himself at least half a dozen times. Hope was what kept a man alive in life, and especially in prison. When his prison term drew to a close, Layton thought of committing suicide upon release. He had no family, friends, or profession. A dark, terrifying void awaited him. Why go on? But again, the thought of seeing Ronald kept him going, irrational as it seemed.

Layton walked slowly along the gravel road, looking at the farm fields that ran along both sides toward the horizon. He reached into his jacket pocket and took out the corn muffin he had smuggled out from his last prison breakfast this morning. Climbing over a low rubble wall, Layton found a place to sit under an elm tree. It was a sheer delight to sit on the grass and savor the muffin, chewing slowly, holding the flavorful crumbs on the tongue. After being in prison, the simplest of pleasures were wonderful. More than that, it was the feeling of being in an open field all by himself. There was no such thing as privacy in prison. One was constantly surrounded and watched by others, stuck in a six-by-eight-foot cell with another human.

Finishing the muffin, Layton lay flat on his back and gazed up into the bright-blue morning sky. A few wispy clouds drifted by. He closed his eyes, took long, deep breaths, and exhaled slowly. When some twenty minutes had passed, Layton rose, made his way back to the road, and started walking west. Except for a passing farmworker with a rake on his shoulder, he had the road to himself. At an intersection of the road was a weathered sign that read WRAGBY — 5 MILES. This town may have a railway station, he thought.

Only when he heard a faint sound in the distance did his head lift up. The murmuring roar was like the growling of an animal. It increased in volume; curiosity won out, and he turned.

On the horizon line in the middle of the road, a small, squat object was coming toward him. Layton stood, mesmerized. At about two hundred yards, he recognized the source of the noise and smiled. It was a horseless carriage. In 1900, when he'd been sent to prison, they had still been extremely rare, more likely to be seen in France or Germany than in England. Although he'd seen pictures, he had never encountered one in person or known anybody who owned one. Not even his rich clients had such a thing. Besides terrifying horses, they were said to be very unreliable. Often, in an ironic twist, horses had to tow a broken-down horseless carriage to a mechanic.

But now, standing at the side of the road, he could see the oncoming vehicle roaring along without trouble, its engine humming steadily. Layton loved anything mechanical, and the machine hurtling down the road fascinated him. It was bright red; its thick rubber wheels had matching red spokes and no top. The driver wore goggles and a long, tan coat and was holding on to the thick wooden wheel with gloved hands. At the front of the carriage were two shiny brass headlights; a sculpted metal ornament was situated atop the engine.

As the machine drove past, the driver twisted his head at Layton and slowed to a stop.

Layton trotted over.

"Hello there. Need a lift, old chap?" the man shouted over the roar of the engine.

Layton nodded.

The driver opened the side door.

"Jolly good of you to stop," shouted Layton.

"Glad to help," said the driver, his eyes fixed on the road.

"This is quite a machine," Layton shouted as they took off.

"It's a Darracq Flying Fifteen from France. Runs like a top."

The feeling of the rushing wind exhilarated Layton. They must have been traveling at least thirty miles an hour! The countryside flew by in a blur; he felt an unfamiliar smile crease his face.

"Motoring's my passion, but you have to watch out these days. Constables are setting speed traps, fining you a quid for going too fast." The driver snorted. "Can you believe that nonsense?"

"It's bloody amazing. These things will put the horses out to pasture," Layton yelled over the roar of the engine.

"I hope so. Be far less shit and piss on the roads!"

"Any English cars?"

"I hear a fellow named Rolls is coming out with one."

"We live in remarkable times," said Layton, touching the metalwork of the vehicle.

"Yes. Soon, we'll be flying these things in the air." The driver saw Layton's look of disbelief and laughed. " 'S true! Two American brothers have created a glider with an engine! It can stay up in the air for a good long time. Before you know it, we'll all be flying about like birds."

In prison, Layton had been entirely cut off from the world. Such isolation was part of his punishment; it was as if he'd lived on one of Jupiter's moons. Martians, like those in H. G. Wells's *War of the Worlds*, could have conquered Earth, and he'd have been the last to know. To think, flying machines had been invented! What else had he missed?

"So you've never heard of the Wright brothers?" the man asked.

"No," Layton said and hesitated. "I've been away for a bit."

The driver glanced over at him. Even with his clothes hidden beneath his motoring outfit, Layton could tell he was an English gentleman, born and bred. He would be far too polite to ask another gentleman why he was out walking on the road.

"How far are you going?" he asked instead.

"Wragby."

"I turn off about a mile before."

"That's fine. So good of you to give me a lift."

"Please," the driver said. "Think nothing of it."

4

As Layton walked the short distance to Wragby, he fumbled about inside his trouser pockets. Among the coins, he felt a house key. A deep sense of gloom descended upon him as he stared at it.

The key to his house. His beloved house, designed so lovingly for his family. Every square inch calibrated to his personal satisfaction.

The wonderful thing about an architect designing his own home was that he didn't have to answer to anyone. Usually, he had to get the client's approval for every aspect of his design. Was this window style all right? Was the shape of the roof to their liking? They were paying for it, after all; they had the right. But when he built his own house, the architect had only to please himself. Every idea could be tried. The smallest detail could be included. No one could order him about. And his house in

West Surrey had been the house of his dreams.

Layton remembered the wonderful day it was finished, standing before it with Edwina and Ronald. The rooms were spacious; the ceilings, high. The windows looked out onto a gorgeous garden designed by Daphne Scott-Thomas, the greatest gardener in England. Layton had enjoyed his home for only two years, but they had been wonderful, especially the Christmas celebrations with his boy. And Edwina's garden parties were some of the most popular society events of the summer season. In 1899, *Country Life Illustrated* even wrote a long article about one of them, including many photos of the house, which led to some new commissions. Layton never tired of compliments on his design, especially from fellow architects; that praise meant the most to him. He had even won an award from the Royal Institute of British Architects. The framed and engraved certificate was no doubt moldering away now in some Surrey trash heap.

In his tiny shared cell in Mulcaster, Layton used to close his eyes and transport himself to the house. In his mind, he walked through its great rooms and garden. He experienced every square foot — the stonework, the paneling, the oak plank floors, the high ceilings. It helped keep his sanity intact during those long five years.

Now the house belonged to someone else. Convicted felons in England gave up their right to property. When the house became part of the divorce settlement with Edwina, there was nothing he could do. Layton's only satisfaction was that the money from the sale would eventually go to Ronald. His son had loved the house, especially when running through its wide, long halls, dragging a length of string that his orange-striped cat, Leo, chased after. He hoped that when Edwina left with the boy, she took Leo with them. It always gave Layton a warm feeling at night to see the cat snuggled in the covers, asleep with Ronald.

To his right, a stream paralleled the road before meandering off into the fields. Layton walked down the bank to its edge. He looked at the brass key once more, then threw it into the slow-flowing stream with a flick of his wrist. It made a faint *kerplunk* sound when it hit the surface. For a moment, Layton stared at the spot where it had sunk. Then he continued on his way.

About fifteen minutes later, the spires of a square, neo-Gothic church tower appeared over the tops of the trees in the distance.

He was almost to Wragby. All market towns in the English countryside had at least one church, which towered over the small cluster of buildings below.

Taking shelter behind a huge tree some ten yards off the road, Layton began an accounting of his capital. Damned lucky, he thought, that he'd forgotten to empty his pockets before he entered prison. The fifty-eight pounds and five shillings made up every last cent he had in the world. This, for a man who'd earned at least five thousand per annum for the past six years. It was what an underbutler on a country estate would make in a year. He knew it would not last long.

Pocketing the cash, Layton walked back to the road. There were more people out now. He saw a couple driving a horse cart, a man on a bicycle. Once in town, he leisurely strolled past the shops, then stood in the doorway of a butcher and watched with great curiosity as the villagers passed by. He hadn't seen ordinary people in five years. A man in brown tweeds and a derby, a woman in a green dress with a scarlet shawl, an old man doddering along on a cane — each had a story, a life full of complications, happiness, and disappointment. What had their lives been like during the time he was in prison? Layton wondered. His jaw tightened. No matter how terrible their sadness and suffering, they had had their freedom. They could come and go as they pleased.

From the right, two young girls came skipping across the road. Of perhaps ten or twelve years in age, they were laughing and chattering away. One had shoulder-length chestnut hair; the other was blond, her locks tied with red ribbons. The second Layton laid eyes on them, his mind snapped like a light switch to the night of the disaster. He saw anew the limp body of a young girl being carried out of the theatre, her long hair hanging over the edge of the canvas stretcher. Perhaps the daughter of the woman outside the prison. A sick feeling swept over Layton; he clasped the corner of the storefront till his knuckles went white. Behind the stone walls of Mulcaster Prison, he had been cut off from the real world. Though the disaster haunted him, there were no sudden jolting reminders of the death he had caused. He turned his head as the girls passed, hoping it would lessen the pain. It didn't.

Layton sat on a bench outside the shop, breathing heavily, his head bent to the stone sidewalk. Directly across the road was a pub called the Yellow Dog, and he made his way to it. It was a Saturday afternoon, and the village pub was crowded with people laughing, joking, and enjoying themselves. When he'd entered the pub, he'd feared everyone would recognize him, that a hush would descend upon the rowdy room. But not a single person noticed. He took his pint to the farthest corner anyway, claiming a small table well out of view. At any moment, he felt, someone's eyes might lock on him, a flicker of recognition might spark. He could hear the whispers now: "Blimey, isn't that Layton, the Butcher of the West End?" People would stare in disbelief, then attack him with fists and bottles.

But somehow, after four hours in the pub, nothing happened. The stout tasted wonderful. Layton ordered pint after pint, prompting the barmaid, who had seen her share of drinking, to comment that he was making the Guinness family even richer today. In prison, he'd forgotten a chief attribute of alcohol: it dulled the mind, made you forget your troubles and feel happy. There were times in Mulcaster when he'd wished he could tear off the top of his skull, reach in with his hands, and rip out the horrible memories. Now, thankfully, he had alcohol to rid him of the torment.

Layton kept drinking and drinking. Each swallow made it easier to forget. At closing time, the publican shoved his near-unconscious body into the street. Totally plastered, he staggered through the streets until he found the railway station, then passed out in a doorway of a grocer directly across the road. He didn't know that a man who had followed him from the pub was standing over him. The burly man backed away, then took a running start and swung his black, hobnailed boot into Layton's stomach.

5

When the dawn came, Layton stirred and opened his eyes, which felt as if they had been glued shut. The first thing he saw was a blurry image of the Wragby railroad station across the street. People were milling about, meaning it was now open. As he rose to his feet, he felt an excruciating pain in his midsection, which caused him to plop back down to the pavement. Taking hold of the doorframe in the entry to the grocer's, he pulled himself up, groaning in pain.

Layton dragged his body into the station and purchased a ticket on the next southbound train. Out of sheer habit, he paid for a first-class seat, though third class would have been one-quarter the price. Fifteen minutes passed, which he spent stooped over on a wrought iron bench, suffering from a pounding headache and blurred vision in addition to the terrible pain in his torso, before the train rumbled up to the platform. Compared to his living accommodations for the last five years, his plush, scarlet upholstered seat in the first-class compartment felt cozy and quite luxurious. Watching the lush green countryside blur by the window soothed him and cleared the cobwebs from his head.

At Mulcaster, his cell had only a two-foot-square window that looked out over a rock-strewn dirt lot. Layton and hundreds of other inmates were sent there each day to crush stone with sledgehammers. In all his time in prison, he never laid eyes on anything verdant. Now, stone cottages, pastures full of cattle, groves of trees, and fields of rye and barley flew by. After about ten minutes, Layton turned from the window to his fellow passengers. One, a corpulent man in his fifties in a black suit who was already seated in the compartment when he boarded, was staring at him. His puzzled look said all too clearly, "Where have I seen this fellow before? The army? The club?" When he saw that Layton had caught him staring, he averted his eyes and pretended to read the *Strand Magazine* on his lap. But his eyes kept flitting up, and he was clearly racking his brain, trying to remember. Layton squirmed in his seat, realizing that every stranger he encountered now was a potential enemy who could identify him. When the conductor came to check tickets, the man began staring again. Unable to bear such intense scrutiny, Layton rose, walked out of the compartment, and found an empty one. His head leaning against the window and the rails rumbling beneath his feet, he considered his options.

Rather, it seemed as if he had only one option. He had no choice but to take on a new identity and try to start life anew. Layton smiled to himself at that thought. A false identity did not trouble him, because he'd been living under a false identity for twenty years; he was as much an English gentleman as the hogs on the farms that the train was passing. *I am a fraud,* he thought. *A charlatan who skillfully hid my common-as-dirt, working-class origins.*

The instant a child in England was brought into the world, he was placed on a rung of a tall, invisible social ladder. And there he stayed for the rest of his life. Layton's rung was located in the village of Puddletown in Dorset, a lush farming country overlooking the English Channel. More specifically, on Cherry Lane, in a thatched-roof cottage of local stone built by his father, Thomas Layton. His late mother, Fanny, was the eldest daughter of a shoemaker in Charminster, a village to the west.

While Layton's rung was solidly on the working-class — and thus lower — half of the ladder, in England, each caste had its distinct parts. Sharp and often cruel divisions existed between those who worked for themselves and those who worked for others. Thomas Layton was a master mason with his own business, albeit a small one, that employed others. He thus enjoyed superior rank. Enhancing his position further was the fact that he was a landholder; he owned a cottage and outbuildings on two acres.

In England's tight-knit rural society, the self-employed looked down on the "work-folk," especially farmworkers. They rarely intermarried or even visited each other's homes. "We don't associate with the likes of them" was a common refrain heard during Layton's boyhood in Dorset.

This was not simple snobbery but part of the system of ironclad discrimination that ruled society. England's class system was not unlike the railways, with their segregated first-, second-, and third-class seating. A man could fall down the ladder — and many did — but almost never did he climb *up*. There was always someone directly above, ready to push him down with his boot. Privilege and status were the only things that determined one's social identity, and all Englishmen knew that, down to the lowliest guttersnipe.

But as a child, these concerns had not touched Layton's mind. The Dorset countryside had been a very wonderful place to grow up. Layton thought often of those long, dreamy days playing in the fields and woods, fishing in the streams, learning the names of plant and trees. It was an idyllic rural life that had changed little from medieval times. Time was measured by the progression of annual festivals and agricultural seasons — Easter, Whitsun, Christmas, lambing time, haymaking, the harvest. Layton had developed the sort of topographical intimacy one gains only by walking everywhere, by knowing every square foot of the land: the ponds; the sandy heaths and chalky downs; the histories, quarrels, and scandals of the occupants of every cottage.

Being the son of a tradesman, he had been isolated from the harsh realities of farm life. Many laborers worked for wages so low, they could barely feed a family. Layton remembered his father telling his mother about a boy on a nearby sheep farm who'd died of starvation; at the autopsy, his shriveled stomach held only raw turnips. Farmers sent children as young as seven to work full-time in the fields.

In contrast, Layton's childhood was solitary — his two brothers were older — but happy. He was part of a close-knit family; ten generations had lived in Dorset, and hardly any had left the county. Both his grandmothers were grand storytellers, inexhaustible sources of country lore. Music was a joy for his family; dancing, singing, and the playing of instruments held important sway in their lives. Layton could still hear the sounds of his uncle's fiddle and see his mother twirling a jig in front of the fireplace. Then there were the obligatory Sunday trips to Stinsford Church, with its time-honored rituals and music of the Church of England.

Due to his family's social standing, Layton attended school, a privilege not accorded to the unfortunate children of the workfolk. From his first day in grammar school in Puddletown, he excelled. His mother and her mother had been voracious readers, and the tradition was passed on. When he showed a talent for drawing, she arranged occasional lessons from a retired schoolmistress. By age eight, he'd won many academic prizes, including a copy of Homer's *Odys-*

sey. At ten, he walked four miles daily to the British School, run by Isaac Glanfield in Greyhound Yard, Dorchester, and there he continued his academic success.

By 1880, Dorchester, a county seat and provincial market town, had expanded well beyond its original Roman fortifications to become a small city with banks, shops, government offices, and a British army garrison. Among the bustle of town, soldiers in splendid red-and-gold uniforms strolled the streets. Layton loved the energy, the change from quiet, rural Puddletown. Dorchester had several entertainment venues, including a theatre and a music hall, which he attended regularly, either alone or with his parents. When Glanfield set up a private academy for older and more advanced students, Layton was invited to attend. There he took Latin and French, read history and the classics. He discovered a wonderful world of knowledge and plunged in with vigor.

Because Layton's father had made some tiny contributions to Stinsford Church, the vicar, Reverend Donald Carter, had invited the Layton family for tea. It was at this repast that the fourteen-year-old Layton met Carter's son Ian, home from his studies at Oxford. Ian was refined, handsome, well dressed, and erudite on all subjects. Layton was completely taken by him, and that was what he decided to become: an Oxford man. He would take a history degree, and he accelerated his studies so that he might qualify for the rigorous entrance examinations at Oxford and Cambridge.

One day in his fifteenth year, Glanfield praised Layton's score on a mathematics exam. Brimming with pride, Layton told the schoolmaster that he had worked especially hard on the topic so that he might be accepted into Oxford. The smile fled Glanfield's face. With an expression of near pity, he explained the facts of British life to the boy — a day Layton would never forget.

In rapid succession, Glanfield spelled out the shortcomings in Layton's education, particularly his minimal knowledge of Greek. But the biggest blow of all was this: he was the son of a stonemason. Even if the boy were superbly trained, when he wrote the university asking permission to sit for the examination, they would reply that someone from his background would find better success in life by following his father's sensible and honorable trade.

"I once had the dream of being a university man," said Glanfield. He sighed. "And the idea was given up years ago." In those days, schoolmasters were not college trained.

Seeing the baffled look on the boy's face, he patted him on the head.

"I've given you the finest education for a boy of your *place,*" he said.

Layton well remembered the long walk back to Puddletown that day in a state of disappointment and confusion.

What Glanfield had said, he realized, his parents had known all along. The prospect of a university education was pure fantasy. Ian was the son of an Oxford-educated vicar whose own father had been to Oxford. Layton's family had the money, and yet, what he was attempting was still socially impossible. Cheeks flushing hotly, he remembered sitting in a pew in Stinsford Church listening to the vicar preach against the presumption of the lower classes who sought to rise into the ranks of the professional class. He hadn't known that applied to him too.

But his father had other plans. When Layton graduated from Glanfield's academy at sixteen, his father told him that he was to be articled for three years to John Hicks, a Dorchester architect, and trained in the architectural profession. Thomas Layton had already paid Hicks the first year's fee of forty pounds for his son's education.

Layton's mind had reeled. As a boy, he had liked to draw, especially portraits of his family and pets, but never expressed any interest in becoming an architect. But his father did the stone- and brickwork for church restorations throughout Dorset, and Hicks's specialty lay in this field. In the end, a business connection determined Layton's future. His father didn't want him to dirty his hands as a mason; in contrast, being an architect was highly respectable and provided a good middle-class income. When a father chose a trade or career path for his son, there was no argument. In the summer of 1886, Layton dutifully reported to the office of John Hicks on South Street in Dorchester.

There were two other pupils in the office, one finishing his tutelage, the other in his second year. Hicks, a genial, well-educated man, took great pride in training young architects, and Layton received first-rate instruction. It was a relief; like many in England, Layton had read Charles Dickens's *Martin Chuzzlewit,* in which the innocent young hero was articled to a villainous and greedy architect, Seth Pecksniff, who lived off his students' fees and didn't teach them a thing. This was not Layton's fate. Hicks's specialty was the restoration of Gothic churches, and Layton took up the same. He was sent all over southern England to draw up floor plans, traveling to the parish churches of St. Mary's, Rampisham, Coombe Keynes, and Powerstock. In the process, he learned all there was to know about medieval construction and design.

Layton's exceptional intelligence and drawing talent proved useful; he soon became an excellent draughtsman. After just a year, Hicks tasked him with designing small parts of renovation projects. When his three-year pupilage ended, Hicks offered him a full-time position, which Layton gladly accepted. His bitterness at being denied a university education had passed. Being an architect made him happy.

Three years later, his life changed again. As he stood in the nave of St. Timothy's Church in Somerset, making some sketches, an elderly man in a rumpled tweed suit approached and asked him about the renovation. Layton took the man around the church, describing the proposed work in great detail. Before starting a project, Layton made a thorough study of a church's history so that he might understand its original construction and alterations over the years. Sitting in a pew with the old man, he enthusiastically told him about this church's past.

After two hours, the man stood and introduced himself as the Marquess of Oxton. His family had donated the funds for the church's restoration, and for the next year, the marquess worked closely with Layton on the project. On the day of St. Timothy's rededication, the old man pulled the young architect aside and asked him to design a chapel on his estate.

All architects dream of going out on their own, but Layton, with his lack of social contacts and low-class standing, had never believed he could. But other projects for the marquess's estate and work for his titled friends soon followed. Layton set up an office to handle the rush of new jobs. The son of a mason found himself dining with the aristocratic and the wealthy — a new life far, far above his station. They valued his advice on architectural matters and liked him as a person.

It was at this point that he began his elaborate masquerade. He would never reveal his past as a workingman's son. Instead, he became a full-time actor, playing the role of a man born into the upper middle class. In England, a gentleman was not necessarily a member of the peerage; land ownership was tied to inheritance and wealth too, and a landowner was also deemed a gentleman. Layton took this path as his story and lied, claiming he had inherited land in the south of England. With expert skill, he learned the accent, manner of dress, and etiquette of his betters. Every day, he took the stage and fooled the world. In England, how one was perceived as a gentleman was absolutely paramount, and Layton had transformed himself into a true gentleman. Within a remarkably short amount of time, he had scaled the citadels of British privilege, even acquiring the most unattainable — a choice marriage to an aristocrat. Lady Edwina, the only daughter of a viscount, Lord Charles Litton, was a classic society beauty with incredible auburn-colored hair. She took an instant liking to Layton, who wasn't such a bad-looking chap in his own right. They had met at a dinner party hosted by Layton's client, Sir Richard Bonneville, who had completed a new home next to Lord Litton's estate. The young architect was smitten with the twenty-year-old girl with the vivacious smile. In real life, a bumpkin like him would never get within one mile of a girl like that socially. With many suitors to choose from,

Edwina's slightest attention was hard-won, and Layton was flattered. He believed she favored him because he actually knew how to do something to earn a living, and she respected that. A proper English gentleman never worked, and she found them boring or silly. Layton fell in love with Edwina and, despite her father's veiled disapproval, proposed marriage. He was incredibly happy — and very lucky.

By connecting with a wealthy aristocratic family, he was able to live and advance even further above his humble origin. How ironic, he thought. Professionally, he excelled in designing ornate facades; in life, he designed a facade too, covering up his real identity. He lied about his parents (long dead), his schooling, and his upbringing. He even shared his wife's snobbery, hiding his true roots so successfully that no one would have believed he came from a thatched-roof cottage on Cherry Lane in Dorset, a million light-years from the ballrooms of Mayfair. He had done what so few in England could: reinvented himself.

Now he had to do it again.

6

"Hello, Dad."

The large, broad-shouldered man filled the doorway, and his head almost touched the top of the frame. The bright light of the lamp behind him silhouetted his father against the dark.

"Would ya like a nice cup o' tea? I just put the kettle on," Layton's father said impassively. Then he turned away.

Layton followed. The second he set foot in the cottage, a feeling of great relief and happiness swept over him. *He was home!*

The room's plastered walls, flagstone floor, and large, open fireplace embraced him with a great, welcoming warmth, like pulling a thick blanket over his body on a cold winter's night. The wooden staircase in the corner still wound its way up to the bedrooms on the second floor. To his right, he saw the extra room his parents had added for his widowed grandmother.

An unfamiliar smile swept across Layton's face. He saw before him the essence of his boyhood, a time when he had no troubles or concerns. If only he could snap his fingers and — just like that — be a boy again, living in this cottage, listening to his grandmother's stories, and playing with his lead soldiers in front of the hearth.

Thomas Layton pulled a cup and saucer from a cabinet and placed it on the blue-and-red-striped tablecloth of the dining table. Layton took the high-backed oak chair as his father began to pour the tea. They sat in silence, looking at each other for a long moment.

"I'm sorry I never visited you at Mulcaster, Douglas. I just couldn't do it."

Layton didn't reply. He just waited, absorbing his father's Dorset accent, which he hadn't heard in years. The sound brought back a flood of warm memories: long days spent sitting in this room, talking to his mother; the clamor of his many relatives. Was his own speech still tinged with that distinctive sound? He'd worked doggedly to get rid of it.

"I understand, Dad."

His father blinked at him with watery eyes. "That sad business of yers, coming on top of Raymond getting killed . . ." He shook

54

his head.

Raymond. Three weeks before the theatre disaster, Layton's older brother had died in South Africa, killed in the Second Boer War. As a sergeant-major in the British Army, Raymond had spent twenty years fighting battles in the farthest outskirts of the British Empire: the Sudan, Afghanistan, Egypt. In the Battle of Omdurman in Khartoum, he'd received the Victoria Cross, Britain's highest decoration for valor. General Kitchener himself had pinned the medal to his chest. Thomas Layton had worshipped his soldier son.

When Layton turned toward the fireplace, he saw Raymond's photo on the mantel. In his dress uniform, smiling that wonderful ear-to-ear grin topped by a handlebar mustache.

There were no photos of Layton on the mantel. Though his father was a master mason who appreciated architecture, soldiering for queen and country was far manlier than sitting at a draughting table. Compared to a soldier with a VC, an architect seemed a poof. No matter how many impressive buildings Layton designed or how many upper-class clients he had, Raymond's achievements mattered more, for Raymond was an empire builder.

Once, when he was just starting out as an architect on his own, Layton had invited his father to a dedication of a library he'd designed in Bournemouth on the coast of Dorset. Because of his charade, he'd had no contact with his family, but in the very brief letter about the new library, he had let his dad know that he'd set up a practice and was doing well but revealed no other details of his life. Like most sons, Layton probably still had the need for his father's approval, and that's why he had wanted him to come. But Thomas Layton had declined, claiming a business emergency. Layton never invited — or contacted — him again. Raymond's feats, he knew, had trumped him once more.

He was ashamed to admit it, but down deep, he had been relieved that his father had refused. The key to maintaining his charade had been never revealing to *anyone* — including his wife — his true background, which meant her family never meeting his family. In England, that revelation would be the kiss of death to one's position. Lord Litton would have looked at his father's rough mason's hands and ill-fitting clothes and snorted in disapproval. What had his beloved Edwina married? So his family wasn't at his wedding, because he never told them about it. Nor was he at his brother's funeral.

Growing up, his father had been stern but kind, and he was proud of Layton's academic successes. But every time Raymond had come home on leave and walked through the door in his uniform, Thomas Layton had almost levitated with excitement. After so many colonial battles conquered by Raymond, his father had come to believe his son invulnerable. A sergeant-major was the most important of the noncommissioned officers, relied upon by the regiment for leadership in the thick of fighting. So when the news came, Layton knew that his father's whole being had been pulverized to dust.

And when his father read in the papers about the theatre accident, the shame of it must have been overwhelming. Because Layton was a native son, Dorset gossiped constantly about the tragedy. His father must have felt like digging a hole and burying himself.

"It's all right, Dad," he said softly. "I understand."

But his father must have heard his stomach growling. "I have some leftover mutton and suet pudding in the larder if yer hungry."

When the food was set on the table,

Layton had to prevent himself from devouring it like a wild animal. He ate slowly and drank a tankard of ale. His father watched silently. Layton set down his fork, about to speak, and felt something at his leg. A solid black cat, purring and rubbing against him. He smiled and picked it up, setting it in his lap, where it curled into a ball.

"Midnight still remembers ya," said his father.

Petting the cat's head, Layton looked across the table.

"It's quite terrifying to face life all by oneself. I had no other place to go, Dad," he said in a low, quivering voice.

"I knew ya was gettin' out soon. 'ow long have ya been out?"

"Two days."

"You'll never get work around 'ere, people knowing who you are." His father was never one to sugarcoat reality.

A harsh voice broke across their quiet conversation.

"Blimey. The black sheep of the family has returned to the fold."

Leaning forward on the thick oak railing of the staircase landing was his older brother, Roger, a tall and gangly man with a shock of sandy-blond hair. He skipped down the rest of the stairs like a seven-year-old.

"Hello, Roger," Layton said tersely.

"I won't bother to ask how things are with you, Little Brother. I can tell by lookin' at yer face." Roger sat down across from Layton, a cruel smile fixed on his face. "You look so different. Thinner, almost like a bloody skeleton. I'm surprised. I 'eard they give you a pound of raw meat every day in prison, like animals in the zoo."

Layton closed his eyes, let the abuse wash over him. Roger had always resented his ability to rise above his station. Now, he wondered if his brother had taken pleasure in his misfortunes too. It wasn't as if he had anything to complain about. Roger was a master carpenter and greatly admired for his skill. People across England hired him to build cabinetry, stairs, and millwork for mansions and other important buildings. And yet. While Roger had a true gift, Layton had never referred any work to him for fear of revealing his family connections. In doing so, perhaps he had hurt Roger more than he knew.

"Douglas here is lookin' for work," Thomas said, turning to Roger, who let out a harsh bark of a laugh.

"Oh, for sure, people'll be bangin' the

door down to give Britain's most famous murderer a job."

"Don't take that tone, boy, or I'll thump ya," growled Thomas.

"What? None of your high-and-mighty friends were waitin' outside Mulcaster to give ya a job? Lord and Lady Bentham didn't have their carriage at your disposal? I'm shocked." Their father was glowering, but Roger continued, undaunted. "You know, we can't blame 'em, Dad, for never coming back to visit. It must have been bloody awkward for our Dougie to associate with his social inferiors."

He leaned over the table and looked straight into Layton's eyes. "But now you're an ex-convict. You're *everyone's* social inferior, mate."

Layton looked straight ahead and continued petting Midnight. Only the crackling of the fire broke the silence in the room.

"You look peaky, Doug. Maybe you should go upstairs and have a lie down in Raymond's room," said Thomas. His tone of voice wasn't compassionate but practical, as if he were telling a drenched man to come in out of the rain.

Layton set the cat on the floor and slowly stood. Like a weary old man, he trudged up the stairs. His torso still ached.

"At least you don't have to share a room anymore — or get buggered," Roger called after him.

"Shut yer mouth, boy," Layton heard his father growl.

The lamp on the nightstand threw out a warm glow, illuminating the many objects attached to the walls, the trinkets and trophies of war that Raymond had brought home for Layton, who worshiped his soldier brother as a hero. A Dervish spear, a Zulu shield almost six feet tall, a jeweled saber from his posting on India's northwest frontier. These strange, exotic objects had fascinated Layton. He had looked forward to Raymond's leaves, to being beguiled by stories of adventures in far-off lands.

Many photographs of Raymond's regiment hung on the walls. Layton could find his brother instantly in every one. Raymond had called the Second Boer War a quick colonial skirmish; the British were expected to march into South Africa and easily whip the Boer farmers in a week. The Dutch-speaking settlers had accepted British rule but refused to let their republics, the Orange Free State and the Transvaal, be annexed when diamonds and gold were discovered within their bounds. To the shock of the world, they had soundly licked the British.

The public had been furious. That mere farmers could beat the best army on the planet! The Boers had used hit-and-run tactics that were deemed cowardly. "Why don't they come out in the open and fight fair?" people had written in letters to the *Daily Mail.*

Reading the *Times* one morning at breakfast, Layton had learned to his horror that Raymond had been cut down in an ambush while leading a night patrol. One Boer bullet to the head ended his bright life. In the photograph of the regiment Raymond had sent his father from South Africa, Layton found his brother, seated in the second row, third from the left, looking confident and proud.

It was the last photo of his brother ever taken.

7

"Never knew you liked the drink so much," said Thomas, handing his son a bottle of Glenfiddich.

"I can drink, or I can weep, Dad. I prefer to drink."

Layton nodded his thanks to his father and broke the seal on the bottle. He took a long, hard swallow of the malt whiskey. With each glass, he forgot the world and passed into a blissful state. It reminded him of the time when, as a child, he'd paid a shilling for a hot-air balloon ride at the fair in Dorchester. The great wicker gondola had lifted him higher and higher over the lush green countryside. Everything on the ground had shrunk away to nothing. He was hundreds of feet above the world and all its unhappiness. It was exhilarating, and he hadn't wanted to come down. The feeling had lingered even after his father had raged at him for wasting a bob on such a foolish extravagance. Like that balloon, the alcohol lifted him up. With each glass, he went higher and higher into the sky, forgetting everything. Layton loved the sensation.

"And drinking is the only way I know to remain unconscious sitting up during the day."

"At this pace, you'll be lying on the floor unconscious — or dead," replied Thomas. "The Irish curse," he muttered with distaste. "Me great-uncle had it, he was a twelve-pint-a-day man, he was."

"I can beat that in a heartbeat."

He had been at home for almost three weeks. Not once had he ventured outside the house. A city dweller might look at the countryside, see the homes and farms so far from each other, and imagine total privacy. But there were prying eyes everywhere. The gossips in the Dorset countryside were faster than a telegraph; they'd alert everyone along the south coast of England that the Butcher of the West End had come home. Reporters would hover around the house like flies on manure.

Not wanting to shame his father, Layton stayed inside.

It was a strange time. Layton was adrift; he had no idea what to do with his life, nor did he care. Becoming a bitter, drunken recluse seemed as good an option as any. Unspoken between Layton and his father was the knowledge that he could stay in the homestead as long as he wanted and be provided with liquor and food. Though he was bored to death, he accepted this as the price for staying safe and out of sight. The little cottage of his childhood had become a fortress, protecting him from the outside world. Since his release from prison, Layton had this constant fear that his freedom was just an illusion that could be snatched away from him in an instant, and he'd be back in a prison cell.

The thick oak door swung open, interrupting Layton's thoughts. In strode Roger, carrying his leather bag of woodworking tools. He had been away in Cornwall, on the far western end of England, working on a job for an estate.

"I see nothing has changed in a fortnight," said Roger, dropping his bag by the fireplace. "Didn't think it bloody would."

Layton lifted his tumbler of scotch in a salute. His brother sat down across from him. Their father took no notice but continued to stir the pot of stew on the stove.

"I'm tired of seeing you get sozzled every night, Little Brother," said Roger. Again, that icy flash of a smile. "So I did me some thinkin'."

"That's a dangerous pastime," Layton murmured. Roger did not seem to hear.

"I recalled our Dougie here being one of them sensitive, artistic types — he could draw real well as a lad." Roger spoke this last over his shoulder to their father.

"So?" Thomas growled.

"Well, I 'appened to run into an old mate in Cornwall. Name of Charlie MacHeath. He'd just finished repairing some doors in a music hall in Nottingham. Charlie told me his nephew got a job in their scene shop — you know, the ones that paint the backdrops — or whatever the 'ell ya call 'em; the things that ya see behind the acts. A London street, a garden in Devon, that kind of thing. Said they was hiring."

The words *music hall* made Layton flinch. But when he met his father's eyes, he could see that Thomas Layton had taken Roger's suggestion to heart.

It was time to go.

8

Layton stood across the street, examining the front facades of the Nottingham Grand Imperial Theatre. It wrapped the corner of Merton and Ward Streets, anchored by a huge, domed tower clad in copper and topped by a tall, gilt spire. The ornate glass and cast-iron marquee also wrapped the corner; above it, letters outlined in lights glowed out GRAND IMPERIAL. The use of white marble gave the front of the theatre great presence.

A very strong design.

Everything had happened so quickly, thought Layton. A good thing, that; it had given him little time to back out. Roger had placed a trunk call from the village to his friend in London and learned the Grand was indeed looking for scenic artists. To keep Layton's identity secret, Roger claimed he had a friend looking for work. From Nottingham, the nephew of his mate had wired that he'd put in a good word. Within a day, Oswald Black, the theatre manager, had granted Layton an interview. As he had no previous experience, he was asked to bring a portfolio of drawings to the meeting. While he didn't have to "be any kind of Rembrandt," Black had cautioned, he had to have some talent. Working late into the night in Raymond's room, Layton made quick sketches of the countryside and streetscapes, then a portrait of Midnight.

Layton chose a new name at random, picking the first and last names from the *Dorchester Times.* He was now Frank Owen. He repeated his new name over and over again. It was interesting, he thought, that one had no say in what they were called. One's last name was inherited from one's father; the first and middle names were bestowed when one was less than a day old and couldn't protest. Not until three or four, when the other children made fun of it, would a child know he'd been given a ridiculous name. Take Beechcrop Manningtree, the name of one of Layton's childhood friends. Didn't his parents know how stupid it was? Why not just plain John?

Layton also assumed a new physical identity. The full mustache and beard he had sported since he was eighteen had been shaved off the first day at Mulcaster because it was against prison rules, so he was already clean-shaven. The thirty pounds he'd lost in prison now became an advantage. To those who knew him before, Layton had always been on the slightly chubby side. To complete the masquerade, Roger had purchased some hair dye, so now Layton had chestnut-colored hair that was swept back with Livesy's Hair Tonic. The final touch was a pair of spectacles that barely distorted his vision. He also gave Roger twelve quid to go into Dorchester to buy him a greatcoat, two suits, and a bare-bones wardrobe.

"Blimey, 'e looks a new man — if ya don't look too closely," his brother had said of his new creation.

Layton was amused by Roger's enthusiasm in helping him out. He knew it wasn't out of brotherly love but to get him the hell out the house.

In spite of himself, Layton liked the fact that he had been reborn. A brand-new name and identity — in a way, it was a clean slate. And now, within a week of Roger's call, he found himself here, about to cross the street for his 11:00 a.m. interview. The job being in Nottingham, a city he'd never visited, pleased him. But for the Robin Hood stories, he knew nothing about the place.

The bustling Midlands city looked like a perfect place to get lost in, with its crowds of people on the lively streets radiating out from its original medieval castle. All Layton craved was anonymity and a chance to get on with his life. Still, he had to be on his guard at all times not to reveal his true identity.

But as Layton stepped off the curb, an image of the Britannia exterior superimposed itself over the Grand in his mind, as if someone had wallpapered a giant photograph on top of the building. They shared many similar features, like a big dome. In a flash, he was back standing on Shaftesbury Avenue that terrible night. He closed his eyes as he stepped back up on the sidewalk. Breathing heavily as he'd done in Wragby when he saw the two little girls, he couldn't bring himself to look up at the music hall, so he glued his eyes to the slate pavement. With his head down, Layton slowly backpedaled until he was right up against the wall of shops. To his immediate right was an entryway to a pub, into which he bolted and ordered a drink immediately. His hand trembling, he lifted a tumbler of whiskey to his lips and downed it in a gulp. Gathering every ounce of his inner strength, he resisted raising his hand to signal the barman to give him another one. The clock in the pub said two minutes to eleven, so Layton picked up the pasteboard portfolio of his drawings and the suitcase he'd borrowed from his father and slowly walked across the street.

The Grand's front entrance was a series of handsome wood and cut-glass double doors stretched under the marquee. Under the morning sun, an elderly charwoman was shining the brass door handles to a brilliant finish. But Layton would not pass through them. Experience designing a music hall had taught him that employees *always* used the rear door, so he walked along the marble facade and turned the corner into an alley.

The deserted alley was lined with garbage cans and crates of construction material. In contrast to the magnificence of the front, the back of the theatre was done in plain brick with simple sash windows. In the center of the wall was a wide, green steel door marked STAGE ENTRANCE. Layton pulled it open and stepped inside. To his immediate right was a tiny cubicle perhaps six feet wide and six feet deep. An old man in a tweed coat and red bow tie sat there in an upholstered chair, reading the *Notting-ham Post.*

Behind him, the wall was lined with wooden pigeonhole boxes like those in a post office. On the flanking walls were shelves piled with papers and glass cabinets holding rows of keys. The old man glared at Layton, seemingly annoyed at being disturbed.

The stage doorman, Layton thought, looking back at him. The master of the guard. It was he who made sure no interlopers invaded the theatre. No starstruck youth looking for jobs, no Piccadilly Johnnies stalking beautiful performers, and no bailiffs handing out arrest warrants to actors. The stage doorman's job was to hand out messages and mail to performers and staff, distribute dressing room keys, and be cordial to everyone — except strangers like Layton.

"Appointment with Mr. Black."

"Down the corridor and up them circular stairs on the right. Not the ones on the left, mind you," the stage doorman growled.

Layton walked down the dimly lit passage. A music hall was made up of two parts. The front of the house was the public area, with the entrance foyer, bars, and auditorium; the back of the house consisted of the stage itself and the backstage area. Backstage was as plain as the front of the house was fancy, and entirely practical and unglamorous. Here, all the functions that created magic on the stage were carried out: the storage for props, costumes, and equipment; the dressing rooms; the workshops for carpenters and electricians. It was a hodgepodge of voids, of dark, tight corridors off of which trailed formless, rabbit-warren spaces. When Layton had been about to begin his design for the Britannia, he'd been shocked to learn that the stage manager and head carpenter would be laying out the backstage, not him. It was a specialized space, and they knew exactly what they wanted. This, he discovered, was how all music halls were designed.

The Grand's walls were made of brick painted dark green up to five feet in height and a sickly yellow ocher from there to the ceiling. Bare Edison bulbs, hung every eight feet, cast a wavering light. Men and women passed Layton in the hallway but looked through him as if he were invisible. At the top of the black spiral stair was a wall with a glass door and tall interior windows that overlooked the backstage.

Layton did not have to knock; a middle-aged man with a shiny, bald head saw him at the door and waved him in. He wore a well-tailored, navy-blue suit, and his attention was focused on a pile of papers on his desk, to which he was furiously signing his name. Standing next to him was a very attractive middle-aged woman in a dark-blue skirt with a white shirtwaist, her sandy-blond hair pinned up. Layton's immediate impression was that she was an actress, but because she was feeding the man business invoices, one after another, he realized she wasn't. Might she be what they called a "New Woman" in England and a "Gibson Girl" in America? These unmarried women who actually earned their livings in offices and lived in their own flats? Layton shook his head in amazement at the thought.

"I tell you, Cissie, someone's robbing us blind." The man shook his head over the latest sheaf of papers. "These bloody prices are higher than Nelson's Column."

The woman smiled. "You're balmy, Ozzie. You're the cheapest bastard in town. No one pays the acts less than you. And the syndicate loves you for it."

Without looking at Layton, Oswald Black extended his free hand, took the portfolio, and placed it on the desk. All the while, he continued to sign.

"Blimey. We have a real Mike Angelo here, Cissie," he said, flipping through the drawings.

The woman leaned in to look over his shoulder and gave a thunderous laugh. "This man has talent, Ozzie," she said. "He can paint better cloths than the ones at the Hackney Empire. But you'll have to pay him more than you do the dancing bear."

Finally, Black looked up at Layton. "No scene painter is going to get paid more than the dancing bear," he said fiercely. "Especially if it's his first job."

"Ever been in a music hall — I mean, the back of the house?" asked the woman, meeting Layton's eyes and giving him a warm smile.

"This is Mrs. Cissie Mapes," Black said, gesturing vaguely in her direction. "She runs the place. Books the acts for the chain. Best mind her, Owen, or you'll be for it."

"No, Mrs. Mapes," Layton said quietly and courteously. "I have had no experience with music halls."

"Well, you'll learn quick enough. Nine — I mean eight — quid a week to start, and we'll see how it goes," Black said. "Start tomorrow morning at eight. Go downstairs and see Albert Stone in the scene shop. He'll show you everything." With that, Black went back to his paperwork.

Layton picked up the portfolio and made to leave, but his new boss's voice stilled his motion.

"Wait. I want you to come to the show tonight. Watch from the front of the house;

75

I'll have you passed through. Pay close attention to the cloths, not the singers' tits."

Cissie burst out laughing. "Don't ask the impossible on his first day, Ozzie."

"The house is filled six nights a week, even Mondays. Frank Matcham, who did the London Coliseum, designed it," boasted Albert Stone, a genial, weak-chinned man of about fifty. He sounded as if he were bragging about his child's academic achievements.

"With standing room, we can fit 2,233 in here. The proscenium opening is thirty-six feet wide, near twenty-eight feet high, with a metal fire curtain."

Layton nodded. He knew of Matcham; the greatest music hall architect of them all, he'd done close to a hundred theatres throughout England. His nickname, "Can't match Matcham," was absolutely true. While there were other big theatre designers such as W. G. R. Sprague and Bertie Crewe, Matcham was king.

Looking out from the edge of the stage, Layton took in the breathtaking beauty of the French Renaissance-style auditorium, with its three curving tiers of column-free balconies, which stepped back as they soared up to the roof. At the ends on the side walls were the private boxes, which were framed by richly adorned arches and flanked by magnificent gilt pilasters. Hanging from the domed, mural-painted ceiling was an immense oval crystal chandelier. From where he stood, Layton could see how the tiers of horseshoe-shaped balconies embraced the stage, making for a more intimate connection between performer and audience.

The irony of it all was that many of Britain's architects looked down upon the men who specialized in theatres. They felt it a vulgar building type and beneath them to design. But Layton admired their skill, and when he'd been offered the commission for the Britannia Empire, he'd snapped it up regardless of the criticism from his fellow members of the Royal Institute of British Architects. Even his father-in-law, Lord Charles Litton, had objected.

But Layton hadn't cared. The music hall represented the joy he'd felt as a child, going to the theatres in Dorchester and Weymouth. Taking that commission was the only time he had retreated back to the working-class roots he'd hidden so well. *And it had cost him everything.* His eyes locked onto the theatre's cantilevered first balcony, and his brain instantly conjured up an image of a fifteen-foot section collapsing down on the seats below. He had to look away, his heart in his throat.

"When are you damn foreigners going to change your music? You've been using the same cues for the last fifty years," shouted an angry voice to the left and below.

"I a wanna the orchestra to play like they've never played before — in tune," answered a heavily accented Italian voice, followed by a bellowing laugh.

"Go to hell, you dago twit," someone shouted.

"Play the goddamn cues," called the Italian. "And be sure to speed up tempo when we finish a trick."

While Stone and Layton talked, the orchestra had filed into the depressed space in front of the stage. "That's band call," Stone said. "Every Monday morning, the acts meet with the musical director and the orchestra. They place their music by the footlights there." He pointed to the piles of sheet music heaped at the edge of the stage. "That's Gino, one of the Flying Donatellos, an acrobat act, and that's Broadchurch, the conductor, in the orchestra pit."

A swarthy, broad-shouldered man was jabbing his finger and yelling at Broadchurch. When the conductor ignored him, waving his baton disinterestedly in front of the equally disinterested orchestra, Gino began stamping his feet to the rhythm.

"All right, you bloody dago, we have it down. Next!" Broadchurch yelled.

"*Bastardo!* You give me hard time because I no give you and band beer money to play."

"That's right, you *don't.* So shove off, wop," yelled a trumpet player.

A pretty girl of about eighteen stepped up to the edge of the stage, a rueful smile on her lips. "We'll start with 'You Are My Honey Bee,' please, Mr. Broadchurch."

"That's Nellie of Nellie, Kellie, and the Two Gents, one of the most popular turns here," Stone whispered. "She's a scrumptious little bit, eh? I'd love to slip her a length. A real saucy number onstage, but the opposite off, if you know what I mean. Colder than an iceberg."

The orchestra played a fast, bright number, and the girl swayed to the rhythm. She then began to dance around and pulled her skirt up a bit, exposing her ankles. All the orchestra musicians kept their eyes glued to Nellie as they played.

"Let me show ya how things work around here," said Stone, though he was clearly reluctant to drag his eyes away from Nellie. He and Layton walked to the rear of the stage, and Stone gestured to the boards below them. "Notice how the floor rises from front to back. That's called 'upstage,' and it's that way to show the swells in the stalls the dancers' feet better."

Layton already knew what *upstage* meant, but he remained silent and followed Stone to a room directly behind the backstage wall. The space was huge, with a soaring twenty-five-foot ceiling.

"This here's the scene shop. Most theatres have to have their scenery done off-site, but we have our own shop. Makes it damn more convenient, I say."

Layton nodded, and Stone continued.

"That's a flat, where we draw out and paint the scenery — or 'cloths,' as they're called."

A big wooden frame the length of the stage was fixed to the back wall, and attached to it was a stretched canvas cloth. A man was painting what looked like a London street scene; Layton could make out Big Ben in the distance. The man wore a gray smock splattered with a thousand different colors of paint. As he worked, he looked repeatedly to a colored sketch on a small portable by his side.

"In the old days, we had to erect scaffolding to reach the upper part because the backcloths were so damn tall. But these flats can be lowered through those slots in the floor to the understage, so you can stand and paint."

Layton nodded, deeply impressed; he wished he'd thought of such a thing for the Britannia. Stone led him back to the stage, seemingly pleased by his approval.

"Now, once the cloths are finished, the tops are fastened to those bars up above us and hoisted out of sight, up into what's called the fly tower. Ours is twenty-nine feet high. The cloths can be raised or lowered from that platform on the sidewall they call the fly floor. The stagehands hoist them by hand with those ropes y'see there and tie them off on the cleats."

Far above his head, Layton could see half a dozen cloths, held in place by ropes like sheets hanging from a clothesline.

"The first thing you'll be doing is transferring a sketch to the cloth and painting it up," said Stone, pointing to the artist already at work. "After a while, you can start designin' 'em yourself. Heard ya were a real bloody Remy-brandt."

Layton smiled at this comment. It would be great fun to design these cloths.

"Do you have digs yet?" Stone asked.

Layton shook his head. He hadn't wanted

to get a hotel room until he was sure of the job.

"Roy!" Stone shouted. A boy of around twenty emerged from the storage closet. He was tall and thin with a potato-like nose. "Take Owen to Mrs. Hodges. Tell her he needs a room." To Layton, he added, "Mrs. Hodges used to be a contortionist in a specialty act. Now she owns a house that only lets to theatrical folks. Keeps a clean place, and she's a damn good cook."

"She makes butter scones *every* day," said Roy with great enthusiasm. "And only one quid a week rent."

9

Layton had a hard time imagining Mrs. Hodges as a contortionist. These were acrobats whose bodies seemed to be made of India rubber; they could be bent and stretched into incredible positions. There were back benders and front benders, and Layton had seen many perform in the Dorchester Place of Varieties while growing up.

In contrast, Mrs. Hodges must have weighed three hundred pounds. She boasted that she'd once been a back bender; she could bend over at the waist until she looked like the letter U and even extend her head under her crotch. A great crowd-pleaser, she chortled. As she wheezed up the staircase, she stopped to show him her photo on the wall. He wouldn't have known it was her. The girl in the picture was skinny as a rail, painted head to toe in silver paint and wearing a turban.

"My stage name was Alethea. Had good

notices in the *Music Hall and Theatre Review*." Mrs. Hodges recited proudly: "Alethea, a beautiful and faultlessly developed girl, is a contortionist whose poses never offend modesty or humanity. All she does is graceful and picturesque."

They continued up, Layton shaking his head quietly at the ravages of time. He was a little worried she'd lose her balance, fall backward, and roll down the stairs like a boulder, crushing him.

"Now, Mr. Owen," Mrs. Hodges gasped over her shoulder. "I like letting rooms to scene painters. They're a rum bunch; don't make no trouble and don't drink."

The last part of the sentence jerked Layton's head up as if it had been pulled by a string. He didn't know if he could stay sober in Nottingham. There were at least two pubs on every block. Already, on the way to Mrs. Hodges's, he'd stood Roy a drink as a gesture of friendship — the boy had turned out to be the nephew of Roger's mate. He just had one pint, but his mouth watered for another.

"Besides stage craftsmen, my house lets only to first-rate artistes." Mrs. Hodges spoke with great pride, as though King Edward VII himself roomed there.

Layton nodded, recognizing the term. Roy

had begun to give him a primer on theatre etiquette. Always call the performers *artistes,* never *actors* or *actresses* — those terms were an insult. Always flatter them and kiss their arses, Roy added, for they had fragile, sensitive egos.

"Here we are," gasped Mrs. Hodges, pushing open a door. The room was charming. Theatre bills and photos, most of them of Mrs. Hodges in her prime, covered the walls. "You'll be next door to Spring & Spring, the Champion Acrobatic Barrel Jumpers. They're just back from an engagement at the Gaiety in Birmingham. If ye hear some thumping around, it's them trying out a new routine."

The room held a bed with an orange-and-blue quilt, an upholstered easy chair in front of the fireplace grate, and a tall window overlooking a garden.

"Yes," Layton said softly. "This is very jolly, Mrs. Hodges. This will do fine indeed."

She handed him a key and turned to the door, trailing a finger over an old photo of herself. The girl in the photo smiled up at the camera, a saucy gleam in her eye. "Mr. Owen, that review wasn't quite correct about my modesty. With all the positions I could bend into, I was a favorite of the gentlemen, if you know what I mean." She cackled and slit her eyes at him slyly. "I'd put a pound to a shilling you're a bit naughty too."

"No, not the least bit."

"I believe you . . . Millions wouldn't. Come down for a cup of tea after you've settled in." She left.

Layton set down his suitcase, stretched out on the bed, and rubbed his hands over his face.

"Owen," he intoned softly to himself. "My name is Frank Owen. My name is Frank Owen."

The sidewalks along Merton and Ward Streets throbbed with people, all illuminated beneath the lights of the Grand's marquee. Men in top hats and evening dress, escorting women in great finery, mixed with working-class men and women in the shabbiest of clothes. Constables stood at the curbs to ensure the crowd was orderly, while beggars and prostitutes worked the perimeter of the throng. Carriage after carriage pulled up to discharge its passengers; "cab glimmers," little boys who opened carriage doors and helped the ladies out for a few coppers, ran up to them in packs.

Layton threaded his way through the mob to the gleaming doors. This was probably the only time he'd ever use them, he thought ruefully. Inside, he stood in the entry foyer and looked up. A beautiful railing of bronze metalwork bordered the dramatic circular cutout in the ceiling. The space was sumptuous, with red granite floors and a wide, white marble staircase that swept up to the dress circle, the first balcony level.

From designing the Britannia, Layton knew that designing a theatre was a class-conscious exercise. While the social classes deigned to mingle on the sidewalk, inside, the strictest of class divisions were maintained. Only those men and women sitting in the best upholstered seats in the house — the stalls at the front of the auditorium and the dress circle — were allowed through the sparkling foyer. The other patrons had their own entrances and exits, designed in such a way that the classes need never meet. Even the toilets and bars were separate.

The highest balcony was the gallery, and its tickets were the cheapest: one bob to sit on wooden benches. Called "the gods" because the seats were closer to heaven than the stage, it had its own plain staircase for the long climb up.

Standing next to the staircase, the house manager, Oswald Black, wore white tie and tails and greeted the upper-class patrons with a toothy smile and hearty handshake. When he spotted Layton, he motioned to a uniformed usher, who gestured Layton forward with a white-gloved hand. To his surprise, Layton was led to the expensive stalls at the front of theatre and given a program and an aisle seat in the fifth row. Of course, he thought; as a scenic artist, he needed a close-up view of the backcloths.

Out of professional habit, Layton craned his neck, trying to take in the complexities of the space. With the house lights on, the plasterwork on the faces of the balconies and boxes exuded a creamy golden glow, which contrasted wonderfully with the royal-blue velvet of the seats. He took in all the details — automatic tip-up seats, bronze light sconces inside the boxes, the beautiful ornamentation of the great proscenium arch framing the matching royal-blue tabs of the main curtain. Matcham was indeed a genius. He could take an immense space and make it into a cozy and intimate world of fun, a welcome escape on a rainy, damp night.

Rising to take off his coat, Layton looked behind him at the pit. This section of bench seats, located under the balcony, on the other side of the low wooden wall behind the stalls, was already packed to capacity with working-class types and a few toffs in top hats slumming with their inferiors. Their seats were the next cheapest in the house. Although they were on the main level, they were far from the stage and had terrible sight lines.

At five minutes to six, the orchestra emerged from a passage beneath the stage. Mr. Broadchurch appeared next, in elegant evening dress, and smiled at the people in the stalls. To the left of the proscenium arch, in a square opening in the stage wall, was a white card with a red number corresponding to the numbered acts on the program. First was the overture. The orchestra started the evening with a lively John Philip Sousa march.

A gentle ripple of applause greeted the end of the piece, and the number board changed from 1 to 2. Then the curtains pulled away, and with a crashing of cymbals, the orchestra broke into a loud, stirring piece. A beautiful white horse galloped onto the stage, ridden by a woman the program described as "Agnes Krembser, Incredible Female Equestrian Juggler." She was lovely, with flowing brown hair, and wore a red fox-hunting habit with a black top hat. A set of gold hoops looped over her shoulder. She smiled and waved to the crowd, which cheered wildly. Then, letting go of the reins, she began juggling the hoops as the horse galloped in widening circles on the stage. Five hoops flew higher and higher; it was an amazing feat, and even Layton started cheering.

He was so caught up in the performance that he almost forgot to look at the back-cloth. Displayed before him was a country scene, mimicking a foxhunt on a great estate. The art was passable, Layton thought, though he would have put a mansion on the hill, overlooking the hunt.

Agnes rose to stand upon the horse like a bareback rider in the circus. Without losing a beat, she continued to juggle. The audience went mad. From this close up, Layton could see the intense concentration on her face. Her assistant stood to the side; he passed her bowling pins to juggle, then flaming torches. The audience roared in delight as, sitting forward astride the horse, she juggled the sticks of fire. Finally, she brought the horse to a halt, leapt off, and bowed. The horse lowered his head and bowed too. The tabs closed, and — to the audience's delight — the horse poked his head through for a final ovation.

The number board changed to 3, and the tabs pulled back. A new cloth had descended. Out from stage left came Perky O'Shea, the "Irish Jester," a diminutive comic in a red-and-white-checked suit. "Hello, Nottingham ninnies!"

"Hello, Perky!" the audience screamed back.

The comic pointed to a man in the stalls a few seats away from Layton.

"You, sir, with the flesh-colored hair. Don't look at the program. Me name's Perky O'Shea. Oh, the man doesn't believe I'm Perky O'Shea. If I'm not Perky O'Shea, then I'm havin' a hell of a good time with his wife."

The audience roared with laughter.

"Speaking of wives, me mate was sitting in a restaurant with his, and there was this bloke, roaring drunk, at a nearby table. He says to his wife, 'Why do you keep staring at that man? Do you know him?' 'Yes,' she says. 'That's my ex-husband. He's been drinking like that since I left him seven years ago.' Me mate says, 'That's amazing. I didn't think anyone could celebrate that long.'"

On and on the little comic went. Layton's eyes drifted to the cloth at his back; this was a front cloth, which dropped directly behind the tabs, giving the stagehands time to arrange the set upstage for the next act.

Someone had painted a large caricature of Perky, along with shamrocks and musical notes.

"We Irishmen aren't great song writers," Perky continued. "We can never get past the *first two bars.* But we can sing and dance a bit."

From the gallery high above, a belligerent voice screamed, "I'm Irish, and me brother once wrote a song, you bastard." The speaker hurled a bag of fish and chips along with his comment, which landed at Perky's feet. The comic picked up the bag and took a bite of a chip.

"Delicious, but needs a lot more salt and a little more vinegar." The orchestra struck up a tune, and Perky danced around the stage with admirable skill, eating the fish and chips as he capered about.

For the fourth turn, the tabs parted to reveal a man in a beret and smock next to an easel. The backdrop for Professor Armand, Artist Extraordinaire, was painted to look like a typical Parisian attic garret with a large skylight. Holding a palette, the performer bowed to the audience and proceeded to paint with great rapidity a still life of a bowl of fruit next to a vase of red roses. The orchestra played a soft minuet; the audience sat in silence, transfixed by this artistic feat. Layton thought the painting damn good, especially for less than ten minutes' worth of work. The man must have been an academically trained painter and could have done a much better cloth than the one behind him.

An all-white cloth came down then, and the footlights turned off. A beam of white light projected onto the cloth from somewhere in the back of the auditorium. A title card appeared on the cloth: THE LATEST WAR PICTURES FROM ASIA. Blurry black-and-white moving images played out a sea battle in the recent Russo-Japanese War. A battleship's guns blasted away. Between pictures were title cards describing the action. The orchestra played a loud, stirring martial tune to accompany the exciting images.

Layton was amazed. He'd heard of such moving pictures but had never seen them in person. It was an amazing sight, like he was in the midst of a great battle on the deck of a ship. Russian officers on the bridge gave commands to their sailors. Returning shell fire from the Japanese ships crashed into the sea, sending up explosions of water. It was like a photograph had magically sprung to life.

Another title card appeared, announcing,

A TRIP THROUGH SWITZERLAND. Taken from the front of a moving locomotive, the film showed views of mountain scenery in the Alps; it ended when the train entered a great tunnel cut through a mountainside. DAMASCUS TO JERUSALEM was the last segment, showing the Holy Land, real Arabs, camels, and an oasis in the desert. For that segment, a mysterious, haunting French horn solo was played.

Layton sat, astounded. He felt as if he'd been lifted out of his body and transported around the world in the blink of an eye. He didn't want the films to end.

The last turn before the interval, called the bottom of the bill, was the second most important act. Here were Nellie, Kellie, and the Two Gents. Just as Albert Stone had said, Nellie was a saucy little number, a sweet soprano and delightful on her feet. The group performed in front of a garden scene with a great fountain. Both Nellie and Kellie showed a lot of ankle onstage.

Perhaps two minutes into their turn, chaos erupted. Two well-dressed women in the dress circle leapt to their feet and started screaming, "Votes for women!"

Layton blinked, shocked. In prison, he'd heard about suffragettes. But to see them in person! The ushers dragged them from their seats, the audience booing and cursing on all sides. The women continued to bellow at the top of their lungs as they were carted off.

"Shut your gobs, you screaming monkeys," yelled a man in the gallery.

"A woman's smaller brain makes her incapable of voting," a man two rows behind Layton said smugly to his companion.

"What would you do with the vote, you bleedin' cow?" another man shouted.

"Same as you," shouted one of the women.

Instead of stopping, Nellie and her troupe kept singing, ignoring the protesters. The crowd admired their determination, and they closed to thunderous applause.

At the interval, the orchestra played, and patrons went to the bathroom or to one of the bars. Alcohol sales were one of the theatre's primary sources of income. For the stalls, the bar, a magnificent wood-carved edifice with scarlet carpeting and a huge marble fireplace, was behind a glass wall off the front foyer.

While Layton sipped a Glenfiddich, he was surprised to see so many women laughing and drinking in the bar. When he'd designed the Britannia, no respectable woman would have been expected to use the bar. Times had certainly changed while he was in prison. The vote for women! Layton had read in the paper there was a group called United Against the Corset. He smiled at the thought. Edwina would never join them. What decent woman does not wear a corset?

Swirling the golden liquid in his glass, he wondered what else was different in this new world he had rejoined.

"I hope you're paying close attention to the cloths, Mr. Owen."

It took Layton a moment too long to realize this comment was addressed to him. He cursed himself mentally; he had to learn to respond when someone addressed him as Owen. Turning, he saw Mrs. Mapes, dressed in a beautiful lavender gown trimmed with white lace. He was so taken by her looks that, at first, he couldn't reply.

"It's been very difficult," he finally stammered. "You book some wonderful acts, Mrs. Mapes, so I'm tempted to look at them, not the cloths."

This pleased her. She took a sip of her drink and smiled.

"Each turn is a separate production unto itself, Mr. Owen. The trick is to make a balanced bill. Each act has to play its part in building the show to a climax." Her eyes twinkled. "I have to do that each and every week . . . for the entire circuit."

"You do a fine job of it," Layton said. "I have never enjoyed the music hall as much as I have tonight."

"Thank you." She waggled her drink at him and said, "Oh, and it's called 'variety theatre' nowadays. Variety is respectable and meant for families, not like the rough stuff in the old music halls. No drunks and whores allowed."

"I look forward to the second half."

"You don't seem like a theatrical type, Mr. Owen." Mrs. Mapes held him in her steady gaze; he could see the quick intelligence in her vivid eyes.

"Just a country boy from Dorset," Layton said easily.

"By way of Eton?" She arched an eyebrow.

Layton laughed nervously. "Grammar school boy, Mrs. Mapes, grammar school boy."

"Is that where you learned to draw?" The house lights started blinking; the second half was about to begin. Saved from having to evade the question, Layton smiled, said good night to Mrs. Mapes, and finished his drink. The whiskey tasted magnificent and warming, and he had hoped to order one more before the end of the interval. It was probably a fortunate thing to run into

Mrs. Mapes to stop him, for he knew he was playing with fire each time he drank. If he wasn't careful, it would ignite a craving he couldn't control, and he'd find himself back at the pub, then passed out in the gutter like in Wragby.

The second half of the show was equally entertaining. A magician named Shang Hi appeared in front of a cloth depicting the Great Wall of China, and a very funny ventriloquist performed with a dummy called the Duke of Idiocy — who looked like the king. Then the Flying Donatellos, including Gino whom he'd seen this morning at band call, took the stage. Three muscular Italian acrobats in white tights used a teeterboard to launch a petite girl into the air; she somersaulted gracefully before landing on their shoulders. Her pink tights showed off her lithe body, and the mouths of the men in the stalls all but watered at the sight. With proper British women dressed in puffy blouses and long skirts, the variety theatre was the only acceptable place to see what a woman's body looked like almost naked.

Great applause greeted the Scottish soprano, Jennie Malone. She was top of the bill — the most important act. Logically, the biggest star would be the very last act, but instead of being the last performer of the night, she was the second to last. It was a time-honored bit of scheduling in the British music halls to follow the star act with a specialty turn, to stop the audience from getting up and leaving during the bill-topper's performance. This was especially important for the second show, when customers wanted to leave early to catch the last tram by 10:30 p.m.

She wore a dark-blue evening gown and stood before a cloth depicting a manor house drawing room with a huge fireplace roaring with an imaginary fire. Her beautiful voice filled the auditorium, and the usually rowdy occupants of the gallery sat quietly, in awe of her talent. The final turn was the El Dorados, whip-crackers who snapped long bullwhips at objects. Their big trick was snapping increasingly short cigarettes from one another's lips.

At last, the first show ended, and the orchestra played as the audience filed out. A second show would start at 8:20, so the house had to empty in ten minutes — 2,233 out, 2,233 in.

Layton was in high spirits. After watching the show, he was confident that he could paint cloths better than the ones he'd seen, and he looked forward to starting the job.

"Topping show, don't you think?" said a stout man in evening dress in the row behind his. "Say, didn't I meet you at Lord Cheltham's house party in Kent?" He squinted at Layton, knitting his brow.

"No, I don't know Lord Cheltham. Sorry, old chap," mumbled Layton. A lightning bolt of panic surged through his body, and he became disoriented, almost losing his balance. He grabbed a seatback to steady himself, then rushed out of the aisle and shoved through the crowd filing out into the street. At the Cat & Hare, Layton downed his third tumbler of Glenfiddich and motioned for the barmaid to fetch a fourth. He *had* met Stephen Madding at Lord Cheltham's.

10

"Come on, luv. How 'bouts some more yellow to match me new frock?"

Layton stood in front of the new cloth he was painting for Mrs. Eddington & Mrs. Freddington, Two Upper Crust Girls. The duo weren't actually women but female impersonators, a very popular type of act. There were also male impersonators, women who dressed and acted convincingly like men; Vesta Tilley was the most famous.

"At the Brixton Empire, they obliged me. Won't you, you handsome sweetie?" Mrs. Eddington, who was actually Cyril Slough, ran his fingers through Layton's hair and put his arm around his waist.

Layton squirmed, his stomach clenching; he didn't want his hair dye to come off on Cyril's fingers, and he also didn't like being cuddled by a poof. Thoughts of prison and its sodomites beat at his brain. With an effort, he pushed them back.

"Leave him be, you old tart. Let him paint what he wants. He's not interested in your tatty frock," said Mrs. Freddington, or Neville Philpott.

"Thank you, Neville," said Layton. He continued his work on the cloth, which depicted the entrance hall of Chiswick House. Eddington and Freddington were two dim-witted upper-class matrons, and the largely lower middle-class and working-class audiences loved watching them make fools of themselves. On the stage, inferiors could insult their superiors without fear of repercussions.

Both middle-aged men were absolutely convincing as women. With their makeup, hair, and costumes, they could have gone shopping at Harrods and not raised an eyebrow.

"You bleedin' cow, mind your business. A little more yellow wouldn't hurt."

"And keep your hands off the man!" Neville squawked. "Next, you'll be travelin' up his bum."

"All right, girls, pull in your claws, and get back to your dressing room." It was Mrs. Mapes, approaching with Elwyn Thomas, the stage manager. Both stepped back to look at the cloth.

"Your scenes are so realistic, Frank," said

Mrs. Mapes. "Really, top drawer. You Dorset lads know how to draw."

Thomas nodded in agreement, and Layton dipped his head in a gracious nod, feeling the praise warm his insides. "Thank you, Cissie," he said.

He'd been on the job for more than a month and was doing the cloths for the next week's turns. In variety theatre, most acts changed weekly, which meant constant designing and painting of backdrops. Sometimes, an old cloth would be reused, but regulars in the audience who could attend two or three times a week would recognize them if they appeared too many times.

From the very first week, he'd found comfort in this fantasy world that revolved around artifice and illusion. People he'd never have associated with in his former life populated the theatre: magicians, acrobats, singers, comics, contortionists, jugglers. They seemed like aliens from another planet. Being backstage with them was completely different from being an architect. In his old job, one had to deal with reality, with the pressure of constructing a building that cost thousands of pounds. Here, everything was make-believe. All that mattered was the unashamed pursuit of delight.

Charlie, the stage doorman, stuck his head

in the doorway of the scene shop.

"Mrs. Mapes, them natives are here."

"Wonderful. Bring them out to the stage, please." She turned to Layton and smiled. "Frank, I'm giving you a special job. Come with me."

Onstage, Layton stopped in his tracks. Before him stood five tiny black people wrapped in blankets. He blinked rapidly, realizing they weren't children but adults. Each was just over four feet in height and barefoot. One carried a spear. A white man in a greatcoat and derby towered over them, and Mrs. Mapes went to him with open arms.

"Professor Evans, how good to see you again. And Mangogo, welcome, sir."

The professor shook her hand; the black fellow smiled, clacked his teeth, and stamped his spear. Stagehands and acts in rehearsal stopped to watch in fascination.

"Frank, Professor Evans & His Pygmies will be with us for a special *one-month* engagement. We'll need two very realistic backcloths."

"They are hunter-gatherers from Central Africa, so a scene of a rain forest will be appropriate." The professor had a refined Cambridge accent and a lecturing tone.

"Maybe some lions and rhinos thrown in,"

added Mrs. Mapes.

"I'll go to the library to look up some photos," Layton said. He couldn't stop staring at the bony little people. Beneath their blankets, they wore only loincloths. The two women looked like the men but had shriveled, prune-like breasts.

"These people use a toilet, right? They won't go shitting on me floor?" growled Elwyn.

"Well, that has been a problem," the professor said. "In the rain forest, they can squat and go wherever they like. But I've instructed them on the use of modern toilet facilities, including toilet paper. It took some doing, but they're jolly good at it now."

"Elwyn, you show them around the place," Mrs. Mapes instructed. "They'll have dressing room six to themselves. Don't see them sharing a space off the bat," she added with a laugh.

Elwyn was clearly reluctant but did as he was told. "Let's go, you bloody savages."

"Come on, Frank," Mrs. Mapes said, tossing him a smile. "I'll stand you a lager at the Admiral Benbow."

In the pub, the publican greeted Cissie warmly and gave them their drinks for free.

They sat at a table in the corner. The widow Cissie Mapes, Layton had learned, was a powerful woman with a fearsome reputation. She booked the acts for the MacMillan Empire chain, the most prestigious theatre circuit in the United Kingdom. She and she alone decided who would perform, and thus she possessed incredible power. Cissie ran the circuit like a general, ordering people about and severely dressing them down for any infraction. She was particularly harsh about the artistes ad-libbing and extending their allocated time onstage. It was an ironclad rule that the show had to stay on schedule.

Twenty years earlier, music halls had been built and owned by one person. Now, at the beginning of the twentieth century, the new huge variety halls were all owned by syndicates; their investors owned chains of theatres and could put up the half a million pounds required for construction. It was likely, Layton thought, gazing across the table at Cissie, that no other woman in England wielded so much influence in big business. The care of her invalid mother and spinster sister required she be based in her hometown of Nottingham, but Cissie traveled to the Great Empire Theatre of Varieties in London's West End once a week to see new acts.

This was the third time Layton had shared a drink alone with Cissie. She did most of the talking, telling stories of her years in the theatre — she had started out at sixteen as a magician's assistant — and gossiping hilariously about the latest acts. Somewhere in her past was a regrettable marriage to a comedian, hence the *Mrs.* Mapes.

Cissie had a beautiful smile and a charming, high-pitched giggle. Independent, funny, and fierce, the total opposite of an English society lady, she was like no woman Layton had ever met. Cissie didn't need a man to support her; she took care of herself and was proud of it. She was a hard-nosed businesswoman, and he liked that.

Layton couldn't help thinking how different Cissie was from his ex-wife. Both were strikingly attractive, and he had loved Edwina to death, but he had to admit that she was like a helpless child. She couldn't do anything for herself. It was because she had grown up with servants around to do everything, for her entire life. They even made sure her bath temperature was always exactly 100 degrees Fahrenheit. Her mother, the late Lady Elizabeth, raised her the way her mother had done, which meant being totally dependent on and completely subservient to a man. Even when they were married, the housekeeper and cook managed their household, although Edwina always arranged the flowers.

But the main difference between the two women was that Cissie came up the hard way and knew the value of a quid. He really admired Cissie's practical nature when it came to money. Edwina, who had unlimited access to her father's fortune, never had to pay for anything out of her own pocket and thus knew nothing about money. When a person never has to worry about what something costs, money has no value. Growing up in Dorset, Layton had been taught that money doesn't grow on trees and should be spent wisely or, better yet, saved. He had wanted to instill that important value in Ronald when he was older but never got the chance. Taking him to a confectioner's shop and teaching him how to pay for sweets and count his change was something he had looked forward to. It saddened him to think that his son would inherit his mother's ignorance of money matters.

Whenever they talked, Layton was careful not to reveal anything about his history to Cissie. He knew he seemed evasive and eventually fabricated a story about working for an engraver in Dorset, where he'd developed his artistic talent. Whenever she started to ask too many questions, he'd veer the conversation toward her.

"You're what they call a 'liberated woman,' " he said gingerly. "She does what she wants and doesn't need a man."

"Bollocks!" Cissie gave a howl of laughter. "You're bloody right I'm a businesswoman, and a tough one at that. But I'm no unfeminine, unsexed man-hater. Do I dress like a man, wear my hair short, and sport a mustache? No! Do you think I'm feminine, Frank?"

The swiftness of her reply caught Layton off guard. "Why, yes! The moment I first saw you in Black's office, I thought how beautiful you were," he blurted.

Cissie smiled at him. "Well, well. Coming from a good-lookin' bloke like you, that's a bloody big compliment."

Layton smiled shyly into his pint of lager. Then he looked her straight in her large, blue eyes, and added, "It's not just your beauty. It's your independence and confidence. You're a woman of *substance.*"

"You're dead-on there, m'boy." She sat back in her seat, taking in the crowd around them. "Most women aren't, especially these society ladies. All fur coat and no knickers."

"You definitely have knickers," Layton said. A second later, his blundered reply dawned on him, and he blushed.

Across the table, Cissie howled with laughter. Layton joined in, his head bobbing to and fro. He hadn't laughed so hard in more than five years.

"Indeed I do, Frank, and many a man has wanted me to drop 'em." She waved her glass in the air. "Jackie, another round for me and my gentleman friend."

She turned back to him. A sudden intensity galvanized her face; it was as if electricity were running through her bones, giving her energy.

"My Pygmies are going to make a packet, Frank. They've played to full houses, and now I've got them under a long-term contract. I'm going to do the same thing with some of the other real popular acts."

"But what do they do?"

"Stand up there and sing and dance while Evans gives a lecture. People love it. They've never seen anything like them before. You see, Frank, there's no shame in an act being nonsensical as long as it has appeal."

"They seem very scrawny," Layton ventured.

"That's how all of them are." Cissie wrinkled her nose. "The problem is keeping 'em warm. They're not used to the English weather. I may have to buy them coats and shoes."

"I'll do some realistic backgrounds for them. They'll feel like they're back home in the jungle. Might make them feel warmer."

"I know you will. I'm glad you've taken to our little world of make-believe, Frank," Cissie said, patting his hand. "What's your favorite act so far?"

"Oh, it's so difficult to say. So many of them are great." He wasn't saying this to curry favor, Layton realized as the words left his lips. He meant it. "The animal acts are very funny, especially Handley's Monkeys. I was really impressed by Agnes, the Equestrian Juggler."

"She's bloody amazing," Cissie said, rapping her knuckles on the table for emphasis. "The sole purpose of variety theatre, Frank, is popular entertainment for the common people. We give 'em a magical place to go, and just for a night, they can forget about their dull jobs, their awful lives."

"You know," Layton said slowly, feeling like an excited child, "I still can't get over the flickers — the moving pictures. Like the one showing the palace of Versailles last week. You felt as if you were really there. What an incredible invention."

"Cost us five quid for just that one film."
Cissie paused, assessing him. "You've never
been up in the projection booth, have you?
What about meeting me up there in the gallery after the second show, luv?"

"Run him out. Run him out," screamed a
man in a derby.

It was sheer bedlam. The crowd in the gallery had gone berserk, standing atop the
wooden benches, cheering their heads off.

"Keep running!" yelled another man.

The object of the gallery's attention was a
cricket match on the stage. The batsman
had just struck the ball and was running
between the wickets. Normally, this
wouldn't have caused much excitement;
cricket was everyday recreation in Britain.
But this was no ordinary match. It was being played by four baby elephants — De
Gracia's Pachyderm Performers.

Layton had climbed up to the gallery to
see how the backcloth he'd painted looked
from "the gods." Now he found himself
caught up in the excitement and cheering
on the elephant batsman, who was slowly
lumbering along. The two elephant fielders
were having trouble retrieving the ball. The
batsman crossed the batting crease; the
fielder rolled the ball back to the bowler,

who snatched it off the ground with its trunk.

His cloth, Layton thought, looked very convincing. He'd based it on the Royal Cricket Grounds, adding spectators and a scoring board. But it was the oversize cricket caps and white jackets the elephants wore that made the act so funny. For elephants, they played damn well.

The audience in the gallery was made up of the poorest of the poor: common laborers, sweatshop workers, clerks, barmaids, and the unemployed. All of them were going crazy with laughter. Each day, Layton thought, this sorry lot fought to survive. Tonight, for eighty minutes, they forgot their troubles, just as Cissie had said. He felt sorry for the acts that had to follow the elephants, which included the top of the bill, Bonnie Bill McGregor, the Flying Scotsman of Laughter.

The show ended with a final turn by Monsieur Slippere, who did a magnificent trick playing on the piano with his toes. The gallery audience filed out quickly; they had to catch the last trams at ten thirty. Layton stayed on his bench, looking around the auditorium. He'd never spent any time up in the gallery. Unlike the rest of the theatre, this section had almost no decoration. The walls and ceiling were plain painted plaster, divided by panels with simple wood moldings. The stage seemed to be miles below.

In the solitude, Layton could admire the entirety of Matcham's exquisite design. He started from the left sidewall of the gallery, taking a 180-degree view to the right. His eyes lingered on the great proscenium arch, then darted back to the right sidewall. He looked to the left again.

Something was amiss. A wood molding toward the bottom of the wall looked crooked. Instead of being laid completely flat, it had a slight but noticeable bulge. Layton saw why — the plaster on the wall itself had a bulge, which meant the brick wall behind it wasn't laid plumb. He was surprised that Matcham would allow such sloppy work. He was well known for his attention to workmanship. Layton started to walk toward it to take a closer look. In his own buildings, he had hated anything out of kilter, even a light shade that wasn't straight.

"There you are," trilled a warm voice. Cissie, standing at the very top of the gallery.

Layton bounded up the steep stairs and stood by her side, facing the auditorium. "There's a loneliness in an empty theatre," he said.

"Or you can hear the echoes of the cheering and laughter. Depends on how you look at life, ducks." Cissie motioned for him to follow. In the back wall along the gallery's rear aisle was a door, which she opened with a key. "*This* is where the flickers come from," she said, turning on the light.

A wooden box with a crank on its side sat before Layton. A kind of telescope stuck out of its end and was positioned in a small circular opening in the wall.

"It's called a Pathé cinematograph," Cissie said. "It projects light through spools of film onto the screen onstage."

Layton ran his hands over the wooden box, smiling. "This is bloody amazing."

"Next month, we're getting a film of a big fire in a warehouse in Lambeth. You see the whole building collapse," Cissie said with great pride.

Layton could see how glad she was to have impressed him.

"They have films showing whole stories now. The Yanks did one called *The Great Train Robbery.* I'm trying to get the circuit to rent it."

The projection booth was tiny, like a telephone call box. Layton and Cissie were crammed together, not quite touching. He had never been so close to her before, and he could smell the scent of her face powder, which was almost intoxicating. He hadn't been this close to a woman since before prison. Being much taller, he looked down into Cissie's face. Her eyes seemed just inches away, but he maintained his decorum, as if they were sitting apart from one another, having tea in a parlor.

Cissie was avidly discussing the different films the circuit would show. One theatre owner, she told him, had abandoned live acts to show only flickers. This, she thought, was nonsense.

"People like the personal contact with a variety act. There's an intimate connection between a performer and the audience. You can't get that anywhere else."

Layton wholeheartedly agreed. Shifting his weight, he bumped Cissie's shoulder.

"Oh, I'm so sorry," he blurted out, getting red in the face.

"My, aren't we the proper gentleman?" Cissie said with a great smile. "Don't you get yourself into a lather. You didn't rip my dress off, you know. And you look very nice when you blush."

Layton laughed nervously. Cissie didn't seem at all uncomfortable. His ex-wife Edwina, he thought, would have fainted dead away. Not from the actual contact, but from the thought of the scandal such a situation could cause.

"Yes, I'm being silly." He had averted his eyes, but now they locked onto hers and stayed there. It was a pleasant sensation. They seemed to draw together like two opposite poles of a magnet, but at the last minute, he pulled back. He didn't want to, but he also didn't want to seem improper, especially with someone who was essentially his boss. An important part of his training as a pretend English gentleman was being a paragon of honorable behavior.

"Well, thank you for showing me the projection booth. I always wanted to see where that beam of light came from. Isn't it odd that a ray of light can transform itself into those wonderful images on the cloth?"

"You have the deepest blue eyes," Cissie said, still gazing up at Layton. "I never noticed that before."

"We've never been so close to each other, I guess." Layton fought to keep his breathing steady. "I inherited them from my mother. She had wonderful eyes. Could put you at ease just by looking at you."

"Mrs. Owen did a jolly good job raising her little boy. He turned out a right nice bloke."

Layton smiled at Cissie, then inched

around her to get to the door. Together, they walked down the gallery exit stair to the first floor.

"The elephant cricket turn was smashing," said Layton rather awkwardly.

"Oh my, yes." Cissie seemed unperturbed. "I thought DeGracia was balmy when he told me he'd trained elephants to play cricket, but damn if he didn't. Next, they'll be playing for the national team against New Zealand."

"Will the circuit be keeping them on?"

"Oh, you can be sure of that, luv. Remember, the owners only respect performers who can put people in seats. Those pachyderms *pack* them in," she exclaimed, pleased with her play on words.

Out in the street, which was now deserted, they turned and faced each other. A few seconds passed in silence.

"Well, I have to get home to bed for a good night's rest. I have a show to put on tomorrow — and so do you, Frank."

"Good night to you, Cissie. Sweet dreams."

11

No one but an architect would give a damn about a crooked wood molding. Even most architects wouldn't care. But Layton couldn't let it go. It was in his nature to be a real fussbudget when it came to architectural details. Anything the slightest bit out of harmony or balance would irritate the hell out of him. When a project of his had almost finished construction, Layton would walk through and make a long list of the tiniest things to be corrected, like a hairline crack in a plaster wall or a sloppy paint drip. He wanted everything to be absolutely perfect. Layton stared at the section of wall for almost a minute. It was indeed odd. Why was there a bulge at the bottom of the wall when the rest of it was so perfectly flat? Why was the one piece of molding so cockeyed?

Layton peered out into the darkened theatre. Strange how a place that was usually so bright and full of enjoyment could look so sinister and evil. He'd waited until the charwomen had finished cleaning the auditorium to return after 3:00 a.m.. Turning on one of the overhead gallery lights, he started prodding around the plaster on the sidewall with his jackknife. He only wanted to probe a little bit, but consumed with curiosity, he kept chipping away. The plaster dropped off, exposing a one-foot-square area of brick. Compared to the wall around it, the mortar joints were sloppily done, and the brick bulged out. Layton easily dislodged one brick, then another and another, revealing a ledge next to a cavity behind the wall. This wasn't unusual; theatres, like other buildings, needed space to run plumbing, gas, and electrical lines.

But when the hole in the brick wall came fully open, Layton noticed an odd smell. It wasn't gas. He struck a match, peered in, and reared up in panic. The match singed his finger; he backed into the edge of the bench across the aisle, sending a jolt of pain through his body. His breath came in hard pants, and his heart was racing. He looked around. Was he alone? With trembling fingers, he lit another match and stuck his head back in the opening.

About six inches away was the foot of a skeleton. He knew it belonged to a human because of a prior experience with skeletons. Seeing the bones unleashed a flood of memories. It brought back his days as a young architect, working for John Hicks. He'd been given the unpleasant task of supervising railway spur construction in the resort town of Bournemouth, on the Dorset coast. The spur passed through a church graveyard, which meant digging up coffins to be reinterred at another location. Some had rotted through, exposing the grisly looking skeletons. As they were lifted from their graves, browned and disconnected bones tumbled free. The skulls looked as though they were grinning at him. It made the hair stand up on the back of young Layton's neck — the same sensation he was experiencing now.

But while Layton was terrified by the sight, an irresistible urge to look inside the opening suddenly took control of him. It was as if the hole in the wall was beckoning him, drawing him forward. Its pull was overpowering. As he gazed at the void, he reached into his jacket pocket and took out another match, then slowly walked toward the wall. He half expected something to leap out at him from the square black hole. Layton was scared but at the same time very elated. Stooping over, he struck the match and stuck it into the opening. The dim, yellowish light shone on a full skeleton lying faceup on the ledge. It looked like it was taking a nap. With his free hand, Layton took hold of the foot and carefully inched the bones toward him.

The skeleton dragged along the ledge of the cavity with a grating, scratching sound. The match burned out, but he didn't need another one with the gallery lights above. The legs emerged, then the pelvis. The rib cage, with the arms by its sides, then the skull squeezed through. When he had dragged the skeleton to the gallery aisle, Layton knelt to examine it. The bones weren't completely bare; the muscle and sinew, still attached to them, looked like varnished leather. The next thing that struck him was the odd shape of the backbone, which curved sharply to the side.

Layton was now sweating and breathing hard, amazed at the sight before him. He suddenly jerked his body around to check again to make sure he was alone. The vast space of the theatre felt menacing and haunted. He sat on the bench behind him and gazed wide-eyed at the bones. He closed his eyes and gripped the edge of bench to calm himself down. Then, taking a big, deep breath, Layton gingerly picked up the bones and eased them back ever so slowly into the hole. But when he stacked the bricks back in the opening, he paused. How stupid of him. It would be plain as day that the body had been discovered. Whoever had put this poor devil here hadn't wanted anyone to know about it.

Layton stared at the hole for almost a minute. He couldn't leave it like this.

He walked down to the backstage and took the spiral stair that led to a vast subterranean space twenty feet high and directly beneath the stage. A complex set of hydraulic-powered machinery lurked before him in the darkness. These devices raised or lowered sections of the stage and operated the traps performers used to ascend or descend during their turns, for, say, a magician disappearing in a puff of smoke. The upper level where the machinery was housed was called the mezzanine. The lower, where crew workshops and storage rooms were located, was the cellar. Here was the building maintenance shop, which held everything that might be needed to make repairs. Two thousand people twice a night, six days a week, put constant wear and tear on a structure, especially the walls.

At the workbench, Layton prepared a large blob of plaster and cement mortar on a hod. Then he took a trowel and walked back up to the gallery. As the son of a mason, he'd learned how to lay a brick wall and plaster it by the time he was ten years old. Repairing the gallery wall was not difficult; he re-created the bulge so no one would know the spot had been touched. But the plaster patch was white, while the rest of the wall was a yellowish-cream color. Touching up paint was another routine maintenance task; Layton went back downstairs and found the right can of color on a shelf. Normally, one would let plaster dry before painting, but of course, he didn't have the time to wait for that.

Finally, he replaced the molding as he had found it and stood back to critique his work. The patch was darker than the surrounding wall, but over time, it would lighten. Besides, the gallery was always filled with clouds of thick cigarette smoke. Nobody would notice. The last thing to do was clean up the plaster he had broken off.

But . . . His heart sank. What about the person who'd buried the poor bugger behind the wall to start with? Who would do such a thing?

As Layton put the tools away, his thoughts returned to the skeleton. If he reported what he'd found to the police, they'd naturally start asking questions about himself — what was he doing up there that time of night? Why did he think something was amiss about the wall and start poking at it? What was his job at the Grand? And who exactly was Frank Owen — where did he come from, and what was his background? The local press who hovered around police stations for big news would be on top of the discovery of the body in a second and hunt down Layton to ask him questions. Their scrutiny would be withering. If they took photographs of him, the jig would definitely be up. Someone in England would see his picture and figure out that Frank Owen was Douglas Layton, the Butcher of the West End. He'd be out of a job, and the press and public would hound him for months as they had before the trial. Layton's life now was on an even keel, and he was happy for the first time in years. No, the mystery was his to unravel.

Why was the man hidden behind the wall? The murderer could have dumped the body in a river or buried it in a forest. But bodies float up or are dug up by animals. The killer must have wanted to be absolutely sure no one would find his victim. Layton slumped on the bench, doing the math in his head. The body must have been hidden while the building was under construction, over four years ago, in 1901.

But who was this man? What had he done to deserve such a fate?

12

Mangogo, the Pygmy, was standing next to Layton stage right, watching the act, but Layton had a hard time concentrating. He kept looking up at the gallery wall. He couldn't stop thinking about the skeleton. When he was onstage during the day, he had to prevent himself from constantly looking up at the burial chamber. Suppose the murderer — or murderers! — noticed. He'd find himself behind a wall too. What a dolt he was to open up the bulge! After leaving the gallery that night, Layton had an urge to light out and catch the next train back to Dorset, but the thought of his brother's taunts and his father's disappointment changed his mind.

"Is there anyone in the audience tonight who thinks they can match my feat of strength?"

"Me," shouted a voice from way back in the pit.

"Then come up here, sir."

A broad man in his early twenties wearing a bowler hat and a shirt without a collar bulled through the patrons on the pit benches. The audience applauded enthusiastically as he made his way to the stage.

"You can do it, mate," shouted a man from the stalls.

Three more strapping young men also made their way down from the gallery. The young man from the pit bounded up the side stairs, waving to the audience, a big smile on his handsome face. On the little table in front of him lay a five-eighths-inch-thick cylindrical iron bar, twelve inches in length, which had been bent into a U shape.

"Please, sir, if you could straighten out this bar that I have bent."

The man grabbed both ends of the bar with his meaty hands and pulled with all his might but couldn't budge them. He tried again and again, his face reddening with exertion. Finally, he gave up. The three men from the gallery had queued, eager for their turns.

"Could you hand me the bar, sir?"

With a sullen look on his face, the man did what he was told. Holding the U-shaped bar aloft, the young, slender, beautiful girl bent the bar straight as though it were made of taffy. The audience went wild. She then bent the bar around her little neck and handed it to one of the waiting men. Each of the three tried and failed to unbend it.

Dainty Amy Silborne was at the moment the world's best strongwoman and, according to Cissie Mapes, the best specialty act in the business. No hairy, hulking giant of a woman, she was as feminine and petite as any society lady in Mayfair. In a burgundy gown adorned with yellow feathers, Dainty Amy looked stunning onstage. Her ladylike appearance made her feats of strength even more spectacular.

From a shelf below the tabletop, she produced a coil of thick hemp rope and challenged the four men to a tug-of-war, which she won handily. As they stewed in embarrassment onstage, Amy picked up a Sears Roebuck catalog and tore it in half.

It was a brilliant act, thought Layton, made better by asking not plants but actual volunteers from the audience to come up. The men provided context for Amy's strength. She took her bows, and the audience cheered wildly. Mangogo let out a shrill call that must have been a Pygmy cheer of admiration. Then he went back to his fish and chips. He always drowned them in HP Sauce, a new condiment Layton thought would never catch on, but the performer loved it. Layton often accompanied Mangogo to the fish and chips shop and tried to get him to use vinegar, but he refused, saying it smelled like leopard piss.

The two had developed a strange bond. Mangogo was no ignorant savage, as most had expected, but an intelligent fellow with a great talent for learning English. The stagehands liked him and got a big laugh teaching him obscene words. Layton taught him more useful phrases, like, "A pleasure to meet you, sir." In the afternoons before the show, performers and crew often took Mangogo to the Prince Regent, their favorite pub. They introduced him to Guinness, which he downed in great quantities to no ill effect. In fact, he could drink any stagehand under the table. Mangogo said that jinwana, a drink from fermented jungle leaves, was much stronger than any British drink.

"Smashing," Mangogo exclaimed now as Amy came off the stage.

Layton smiled and picked a chip out of Mangogo's packet. Fish and chips came wrapped in old newspaper, which he liked; the printer's ink added to the flavor.

"Make good . . ." Mangogo pointed at Amy in the wings, the word escaping him.

"Wife," Layton volunteered.

"Strong, do much . . . zocancho."

"Work."

"Jolly good — much work."

"Do you have a wife?"

Mangogo raised his hand, showing four fingers.

"Four?"

"Four jolly good for Mangogo. Do much work."

Layton burst out laughing and slapped the little man on the back, and Mangogo happily stamped his spear on the stage boards. Mangogo was actually the first black man Layton had ever known. There had been no blacks in Dorset and none in British high society, although the thought of the latter amused him greatly. Tomorrow afternoon, he planned to take Mangogo to lunch at Pearson's, Nottingham's poshest restaurant. How astounded those upper-crust patrons would be to see him dining alongside them! But nobody would ask him to leave; his spear, which he took everywhere, made sure of that.

The other Pygmies were still scared and unsure of their new environment. They kept to themselves in their little flat in the center of Nottingham and never ventured out. In contrast, Mangogo was preternaturally sociable and outgoing. And he was far more interesting than any of Layton's aristocratic clients had been. He told Layton many exciting stories of the jungle, dealing with leopards, giant poisonous insects, pythons, and bull elephants. He was so short and slight of build, but his courage seemed inverse to his physical stature. Mangogo was born a brave fellow, thought Layton.

Mangogo offered him a chip not slathered in HP Sauce and waved goodbye. He was on after the next act.

"Remember, tomorrow afternoon, lunch at Pearson's," Layton called after him.

"Steak and . . . kidney pie," Mangogo said, rubbing his little brown belly under the burnt-orange-colored blanket he always wore.

"I'll make a proper Englishman out of you yet, you'll see."

The act onstage was Eddington & Freddington, the two posh nitwit female impersonators.

The English country manor drawing room backcloth Layton had designed fit the act perfectly, and in no time, he was choking with laughter, even though he'd seen the act many times. Cyril and Neville were hilarious, and audiences loved them.

The rest of the night stretched pleasantly

ahead of him. After the second show, he and Cissie would go to the Prince Regent with Cyril and Neville and stay until last call, listening to the duo's stories and jokes. The two flaming poofs had become close friends of his, as had other performers and stage crew. He enjoyed being invited into this warm circle of friends from this magical world. It gave Layton great comfort after all he'd been through.

The torment of the disaster and losing his family still hounded him, but being with friends in the pub controlled Layton's drinking a bit. Although he still drank by himself in his digs, he found he didn't need the alcohol as much after joining the music hall. After closing, he would often go to Cissie's home and have just one drink with her sister, Daisy, and her mother, Rose, whom he liked immensely. Cissie's presence had become the most important thing in his life; it felt like a life preserver thrown to a man drowning in a raging sea. Her jolly nature and keen sense of humor had kept him from being consumed by his sorrows. The bad memories still tormented Layton, but they weren't as frequent, and the pain wasn't nearly as acute.

Down below, Eddington & Freddington were trying to change a light bulb in a table lamp. They were too stupid to manage it; complete chaos ensued, and the audience in the gallery howled with laughter. Osborne, their elderly butler, tottered out onto the stage.

Eddington: Osborne, how many Englishmen *does* it take to change a light bulb?
Osborne: Two, m'lady. One to mix the gin and tonics while the other calls an electrician.

In his short time in the theatre world, Layton had discovered that a tangible transfer of energy existed between performers and audience. It was much like an electrical circuit. Songs and jokes flowed out to the audience, generating pleasure, and laughter and applause flowed back to the stage. The applause gave the performers confidence, invigorating them with energy. Layton could see it happening right now.

The orchestra broke into a pounding drumbeat, the brass section screeching out what sounded to British ears like exotic jungle music. The audience broke into applause, a clear sign that the act was popular: the theatregoers knew the intro music. The tabs pulled away, revealing Mangogo's act, Professor Evans & His Pygmies, in front of a jungle scene Layton was quite proud of. The music stopped, and Professor Evans, in a tan pith helmet and khaki outfit, started explaining the ways of Central African Pygmies.

When Layton had first seen the act almost four weeks ago, he'd thought the audience, especially the pit and gallery crowd, would find it a big joke and heckle. But as the professor lectured and Mangogo and his fellow tribesmen stood, smiling silently, the people in the gallery froze, transfixed, uttering not a sound. Layton could see fascination and awe in their faces. When the Pygmies started dancing and singing, they were even more astonished. Aku, the youngest of the group, beat out a rhythm on his tom-tom, and the orchestra joined in. At the end of the nine-minute turn, Aku produced a small Union Jack from under his blanket and waved it, to the delight of the crowd. Amazing, thought Layton. But after all, the Pygmies were part of Britain's great colonial empire. Maybe all these white Englishmen felt connected to them.

Before Layton returned to the scene shop, he stole a glance at the gallery wall, then looked quickly around to see if anyone noticed him looking.

13

"Excuse me, mate."

The cloth before Layton depicted Trafalgar Square. His hand was moving fast, giving a vivid sheen to the water that filled the fountain. Still shaken by his discovery of the other night, he was painting in a trance and hadn't heard anyone enter the scene shop. Now, he turned to see a skinny, middle-aged man.

"How can I help you?" Layton asked.

"Can you tell me where the pot is? I was on me way to use the one at the main entrance, but that clot of a theatre manager told me the help has to use the one backstage. Can you believe the cheek of that wanker?"

Layton smiled and wiped his hands with a rag. "Yes, yes I can. Let me show you where the convenience is located."

"You're a good bloke, you are." The man shook his head ruefully. "Think I got the tandoori trots from me spicy curry. I'm about to explode, if ya get my meaning."

"I had a case of it myself a few weeks back. We British have a delicate constitution."

The man laughed. "That we do, mate."

"So, are you a new act?" Layton asked as he led him down the narrow brick corridor.

"Nah, I'm a Pathé projectionist. I show the flickers in the first half of the bill."

Layton stopped, wonder on his face. "You don't say! What an incredible invention. I love all the acts, but the flickers are my favorite. They're bloody amazing."

"Harry Aubrey's the name. I was showing 'em at the Hippodrome. Just got assigned to the Grand yesterday."

"Here we are," said Layton, pointing to the loo.

"I'll be out after I make a deposit. Don't go away. We can chat a bit," Aubrey said, bolting through the door. A few minutes later, he emerged, looking very relieved.

"So you was sayin' how incredible the flickers are. Let me tell ya something. One day, they'll have whole big theatres just to show moving pictures — no music hall."

"I've heard that," Layton said.

"Well, you best believe it, mate. Tonight, I'm showing *The Temptation of St. Anthony* and one about the assassination of the Grand Duke Sergius in Russia — not the real assassination, but what they call a 'reenactment.' "

"All on that little strip of celluloid." Wonder sounded in Layton's voice.

Aubrey gave him a cheeky grin. "If it weren't for you, I'd be wandering around with a load in my drawers. Come on up fifteen minutes before my turn, and I'll show you how the whole caboodle works."

"That's right, just thread the film through there, then down under here. Give a bit of slack. There, you got the hang of it. All the pictures are on one reel."

Layton was so excited to learn to run the projector that he barely thought about the skeleton that was fifty feet away in the gallery wall.

Down on the stage, the baritone, George Robey, was finishing up his rendition of "Keep the Fires Alight." The flickers were next on the bill. Aubrey switched off the overhead light and placed his finger on the projector's toggle switch. The orchestra struck up an introduction.

"And 'ere we go," Aubrey said softly.

A beam of white light shot out of the varnished wood box, and Aubrey started turning the crank. On the screen below, Satan tempted St. Anthony with the beautiful Sirens. "You take over, Frank," Aubrey whispered, and Layton began cranking in complete synch. It was like he was a magician, producing moving images with light.

Grinning from ear to ear, Layton kept up the steady cranking through a Swiss tobogganing scene, a warehouse fire, a clown trick, and finally the duke's assassination.

While he was cranking away, the audience below oohed and aahed at the various scenes; the tobogganing scene in particular was exciting, because the camera had been mounted in the sled, giving them the illusion of being in the driver's seat. Layton wondered if Ronald had been to the flickers; he imagined his son absolutely loving them. Layton had noticed that British society had become less staid and attended the music hall performances now, which wasn't so before the disaster. Edwina and he never went; music halls were considered common by Lord Litton. But maybe Ronald had been to one.

Before he went to prison, Layton had always read his son stories at bedtime. With Ronald sitting in his lap in the bed, together, they turned the pages of the book, admiring the wonderful illustrations. Ronald would point his little finger at a picture of a knight and expand on the story, explaining that the great warrior had already slain four dragons and one witch and was the bravest man in all of England. Every night, a story would be read, and sometimes it was hard to keep up the supply of books.

One night, on a whim, Layton found a book of paintings in his library and asked Ronald to explain what was going on in a picture. For a painting by Sir Alfred Munnings of a little girl and boy pushing a punt along some reeds in a river, Ronald concocted a marvelous story of why they were there — the children wanted to gorge themselves on sweets out of sight of their nanny. For Layton, this form of storytelling was far more enjoyable, and it became a ritual for the two of them. It delighted Layton that his son was so imaginative for being only four years old. Yes, the flickers would definitely excite Ronald's vivid imagination. Layton wished he could sit next to him in the darkened theatre and just enjoy his reactions at the magical glimmering images up on the cloth.

"Well done, Frank, me boy," Aubrey crowed when the reel reached its end. "Did you enjoy that?"

"Yes, I did," exclaimed Layton.

"Come up anytime and be my assistant. You're always welcome. One night, I'll show you how to run the flickers backward. It's funny as hell to see."

Layton immediately thought Ronald would find that sidesplitting.

There was the sound of feet on the stair outside, and the projection room door swung open, revealing Cissie. "They told me I'd find you up here," she said.

"Just teaching 'im all about the flickers, Mrs. Mapes," Aubrey said jovially, taking the reel off the projector and stowing it safely in its container.

Cissie smiled at Layton. "This chappie does love the flickers."

"Now, if you'll excuse me, I got me a little crumpet waiting for a slap and tickle. See ya tomorrow, Frank." Aubrey put the reel in a cupboard, locked the padlock, and hurriedly pulled on his jacket. "Do me a favor — turn off the light and lock up."

Cissie rolled her eyes as Aubrey hurried out, then stepped into the tiny booth to stand beside Layton. "She's probably a cow, but they're all the same in the dark, eh?"

Music sounded for the next turn; the applause in the gallery erupted around them. Cissie peeked out the window and gave Layton a wry smile. "Laura Bennett, the

Yankee Country Girl. Pretty little trick, but not the best of voices."

"So why'd you hire her?"

"I saw potential, Frank. Someone who could turn out to be a star. I'm very good at seeing potential — at finding good things in people."

"That's an admirable talent." Layton looked straight into Cissie's eyes, which were just inches from his. She was a magnet, drawing him in, and it felt wonderful. He desperately wanted to feel love for someone, to let go of the emotions his present masquerade forced him to keep in check. Over the last five years, he'd lived in a wasteland of stifled emotions. And now, this odd woman — so different from the world he was used to — had won his heart with her kindness, brashness, and raucous humor.

"Do you see any potential in me, Mrs. Mapes?" Layton asked in a low, tentative voice.

"A great deal, Mr. Owen," purred Cissie. "Potential for great happiness — in my life."

Music piped up from the orchestra for the duet act onstage, but neither Layton nor Cissie paid attention. Everything had left their minds except their feelings for each other. Layton leaned over and gave her a long, slow kiss. Then he locked the door of

the small, cramped room from the inside
and switched off the light.

14

"What's wrong, luv?"

"Nothing." Layton's annoyance at being pestered was clear from his voice. "Nothing at all."

"Oh yes there is, Frank. You can't fool your Auntie Cyril, dear. Why do you keep looking up in the gallery? Is there someone up there you know? An old sweetheart, I bet."

Eddington & Freddington, the next turn, stood in the wings, costumed in sequined evening gowns, feathered boas, and strings of pearls.

"Leave him be, you old tart. He's Cissie's property now," cackled Neville. "They're having a proper twinkle."

"I don't blame her," Cyril said, touching Layton's behind.

Layton jerked away, and Cyril let out a cackle of laughter.

"Shove off, Cyril. Remember, I told you

I'm not a sodomite."

"But you should consider it, luv. You don't know what you're missing," Cyril cooed into Layton's ear. Then, with a wink, he gave Layton's earlobe a playful tug.

Layton swore and stepped away, annoyed with himself for showing his cards. He was troubled by something up in the gallery.

"Tell Auntie Cyril what's the matter. A good talk and a nice cup of tea will do you good."

Layton ignored him. Sakuru, the Japanese Juggler, was about to do his brick trick, which meant he was almost finished. His backdrop was an abstracted Japanese garden scene with Mount Fuji in the background; Layton had drawn on the Japanese block prints he'd found at the main library in Nottingham for inspiration.

Sakuru, a husky Asian in a crimson kimono, eyed the tower of twenty-two bricks on the table in front of him. Atop the bricks was a glass of water. With a look of intense concentration on his face, Sakuru slowly worked his hand under the bottom brick and lifted the entire stack of bricks off the table. The tower leaned like it was about to topple over, but he ran across the stage, regaining its balance point, to the delight of the audience. He held it with his right hand, his left arm flung out in a flourish, then tossed the bricks up into the air. As they came crashing down, he caught the glass of water and drank it down to a rousing finish from the orchestra. He took his final call, bowing first to the gallery, then to the balcony circles and the stalls, and exited into the wings.

"How do you like that applause?" he said to Cyril in perfect English. "Won't be anything left for you, you bloody poof."

"You yellow Jap, how do you like this?" hissed Cyril, grabbing Sakuru's crotch.

Then Eddington & Freddington's cloth tumbled down from the fly tower, and they were on.

"I just heard that two Englishmen have been rescued after two years on a desert island in the Pacific," Eddington began.

"They must have been sick of each other after all that time together," Freddington said.

"Not at all. They never once talked to each other."

"Why on earth not?"

"They simply couldn't. They were never formally introduced!"

As laughter engulfed the theatre, Layton walked to the stage manager's desk. From here, Elwyn oversaw the performances, like a field general barking out orders to the troops. The fly floor was directly above.

"Get ready with Bimba Bamba's cloth, lads," Elwyn called up to the stagehands. To Layton, he said, "Nice work on the magician's cloth, Frank. Mr. Black likes your designs. Not the usual tripe. Very modern and progressive, but you keep 'em artistic."

"Thank you, Elwyn," Layton said, smiling. Painting the cloths had given him new confidence and taken his mind away from his demons. When you were engrossed in doing something you really enjoyed, he discovered, you didn't dwell as much on bad things. With Cissie and his job, he had been on the way to a new, happy life. Then Layton shot a glance at the wall in the gallery — the other night's ghastly discovery threw a roadblock in that path. Why couldn't things ever work out? Layton thought wearily. He just wanted to lead a normal, anonymous life. He shouldn't have poked his nose where it didn't belong. *But if no one discovered that he'd found the body, he might be out of harm's way.*

Bimba Bamba, whose real name was George Formby, approached. In his gold robe and turban, puffed, blue silk pants, and black satin slippers with the toes curled up, he resembled a Turkish sultan. George was a successful conjurer who'd toured the country for years; it was said he made £200 a week. In his most famous trick, his assistant climbed into a bejeweled box suspended ten feet above the stage. George shot three times with a pistol, the four flaps of the box collapsed open — and the girl was gone. Layton still couldn't figure out how it worked. It was a well-kept secret by Formby.

"Hello, Frank," said George as Fiona Pratt, his assistant, tripped up behind him. She was costumed as an exotic Middle Eastern wench in a turban and very low-cut red satin blouse, an amazing transformation for a girl from the slums of Brixton. Both had darkened their skin with makeup, and George wore a fake black mustache that curled at the ends. "Let's try that new cloth, the Persian rug with my face in the center. But make my head bigger, more evil-looking."

"Your head's big enough already," said Fiona, giving Layton a wink.

"And your bottom's too big," George growled back. "You had trouble getting it into the box last night. Keep it up, me girl, and you'll be out on the street. Now, go help Richard with the props."

Fiona scowled at George, then turned to

Layton and gave him a wink. "Frank, you should come to me digs for a cup of tea. Maybe I'll tell ya how the disappearing girl trick's done."

George sighed, watching her skip off.

"She's actually the best assistant I've ever had," he said. "And a decent shag to boot. She was thin as a bean when I first hired her. 'Twas right after the Britannia Empire disaster."

Layton blinked, fighting to keep his voice steady. "Were you there that night?"

"I was on the second half of the bill. Was backstage when the balcony came down, but I saw the results — all those poor buggers, screaming in pain. We artistes ran out into the auditorium." George shook his head. "Helped pull people out. Saw a fellow with his head squashed like a melon. Should have beheaded that bastard architect."

"I'll take care of the cloth, George," Layton said quietly and walked away.

But Charlie, the stage doorman, intercepted him in route.

"Mr. Black wants ya in his office, Frank."

"We're in a bit of a pickle, Frank." Black sat behind his huge desk, smoking a pipe. "Flanigan & Cobb are topping the bill at the Queen's Palace in the West End in a week, and they're making a big row about their cloth. They want you to design it."

Flanigan & Cobb were a hugely popular comedy act on the variety circuit. Cobb played a pompous toff, refined and debonair; Flanigan was the sloppily dressed working-class funny man, always undermining his social better. They had done a popular two-week engagement at the Grand last month, and Layton had painted twenty-foot-tall caricatures of their heads on either side of the cloth, with the Strand between.

"You can leave in the morning for London. I'll arrange your train fare and digs. It's only seven thirty now. Go home and pack."

Layton nodded. He could tell from Black's tone that the decision was final.

"You should be flattered, Frank!" Cissie said, sipping her pint of ale. "A West End theatre — that's the big time. So what's the problem? You don't like London?"

Layton gazed down at his glass. They were sitting at the little round table in the dress circle bar. This intimate, elegantly decorated area, with its cozy fireplace and mirror-hung walls, had quickly become their favorite spot for a drink during the performances.

"I've spent some time there," he said, try-

150

ing to keep the tremble from his voice. "Just some bad memories, that's all."

"Sounds like a woman's involved," Cissie said with a big smile. "An old sweetie pie, m'lad?"

Layton gave her a wan grin and took a sip of his Guinness.

"I'll be down to London in a couple of days," she said casually. "I need to meet with the solicitors about the new barring clause in the contracts."

"What's that?" Layton asked, eager to steer the conversation away from his past.

"It's a clause that will prohibit an act from appearing in any rival theatre within a radius of a mile, either sixteen weeks before an engagement or two weeks after."

"That's rather harsh," Layton said, sitting back slightly from the table.

"If you want to be more successful than the Hall Syndicate, you have to be harsh," Cissie snapped.

MacMillan and Hall were Great Britain's two largest chains — and great rivals. Together, they dominated the variety circuit, and they regularly tried to pilfer artistes from one another. In the past few years, MacMillan had topped Hall in attendance and popularity.

"You get too tough, and they'll form one

of those unions," Layton said, his voice carefully neutral. "I hear the government is going to force people to give servants health insurance. They say Labour will win the next election, and they favor the poor."

"Let those champagne socialists bloody well try," Cissie said. Her smile looked almost evil. "There are a million acts and just a few spots on the bill. If they don't like the rules, we'll get replacements in a heartbeat."

While Cissie was a very attractive, goodhearted woman, she had a hard-as-nails side when it came to business. Most women in Layton's former life were like Edwina — they knew nothing about business; it was a man's preserve, and they were content to stay away. Of course, there were women in England who ran small shops in villages and cities, but Cissie was different. The business she ran was an entertainment empire; the men who owned the circuit so valued her skill and knowledge that they had granted her the power to make huge decisions entirely on her own. Her savvy and toughness had made MacMillan number one.

When he and she were alone together, they did just two things: make love and talk about the theatre, which was the center of her life. Layton was always amazed how much she knew about this business of fun and fantasy. Cissie was totally dedicated to making people happy for two hours every day but Sunday, always trying to find unique (and money-making) acts to present to them. Layton thought he had an excellent memory, being an architect, but she had an incredible memory and could remember the exact sequence of a bear act from eleven years ago.

"What about a quick cuddle before I'm on my way?" asked Layton in a low voice.

Making love to Cissie was a revelation, a shattering of the staid sexual universe Layton had lived in his whole life. Who would have believed that sex could be so intoxicating, so uninhibited and exciting? While they lay in bed caressing each other after making love, Layton would invariably compare his former sex life with the present. He had truly loved Edwina, but like many society girls, she was taught by her mother that sex was a duty and not something to be enjoyed. "Just close your eyes, grit your teeth, and think of England" was the common advice of society mothers to their daughters, and that's exactly what Edwina did during their lovemaking. For Cissie, it was pure, unadulterated enjoyment. While Edwina had a beautiful figure,

Layton only saw glimpses of it under her nightgown. Cissie would stretch out unashamedly naked on top of the bedcovers.

Layton realized that the sorrow of losing Edwina was lessening bit by bit every day, just like the torment of the disaster, something he hadn't thought would happen. Sometimes, he felt quite guilty about it. When Edwina had abandoned him after only six months in prison, he was angry and hurt, because he had truly loved his wife. But slowly, Layton understood that she had done what any British society wife would have done: avoid scandal, no matter the hurt inflicted. Her life had become what the toffs describe as "untidy." Besides, Edwina always did what her father commanded. In this case, divorce him and start life anew with their young son. She had to follow their caste's strict rules or "be talked about," which was the worst thing that could happen to a society woman. The loss of his son, though, had not diminished at all.

Cissie shook her head at his suggestion. "Off you go to pack, luv," said Cissie. "Can't miss your train."

They bid each other an amiable goodbye, and Layton walked out of the bar. At the door, a short, pudgy man with greasy, black hair parted in the middle approached him.

"Dougie? Dougie Layton? It *is* you. I was sitting in the bar and saying to meself, 'I know that bloke over there.' I wasn't sure of it, but bless me, it's me old mate from Mulcaster, Cell Block D."

Archie Guest had been the very lowest creature in the prison kingdom — a common thief and a pedophile, serving eight years. His face was weather-beaten with tiny, yellow eyes that reminded Layton of piss holes in the snow. He was a loathsome man whom Layton had scrupulously avoided. The inmates hated so-called kiddie fiddlers; such men were often beaten and sometimes murdered.

"I'm surprised to find you in the dress circle bar, Archie. I thought the gallery was your natural milieu." Layton felt a scowl crease his face. "Let me guess: you nicked a wallet and got the five-bob admission."

"Always was the gentleman with the fine words, eh?"

Layton walked away, but Guest followed, right behind him, and kept whispering in Layton's ear.

"While I was watchin' ya gabbing with that fine-looking wench, I thought, well, well, ol' Dougie's gone to the trouble of changing his appearance and all. With that new hair color and them specs. Wonder why,

155

I said. Then I remembered all that fuss about ya killing them people in that music hall. Folks were a bit upset, eh? Ya wouldn't want people knowin' who ya was."

"It's been great fun seeing you, Arch, but I'll be on my way." Again, Layton made to leave.

Again, Guest barred his path. "Ah, you're not going to stand your old mate to a pint?"

"Maybe another time."

"You can bet it on it, lad. I've got an interesting business proposition for you."

Layton already knew what it was.

15

Like images from a Pathé cinematograph projector running ceaselessly inside his head, the terrible scene he'd witnessed from this exact spot on Shaftesbury Avenue almost six years ago played over and over. But this film had sound; the screaming and wailing of the survivors blared through his skull. Layton put his hands to his temples and squeezed, trying to stop the projector, but it just cranked on and on.

I was a bloody fool, he thought bitterly. *I should have never come back to London and never ever returned to the Britannia.*

Unable to bear it any longer, he retreated down the street toward his original destination. The Queen's Palace of Varieties was also on Shaftesbury, a few blocks east of the Britannia. When he came to the corner of Frist Street, Layton stopped. It was a typical foggy, pea-soup day in London; a damp mist had mixed with the noxious, sulfur-laden smoke from the factories to tint the air a sickly, sooty yellow.

But ahead through the fog, he could make out the theatre. As he started walking down the street, he paused in front of the Elephant & Castle, one of the many pubs that lined both sides of Shaftesbury. As a man came out, Layton slipped in the door. After his second Glenfiddich, his nerves, which had come unraveled in front of the Britannia, were steadied a bit. Taking a deep breath, Layton rose from the corner table and made his way to the street. On his way to the theatre, he stopped at a tobacconist's for a pack of Altoids for his breath.

The Queen's Palace was immense even by West End standards, with a colossal dome that seemed as big as St. Paul's. A huge cupola supported by slender stone columns and capped with a bronze statue of Mercury topped the vast edifice. Both sides of the building were magnificently done up in different marbles: one for the walls, one for the base, another for the trim and decorative work. Twinkling electric lights outlined the ribs of the great dome. It was a palace for the common man.

After taking in the entirety of the theatre, Layton went down Frist to the alleyway behind the building. The stage doorman, a man of about a hundred, seemed to know he was coming and directed him to the stage, where a ladder act was rehearsing. Two men each balanced atop eight-foot-tall, unsupported ladders, juggling gold hoops. As they practiced, they discussed the coming year's chances for the national cricket team.

Flanigan of Flanigan & Cobb was stage right, smoking a cigar. He spotted Layton and beamed.

"There's me boy, come to save the day," he shouted to a man in a brown tweed suit standing a few feet away. "This is me ten percenter. Dan Logan, Frankie." A ten per-center was a theatrical agent, so called because he got ten percent of the artiste's salary as a fee.

Logan nodded at Layton.

"Now, Frankie," Flanigan continued. "We want a cloth with cartoons of us, but holding sledgehammers this time, as if we're about to attack each other."

"Anything between you?" Layton asked. "A street — maybe a fence?"

Flanigan perked up. "Maybe one of those horseless carriages."

"Why the hell would you want one of them on your cloth?" Logan exclaimed.

From Cissie, Layton had learned that

agents were typically the brains of the outfit. Artistes, no matter how skilled and talented, were often stupidly impractical, especially when it came to money.

"Because I was thinkin' of gettin' one," Flanigan said.

Logan rolled his eyes.

"I'll do a street scene and put some in," said Layton, attempting to make peace.

"You're a corker, Frankie. Go see Dash. He'll set you up in the scene shop. *My* cloth has first priority."

The Queen's Palace had an even bigger scene shop than the Grand, which could handle four cloths at once. Three artists were working away. Dash, a sourpuss Scot, had a brand-new blank cloth ready and waiting for Layton.

"Laddie, the head office told me to tell ya to stick around after you finish. Need you to do a cloth for Olly Olsen & His Seals, and the Wolenzas, an Arab act. They'll be here tomorrow morning to tell ye what they want."

The latter of these intrigued Layton. An Arab act was a loose form of tumbling, with pyramid building and side somersaults. Maybe sand dunes and a yellow-orange sunset or a night sky with twinkling stars? Layton took off his jacket, put on a smock, and got to work. He always sketched out the design with a stick of charcoal first; if he made a mistake, he could rub the line off easily with a rag.

He began with the cartoons of Flanigan & Cobb, leaving the street scene for last. In the stagehand workroom were old copies of the *Illustrated London News* with Oldsmobile advertisements. Using them as a guide, Layton drew out the automobiles Flanigan wanted. The man was making £200 a week performing; he could easily afford the £150 price.

After a while, Layton took a break and went to a pub. He drained a glass of Glenfiddich, then ordered another one and then another one. He wanted to keep drinking, but he had to get back to work. As Cissie said, this was a great opportunity, and he couldn't succeed by stumbling back drunk as a fiddler's bitch. It was best for him not to drink so much on an empty stomach, so he ate a shepherd's pie and returned to the theatre and his cloth. He worked to the sounds of music and applause coming through scene shop walls from the second show. Right after ten, the place fell silent. It was long past midnight when he stepped back to give the cloth a final look. Satisfied, he wiped his hands with a turpentine rag and then washed with soap and water to rid himself of the smell.

Before he returned to his hotel room, he wanted to do one more thing. That morning, when he'd seen the dome of the Queen's Palace for the first time, he'd told himself that he had to climb up to that cupola. Now, with no one about, was the best time.

The dome was actually a double shell. The outer part was copper roofing; the inner was the plasterwork and paintings seen from the auditorium below. Between these shells was the winding metal stair that led to the cupola. Unbolting the latch, Layton stepped up — and broke into an enormous smile.

The usual night fog had subsided, and he had an exhilarating 360-degree view of the West End and beyond. To the west, he could see Piccadilly Circus, where Shaftesbury Avenue, Coventry and Regent Streets, and the Haymarket all collided at the great circle. There stood the Shaftesbury Monument, with its statue of Eros. At this hour, the streets were deserted. By day, they would be choked with people and vehicles.

In all directions, some lights still burned, but most of London was asleep. The electric streetlights along Shaftesbury bounced off the great advertisement signs on the buildings: Dewar's, Cadbury Cocoa, Schweppes. Off to the south was Matcham's newly built London Coliseum, with its lighted sphere; beyond it loomed the Houses of Parliament and the Thames. Layton could even see the lights in Green and St. James's Parks.

Layton lit a cigarette and leaned over the marble railing. You could actually see the stars tonight. It occurred to him that Ronald probably lived not far from here in his grandfather's house in Mayfair, and he could be looking up at the same night sky as he. Many times, Layton wondered what his son was doing at this exact moment — playing with his soldiers in his room, having breakfast, looking at his storybooks at bedtime. He tried to picture in his mind Ronnie doing all those things.

The damp night air felt intoxicating; he closed his eyes to better enjoy the cool sensation. The cupola was at least eight feet in diameter and solidly built, with six marble columns supporting the dome above. Layton ran his hand over one of them, following its tapered shaft up to the architrave. Looking at the large, pie-shaped, blue-glazed ceramic tiles forming the cupola ceiling, Layton felt his heart plummet to his feet.

The color and the tooling of the mortar

joints on one wedge clearly didn't match the others.

Finding the wobbly stepladder in the cellar took but a few minutes. Nervously, Layton looked about before ascending it. Only a bird would see him up here. He placed the palms of his hands on the tile and pushed up with all his strength. It dislodged easily. He reached into his pocket for an electric torch, another of the marvels invented while he was adrift in Mulcaster. Then he climbed up two more steps, until his upper body was above the ceiling.

He knew full well what he was going to see. And he was right. About three feet away lay a skeleton.

Layton pulled himself up until he was standing on top of the ceiling. It was constructed of small metal beams and would hold his weight. He knelt and examined the remains. Again, brown, leathery muscles still covered the bones. He flashed the light around the space; yes, this was the only occupant. Whoever had killed and hidden these people had stripped off their clothes, leaving no chance of identification.

This skeleton's left arm stuck out at a forty-five-degree angle from the body; Layton followed it to the fingertips, and something caught his eye. He carefully lifted up the hand. A tiny ring — a very thin gold band inlaid with a red jewel — gleamed on the third finger. The murderer must have overlooked it when stripping the body.

Layton brought the bony hand closer. The jewel, he saw, was a tiny ruby. Something stirred in his memory, and slowly, he saw the hand of a newly married architect in his old office, showing off his ring. His bride had set the ruby, which she claimed used to be owned by some Indian maharajah, into a gold ring. Layton's brow furrowed; he pulled the ring off the bone and shone the light on it. On one side of the ring was inscribed *Peter,* and on the other, *Alice.*

Layton's mind screamed out, *This is Peter Browne, my chief assistant architect!* His whole body felt chilled, as if he'd been dipped in ice water. How had Browne ended up here, dead and interred? And why? Frantic now, Layton combed his memory, trying to remember every detail about the man. Peter had been an excellent architect; Layton had quickly come to trust his talent. An architect cannot do a building alone; dependable assistants carried the workload, executing the design under their superior's supervision.

In the old office, Peter had assumed more

and more responsibility, working out the drawings for many big projects, including the Duke of York Hospital, the Foreign Office extension in Whitehall, Lord Delvin's country estate, *and the Britannia Empire.*

Something inside Layton's brain clicked, like the flywheels of a watch set in motion. His eyes widened in astonishment; his mind flew back to the body in the gallery wall at the Grand. Had that been an architect from his office too?

That skeleton's only distinguishing trait was a curved spine like that of a hunchback's. Layton racked his brain, trying to make a connection between the two bodies. No one in his office had been a hunchback. The only hunchback he knew of was King Richard III in English history and Shakespeare's play.

Ten minutes passed; he hunched over the body in the cupola, grinding through his memories. Then, as if emerging out of a dense fog in his mind, a memory appeared. Layton had known a Richard III, but it was a derisive nickname that people called an actual hunchback behind his back. Where had he met him? It had to be work. In London society, no hunchback would ever appear in public; the family would keep them locked away like an insane relative. If it wasn't his office, then where? Layton sat down on the floor next to the skeleton and rubbed his hand over his face. Two minutes later, it came to him — John Reville.

Reville wasn't a real hunchback like Richard, but he had a deformed spine. A consulting structural engineer, he was an expert in designing beams, columns . . . and trusses. *Like the ones in the Britannia balcony.* Layton's mind was reeling.

With the new advances in steel and structural engineering, theatre balconies no longer had to be supported by tiers of metal columns, which had obstructed views in the past. Now, balconies could soar out fifty feet from the walls, using riveted steel trusses bearing on cantilevered deep plate girders. Reville was one of England's leading engineers in the intricate new steel technology that buildings were now using instead of wood and cast iron. Despite his handicap and the ridicule heaped upon him for it, the engineer was quite highly regarded in the architecture and engineering worlds. Reville was brilliant, the man to call to design a complicated structure. An architect would show Reville his design, and he would figure out its structure. It was very much like a general physician consulting a specialist on a case.

Layton now connected the dots — both Reville and Peter had worked on the complicated structural detailing of the Britannia balconies.

Layton crouched down, pulled out a cigarette from his gold case, and lit it. He wasn't panic-stricken as he had been with the first body in Nottingham. He didn't have the urge to run away this time. Exhaling a billow of smoke, he tilted his head up to see the steel ribs of the underside of the cupola dimly lit by his torch. This ghostly setting reminded him of the catacombs with its piles of bones he had toured in Rome. Deep in thought, he puffed away. After fifteen minutes, the pieces of a puzzle began slowly to fit together, forming a horrific image in Layton's mind. He dropped his chin to his chest and groaned at the awful realization: somehow, Reville and Peter had engineered the balcony failure.

But could it be? It was too monstrous to believe that they would have intentionally murdered fourteen people. Layton racked his brain again, thinking why they would do such a thing. Why would an architect and engineer do that? What would they gain by it? Then it dawned on Layton that the only reason could be that someone *paid* them for their structural expertise to bring down the balcony. And now Peter and Reville were *both* dead. It was clear that somebody had murdered the men to silence them forever. But who?

Amid his shock, a feeling of wonderful elation swept over Layton. The joy he felt seemed to lift him several inches in the air.

"I didn't kill all those people . . . *It wasn't me.*"

Tears welling up in his eyes, Layton pointed the electric torch at the thin, gold wedding band in the palm of his hand.

He smiled and placed the ring in his pocket, then shone the light again on the skeleton from whose finger he had taken the ring.

"I don't know why you did this to me, Peter. But thank you for giving me back my life."

By the time Layton had put away the ladder, his joy had diminished, replaced by grim determination. No matter the cost, he was going to find out who had framed him for the Britannia disaster.

16

"Mr. Owen, I'm sure you can see the difference between Felicity and Molly."

Layton couldn't. Both of the seals looked exactly the same.

"Yes, they're quite different," he lied, doing a quick sketch of Molly, who lay placidly before a blank cloth in the scene shop of the Queen's Palace. He petted her back, and she barked appreciatively. Seals had such soft fur; he could see why people wanted sealskin coats. But he'd never say that to their master, Olly Olsen. It'd be insulting.

"Molly will be on the left," Olsen instructed. "And Felicity on the right. Each must be bouncing a ball off her nose, and the ball has to be red, orange, and purple, to match the real one. For the background, the wild, rocky Cornish coast. Each girl on her own rock. And they have to be smiling."

"Righty-o," Layton said easily.

"We feel heaps better that you're doing

our cloth, Mr. Owen," said Olsen, putting his arm around Felicity, who gave out a low grunt. "You're a real artist."

"That's very kind of you, Mr. Olsen. I'll get right to it."

The words came easily, but Layton's mind was a billion miles away. He'd spent the previous night thrashing about in bed, trying to determine who could have done this to him. The five years in prison, the loss of his family and his livelihood — none of that was the worst of it. No, it was the constant torment and shame, the daily agony of guilt at having killed and maimed all those people.

The irony hit Layton as he sketched out the two seals in charcoal; he felt the corner of his lip twist in a wry smile. He'd been so distraught over the discovery that he hadn't had a single drink today. The revelation had taken that monkey off his back — for now. Again and again, the question pounded through his mind: What kind of monster could do this?

Peter and Reville had definitely supplied the technical expertise; of that, Layton was sure. They'd had the knowledge to carry off the collapse.

He sketched a typical balcony truss on the canvas cloth, stared at it for a long moment.

Only the front, cantilevered section of the Britannia balcony had failed. There, the trusses sat on a curving, four-foot-deep girder that spanned between the auditorium walls. He drew it in. The tampering must have occurred *between* the girder and the end of the balcony truss.

Structural failures were the architect's and engineer's worst nightmare, and over the years, there had been plenty in Britain. But by pure luck, many had happened at night, when the buildings were empty, like the Ripton train shed failure, which had occurred at two o'clock in the morning.

Ralph Sims, one of the theatre's scenic artists, was approaching. With the sleeve of his smock, Layton wiped out the truss sketch. He had another cloth to do for the tumbling act, and he threw himself into the work, hoping it would take his mind off the problem. But he couldn't stop thinking about it.

A few hours later, as he was putting the finishing touches on the seals' rocks, he felt a sharp tap on his shoulder.

"Blimey, I called your name three times, and you took no notice. You must love painting seals." Cissie stood behind him, hands on her hips, one eyebrow raised.

"I'm sorry," Layton said weakly. "I didn't

hear you."

"I sure as hell know that. Looks like you're all finished. It's nine o'clock. Let's knock off for the night."

Instead of going to a restaurant, they went back to Layton's hotel, near Oxford Circus. Layton went up to his room alone; Cissie slipped in ten minutes later. Even though she was naughty, she said with a wink, she was still a lady. Layton ordered room service, and they had their evening meal of bangers and mash in front of a roaring fire. A good Englishman eats breakfast three times a day, Cissie told him. Layton tried to be of good cheer, but he knew he seemed preoccupied. Cissie also seemed distracted; maybe, Layton thought, the new contract hadn't worked out as she had hoped.

By eleven, they were in bed, but Cissie said she couldn't make love because her monthly visitor had arrived early. He didn't mind, for he just loved the warmth of her body next to his, and he took in her scent as he drifted off into sleep.

At first, Layton thought the sobbing and sniffling was part of a dream. Then he felt a drop of moisture on his face. As he struggled back to wakefulness, he felt something heavy pressing on his chest — and something sharp against the side of his neck.

He was more bewildered than frightened. He opened his eyes, took in the bluish-black darkness of the hotel room. A dark shape sat atop his chest. Again, there was the sound of sobbing. His eyes widened in horror: it was Cissie, sitting astride him, fully clothed — and holding a straightedge razor to the soft skin of his neck.

"Damn you," she whimpered. "I don't want to do this. But I *have* to."

"Cissie!"

"My husband was in the Britannia that night, Douglas Layton." The words seemed to flow out of Cissie like a river, long dammed, that had burst its banks. "Johnnie was a comedian, and a bit of a bastard, really, and he always had a bit on the side. Still, I loved him. We had many a laugh and a cuddle. After he died, there was nothing but sadness and loneliness inside me. *Until you came into my life.* I was so happy. You made me want to live again — *and then you turned out to be the man who murdered my husband.*"

With the razor at his jugular, Layton lay completely still. He could not speak.

"When you came into Black's office that morning, I knew something was off. A gentleman, wanting to be a scene painter? I

174

did a little checking, but I came up empty. And you turned out to be such a nice, good-looking bloke, even if you were a specky four-eyes. I took a fancy to you right off. But . . . I had my doubts. For someone who'd hardly been in the theatre, you knew a lot of technical things. I told myself you were just a clever boots. And your gold cigarette case wasn't something a Dorset country lad would have."

"Please," Layton rasped out. "Listen to me, Cissie."

But she continued, undaunted. "Just a few days ago, I was cleaning out my mum's attic. I'd kept a box of newspapers from the time of the trial. There on the front of an old copy of the *Daily Mail* was a picture of you. My heart was broken, Frank — or should I say Douglas?"

Cissie wiped her eyes with her free hand and sniffled. She bent closer to Layton's face, until he could feel her warm breath. Her next words were a muffled shriek.

"Five years ago, I told myself I'd kill you if I ever met you. I was going to cut your throat while you slept. The police would think it a robbery. But now I don't know if I can do it." She began weeping uncontrollably.

"If you put down the razor," Layton said

in a frantic whisper, "we can sit and talk. I have something important to tell you."

"You made me so happy, Frank. But Johnnie was my husband — and all those poor people you killed! Some of them were just children," she whimpered.

"Someone else caused the balcony to collapse," Layton said. His voice was louder now and preternaturally calm.

"You're a bloody liar," Cissie snapped. "You didn't say that at your trial."

"It wasn't until yesterday that I knew I'd been framed for the disaster." Layton sat up just slightly, feeling the blade pressing against his throat. "Look, the condemned is always allowed a last request. Please, let me show you something."

Cissie reached the bottom of the stepladder in the cupola and looked directly into Layton's face. Her eyes were on fire, burning with anger.

"We're going to kill the person who did this to us."

Without a trace of emotion on his face, Layton nodded.

17

"The Britannia, the Grand, and the Queen's are all under the same ownership. The Mac-Millan Empire circuit is controlled by Sir John Clifton and his partner, Lionel Glenn." Cissie's voice as she recited these facts was choked with anger.

Layton stared down into his pint of Guinness. He'd had only a sip; Cissie hadn't touched her gin and bitters.

They sat quietly at a corner table, amid the din of the Eagle and Hawk on Frist Street.

"Oh, Frank, they destroyed your entire life." Tears were welling up in Cissie's clear gray-blue eyes. "They made you the most hated man in the British Empire."

"Indeed. Probably even the Africans in darkest and deepest Nigeria knew of me," he said with a wan smile. "The Butcher of the West End."

"And you never heard from your wife and

child? Not in all this time?" She stroked his hand gently, as if to soften the pain of the question.

"Just the divorce papers." Layton sighed. "It's strange. They're likely living in her father's house in Mayfair, just five minutes from here."

There was a long silence. Finally, Cissie spoke. "Who would do such a terrible thing?"

"I don't know, Cissie," Layton said.

"Yes, one of the owners could have arranged it. That's a logical place to start looking."

"They would certainly have the money to bribe Peter and Reville. But why? I don't know where to begin." The weariness in his voice surprised Layton; he realized he'd spoken the truth. Though his entire being was filled with rage, trying to find the real killer seemed an impossible task.

"Frank. You don't mind me calling you Frank instead of Douglas?"

Layton shook his head.

Cissie's voice grew more urgent. "Listen. You must stay the week in London. I can fix it so that you work at the scene shop at the theatre."

"Why?"

"Because we're going to a house party in

178

the country this weekend, luv." Cissie's smile was bright and false. "The Duke of Denton is one of the largest investors in the syndicate. Every September, he invites Clifton and Glenn to his estate in Wiltshire. He loves the variety theatre, so he also invites a few artistes to entertain his guests. I'm management, so I always get an invitation — and I can bring a guest. They don't care if it's a man; they think all variety hall people are immoral."

Layton nodded slowly, mulling it over in his mind. Variety hall entertainment had been big business since the 1890s. The theatre chains owned more than a thousand theatres in every city, town, and suburb of Great Britain. From his experience designing the Britannia, Layton knew that the syndicate businessmen had even lured the peerage into investing in variety halls. With more and more upper- and middle-class people attending shows, the variety theatre had become socially respectable. And it was far more exciting than investing in a railway bond.

"Yes," he said slowly, a determined look on his face. "That would be the place to begin. The murderer could be in the very house with us."

"You'll need to rent some evening

clothes," Cissie cautioned. "It's a swank event."

"I'll need clothes anyway for a weekend in the country. A three-piece tweed suit, a cap, and some . . ." Layton got the cold shivers; his body trembled in his chair.

"What's wrong, luv?" Cissie asked, eyes widening.

"If the MacMillan Empire management are guests this weekend, won't Basil Dearden be there? He was the theatre manager for the Britannia. I worked closely with him on the design. He's the only one from the circuit I had contact with, but he's sure to recognize me."

"Oh, no, luv, you don't have to worry about that. Basil died two years back. They —"

Cissie and Layton looked at each other with startled expressions.

"They found him lying dead on the floor of his house in Bayswater," Cissie said in a low voice, her eyes wide with fear. "Natural causes, they said it was. Came as a shock to everyone. He was only thirty-four."

As an architect, Layton had been to many weekends in the country hosted by clients and friends of Edwina and her father. Thankfully, he'd never been to Eversham, the ancestral home of the Duke of Denton. But he knew where the long, tree-lined drive of the estate led, and he knew exactly what was about to happen. All country weekends of the peerage and gentry were the same.

The official London season, the social scene of fancy dress balls, opera, and sporting events, began in May and ended in August, after the regatta at Cowes. Then came the country house season, with its house parties, hunting, fishing, banquets, and balls, which lasted until winter. The English social elite loved the country; the invention of the motorcar and the improvement of Britain's roads made the country houses more accessible and thus even more popular.

Eversham appeared in the distance, artfully framed by a canopy of oaks. It was a well-designed entry to the estate, thought Layton, and he should know; he'd designed a few himself. The house was an enormous Palladian composition, on the same scale as Blenheim Palace, with a temple-fronted center section symmetrically flanked by curving wings. The late-afternoon sunlight made its sandstone exterior glow like gold.

Their motorcar crunched along the pea gravel of the circular entry court. Up ahead, Layton could see the arriving guests, all dressed in the required tweeds. George Formby, also known as Bimba Bamba, was walking up the wide stone steps to the door. That meant there would be magic tricks tonight. Dainty Amy, who followed behind him, was in her country lady's outfit of an olive tweed skirt and a brown tweed jacket. At a rakish angle on her head was a burgundy-colored cap with a long feather attached. Cissie told him that Laughing Luigi, the Italian Juggler, the comic Timmy Donovan, and a few singing acts had also been invited.

The butler, the highest-ranking servant, greeted each guest as they got out of their motorcar. Standing next to the rotund, gray-haired man was an exceptionally tall, sandy-haired young man, whom Layton knew must be the first footman. Every estate wanted a tall first footman; it was an upper-class sign of prestige. The taller he was, the higher his salary. A man over six feet could get ten pounds more a year than one under.

"Welcome, Mrs. Mapes," said the butler in a strong, stentorian voice.

"Good to see you again, Wilcox," Cissie chirped. "You get handsomer every year."

"I always look forward to your weekend visit, ma'am. Phillip will show you to your rooms. Drinks in the Chinese drawing room at seven, and His Grace said to inform you that we'll be dressing for dinner this evening."

They were taken through the great entry hall to the east wing and down a long, red-carpeted corridor lined with paintings and sculpture. Layton and Cissie had adjoining rooms, which was typical; country house arrangements were very understanding of nocturnal trysts. No one cared if you cheated on your spouse, as long you were discreet.

When they entered the Chinese drawing room — so-called because of its red-and-black-lacquer decor — many guests had already arrived and begun imbibing "cocktails." This new American trend combined alcohol with sugar, mixers, and bitters to produce drinks with odd names. Before Layton's time in prison, the drinks at these social events had been limited to sherry and brandy.

As requested, all the men were in the exact same evening attire with white tie, shirt, and waistcoat. The women, including Cissie, were dressed to the nines in gowns of a great variety of colors and materials.

At the grand piano, Angus McLean, the handsome Scottish tenor, was softly singing a ballad to a group of admiring young women. Across the room, comedian Timmy Donovan was regaling a group of toffs by the massive, ebony-faced fireplace.

"A widow's lookin' to hire a handyman. So she says to the applicant, 'I want a man to do odd jobs about the house and run errands, one that never answers back and is always ready to do my bidding.' The applicant says, 'What you're looking for, ma'am, is a husband.' "

The upper-class guests roared with laughter. Donovan swilled down his drink, one of many, Layton knew from experience with him in a pub, that he would be having tonight.

"It must be so exciting, Mr. Donovan. Being up onstage, holding the audience in the palm of your hand." The society lady who spoke wore a bright-yellow gown trimmed with ostrich feathers. The light from the chandelier reflected off her diamond necklace in bursts like little twinkling stars.

"Call me Timmy. And you're right, m'lady. Being onstage was the only thing I could do. I wasn't any damn good in school, especially spelling. But so what if I can't spell Armageddon? Hell, it's not the end of the world."

Another wave of laughter convulsed the Chinese drawing room.

This was an unusual country weekend, Layton thought. Because the guests were all variety-hall performers, they were *interesting*. Most of the time, these events were excruciatingly boring; as he had discovered, the rich were incredibly dull. More times than he could count, he'd wished for a country dance back in Dorset, with all its fun and gaiety. The higher one went up the class ladder, Layton had learned, the less fun one had.

Wilcox was behind the drink cart, and he concocted them something called a *pirate.* Layton thought it quite good. More guests entered. The paunchy, cigar-smoking, middle-aged men were probably theatre managers for the other variety houses in the circuit; Oswald Black of the Grand was among them, laughing and chatting.

Luigi, the handsome juggler, was talking to a beautiful young woman. Though he was married with three children in Manchester, he used his native Italian charm and accent to great advantage with the ladies in every city he played.

"These cold-climate Englishmen are afraid to show sentiment," he was saying earnestly to the girl. "Only men from a southern climate know what pleases a woman." From the look in the girl's eyes, Layton knew he would be visiting her room tonight.

The Duke and Duchess of Denton finally entered and began enthusiastically greeting their guests. The duke was an imposing man in his fifties with swept-back gray hair, the very model of an aristocrat. His wife, though older, was still a great beauty; she wore a magnificent scarlet-and-green gown.

From his marriage to Edwina and his commissions for the aristocracy, Layton had learned the peerage titles by heart. Dukes, like their host, were the highest, followed by marquess, earl, viscount — like his former father-in-law — and baron, the lowest on the chain. In all families of the peerage and even among the landed gentry, only the oldest surviving male could inherit the family fortune. The duke's oldest son would get all of Eversham and become the Duke of Denton; his brothers and sisters would be left to fend for themselves.

As Cissie and Layton sipped their drinks and talked to Lady Emerson, who was gushing on about a show at the Lyric Theatre, two men approached. Cissie lit up like an Edison bulb.

"Lady Emerson, have you met my employers, Sir John Clifton and Lionel Glenn?"

"Yes, Mrs. Mapes, we've had the pleasure," said Clifton with a polite bow. "So nice to see you again, Lady Emerson."

Layton recognized Clifton, a tall man in his forties with a pale, cadaverous face, from a photograph in an Empire program. He looked more like a schoolmaster than someone associated with the entertainment business, much less a managing director of the circuit. It was hard to picture him standing next to magicians and scantily clad female acrobats. Clifton was formal in his manner and speech, like a stiff-backed character out of Dickens, and seemed to lack a sense of humor, making him even more incongruous within the world of variety theatre. He looked quite at home here in his evening dress and pince-nez glasses, walking around the room with a glass of sherry. He didn't seem the type to prefer a highball; it was far too modern.

"So exciting to have so many entertainers around, Sir John," said Lady Emerson. "It must be a frightfully interesting life you lead."

"Not really, m'lady. I run the business end of the theatre circuit, and these are my employees, much like workers in a textile factory whom I have to pay much too much for their services," replied Clifton in an icy tone. "In business, Lady Emerson, one must deal with unruly workers, and we have unfortunately quite a few." Clifton looked over at Timmy Donovan knocking down one drink after another, which brought a look of disgust to his sallow face. "But they make the circuit profitable," he added in a voice of resignation.

Glenn, on the other hand, had a jolly personality that seemed a natural fit for his short, rotund body and plump, kind face. He looked as though he might have been a comedian in his former life. He appeared totally out of character in evening dress. Layton saw him more at home in a green-and-white-checkered suit.

"Ah, m'lady, these artistes are a handful. Like children they are," bellowed Glenn.

"Sometimes, we wish we could give them all a good caning," added Cissie, which brought a slight smile to Clifton's razor-thin lips.

"Sometimes, I think they deserve a worse punishment," said Clifton, still smiling.

"We've an exciting new act that our Cissie discovered — Gregor, a Russian giant who's nine feet, four inches tall," said Glenn enthusiastically, waving his big fat cigar around.

As he chattered on, a strikingly handsome boy in his midtwenties escorted by a very pretty blond in a light-blue gown walked up to Clifton, who smiled at them.

"Hello, Georgie," said Cissie.

"My son, Lady Emerson," said Clifton proudly. "And his wife, Lady Diana."

"What a splendid-looking lad," the woman blurted out. "With your looks, you should be onstage."

George looked down at his shoes bashfully. His wife beamed.

"That's what all the girls say about our Georgie," Cissie said with a laugh. "Before he was married," she added with a wink at Lady Diana.

Clifton shifted, clearly uncomfortable; Layton could see that no son of his would ever wind up onstage.

"My son took a second in history at Oxford, Lady Emerson," said Clifton with an air of pride. "George did not join me in the variety business in any capacity."

While they talked, Layton inched away and melted into the crowd. He didn't want to risk Clifton and Glenn recognizing him. He stood alone by the fireplace, sipping his drink, observing Clifton and Glenn.

After about ten minutes, Cissie rejoined him.

"They're an odd lot," Layton whispered, looking over at the two owners still chatting with Lady Emerson.

"If one of those buggers did do it, you wouldn't know by the look of them." Cissie's whisper was fierce and strong.

"One of the many things I learned in prison," Layton said slowly, "is that you can't know what evil a chap is capable of by looking at his face. I've seen men with the faces of angels who've beaten a fellow to a pulp because it gave them a lark."

"Why, here's the lady that makes us wealthier year after year!" The duke, booming and boisterous, approached Cissie, grabbing both her hands.

"You're too kind, Your Grace," Cissie said weakly. "Thank you for inviting me. This is my good friend, Frank Owen."

"A pleasure to meet you, Mr. Owen. I hope you shoot. We have plenty of good sport here at Eversham."

"I do," Layton said. "And I'm very much looking forward to it."

"Good show. Start at nine o'clock sharp tomorrow morning. We'll fit you out with a gun if you didn't bring one."

Shooting, Layton knew, was the main event of any country house weekend. He didn't like the sport but was quite skilled with a gun. One definitely had to shoot to blend in with the upper classes. He'd already been taught to handle a gun by his father. It was an essential skill passed on by generations in Dorset. He remembered fondly tramping through the countryside with his father, hunting rabbits and birds, and the excitement of bagging his first quail. It was one of the very few times he had had his dad all to himself. Though they hunted in complete silence, he had felt very happy just walking alongside him. Layton bowed slightly and shook hands with the duchess, whose eyes barely rested on him.

"Cissie, we must talk later. I want to know what artistes you have lined up for the spring." The duke spoke in a conspiratorial tone, as if he were requesting top-secret information from the Foreign Office.

What a change had occurred in society, thought Layton. To see a peer welcome variety theatre performers into his home! The duke's unsnobbish acceptance produced an immediate feeling of affection. Of course, the man might be an anomaly, but before Layton had gone to prison, 99 percent of society had looked down their noses at theatre folk, thinking them common as mud. Did mainstream architects still regard music hall architects as commercial hacks? Layton wondered. The question stirred something in his heart, which he pushed away.

As if sensing his distraction, Cissie took Layton by the arm, kissed his cheek, and led him to a love seat in the far corner. For his part, the duke made his way to the piano, where McLean belted out "The Nipper's Lullaby" to the delight of the duchess, who was clapping her white-gloved hands. Soon, Luigi the Juggler barged in, singing "Santa Lucia." As he did, he picked up three large Chinese jade figurines from the fireplace mantel and began juggling them. A look of fear came over the duchess's face, but Luigi handled them effortlessly, even catching them behind his back. Dainty Amy took an iron poker from the great fireplace and bent it into a U as though it were taffy, then unbent it to return it to its original shape.

The skill of the artistes, how easy they made their tricks look, never ceased to amaze Layton. To him, watching from the wings, these men and women of the theatre seemed superhuman in agility, strength, and concentration. He sometimes wished he had skills akin to theirs and lived in this world of fun. Architecture had been such a damn serious business where fun wasn't allowed. His former office with its rows of draughtsmen was always dead silent, except for the scratch of inking pens and pencils on paper.

Hicks's office had been the exact same way.

The tall first footman entered the room and whispered something into Wilcox's ear, which made him light up, smiling. He transmitted the message to the duke, whose face flushed red. Then the duke grinned and nodded to Wilcox, who stood erect as a soldier and announced in a loud, clear voice, "Your Grace, lords, ladies, and gentlemen — His Majesty, the king."

In strode King Edward VII, sovereign of Great Britain and the British Empire and Emperor of India. He wore evening dress and puffed on a long cigar. Stunned into silence, the guests bowed and curtsied in complete unison.

The king smiled, waved his cigar at them nonchalantly, and gave the duke's hand a hearty shake. "Sorry I'm late, Harold," he drawled. "The damn motorcar stalled out. Give me a good horse any day."

The guests laughed at this jest. Then the king kissed the duchess on the cheek, murmuring that she hadn't changed since he'd laid eyes on her at Ascot in 1875.

Standing directly behind the king was Alice Keppel, his mistress, and Sir Francis Knollys, his private secretary. Mrs. Keppel, London's most famous society hostess, was an incredible beauty, all wide blue eyes, chestnut hair, and a magnificent bust that contrasted sharply with her tiny waist. She had been Edward's lover and confidant since 1898, when he forsook his previous paramour, the Countess of Warwick. Rumor held that he was a much pleasanter "child" since changing mistresses, and Mrs. Keppel's influence was such that statesmen and politicians tried to talk to her of government matters first.

Before succeeding his mother, Queen Victoria, to the throne in 1901, the king — then the Prince of Wales — had been a well-known attendee of the variety theatre. It was for this, and other reasons, that he was so greatly popular with Britain's people; he wasn't a stuffed shirt, and he enjoyed many of the same pursuits as the commoners did: racing, cricket, the music hall. He liked a good song and a hearty laugh.

Now, the king made his way about the room, chatting with the upper-class guests, granting especial favor to the artistes. Luigi renewed his song and juggling, to his ruler's delight. When McLean's turn came, he sang a rousing Scottish song — the king, as all in attendance knew, favored his castle, Balmoral, in the Scottish Highlands, and loved anything Scottish. He knew McLean's song and joined in, horribly off-key.

As the revelry proceeded, a short, bald man with a wide mustache and a Vandyke slipped into the room. Cissie nudged Layton and whispered, "There's the Israelite."

"Ernest, what do you know about investing in the variety theatre?" bellowed the king.

"Not your usual investment, Your Majesty," sniffed the man. "Steel and shipping are more my line."

Clifton and the Empire investors exchanged quick, disappointed glances.

"Harold said he had a twenty-five-percent return the past year. What do you say?"

Sir Ernest Cassel gave a slight, polite smile. Aside from Mrs. Keppel, he was the king's closest advisor; under his influence, the king had grown yet richer. As a Prussian-born Jew, his presence in the inner court circle would have been unthinkable even a few decades before. But the king differed from his mother and from Britain's previous rulers; he wasn't an anti-Semite and had Jewish friends, as well as many commoners — men whom the aristocracy called *lowborn.* The king was said to admire those who rose from nothing, like Cassel, who had come to England penniless and was now thought to be the richest man in the empire.

"Talk to Sir John here. He can give you

the figures. A lot more fun than putting my money in a coal mine, eh?" The king gave Cassel a wink, nodding toward Sally Everett, the beautiful singer standing to his right. Obligingly, she launched into the American ballad "Jeanie with the Light Brown Hair."

When she finished, Wilcox announced, "Dinner is served, my lady."

The guests separated into two groups, creating a wide path for the king, who took the duchess's arm to escort her to the dining room. They moved forward, whispering, when the king stopped abruptly, and said, "Why, hello! Where did you and I meet?"

All eyes fell upon Layton, whose face flushed red.

"Was it a cornerstone laying or a building opening of some kind?"

"I don't believe we've ever met, Your Majesty," Layton murmured deferentially.

"You sure about that? You look damn familiar," the king said and moved on.

Layton tried not to look as crestfallen as he felt. Truly, his attempt to change his identity had been a complete failure; both an ex-convict and the king of England had seen through him in an instant. The king was right; they had met, briefly, when the then-Prince of Wales laid the cornerstone of St. Margaret's Children's Hospital, which

Layton had designed. The king's memory amazed Layton; the monarch had barely laid eyes on the architect at the dedication.

On every side, people were staring, envious that the king had paid him personal attention. Even Cissie looked baffled. Sighing, Layton led her into dinner.

The king sat at the head of a fifty-foot-long table set with flowers and an extravagant epergne, or ornamental centerpiece. Servants brought forth a ten-course meal *à la russe:* hors d'oeuvres, soups, salads, poultry, pork, seafood, puddings, breads, fruits, and sweets. The pièce de résistance was pâté de fois gras stuffed inside a truffle, which was itself stuffed inside a quail. The duke had acres of forestland, which meant an abundance of game — pheasant, partridge, hare. Different wines accompanied each course: Chablis with oysters, sherry with the hors d'oeuvres and soups, burgundy with meat, and claret with game.

Layton was glad to find himself at the far end of the table, away from the king. But he could still see evidence of the man's legendary appetite. In a ten-course meal, most guests did not partake of every dish. King Edward did, wolfing down prodigious amounts of food and quaffing an extraordinary amount of wine. Clients had whispered to Layton that even after lavish dinners such as this, at bedtime, hostesses would send up a late-night snack to the king: a plate of sandwiches, perhaps, or a whole chicken.

Instead of the men and women breaking up into separate groups, as was usual after a dinner party, all returned to the drawing room to be entertained by the artistes. Luigi juggled; Timmy Donovan told more jokes.

"Your Majesty, you know what the dwarf said to me when I asked him to lend me two bob? 'So sorry, I'm a trifle short.' "

The king convulsed with laughter, turning beet red and alarming Mrs. Keppel, who feared he'd have a heart attack there on the spot. There were more songs, until at last, at one in the morning, Sally Everett sang "Goodnight, Ladies," and the guests retired.

Swept up in the infectious laughter and gaiety, Layton realized he'd forgotten that he was there to find a murderer. He bid good night to Cissie, though he planned to slip into her room later to talk about Glenn and Clifton and what they would do next.

He was almost to his room when a low voice called out from down the hall.

"Doug?"

Layton froze, paralyzed. Then he turned, slowly, to see a manservant in a black suit. Layton stared at him for a few seconds.

Then a wave of relief swept over him.

"Hello, Daniel," he whispered. "It's so good to see you."

Growing up in Dorset, Daniel Harker had been Layton's best friend. They'd spent many a lazy, sprawling afternoon exploring the downs around Puddletown. At about the same time Layton had gone for his architectural training, Daniel had been sent off into domestic service. The work was highly valued by the working class, especially the girls, and Layton had almost burst with pride for his friend's new opportunity.

From the 1880s until the turn of the new century, England had labored under the crippling weight of an agricultural depression, and many children of Dorset farmers had left home to find work as servants. Edwina (or rather Mrs. Hopkins, the housekeeper) had managed a large home, so Layton knew firsthand about the world of housemaids, butlers, cooks, and footmen. In a year, a servant might make as much as seventy pounds, with free room and meals — a far better life than that of a farm laborer. Standing in the dim hallway, looking at Daniel, Layton thought that if things had worked out differently, he might have been standing there too, wearing the nondescript black suit, white shirt, and black tie of the serving class.

"I'm Sir John Clifton's valet," Daniel said simply. "That's why I'm here. Been working for Sir John for almost nine years."

"You recognized me," Layton said.

"We grew up together, Doug. At first, I thought I was mistaken, but no." Daniel shook his head, looked down at the red carpet. "I was awfully sorry about what happened to you, Doug. But just think, before that terrible night, of all the important buildings you did. Look how far you came — from that little cottage in Puddletown. We were all so bloody proud of you, especially your dad."

"My dad?"

"Why sure." Daniel seemed taken aback at the surprise in Layton's voice. "He'd tell the neighbors all about the latest buildings you were doing, every time."

Layton was puzzled at this remark, but Daniel's concern, the warmth in his voice, touched something deep inside him. It'd been twenty years since he'd last seen him, but in all that time, he'd probably never had as good a friend. He swallowed hard, surprised by the lump in his throat.

"Doug, your secret's safe with me," Daniel was whispering. "I can understand why you took a new life. I'd've done the same thing."

"You scrub up well in that outfit, mate," said Layton with a smile. In Puddletown, Daniel always wore a flannel shirt and canvas pants.

"Haven't done too bad for meself," Daniel said, smiling back.

"After you've put your master to bed, come to my room, and we'll have a gab," said Layton enthusiastically. He saw the answering gleam in his old friend's eyes.

At nine sharp the next morning, a line of men holding double-barreled shotguns formed at the edge of a clearing. They were dressed almost identically in tweeds; next to each stood a gun loader, holding another shotgun. The king was at the beginning of the line; Layton made sure he was at the very end. To Layton's amazement, there were some women on the shooting line. He had never seen such a sight, but dressed in tweeds with their own shotguns and loaders stood six females, including Lady Emerson, Joan Basswell, and Dainty Amy Silborne. The king acted as though this was completely normal and chatted with the ladies, telling them about a new shotgun shell he was using. Layton shook his head slowly from side to side. Women smoking, drinking in bars, supporting themselves, trying to get the vote, not wearing corsets, and now the unthinkable — they were shooting their own guns. Some probably drove their own autos.

A low whistle sounded, and fifty yards away, the beaters — village men recruited by the estate gamekeeper — started walking forward, stirring up the underbrush with long sticks and uncovering pheasant, woodcock, and quail, which flew off in terror . . . straight into the sights of the shooting party. The king, given the honor of the first shot, blasted a bird out of the sky with great skill. Then, a continuous, ear-shattering blasting commenced, and down the birds rained. As they fell to earth, the beaters snatched them up, thrusting them into the canvas sacks they carried.

When a man had shot off both barrels, he exchanged his weapon for a newly loaded one. Each loader also kept count of his gentleman's kill. Some owners felt this unsporting, but the duke didn't mind.

Layton looked over at the women shooters; they all handled their weapons with great skill, bringing down their share of birds. The elegant and refined Lady Emerson was blasting away with gusto. If she was shooting, then all British society ladies would know it was acceptable for them to shoot.

Once the beaters had covered a hundred yards, the shooting stopped, and the group shifted to the right, where the massacre began again. After a time, they paused for lunch, which was served by footmen under a great tent in the field on silver platters. The repast was lavish: cold meats, puddings, strawberries with crème, and crystal glasses full of wine or champagne. The women, and those few men who didn't shoot, came down from the great house for the meal; when it was finished, the slaughter continued. Scores of dead birds hung from racks atop a wagon pulled by a stocky old horse.

Just before shooting ended for the day, Layton was taking aim at a bird when he felt a bullet graze his hair. Startled, he stumbled back, looking about in fright to find the source of the shot. But there was no one behind him.

A loud cry of agony rang out fifty yards ahead. A beater lay in a thicket with a bullet lodged in his thigh.

18

"We have to be in London to get to the bottom of this, Frank."

"I know," said Layton, staring into his teacup. They were in the parlor of Cissie's home in Nottingham. "But how can that be?"

"Simple," said Cissie. "They've been after me for years to come back to the head office. Once I'm there, I can get you a new position at the Queen's Palace or any other circuit theatre you want."

"But your mum and sister? I thought you had to stay in Nottingham for them."

"They'll get used to a nice house in South Kensington or Pimlico just fine. But for now, you and me will be in theatre digs in London. I know a Mrs. Cooper who used to be part of a unicycle act, runs a first-class place in Bayswater for only top of the bill artistes. No riffraff. I'll ring up this afternoon and book us two nice rooms."

Cissie came around to the back of Layton's armchair, put her arms around him, and kissed his cheek. "Don't look so down, luv," she said gently.

"Cissie, you said you'd kept a box of newspaper clippings about the trial. Is there a chance I might see them?"

Layton stared at the list of the dead in the *Daily Mail.* Fourteen names, in alphabetical order, with their ages in damning black ink beside.

All the newspapers had focused on those terrible deaths. And they'd run story after story on the maimed and injured too, spreading the horror throughout the empire. Men and women who would never walk again or hold a job because they'd lost a hand or leg. Each detail made Layton more hated and reviled.

In those days, he'd seen the list but couldn't bear to read about the victims of the disaster. What was the use? He couldn't bring them back to life.

Now, he ran his finger down the list on the brittle, yellowed pages. He thought of the daughter of the woman waiting outside the prison. They would be the younger victims, all the nascent promise of their lives extinguished in an instant.

He stopped for a fraction of a second at John Mapes, 41, then continued on, not daring to look up at Cissie.

Denys Blair, 78
Ronald Cass, 52
James Croyden, 37
Robert Davidson, 12
Shirley Finney, 19
Daphne Foster, 46
Ted Hardy, 44
John Mapes, 41
Isabel Massey, 14
Hugh Rice, 53
Sir John Richardson, 54
Jocelyn Shipway, 31
Trevor Stanton, 42
Sibyl Treadwell, 36

"Why would Clifton or Glenn want to kill one of these people?" Cissie asked.

"No one would go to all this trouble for just one person," Layton said, more to himself than her.

"You're saying that they wanted to kill a few people — all at once?" Cissie blinked, shocked at what Layton had just suggested.

"If you wanted a group of people dead, what better way to murder than to kill all of them in what seems like an accident?"

Layton replied, his face drawn and tense. "It's quite ingenious, really. Instead of killing four or five people individually and then having to dispose of their bodies, you murder them all in one shot in broad daylight."

"The bastards!" Cissie took the paper from Layton and gazed at the list. "Poor Johnnie," she sighed. "He never did anything to Clifton or Glenn."

"Did he ever meet with the partners?"

"Only at the annual weekend parties. Clifton and Glenn kept their distance from the artistes. It was all right to make money off them but not to socialize. Clifton had been knighted, so he's only around the hoity-toity."

"Johnnie never talked about them?" Layton pressed.

"Just that they were cheap shits," Cissie said with a laugh.

"Can you fetch me some writing paper and a pen?"

On the tea table, Layton made a copy of the list in neat, careful cursive.

"These people are in some way connected to Clifton and Glenn, and we have to find out how. It's the only way we might discern a motive. If we find some connection, we'll write it next to their name."

Layton saw the confusion in Cissie's eyes and leaned forward, spoke more passionately. "Cissie, we're beginning a thousand-piece jigsaw. It's just a jumble now, and it doesn't make any sense, but when the pieces start to fall into place, only then will we see the full picture."

Cissie nodded, and he saw the determination dawning in her eyes.

"I have an idea of where to start," Layton added. "With an old friend."

19

"Yes, Shirley Finney was a parlormaid in Sir John's London house in Mayfair." Daniel Harker's eyes were distant as he searched his memory. "Nice lass she was, ever so cheerful. Hard worker too. The downstairs staff are always sniping about each other, but none ever had a bad word for Shirley."

Layton and Daniel were huddled together at a table in the rear of the General Gordon, a popular London pub. They'd met again after Layton finished his work at the Queen's Palace, Cissie having secured him a permanent job in the scene shop just as she said she would.

Although Layton had an ulterior motive, he was thoroughly enjoying himself. Daniel transported him back to his Puddletown boyhood, the happiest time of his life. Smiling and laughing, the two men relived the wonder of exploring downs and forests, wading in streams, and sprawling in fields of new-cut hay, gazing up into the blue sky. They shared their first cigarette and first jug of ale. Even when Layton embarked on his ill-fated quest to become a university man, he'd found time to spend with Daniel, who'd been taken out of school early to work the fields before he went into service.

As Daniel had worked for Clifton at the time of the accident, Layton had thought he might recognize some of the names on the list. He disguised his motives, telling Daniel that he wished to send each victim's relatives a heartfelt apology and plea for forgiveness. The weight of the guilt was too much, he whispered, eyes lowered. He couldn't go on unless he found some way to atone. He showed Daniel the list, and to his luck, his friend's eyes lit upon Shirley.

"The staff was bowled over when we found out about the accident," Daniel continued. "Couldn't believe it. She was just this pretty little thing — goes out for a special night and gets crushed to . . ." He stopped and looked down at the table in embarrassment.

Shame hit Layton like a wave; milking his dear old friend in this manner made him vaguely sick. And yet he couldn't tell Daniel of his suspicions. He would never believe Clifton capable of such a heinous act, would think the very suggestion mad.

"Sir John and his wife, Lady Eileen, were terribly upset about her death," Daniel said, sighing heavily. "They gave Shirley's family her full year's wages."

"To whom do you think I should send my letter?" asked Layton in a quiet voice.

"Well, her people are from Leeds, but I recall she came to London with her sister, Agnes, to work in service. Last I heard, she was with a family in Belgravia." Daniel knit his brow and squinted, combing his memory. "Mrs. Wilberforce, our housekeeper, was fond of Shirley. She's kept in touch with Agnes since . . . well, since the tragedy." It came to him in a rush, and he blurted, "Clarence, that's it! Clarence is the family."

Layton leaned forward confidentially and said, "I want to thank you, Danny, for your help. At the duke's, the mere sight of you lifted my spirits."

"We were best mates, Doug. That's something that doesn't ever go away."

"Can we meet again for a drink?"

"Why, sure. How about same time next week?"

"It's a date — every week, mate." Layton sat back and slapped his palms gently on the table. "I've just moved to London from

Nottingham last week. It'll be a regular thing."

"That's wonderful! It'll be nice having you around again, just like the old Dorset days. And, Doug." Daniel leaned forward urgently. "I'll *never* reveal your secret. You can count on me. You had to get on with your life as best you could. I understand."

Tears sprang to Layton's eyes. He wiped them away, cupped his hands around the empty pint glass.

Agnes Finney wasn't what Layton had imagined. In fact, she was a bit of a tart — but that only made his task easier.

Servants were allowed one afternoon and one night off per week. By bribing the footman at Agnes's employers' residence, Layton learned that Thursday was her night off. Two days after meeting Daniel, he waited across from No. 7 Chapel Street and followed her.

Agnes took a bus across the Thames to Lambeth, a decidedly lower-class neighborhood, and walked to a pub on Frasier Street. Most pubs in London would not allow unescorted women, but in Lambeth, such rules were thrown to the winds. Depending on the household, Layton knew that maids had a rough time of it; they were often up at five to set fires, heat water for baths, and start dusting. With these rigors as her daily lot, Agnes seemed to want as much of a good time as she could have in a single evening.

She was clearly a regular at the pub and heartily welcomed by all. Layton took in the scene from the entrance and then walked slowly up to the bar, moving as if he owned the place, smiling and greeting complete strangers. Because he was a gentleman, the customers paid him the proper respect. Agnes took notice and began chatting him up.

"Buy me a drink, 'andsome?" she said, batting her lashes at him.

"Whatever this radiant beauty desires, barman. And may I share some refreshment with you at that table over there while I'm waiting for my sister to come?"

Agnes agreed enthusiastically, and they settled in a far corner. Layton peppered the conversation with compliments, paying ode to her auburn hair and alabaster skin. It was evident that she enjoyed the attention of a proper gentleman instead of the usual drunken louts; by the third gin and bitters, her tongue was loosened, her guard down.

Layton looked over at the door of the pub and shrugged. "I suppose my sister had to work late tonight so she couldn't meet up for a pint," he said in a voice of disappointment. "Shirley's a good lot. You would've liked her."

"I used to have a sister named Shirley," slurred Agnes.

"Oh, she's passed on?" asked Layton with great concern.

"She died in the Britannia disaster."

Layton's eyes widened, and he put down his drink. "Oh my God, that's terrible." He patted her hand in sympathy.

"I still can't believe she's gone. She was a lovely girl." Her eyes filled, and she sniffled, swiping roughly at her nose. "Smashed to pieces, she was. That architect shoulda been hanged, the shit."

"Was she in service too?"

Agnes was too upset to hear. She covered her face with her hands and cried, her whole body shaking with silent tears. After a few minutes, she composed herself and looked at Layton.

"She was me only sister. You know, I was to become an auntie?"

Layton jerked his head in surprise.

Agnes nodded. "Yes, that's right. Shirley was in the family way when she died."

"She was married?" Layton asked gently.

"Nah, servant girls can't be married."

"Oh," replied Layton, acting embarrassed. "Then . . . another servant . . . ?"

"Someone *upstairs,* not downstairs," snapped Agnes.

He braced himself for the answer to his next question. "Was it . . . the master?"

Agnes sniffed and wiped her nose with her sleeve. "His son. You know how it is; the boys play with the maids like we're their very own toys. Bonk 'em over and over. Then when they's knocked up, they won't have nothin' to do with 'em."

"Did the master know?"

"Yes, he did." Agnes narrowed her eyes and shook her head sadly. "Shirley told the head butler, Mr. Millgate, who, bless his heart, told Sir John about it. But the bastard refused to believe his precious son would do such a thing, especially with a servant girl. One day when she was cleaning out the fire grate in the study, she up and asked Sir John face-to-face for help because she would be showing soon. He said it wasn't his concern. I pleaded with her, but Shirley wouldn't get rid of it. Me, I went to see a woman in Spitalfields when I was in the pudding club. But she wanted the brat, bless her heart. She would've made a wonderful mum. Didn't know how she was going to manage it, though."

"Did you know she was going to the theatre that night?"

"No, but she loved the music hall and went lots of times, 'cause she worked so close to the West End."

"Perhaps someone gave her the ticket," said Layton, gripping his empty glass so tightly, he felt it might shatter.

" 'ow about one more drink for the road, ducky?"

Another round in, Layton steered Agnes's wobbly body out to Westminster Bridge Road and hailed a taxi. As he helped her in, he slipped a one-pound note into her pocket.

To great applause, Bimba Bamba completed his grand finale.

With a roar, he shouted out something that sounded like Hindustani, and his turbaned assistant, Fiona Pratt, vanished from the middle of the stage in a huge cloud of green smoke. Cymbals crashed triumphantly. The audience screamed and cried in amazement. Layton stood in the wings with Mangogo.

Set in the stage floor were trapdoors shaped like pie wedges. At Bimba Bamba's call, a stagehand below pulled a lever, and the wedges came apart, creating a hole through which the assistant fell, landing on a big cushion below.

Mangogo didn't know about the trap-doors. Rather, he thought Bimba Bamba had magical powers, of the sort possessed by shamans back in Africa.

"Smashing," he cried and stamped his spear on the floor as the house applauded.

In her move to London, Cissie had taken the Africans with her. She felt the Pygmies might make the chain more money at one of the West End theatres, and this gamble had paid off. The troupe was now playing the Queen's Palace indefinitely, and they had become a hit as Cissie said they would. Layton was very glad for Mangogo's continued company. Excepting Danny Harker, he had become his closest friend.

Cissie came up behind Mangogo and patted his woolly head.

"Remember, you devil, no ad-libbing. Stick to the script."

Even for the Pygmies, improvisation remained a breach of contract. And Cissie's warning had merit; Mangogo had once broken into an unscripted dance for a full five minutes and thrown off the timing of the whole show.

"No ad-lib," he said now and flashed Cissie a white-toothed smile as he headed backstage to prepare for his act.

As Cissie and Layton watched from the wings, he murmured, "So Sir John's son, George, was having a go at Shirley Finney. And there's more. Around the time of the accident, he was engaged to be married to Diana Finch, the Earl of Wickford's daughter."

"Fathering a bastard would've thrown off his plans," Cissie said, nodding. "And I imagine Lady Diana had quite a fortune?"

"You would imagine correctly. A great deal of which could be invested in the MacMillan circuit if needed."

"Maybe Shirley couldn't be bought off and was going to make a stink. She needed to go," said Cissie with her eyes still fixed on Bimba Bamba on the stage.

Layton could tell she had found something about the performance to criticize. Cissie was incredibly tough on performers, never praising them but dwelling on some slight error.

"What are your plans?" Layton asked.

"Tomorrow," Cissie said, "I'm taking a short trip to Stevenston which is just outside London. To enquire about a certain deceased vicar."

20

Not a single person was looking at the paintings in the National Gallery. Everyone was staring at Mangogo.

At Layton's side, the tiny African was admiring Thomas Gainsborough's *Mr. and Mrs. Andrews.* The gentleman in the portrait wore an elegant gray topcoat and held a gun in the crook of his arm. Beside him, his young wife was resplendent in a sky-blue satin dress and dainty silver slippers. The couple was posed by a tree in the country-side, a building — likely their estate — in the background.

"Who are man and woman?" asked Mangogo.

"Mr. and Mrs. Andrews of Suffolk."

"Mangogo tribe Mbuti. What tribe they?"

Layton laughed. "They belong to the English gentry. Big bosses in England. They, along with a tribe called the aristocracy, tell everyone what they should do."

"Mbuti no have boss man. Everybody same, even woman."

Layton found this interesting. Those persons the British would regard as savages had a more equal society than that belonging to Britons at home.

"Woman not look like can do much work, like hunt with net or get water. Can woman cook?" Mangogo asked, stepping forward to look at the painting more closely.

"No, women from that particular set are essentially useless," Layton said, laughing. "They have servants to do all that."

Mangogo sniffed. "Mbuti forest has many more . . . trees. So many you not see the sky."

The professor had told Layton that Mangogo's tribe was nomadic; they built temporary huts as they wandered the rain forest, hunting and foraging for food. They had an incredible knowledge of the land and how to live off it. Both men and women cared for the children, which was certainly different from England: no nannies for the Pygmies.

"Mbuti, children of forest. The forest is our god," said Mangogo with great seriousness.

"Mr. and Mrs. Andrews belong to the Church of England," Layton said. "Which means they don't believe in anything, really."

As they moved on to the next painting, a child approached Mangogo and asked, shyly, to shake his hand, to which the Pygmy heartily acquiesced. He even let the little boy hold his spear.

The Pygmy act had become a sensation in London, and Mangogo was its star. On the street, people would shout greetings or call out his name; one man asked to take a snap of him with his Kodak Brownie, another to rub his head for good luck, all to the great pleasure of Mangogo.

They paused in front of *The Fighting Temeraire* by J. M. W. Turner. The seascape showed a tugboat towing a famous ship, wrecked in the Battle of Trafalgar, to be broken up. At the right side blazed a magnificent sunset, all hot oranges and reds.

"Turner is one of England's greatest painters," Layton said. "Pictures of the sea were his favorite."

"Our forest not have that much water. Much fish in there, yes?" asked Mangogo, pointing the tip of his spear at the grayish-blue waves.

"Indeed. That's where your fish and chips come from."

"Mmm. With HP Sauce . . . smashing,"

said Mangogo, rubbing his little potbelly.

It was November, and the weather was beginning to cool. Mangogo wore a white shirt, minus the collar, under his burnt-orange blanket. Though he still refused pants, he now sported low-cut hobnail boots with thick leather soles, which clomped loudly on the wood floors of the exhibition rooms.

As Mangogo examined the Turner more closely, Layton drew out his watch. He had tried to teach his African friend to tell time, but the Pygmies knew only the rhythms of sunrises and sunsets. "Elevenses," he said, tucking his watch away. "Time for tea."

They found a teashop on the Strand near Charing Cross Station. The proprietor, a prim-looking lady with spectacles, was at first alarmed, but when two customers called out Mangogo's name — fondly, as though he were an old classmate from Oxford — she relaxed and showed them to a table.

"Thank you, madam," said Mangogo in a loud, clear voice, startling the woman.

A timid waitress brought their tea, backing away as soon as she'd set down the plates. Mangogo nodded to her and smiled, then dug into a scone, upon which he heaped a large serving of butter. Whenever they took tea together, he insisted on pouring as Layton had taught him, the way the upper classes did: tea first, then milk and sugar — never put the milk in first!

Layton watched as Mangogo carefully stirred his tea. *I'm turning him into an upper-class Englishman,* he thought with a jolt of amusement. Like he had done with himself.

A man and his wife came up to Mangogo to shake his hand. He stood up and bowed to the woman, to her delight.

"Do you miss the food of the forest?" the man asked.

Mangogo swallowed his mouthful of scone before answering. He no longer chewed with his mouth open.

"Yes, no antelope or chakka leaves in England," he said, a touch of sadness in his voice. "But like Marmite. Remind me of beetcha. Mashed beetle pulp."

Marmite, a thick, brown paste made of yeast that Englishmen smeared on toast, was another delicacy invented during Layton's time in prison. All the Pygmies in the troupe loved it and ate it right out of the jar, using their fingers as spoons.

The more he got to know Mangogo and the more he enjoyed the little man's company, the more Layton ached to help him adjust to his new life. Backstage one night, the professor had told him a sad story; now Layton struggled to get it out of his mind.

Years ago, in 1903, an American explorer had brought a Pygmy from the Central African rain forest back to the United States to be displayed in the monkey cage at New York's Bronx Zoo. Forty thousand people a day had come to see him. But one morning, the zookeeper had found the Pygmy dead. He'd hanged himself with strips torn from his blanket. At the thought of this being Mangogo's fate, a shudder rippled through Layton.

Of course, while it was true that Cissie and the circuit were making a packet off the Pygmy act, they weren't treating them like zoo animals. A share of the profits had even been put aside for them, though they had no concept of money; to Mangogo, a monkey hide for barter was far more valuable than any coin or pound note. Marmite was even more valuable. While Cissie had found them a flat in Southbank, most of the time, the troupe stayed in the cellar below stage. It reminded them, Mangogo said, of their dark, windowless huts at home.

"Owen heartsick," announced Mangogo out of the blue.

"Why the deuce would you say that?" Layton said with an astonished smile.

"Mangogo know." His voice was grave, and he wasn't smiling.

His concern touched Layton.

"Do the children of the forest read minds?" he asked gently, impressed by his friend's perspicacity. Despite his troubles, he tried to always be jolly when with Mangogo. And all the time he spent with him, he enjoyed himself so much that he forgot his woes for a while.

"Read minds?" Mangogo repeated.

Smiling, Layton took his finger and drew an invisible line from the Pygmy's forehead to his own.

Mangogo nodded. "Yes. We know what animal think — like viper and leopard."

"And I'm unhappy?"

"Owen in Queer Street," he said. "Why?"

He was right; Layton *was* in trouble. An incredible urge to tell Mangogo everything surged up inside Layton. But he held his tongue. He didn't want to endanger his friend. Besides, it was a complicated story, and Mangogo might not understand. Or if he did, he might do something rash. Unlike the British, who were masters of repressed emotion, the Pygmies acted on impulse if loyalty demanded it.

"No, I'm in no trouble. I am right as rain, I assure you."

Mangogo shook his head. "Bollocks," he said, repeating a word he'd heard many times from Cissie. It suited him.

Layton exploded with laughter.

"Mangogo keen as mustard to help." He rummaged inside the leather pouch he wore always around his neck. Removing what looked like a piece of blackish-gray tree bark, about seven inches long and five inches wide, he held it out to Layton. "Loktiki tree — big magic," he said excitedly and broke off a piece.

Layton plucked it from the palm of the African's bony little hand and clutched it tight. "Well, thank you," he said. Touched by this kind gesture, he made to put it in his side coat pocket.

"Eat," Mangogo insisted, making a chewing motion with his teeth.

Layton hesitated, then smiled and put the bark in his mouth. His first sensation was that this was the closest he'd ever come to eating feces. He swallowed, trying to disguise his grimace of disgust.

"Owen keep pecker up — bad will go away. More tea, white British chap?" asked Mangogo, as politely as any upper-class matron. He lifted the white-bone china pot, ready to pour.

21

"What was the name of your organization again, my dear?"

"The Central African Christian Movement. We bring the word of Christ to the heathens of the Dark Continent. Here's a picture of our most recent converts." Cissie leaned forward and displayed for the old woman a publicity photo of Professor Evans & His Pygmies.

"The white fellow is Reverend Hoskins. He's had a tremendous success rate."

Impressed, Mrs. Blair asked Cissie in. Her home was a quaint, charming cottage in the village of Stevenston, Hertfordshire, twenty miles from London. Constructed of native stone with a red tile roof, it was just the right retirement home for a vicar's widow.

In the parlor, Mrs. Blair picked up a brass bell and shook it violently, screaming, "Mabel!" In strode a slatternly girl of about sixteen in an ill-fitting black-and-white maid's uniform. "Mabel, bring us some tea and those blueberry scones."

Without even a "yes, ma'am," Mabel turned and stomped out of the room.

The women settled into armchairs across from each other.

The newspapers had written that seventy-eight-year-old Denys Blair, the former vicar at All Christ's Church, was survived by a wife, Mary, and a daughter, Alma. Tracking down the widow, who was in her eighties and becoming disoriented, had been simple for Cissie.

"I'm just back from Africa," Cissie said, "and my very first task is distributing gifts to our loyal supporters. When will Reverend Blair be returning?"

"I'm afraid Reverend Blair died more than five years ago." Mary touched the corners of her eyes with her lace handkerchief. "In that horrible Britannia Theatre disaster. A balcony collapsed — it fell on top of him. Denys frequently took the train in to London to attend the variety theatre, although I never accompanied him. I found music halls to be vulgar," the old woman sniffed.

"Oh, heavens," gasped Cissie, gloved hand to mouth. "But if there's one man who is in the kingdom of heaven, it must be Reverend Blair."

"Well, I don't know about that," said Mrs. Blair. She looked rather uncomfortable now. "They do say God is merciful toward sinners — even the worst."

"What a shame. I had a gift for him: a King James Bible, bound in Moroccan leather. Now it's for you to treasure, as a memory of your late husband." Cissie handed the Bible to the widow reverently, holding it in both palms, as if it were a gold plate.

Mabel stomped in with the tea and set it roughly on the table.

"That's all," snapped Mrs. Blair. But as she leaned forward to pour, a grimace came over her face. "Stupid girl. She forgot the scones. If you want something done right, you must do it yourself. Excuse me, Mrs. Ludgate."

In her hostess's absence, Cissie got up and walked about the parlor. The fireplace mantel held a charming collection of trinkets collected from holidays on the coast of England — a little windmill from Blackpool, a ceramic Japanese doll from Bournemouth. Mementos of the widow's life with the vicar were scattered about too: his framed divinity degree from Oxford; an image of the church's rededication, likely after some restoration project; and photos of the vicar sitting with the choir, the dates written in white ink at the top.

In each, a dozen boys surrounded Blair, then a tall, vigorous man with a flowing mane of hair. All the boys had carefully combed hair, wore choir robes, and stared vacantly into the camera. Their names were listed by row at the bottom of each photo.

As Cissie glanced over them, something caught her attention. In the 1872 photo, the boy at the end of the first row was labeled as Lionel Glenn. Her eye darted to his face: yes, a pretty blond boy with plump cheeks and a serious expression. Cissie put her eyes right up to the tiny image and stared. The Lionel Glenn she worked for was fat and bald, but the resemblance still shone through in certain features — those wide eyes, the nub of chin.

Something was beating urgently inside Cissie's mind, but she couldn't put her finger on it yet. She scrutinized the other boys' faces more closely. All about the same age. The widow must have been giving Mabel hell indeed; Cissie darted to her purse, pulled out the list and a pencil, and scribbled the names of the other boys on the back of the paper. Just as she finished, Mrs. Blair returned, carrying a plate heaped with scones.

"There," she said. "Now we can have a proper tea."

As they ate and drank, Cissie tried to make conversation about the choir, but the widow only talked incessantly about the vicar's matchbox-collecting hobby. When Cissie at last made to depart, Mrs. Blair insisted on contributing five pounds to her cause, which Cissie had no choice but to accept.

Outside, it was midafternoon, a cool fall day with plenty of light left. Cissie found her way to All Christ's Church, which stood at the far end of the village. It was the usual medieval English parish church, with heavy stone walls and a steep slate roof. The light inside shone through stained-glass windows; the ceiling was a series of handsome oak hammer beam trusses.

As Cissie stood, taking in the feel of the space, a door opened behind the pulpit, and out came an elderly caretaker, stooped and mumbling. When he saw Cissie, he waved and, in a croaking voice, called, "Welcome."

"Thank you, sir. What a beautiful church."

"Yes, we're quite proud of it. Originally from the 1300s; restored in 1881."

"In fact, my uncle lived in Stevenston. He attended this very church." Cissie spoke in her jolliest voice. "He heard I was coming through and asked me to look up some old mates of his. You know, for old time's sake."

"I've been round here all my seventy-five years." The old man snorted proudly, as if he were boasting about his ability to recite every king and queen England had ever had. "I know everyone."

"Thomas Swain, Nigel Blunt, Joseph Durham, Derrick Carr, Alexander . . ." Cissie began, reading off her list. But one of the names had caught the old man's attention.

"Why, Derrick still lives on Standish Street, by the tobacconist's!"

"Why the hell would I want to give money for a bunch of bloody darkies in Africa? I got me own problems. They can swing from tree to tree and eat coconuts for all I care," Derrick Carr snarled. He was in his early fifties and as wide as he was tall.

It hadn't been easy for Cissie to get inside his house; she'd practically had to shove her way past him at the door. Like most people, Carr hated door-to-door salespersons, especially do-gooders asking for religious donations.

"But we are striving to bring them to Christ," she entreated, using her most innocent tone and opening her eyes wide.

"You're wasting your bloody time — and mine, woman."

"Mrs. Blair, the wife of the late vicar, said you might make a small contribution."

This caught Carr's attention. He didn't speak but gave Cissie a withering look.

"She said you were in the choir when you were a lad."

Carr walked right up to Cissie and put his face to hers. "That I was, and I'll never forget it. I turned my back on God after that." His voice rose; color flushed to his cheeks. He was getting angrier by the second. "The wife of that bloody bugger has some nerve sending you here. She knew full well what was going on, and still she chose to look the other way."

"Bugger?" Cissie echoed. A religious zealot shouldn't know the word — not like an experienced theatre woman.

"He never did me; guess I was lucky I wasn't pretty enough. But he gave it up the bum plenty of times to them others in the choir. Especially Philip and Lionel, poor devils. Wouldn't keep his hands off 'em. Every couple of years came a new set of boys. He was vicar here some thirty years, the filthy bugger. Do you know how many boys that added up to?" Carr was fully red in the face now.

Cissie knew she had to leave or be pitched out on her head in the street. Prudence reigned; she turned and fled.

"Man of God," Carr shouted after her. "What a bloody pile of manure."

22

"Hello, Dougie. Bet you thought you'd never see me again."

On the contrary, Layton thought wryly. He wasn't at all surprised to see his old prison mate, Archie Guest. After five years in Mulcaster, he knew the criminal mind inside and out; when there was easy money to be had, a criminal never gave up the chase. Abruptly moving to London from Nottingham wasn't going to shake this rotter. He'd known damn well that Guest would follow him here.

It was early Tuesday morning. Layton had been approaching the stage door when Guest appeared at his right, a big grin on his leathery face. Other stagehands were coming down the alley, along with a few performers hoping to rehearse before the evening show.

"Am I imagining things, or was me old pal trying to give me the slip?" Guest was salivating for fear and panic from his victim.

Layton just smiled and put his arm around the man, as companionable as if he were an old Eton classmate. "Archie, have you ever been backstage at a music hall? It's a fascinating world." He didn't wait for Guest's reply but guided him gently through the stage door. "The gentleman in that little cubicle is the stage doorman, who stands guard to keep out intruders. Since you're here with me, there'll be no problem," Layton said and nodded to Simon Blaine, the doorman.

The two men walked leisurely through the bleak brick-and-plaster hallways. People came and went on all sides.

"You've always been an observer out in the audience," Layton continued in an eager-to-please tone. "Now you've crossed an invisible threshold, and you can see where the magic is made."

Though Guest remained silent and listened, his eyes darted about frenetically, as if he were desperate to figure out Layton's plan.

"This is the stage from the performer's point of view," Layton said. "Looking out into the auditorium. Quite a sight, am I right?"

He guided Guest to the side of the stage.

The Bouncing Bobos, a tumbling act, was rehearsing at center stage. Four men held the corners of a large blanket, tossing a pretty young girl in red tights up into the air. She turned multiple somersaults before landing each time. Layton gestured up, drawing Guest's eye.

"That's the fly tower above our heads. The cloths I paint are flown up by ropes from that gallery on the side." Layton led Guest into the wings and gestured left and right. "Back here we have dressing rooms, the scene shop, and a carpenter's shop. Don't these poky corridors have a charm and fascination all their own?"

"Sure, sure. It's all very bloody interesting." Guest shook his head, refocusing on his task. "But, Dougie, you and I have some business to attend to. Remember?"

"Of course. Why don't we go somewhere more private? Follow me."

With Guest following behind, Layton descended a spiral stair to the understage and led Guest behind a large wooden wheel that operated one of the traps in the stage.

"Now we have some privacy."

"All them people up there would be surprised as hell to know they're working alongside the Butcher of the West End. They'd be bloody mad, in fact." Guest

237

waggled his eyebrows, shook his head. "You got some cheek, mate, getting yourself a job with the very circuit you built the Britannia for."

"How much?"

Guest blinked, folded his arms against his chest. It was a dramatic gesture to show he meant business. "Since we're old friends, I'd say twenty quid a month is fair."

"Agreed," Layton said cheerfully.

"Well . . . Dougie," Guest stammered, "I'm right glad we could come to an agreement without a lot of fuss, two Mulcaster gents like us."

"I couldn't agree more, *Arch*. And I bet you want your first month's payment?"

"Why . . . yes. That's what I was thinkin'."

"How about this? Since it's nearing the end of the month, I'll give you ten quid, and we'll start afresh next month. That's fair, isn't it?" Without waiting for an answer, Layton stuffed a ten-pound note into Guest's pocket.

A smile came over the ex-convict's face. "That'll do nicely, m'lad. Very nicely . . . for now."

"I'll see you to the door."

As they walked down the corridor, they saw Cissie, talking to the stage doorman.

"Mrs. Mapes, let me introduce you to a

very old school chum of mine, Archibald Guest."

"Glad to make your acquaintance, Mr. Guest."

"Mr. Guest is a lover of variety theatre entertainment. Could we leave a weekly pass for him?"

"Anything for a friend of yours, Mr. Owen."

As they waved him out the door, Cissie smiled and whispered, "So that's the piece of shite, eh?"

"Indeed it is, Mrs. Mapes."

"What's his price?"

"Twenty quid a month."

"Once he knows he has you under his thumb, you know it'll go up to at least fifty. What will you do then?"

Layton shook his head, and for the first time, the easy smile dropped from his face. "I don't know, Cissie. I don't know."

23

"I thought the seals were funniest," nine-year-old Ronald Layton piped up. "Didn't you, Nanny?"

"Eddington & Freddington were funniest for me, Master Ronald. Those two toffee-nosed girls were a real hoot."

"What does 'toffee-nosed' mean, Nanny?" Ronald asked, confused.

"Stuck-up, hoity-toity. The kind that looks down on others."

Mrs. Hawkins had been Ronald's nanny since his birth. He was a good, thoughtful lad who never gave her any trouble. His divorced mother, Edwina, was recently engaged to remarry. Soon, Mrs. Hawkins thought, another child would be on the way and destined for her care.

Like all upper-class British boys, Ronald had been sent to boarding school at age seven. Now he was home on holiday, and Mrs. Hawkins had thought she might introduce him to the pleasures of the variety theatre. It was all wholesome fun these days; the bawdiness and drunkenness of the old music halls had passed, but she still hadn't told Lady Edwina where they were going this afternoon.

Nannies were in effect the real mothers of children of the peerage and the upper classes, whose parents were too caught up in their social worlds to pay their offspring much attention. Mrs. Hawkins — she had never married, but all nannies carried the title "Mrs." — felt it her duty to show Ronald the real world outside his family's London town house in Mayfair and country house in Kent. Imagine, him turning into an upper-class twit like Eddington & Freddington! Not if she had any say in the matter.

And Ronald already had a measure of independence. He wasn't a baby anymore and was allowed go out alone and play in the park with friends.

The first show had finished; Ronald and Mrs. Hawkins filed out of their seats onto crowded Shaftesbury Avenue. People lined up for the second performance were eagerly asking the departing audience about the show. The buskers, street performers in gaudy costumes, danced and played instruments to entertain those waiting in hopes of a few spare coppers. Mrs. Hawkins kept firm hold of Ronald's hand. They'd go next to a fish and chips shop — not because she thought Ronald should try commoner's food, but because she loved a good fish and chips drenched in vinegar.

As they shuffled along with the crowd, a man emerged from the alley behind the theatre. Mrs. Hawkins stopped dead in her tracks.

"Crikey," she blurted. She froze, wide-eyed, but caught herself an instant later. Ahead, the man crossed Shaftesbury Avenue. Mrs. Hawkins took hold of Ronald's hand and abruptly turned the other way, glancing occasionally over her shoulder. When the man was out of sight, she turned and walked toward their original destination.

At the fish and chips shop, Mrs. Hawkins seemed very distracted. Ronald, a bright and inquisitive boy, sensed something was wrong, but when he tried to question her, she steered the conversation back to the acts they'd just seen. Undeterred, he kept pressing the matter in the carriage ride back to Mayfair.

"I'll lay a shilling to a pound it was someone you knew once," he said, racking his mind to think of a likely candidate. "One of your children from another household?"

With her nerves raw and jumping, Ronald's precociousness was aggravating in the extreme. Still, Mrs. Hawkins kept her temper in check.

"Yes, Master Ronald, it was someone from my past," she said, hoping to end the conversation there.

"Why didn't go up to him and say hello? He'd have liked that."

In spite of herself, Mrs. Hawkins smiled. Yes, Mr. Layton would have indeed liked that. They'd always been fond of one another; instead of being toffee-nosed, like most employers in her long career, he'd been kind and caring. He was so different in character from all the upper-class people she had known. When her mother was dying up in Liverpool, he'd paid Mrs. Hawkins's train and hotel fare, so she and her ma could spend her last days together. When Mr. Layton found out she was going to spend her holiday alone in the country house, he treated her to a week at Bournemouth, a place he'd loved as a child.

"It's too bad," said Ronald. "I'd have liked to meet one of your friends."

Mrs. Hawkins didn't smile at this comment. Because she knew the man would have liked to meet his son too.

It wasn't right, she thought fiercely. Having told Ronald his father had died in his youth, Lady Edwina and her family had obliterated all traces of the man from his son's life. Not a single photo remained. Douglas Layton had been a loving husband and wonderful father who had spent time with his son whenever he could, despite his busy career. And yet, once he was convicted and sent to prison, he no longer existed for the Litton family. Lady Edwina had gone abroad with her son for a year, returned when the dust had settled, and proceeded to live a life entirely absent of one Douglas Layton.

Mrs. Hawkins shook her head. Those people had died in an *accident*. Mr. Layton hadn't done it on purpose. He was a good and decent man, yet the press had turned him into a murderous beast, whom all of Great Britain and the empire hated. In the face of such scorn, Lord Litton's embarrassment and humiliation had been unbearable. He had raged at his son-in-law for bringing disgrace on the family. Douglas shouldn't have taken the job in the first place, he had fumed. Designing a music hall was no work for a gentleman architect.

The next day, at tea in her room at the

Mayfair house, Mrs. Hawkins did something she knew was forbidden.

"Ronnie," she asked. "Do you have any memories of your late father?"

"Barely, Nanny. I kind of remember him reading stories to me." Ronald spoke in a matter-of-fact tone. "Mummy never says a word about him, so I don't ask."

Mrs. Hawkins took a long sip of her tea and set the silver cup down on the tray. She watched Ronald gulping down his buttered scone and felt affection well within her.

"Would you like to see what he looked like?" she asked in a low voice.

Ronald stopped chewing, and his eyes widened.

"Why, Nanny, do you have a picture of him?"

Surreptitiously, she nodded for him to follow. In most houses, the nanny's living quarters were next to the nursery, which ceased to be used when the children went off to school. Now, Mrs. Hawkins had a warm, inviting suite of rooms in which she and Ronald had spent many an hour talking, reading, and enjoying each other's company. On the fireplace mantel were formal photos of Ronald at different ages: a toddler, a chubby five-year-old in a sailor's suit, a boy in his school uniform with an unhappy expression.

Ronald watched intently as Mrs. Hawkins took down one of the framed pictures and produced a Kodak snap from the back of its frame.

"I took this of you and your father with my Brownie when you were three," said Mrs. Hawkins, placing it in the boy's hands.

He stared for almost thirty seconds before handing it back.

"You and him are standing in a field of poppies behind the old house in Surrey. You loved to run through them."

"He seems likes a nice chap," he ventured, striving to keep his voice level. "Were you fond of him?"

"He was a first-rate fellow," Mrs. Hawkins said. "I see a lot of him in you, Ronnie."

Flattered, Ronald beamed a big smile at his nanny and asked, "Why don't you have the snap in its own frame like the others?"

"It's my special hiding place for a very special picture. You won't be giving me away now, will you?" She arched an eyebrow, knowing Ronald's love of secret pacts.

"Of course not, Nanny. It'll be our secret," the boy cried enthusiastically.

For the second afternoon in a row, Ronald had paid Cedric Hardwicke two bob to say

246

he'd been playing with him in Hyde Park. He hadn't. Instead, he'd stood in a doorway across from the alley that bordered the Queen's Palace of Varieties.

The theatres in the West End weren't that far from Hyde Park; it was just a short walk down Piccadilly. Just like the day before, at 2:00 p.m., the same man walked out of the alley and joined the steady flow of people in the street. At 3:00 p.m., he returned, accompanied by a woman in an olive-colored dress. They laughed and chatted away like the best of mates.

After so many years together, Nanny and Ronald could sometimes read each other's thoughts. When Nanny had shown him the snap of his father, he'd known that in her mind she was saying, "You know what to do." And he had.

Looking at his father was strange. Until now, he had been a ghost to Ronald. And now he was real. He was tall, which made Ronald happy. Maybe he'd grow up tall too. And he had excellent posture and a bright smile, the kind that made people feel good. Watching him, Ronald wasn't scared or nervous, just fascinated and excited, the way a scientist would feel observing a rare species in the wild.

Today, as his father, whom Ronald knew

was named Douglas Layton, walked down the alley, Ronald scampered after him across the street, dodging carriages and wagons. At the stage door, his father greeted a man in a three-piece suit on his way out. Then the heavy, green metal door shut behind him and the woman.

Ronald stood at the intersection of alley and street and watched other people come and go from the theatre. These were probably the performers, he decided, but without the exotic costumes they wore onstage, they looked like ordinary people.

Was his father a music hall performer? Ronald wondered abruptly. It was an exciting idea. Perhaps he'd seen him that evening with Nanny. He could have been an acrobat, a tumbler, or one of the trainers of the seals he'd liked so much.

Galvanized, Ronald walked to the front of the Queen's Palace and scrutinized the bill advertising that night's acts. The Lancashire Lads, the Kings of Clog Dancing; Jack & Jill, Songbirds of London; Professor Evans & His Pygmies; Sam & the Crazy Gang. There was no Layton listed. Probably because he used a pretend name!

It was late afternoon; he had to be getting home. But as Ronald made his way through the bustle of Piccadilly, he felt like he was floating a finger's breadth above the pavement. He had a father! The discovery excited everything in him. He'd always been ashamed of his father's absence, which made him feel inferior among his friends. His mother's upcoming marriage to Percival Tree, the Earl of Gainsford, would correct the situation, but then, Lord Percival didn't seem to care much for being a father. And after today's discovery, everything was different.

Dreams of being backstage, helping his father with his act, filled Ronald's mind. He couldn't stop smiling. He'd be the envy of all the boys at school. Their fathers were a bunch of boring dukes, earls, and bankers. His was a music hall performer!

24

"Come in, you dear, dear boy."

Eddington & Freddington had just finished their turn and were taking off their makeup in the dressing room. It was a shared space; only top-of-the-bill performers like Dan Leno or Marie Lloyd were given a personal dressing room. Not that privacy made much difference. The dressing rooms were a collection of cramped, windowless boxes off the maze of backstage corridors. They'd remained unchanged — and poorly lit — for centuries; only recently had their table mirrors been outlined in small electric light bulbs.

Neville gestured for Layton to come nearer as he removed his stuffed brassiere.

"Frank, darling," he crooned. "We're trying out new material for tomorrow night's show. Tell us what you think."

Eddington: I just attended the races at Ascot.

Freddington: And how did it go, my dear?

Eddington: I was looking around the paddock when a stable boy threw a saddle on my back.

Freddington: Oh dear! What did you do?

Eddington: What could I do? I came in third.

Cyril and Neville cackled with uproarious laughter. Noel Talbot, the Welsh Tenor, who was changing into his street clothes at the end of the room, was less impressed.

"That one's as old as the shit on your teeth, you bloody fairy," he snarled.

"No one asked your opinion, Taffy," Cyril cut back.

"Taffy was a Welshman, Taffy was a thief; Taffy came into my house and stole a side of beef," sang Neville.

"Stole a song, more like it. Frank, did you know these singers don't write their songs? They buy them. *We* write all our own material," Cyril said proudly.

"Ignore him. Yes, Cyril, I would definitely use it," Layton said, smiling. He'd come to really like the duo — especially as Cyril was keeping his promise not to touch his bum. Their act was just starting a monthlong engagement at the Queen's Palace; a West End theatre was a big opportunity for them, and they hoped to land at the top of the bill.

"But really, we didn't ask you here to test out jokes, Frank. We want to take you for a drink, show our appreciation for those new cloths you did. They're works of art."

"Indeed. They give us class, m'boy," added Cyril, nodding proudly at Neville.

"Class my ass," said Talbot, stomping out the door.

"Filthy Welshman," Neville shouted after him. "You sing like a hinge!"

When Cissie had secured Layton the job at the Queen's, he'd decided that he would become the head artist — this despite the troubles surging around him. He had to rebuild his life. With that in mind, he'd continued to put great thought and care into his backdrops. Cyril and Neville's had been major efforts: one, a garden in front of Lord Burlington's Chiswick House; the other, the interior of the Banqueting House in Whitehall by Inigo Jones, complete with a representation of the ceiling by Rubens.

"I'd enjoy that very much," Layton said, smiling at Neville and Cyril. "I'll be waiting by the stage door."

But by the time they were ready to leave, it was after eleven, when most pubs had closed for the night.

"Everything's shut up. Where we will go?" Layton asked. He sighed; he'd been looking forward to a pint of Guinness.

"Oh, have no fear, my friend. A special, *secluded* spot we know of is open all hours," said Neville in a conspiratorial tone. "Follow us."

They walked down Shaftesbury Avenue to Piccadilly, both deserted now, and turned left on St. James's. There, they entered a building half a block from Pall Mall, whose entry led to a long, dank hallway still lit by gaslight. At its end stood a metal door, upon which Cyril gave three knocks, a single knock, then three more knocks. They heard the sound of a bolt slamming back, and then the door opened into a surprisingly ornate lobby with paneled walls and a marble floor covered with oriental rugs.

"Welcome to the Abdullah, Frank. It's got a dangerous Oriental aura we just *adore.*" Neville spoke as proudly as he would have in showing off his own home.

"To the left is the bar, and down that spiral stair are the Turkish baths, which are quite stimulating," Cyril said.

"I'll attest to that. And in more ways than one." Both Cyril and Neville chortled at this little aside.

Then the trio walked into the bar, a deceptively large room full of round tables. Each had an electric lamp with a red shade, which gave the space an eerie, mysterious feel. Thick cigarette smoke filled the air, along with the scent of incense. Along one wall was a bar; at the opposite end of the room, a four-piece band played a fox-trot to which couples — all men — were dancing.

When Cyril and Neville entered, applause broke out roundly. They acknowledged it enthusiastically, and then all three sat at a booth along the wall. Layton had known from the moment he entered that this was a poof bar; out of respect for the artistes, he pretended not to notice, but he found himself ill at ease. From time to time, the police raided establishments like this one, and he'd met a few fairies at Mulcaster serving time for gross indecency. He didn't want to end up like Oscar Wilde, who had been sent to Reading Gaol and forced to walk a treadmill drum, which operated a flour grindstone, for sixteen hours a day. Humiliation, then death, had met the great author. Layton would do anything to avoid a similar fate.

A man in ill-fitting evening dress and a red fez cap took their orders. While they talked, a young, rakish-looking man in a scarlet velvet coat and a gold cravat approached the booth.

"Cyril, would your friend care to rumba?" asked the youth, nodding at Layton.

"No, he would not. Go away, Desmond," Cyril snapped.

"A very naughty boy, Frank," Neville whispered. "Keep away from that sort."

"You're a fine-looking chap, Frank," Cyril said, patting his hand. "You have to expect that kind of attention here at the Abdullah."

Layton smiled, amused but not at all shocked. Between prison and the theatre, he'd seen every type of sodomite there was.

As he, Cyril, and Neville drank into the wee hours, many men came and went, some alone, some with companions. The only women present were men *dressed* as women — often convincingly. One looked amazingly like Mrs. Keppel, the king's mistress.

Layton was enjoying himself immensely, and the alcohol gave him a warm, fuzzy feel. It was great to be among friends, laughing, trading jokes, and gossiping.

After three hours, his bladder needed emptying. In the restroom, standing at the long urinal trough, he stared at the plaster wall in front of him. Names and obscene comments covered every inch.

Layton's urine stopped midstream when he saw, among the crude scrawls, *Ted Hardy R.I.H.*

"Say, old chap, maybe you can help me." Layton leaned forward over the bar and spoke in a hushed voice. "I've been away in India on an engineering job. Just came back a week ago, but I used to come here quite a bit. And now I'm trying to look someone up."

The barman, a skinny man with a protruding Adam's apple, wiped down a champagne glass and eyed Layton with suspicion. It was midafternoon at the Abdullah, and the place was quiet. Only one other man sat at the end of the bar, nursing his drink.

"Didn't I see you here last night?" the barman asked.

"Why, yes. You're most observant. I was sitting over there with my friends." Layton gestured to the booth he'd shared with Cyril and Neville. "Two rather well-known music hall performers. Brought me as their guest."

Without speaking, the barman set the glass down and began wiping another. Layton understood his reticence. In London, the police would often send undercover officers to entrap fairies. However, this establishment, according to Neville, paid off the police quite well and had a very influential clientele, both of which ensured that such stings never happened. Tory cabinet ministers, an archbishop, and an officer of the Bank of England were all regulars at the Abdullah.

Having given Layton the once-over, the barman relaxed and smiled.

"Might I get you a drink, sir?"

"A gin and tonic would fit the bill."

As he mixed the drink, the barman politely asked, "And who was the gentleman you were asking about, sir?"

"Ted Hardy."

"Ted Hardy!" cried the man at the end of the bar.

The barman stopped mixing the gin and tonic, and he and the Abdullah's sole patron exchanged incredulous looks.

"Yes, Ted Hardy," said Layton. His puzzled expression wasn't an act; he hadn't expected such a reaction.

"And you said he was a friend of yours?" the barman said dubiously.

"With friends like that, lad, you don't need enemies," the man at the bar said, gulping down his shot.

"Well, he was more of an acquaintance,

really," Layton said.

"I'm sorry to tell you, sir, that Ted Hardy is dead." The barman shook his head. "Killed in that Britannia Theatre disaster some years back."

"Good riddance," the man at the bar said bitterly. "God did us a favor."

"Even a blighter like him didn't deserve such a horrible death," the barman said, shaking his head.

"The Britannia." Layton shook his head. "I heard of that while I was in India. What terrible news."

"What's your angle? Did Teddy Bear put the bite on you too?" asked the man, rising from his seat.

He was completely drunk, Layton realized, and unsteady on his feet.

"Oh, I didn't know him very long," he said hastily. He didn't want these men to think him unsavory too; rather, he hoped they'd assume his connection to Hardy a mere one-night encounter — rather the norm for poofs.

But now he understood the "R.I.H." on the wall. It was no spelling mistake; it likely stood for Rest — or Roast — in Hell.

The barman handed him his drink.

"No matter what you think of that man, it's a horrible way to die," Layton said. "His family must have been devastated."

"I bet they said good riddance to bad rubbish," the man down the bar mumbled.

"If he had any family," Layton added, pressing his luck.

"Didn't he have a mother who had a flower stall at Covent Garden?" the barman said idly.

"If she's alive, then I spit on her for giving birth to such a shit," slurred the drunken patron.

Layton did the arithmetic; Hardy would have been fifty-one if he'd lived, meaning he probably had a mother of seventy or so years.

Standing by one of the skinny cast-iron columns that held up the great glass-and-iron roof of Covent Garden Market, he surveyed the rows of flower stalls. It was an amazing sight, a continuous vista of flowers of every description, in every color one could imagine. The wonderful smells that floated above them were yet more captivating.

Down the center aisle, well-dressed society ladies stopped at each stall to examine the vases and buckets of flowers. Women from Mayfair, Belgravia, and Kensington came here weekly; while ladies of the upper class and aristocracy had servants for the house-work, selecting and arranging flowers was the domestic chore they reserved for them-selves. Edwina had adored flower arrange-ment.

When a lady stopped at a stall, the head of a man or woman would pop out from the bunches of flowers, ready to make a sale. Layton watched for almost five minutes; at last, he saw a gray-haired old woman rise up from behind a bouquet of red carnations.

"What kind of flowers ya lookin' for, guv?" She was a tiny, spry thing in a dark, tatty men's cardigan. "Something for your sweetie?"

Layton didn't respond but carefully touched several bunches of flowers, bending low to sniff them. Seeing his serious man-ner, the woman reined in her good cheer and fell silent.

"Nina loved cornflowers," said Layton, more to himself than to the vendor. He stroked the tops of a nearby bouquet. "Yes, I'll take a bunch, please."

The woman smiled, wrapping the flowers up in newspaper so as to sop up the water from their stems. "Sixpence, sir."

As Layton handed her the money, he murmured, "I always put fresh flowers on my daughter's grave. I think she'll like these."

"That's a fine thing to do, guv."

"It's going on six years now since she died. In that Britannia Theatre collapse."

The old woman raised her hands to her mouth, as if stifling a shriek.

"Blimey, sir," she muttered. "Me son, Teddy, died in that same accident."

Layton's eyes widened in surprise, and he dropped the flowers. "You're the first person I've met that lost someone that night too," he exclaimed, putting his hand on her shoulder.

"The same." She put her hand on top of his and looked into his eyes. "I can't believe my Teddy is gone. I always expect to see 'im strolling up this aisle, waving."

"When I come home at night, I half expect Nina to come bounding down the stairs to greet me."

"The worst thing a mother can do is bury her child." Tears filled the old woman's eyes. "Teddy was no saint, mind you, but he was me only child. Now I'm alone."

Layton smiled and squeezed her shoulder. "My name is John Clive."

"And mine's Connie Hardy. Mighty pleased to meet you, sir. I've been longing to meet another parent who lost a child that horrible night. Makes me mad as hell that they only gave that architect fellow five years."

"Yes," Layton said fiercely. "A travesty of justice. He should have hanged."

"I'd've given all my savings to watch the bastard strangle at the end of the rope. Every single day, I think of me Teddy." Other customers had approached, but Connie Hardy ignored them and kept her eyes fixed on Layton.

"I too have always wanted to talk to another parent," said Layton in a forlorn voice.

"Say, I don't live far from here. I'll get Eddie to keep an eye on me stall and fix you up a nice cup of tea with some biscuits. What d'you say to that?"

Layton agreed, and off they went up Drury Lane. As they walked, Layton fought back feelings of guilt — it felt dirty, fooling an old woman.

The two turned right on Parker Street and reached a small three-story building. It wasn't the hovel out of Dickens that Layton had expected but a tidy, respectable place that might have passed for middle-class lodgings. Mrs. Hardy's flat was small but clean and nicely decorated. It seemed she did well with her flower stall.

The old woman brought out a plate of biscuits and sat on the green-and-red sofa. Layton helped himself to one. "Kettle'll be ready in a jiffy."

"So, what line of work was Ted engaged in, Mrs. Hardy?" asked Layton in the most matter-of-fact manner. "Delicious biscuits, ma'am."

"My Teddy tried his hand at all sorts of things. Just couldn't make a go of it, poor dear. It was almost that he was too handsome for his own good. He got himself in trouble. Mucked up most everything he did."

Layton looked at Mrs. Hardy and saw the shame on her face.

"He could be a naughty boy, but he was me son, and I had to love 'im, no matter what. I can't count all the money I used to give to get him out of trouble, Mr. Clive."

Layton could imagine what that trouble had been. In that instant, his heart went out to the old woman. She had deeply loved her son and accepted him as he was.

"I kept his room exactly as it was. I'll show you," she said, pointing down the hall. "Once in a while, I go in and just sit on 'is bed, hold a piece of his clothing to me cheek, and have a good cry."

Like the sitting room, the bedroom was

small and intimate. A single bed with a checkered quilt sat beside the window, with a desk and chair pushed up against the opposite wall. Drawings of hunting scenes decorated the walls. Layton was surprised by how conservative and refined the space was; in contrast, Neville and Cyril decorated their dressing room area with all sorts of beads and spangles.

The whistle on the kettle went off.

"There we go. Let me fix you a nice cup of tea," Mrs. Hardy chirped and rushed out of the room.

Having made sure she was gone, Layton went to the desk and opened the drawer. Among the bric-a-brac was a packet of papers bound by a string, mostly letters. Layton glanced at the salutations, but nothing caught his eye. But as he slid the drawer shut, Layton saw, in the far left corner, some crumpled admission receipts for the Abdullah Turkish Baths. He stuck one in his pocket.

"Your tea is ready, Mr. Clive."

The air was hot enough to strangle. But Layton had slowly grown used to it.

This was his third straight night in the warm room of the Abdullah Turkish Baths. In the first of a three-step process, hot, dry air roasted the bather until he sweated like a pig. With a towel wrapped around his waist and another in hand to continuously wipe the perspiration from his face, Layton watched men come and go.

Though it was 3:00 a.m., the bathhouse was full. Some men sat by themselves; others chatted. He had come here for information on Ted Hardy, but the bathers weren't interested in talking. Layton learned quickly that this was a place of intimate contact. A man next to him would stretch his legs out on the bench, brushing Layton with his toes. Without looking at the man, Layton would slide farther down the bench, out of reach. Several times, his pursuer did the same.

Other men huddled next to each other, slipping hands surreptitiously under towels. Certain couples would retire to the so-called bachelors' quarters, little rooms one could rent for what was presumably more aggressive action. As he had on all three nights, Layton prayed Neville and Cyril would not enter and get the wrong impression.

Tonight, rather than proceeding to the cooling room, Layton stayed put.

Hours passed. Layton was about to go on to douse himself in the blessedly cold water and call it a night when two men came in, laughing and talking. The taller, older man had his arm around his good-looking friend's shoulder, and neither man had a towel around their waist. They sat down about ten feet to Layton's right.

Frustrated about another unproductive night, Layton glanced again at the older man — and a flicker of recognition ignited in his brain like a tiny spark struck off a flint. He realized it was Sir John Clifton, who was now enthusiastically rubbing the inside of the younger man's thigh and laughing. He was no longer the stern, unsmiling schoolmaster with pince-nez specs from a Dickens novel. He was stark naked and clearly enjoying himself.

Panic surged through Layton at the sight of the MacMillan theatre circuit owner for fear of being recognized, and he draped the towel over his head like the hood of a Cistercian monk. After a few minutes, he made slowly for the door.

Now he understood what the drunk at the bar had meant when he'd asked if Hardy had put the bite on him. Many prominent men in business and public life were queers, but if they were exposed, certain ruin awaited. The 1895 trial of Oscar Wilde had put terror in the hearts of many a man. One of Britain's greatest writers, destroyed both

266

financially and physically; in 1900, he died alone and penniless in Paris.

Ever since, some men who were exposed had put a bullet in their head to avoid the humiliation and shame they'd brought on their families. It was likely that Hardy, a rotter through and through, had been blackmailing Clifton. From his dealings with Archie Guest, Layton knew firsthand that blackmailers never went away. They always wanted more to keep quiet.

Sir John Clifton, he thought grimly, had needed Hardy to go away.

25

"It's the first of the month, Dougie. Happy November."

Guest had arranged a meeting at the corner of Fleet Street and Whitefriars, which was fine with Layton. He didn't want to be seen with him around the Queen's Palace, or anywhere else in Theatreland, as the West End theatre district was called.

Sighing, he handed Guest a plain white envelope, which the blackmailer stuffed in his pocket. He took out a cigarette and lit up, not bothering to offer Layton one. His next words were casual but pointed.

"You know, Dougie, London is a bloody expensive place to live. Even a pint costs a helluva lot more."

"Yes, I know. I just moved here from Nottingham."

"Then you know how tough it can be for a bloke to get by."

"Especially a bloke that doesn't wish to

get a job."

Guest's thin lips quirked. "Honest work doesn't suit me, Dougie. Maybe it's in me blood. Me dad and his dad and me mum's dad was all in the criminal line."

"You inherited that inclination, Guest. I suppose you can't fight nature. Just like you can't fight your craving for small boys."

Guest glared at Layton but kept his temper in check.

"Exactly. I knew me ol' mate would understand."

"But there's plenty of big pickings here in London. A talented thief like you would do well. Like shooting fish in a barrel."

"Oh, I'm reviewing my prospects, as they say. But I need some more working capital to set up." Guest patted his pocket and took another long drag on the cigarette.

"I see. And you need some additional funding each month, eh?"

"That's the ticket."

"But a deal's a deal. We agreed on twenty quid."

"Forty."

"Impossible."

"You know why I asked you here?" Guest gestured expansively around. "Because Fleet Street is where all them London papers have their offices. See. The *Daily Mail.*

The *Daily Telegraph.* All them would love to know that you're in town, working right under their noses, at a bloody music hall, of all places."

It was true; the Butcher of the West End's whereabouts would sell a lot of papers. At least until people lost interest, Layton thought, as they always did.

"They'll pay a pretty penny for that information, lad," Guest said, pressing his case. "Or you could pay forty quid a month from now on."

Layton smiled and pulled out a cigarette.

"Again, that's quite unreasonable, Archie."

"Sorry, Dougie. Forty, or your face will be on the front page of the Sunday *Daily Mail.* Think about it, mate. I'll send a message as to where we'll meet next."

Layton threw down his cigarette, stamped it out, and watched as Guest walk down Fleet Street. There was a bounce to his step, like a man who was on top of the world.

The time had come. Layton knew what had to be done.

"Good to see ya, Doug. I was hopin' we'd meet up again."

Reggie Ash was a career criminal released from Mulcaster a year before Layton. A giant bear of a man with a shiny, bald head and light-blue eyes that almost seemed to twinkle, he didn't look like he'd hurt a fly. But in thirty years as a robber, gang enforcer, and extortionist, Ash had left a trail of damaged bodies — and, rumor claimed, a few corpses — along the way. He'd served five years in Mulcaster for robbing a mail train outside of Bristol, a bold crime that won the admiration of the British criminal world. The nontraceable cash was thought to be hidden in the Scottish Highlands and destined to someday serve as the gang's pension fund.

The rub was that Ash would have gotten off scot-free if a drunken accomplice hadn't bragged about the caper in a pub. This accomplice, who was sent off to prison with Ash and the rest of the gang, had met with an untimely accident, "falling" into a scalding vat of water while working in the laundry. Big mouths paid a hefty price in Mulcaster.

"I'm in real trouble, Reggie," Layton said.

"Well, didn't I say to look me up when you finished His Majesty's pleasure? I swore if you ever needed help, I'd be there for me ol' mate."

When he'd entered prison, Layton had learned quickly that it was an animal world, akin to life in Africa or the Amazon. The brutality of the place was horrifying. Layton had been totally unprepared for this barbaric existence. The strong terrorized the weak, like a python gobbling up a mouse. Layton had thought the guards, in their smart, black uniforms, would keep order. But they were often more brutal than the inmates and could be bribed to turn their backs on the constant violence.

For Layton's own lot, no one had cared that he was a murderer. They *did* care that he was a gentleman and therefore presumably weak. As in the outside world, prisons had class prejudices too, but instead of snubbing those they didn't approve of, they thrashed the hell out of them on a regular basis. Or much, much worse: buggered them. Sodomy was what Layton feared most; he'd rather be killed outright.

At first, he was met with evil looks. Then came roughing up when the guards weren't about — punches to the stomach, hard slaps to the face. This was a shock to Layton. Violence was something one read about in the newspapers; it happened in the East End or the city's other pits of degradation, not among the middle and upper classes. His own father never laid a hand on him. Though he knew he had to stand up to his assailants, acting tough wasn't in his nature.

It was just a matter of time, he'd thought in terror, before he'd be getting it up the bum like clockwork.

Shortly after his arrival at Mulcaster, he was given a job in the prison library, to be completed in the evenings, after the day's hard labor. Layton was chosen because he looked educated; most of the inmates hadn't attended so much as grammar school. This position gave him a way to be around the prison's highest-ranking inmate — based on the brutality and severity of his crimes — one Basher Grimes.

Grimes was serving a life sentence for killing and dismembering two people, one of whom was his brother, who had cheated him out of his share in a robbery. Layton had heard through the prison grapevine that Grimes was a true hater of the British upper classes, and he believed that they should have their own prisons. Out of pure principle, Grimes had given the denizens of Mulcaster his approval to go after Layton.

One day, Layton saw one of Grimes's henchmen reading the sports page in the *Daily Mail* aloud to him. It was evident that Basher didn't know how to read. With time running out, Layton made a desperate move.

Boldly, he approached Basher in the dark

and cavernous prison dining room, smiled, and held up a book from the library. Hundreds of prisoners and guards watched, in awe of his nerve.

"Mr. Grimes, I believe that you may find this new book quite entertaining. May I have the honor of reading it to you?" Layton held a copy of *The Wonderful Wizard of Oz* by L. Frank Baum.

Grimes scowled and grabbed the book away. But instead of tossing it aside, he fanned the pages, stopping at each illustration. Like a chimpanzee fascinated by a piece of sparkling jewelry, he kept perusing the volume.

Finally, he snarled, "Tonight at seven."

Thus began five years of reading to Basher Grimes. The Oz book hooked him like a trout. "That witch better not harm one goddamn hair on Dorothy's head," he'd shout. Grimes had a peculiar habit of transporting himself mentally into whatever book he was reading; he'd scream for a character to look out or warn a villain to leave the hero alone. In Conrad's *Lord Jim,* he became especially agitated at Jim's decision to sacrifice his life in the end. "No, Jim, you don't have to do that," Grimes begged at the top of his lungs.

His closest confidants were allowed to listen, which led to impassioned discussions

— and sometimes fisticuffs — over characters and plot twists in books like Jack London's *The Call of the Wild,* which saw Buck the dog taking off to mate with a wolf. Basher's best mate, Reggie Ash, argued it was the natural dog thing to do; Basher felt Buck should have remained loyal to his master. The difference of opinion got so out of hand that the guards had to break it up.

After that first reading, no prisoner dared touch Layton. His friendships with Basher and Ash didn't erase the shame of being in prison, but they made life at Mulcaster bearable. He didn't wind up murdered or buggered, and he taught a score of men how to read. Not Basher, though. He preferred the oral tradition.

Pushing back against the flood of memories, Layton looked around the smoke-filled pub in Whitechapel in the East End, where he and Ash sat at a dirty, scored table.

"Remember Archie Guest?"

"Who can forget a shit like that?"

"He's putting the bite on me, Reggie, threatening to tell the newspapers who I am. I've just got my life in order, and along comes this rotter trying to destroy it."

"How much?"

"Forty quid a month."

"The cheeky bastard," said Ash disdain-
fully.

"By sheer coincidence, I've got a job in a
music hall in the West End. You know what
a stink it'll make if I'm found out."

On his way to the pub, Layton had considered telling Ash about the bodies he'd found
and his belief that Clifton or Glenn had
caused the Britannia accident. In the end,
he decided not to. His true dream, though
he hardly dared admit it to himself, was to
clear his name and become an architect
again. And see Ronald again. That meant
gathering incontrovertible evidence and
bringing it to Scotland Yard. His desire to
win his revenge by killing Clifton and Glenn
had diminished; in death, the two men
would escape their guilt forever.

"The Basher and me wanted ya to put this
all behind ya, Doug. You're a proper gentleman, and you didn't belong behind bars. It
was terrible about those people, but it was
an accident, plain and simple." Ash shook
his head. "You know, when I got out, I
found out that Hughie Rice died that night.
Couldn't bloody believe it."

"Who's Hughie Rice?" Layton knew the
name from the list of the dead. But the
papers had said only that he was a business-
man.

"He ran the Brick Lane gang here in Whitechapel. Good bloke, he was. Top moneylender in all of London. A bleedin' powerful man and rich as Croesus. God help ya if ya owed him money and didn't pay up."

Layton blinked, perplexed.

Ash mistook his confusion for something else. "Don't have kittens, Dougie. I'll have a talk with ol' Archie. We'll come to an understandin', I promise ya."

"I wasn't thinking of anything too rough, Reggie," Layton cautioned.

"Nah, just a talkin' to, that's all. I promise on me dead mum's soul that he won't bother ya again, me boy. Now, I'm going to take ya out for a nice meal, what do ya think of that? We'll have a spiffin' night out. How 'bout roast beef and Yorkshire pudding?"

November 5 was Guy Fawkes Night, a commemoration of the failed Gunpowder Plot to assassinate King James I in 1605. Great bonfires were lit all about London, and fireworks were set off throughout England. People competed to build the biggest bonfire; some were as high as a three-story building and resembled an inferno straight from hell.

Layton and Cissie watched the festivities

around Belgrave Road. Thousands filled the streets, laughing and rejoicing, shrieking as sparks leapt from the massive fires.

"Was the MacMillan Empire ever in financial trouble?" Layton asked.

"Yes, about six or seven years ago," Cissie said. "They almost went under."

"Ever hear of a fellow named Hugh Rice?"

"From the list." Cissie searched her memory, shook her head. "No. Who is he?"

"Our first possible connection since Hardy, Finney, and the vicar," Layton replied. Working off the list, he and Cissie had come up blank on eight of the victims in addition to the children. None seemed to have any connection to Clifton or Glenn in any way. But maybe Rice knew the owners.

Layton took Cissie's arm and led her off into the night's revelries.

Almost directly across the Thames, in Lambeth, one particularly large bonfire burned near the intersection of Black Prince and Kennington Roads. It roared through the night, hungry for fodder. And in the morning, among its glowing orange embers, some brass buttons and shards of bones caught the morning light.

The only surviving pieces of Archie Guest.

26

"Dodd, if you don't gather your ape, you'll never work London again," screamed Henry Wilding, the stage manager.

As the Dodd Chimpanzees, costumed in evening dress, took their final bow, Mickey, the youngest chimp, had bolted toward the audience. Leaping from the stage, he charged a woman in an aisle seat in the stalls. Landing in her lap, Mickey plucked her feathered hat from her head — colorful ostrich plumes were all the fashion — to the sounds of her screams.

The audience went crazy with laughter, thinking it all part of the act. But instead of returning to the stage, Mickey leapt from seat to seat in the stalls, grabbing hat after hat. Finally, he jumped into the aisle and raced for the back of the theatre, with Dodd, a man of about sixty, puffing frantically behind.

For Wilding, this was a stage wait, the very

worst thing that could happen. The artistes gathered in the wings weren't amused either. It was a Saturday night, and they wouldn't be getting their weekly pay until the second show concluded — a necessary measure to prevent the less scrupulous from skipping out on the final performance. Now the show was delayed, and that meant the bookies and creditors who waited outside the stage door on Saturday nights to get paid up would get restless. For the big wages they were paid, Layton had been surprised to learn that so many artistes were broke, never a penny in their pockets. Bimba Bamba had even tried to borrow money from him.

The house lights were on full now, so Dodd could find Mickey. Layton, standing stage right in the wings, sighed and tapped his foot impatiently. At long last, the monkey was recovered, the lights dimmed, and the show resumed with the top-billed act, "The World's Greatest Juggler." Of course, every performer called him or herself the greatest, Layton thought wryly. This man, the American headliner W. C. Fields, had a bulbous pink nose, the fumes of alcohol coming off him thick as a storm cloud, and he looked unprepossessing at best.

Pushing a cart filled with all kinds of

objects onto the stage, Fields got five cigar boxes revolving in the air. Then bunches of bananas, then five full milk bottles. The crowd broke into applause. Even Layton was impressed. By this time, he'd seen many a juggler but never one with such ease and nonchalance. That was the secret, he thought. The great ones were so good, they never broke a sweat.

Onstage, Fields kept juggling and puffing away on his massive stogie. He'd chastise the objects in a nasal American accent if they didn't land smoothly in his hand, shouting, "Damn you, behave! Do what you're told!"

One act later, the show wrapped, and Layton walked out the stage door to go back to his digs. Cissie and Layton had suites with a sitting room and bedroom, meals and tea included. At breakfast and dinner, they sat at a great table with other top-of-the-bill artistes currently performing in the West End. Voltaire, a French illusionist; Nell Swan, a singer; the Menjou Brothers and Juanita, a dental aerial act, which performed by gripping with teeth instead of hands and legs; and Hetty Hudson, a famous male impersonator, all lived there. Layton had thought architects vain, but they were nothing compared to variety performers. The lodgers bragged constantly about past performances, a daily litany of "I remember when I played the Royal Hippodrome in Liverpool" or "Like the time I was top of the bill at the Tivoli!"

Layton walked along the dimly lit alley behind the theatre where a few people hung about, smoking and talking. A few audience members stood around, hoping to meet their favorite artistes and ask for an autograph.

"Don't give me that load of shite, you stupid wee lassie," came a shrill voice to Layton's right. He saw a man in a brown suit and derby grabbing a woman by her wrist and violently shaking her.

Layton paid no mind; the alley behind a theatre had a drama all its own: arguments between lovers, Piccadilly Johnnies hounding female stars, and would-be actors trying to talk to agents.

"Where's me money? Stump up. I've been too patient with ya, lassie," snarled the man. As the woman struggled to break free, the electric light post in the alley illuminated her frightened face: Beryl Wheeler, Voltaire's assistant, a girl of about twenty.

"Hello, Beryl. What's all the noise?" asked Layton in the friendliest of voices.

"Shove off, mate," shouted the man. "This

is business, and it's between me and her."

Layton wasn't eager to get his head busted open for Voltaire's tart, but there was something else . . . He paused and stared at the man for a few seconds.

"You're a moneylender, aren't you?" he asked.

"That's one way of puttin' it. Be glad that you don't owe me money, guv."

"What's the amount in question?" Layton asked, as if he were a City of London banker at a loan interview.

"This slut owes me two quid for the last four weeks. It's time to pay up, and I ain't taking payment in kind — if you know what I mean," said the man, giving Beryl's shapely body the eye.

With a sigh, Layton pulled out his wallet. "This will settle the debt."

"Oh, Frank, that's ever so nice of you," gushed Beryl.

"Off you go," said Layton, and she fled down the alley. The man made to follow, but Layton held up a hand. "Hold on. I helped you collect a debt. I want a commission."

The man was at first puzzled, then angry. "On your way, arsehole."

"Not monetary compensation. Just a little information."

This interested the man. He studied Layton, then nodded.

"Ever hear of Hugh Rice?"

"Everyone in London's heard of Hughie Rice," the man said with a great laugh. "In fact, I used to collect for him." His eyes narrowed. "But he's dead, if ya happen to be lookin' for him."

"I know that." Layton leaned forward and lowered his voice. "How much did you know of his business dealings?"

"Quite a bit, guv."

"Did he ever do business with theatre people — not actors and that lot, but the men who owned the theatres?"

"Aye, Hughie was rich. He lent money to all sorts of businesspeople, the ones that could not get credit and were bloody desperate. Factory owners, shipping companies, you name it." The man's coarse face broke into a smile. "I do remember he helped out some theatre fellas when they were in a bad way, 'cause they let him go to the theatre all the time for free."

"If they came to Hugh Rice," Layton said slowly, "then they had nowhere else to turn."

"That's the long and short of it, guv. The lender of last resort, as they say."

"I imagine the interest on such a loan was

quite high?"

"Sky's the limit," said the man, nodding.

"And there was a late-payment penalty, I suppose."

"Indeed, there was, guv." The man took a set of brass knuckles from his side pocket and gave them a long, loving caress. "I believe with the theatre people, we had to apply the penalty more than once."

"Johnnie told me they were in over their heads. They were building the Britannia, the Fulham, the Grand, and the Vauxhall Hippodrome, all at once! No wonder they were hard up."

Layton was sitting on the bed in Cissie's room. In theatrical digs, certain items of propriety were ignored — such as gentlemen being allowed in a lady's room after ten.

"Back then, Clifton and Glenn had trouble making the payroll and paying the bills," Cissie said. She was pacing back and forth in front of Layton, her hands on her hips. "And they were on me to pay the artistes way less, to be tougher in negotiating. That's always a bad sign."

"If no one would lend them money to cover the shortfall," Layton said, "the circuit would have gone bankrupt. They'd have lost everything."

"They must have turned to Rice to bail them out," Cissie said, pausing at the window. The pale glow of the lamps outside glistened on the dark, slick street. "Not exactly the Bank of England. Much higher interest rates."

"I believe it's called usury," Layton said, lying back against the pillow and lacing his fingers behind his head. "Did things get better after the accident?"

"At first, no one would go near a Mac-Millan circuit theatre for fear it would collapse. It was a few months before things got back to normal. But then they made money hand over fist, let me tell you."

Layton had learned much about the criminal world during those five long years in Mulcaster. Extortion, he'd found, was perhaps the most lucrative of crimes, offering a long-term stream of revenue. In most cases, the victim had nowhere else to go and would agree to the loan and its incredibly high interest rates. But the transaction wasn't executed on paper; its terms were stated verbally, often with veiled threats about the consequences of missing a weekly payment. With interest piling up, the loan was impossible to pay off. Where a bank would file suit, a gang would use violence to collect.

This violence, Layton knew, was the foundation of the criminal life. Once a gang got its hooks into you, it never let go. The partners hadn't been able to get Rice off their backs. They'd realized he was going to bleed them dry.

"Clifton and Glenn were trapped, but they couldn't go to the police, or Rice would murder them," said Layton.

"And the investors would find out the circuit was broke."

"So they murdered Rice — along with all the others." Layton shook his head and gave a low whistle. "*Both* Clifton and Glenn had to be in on this."

"The bastards," Cissie breathed.

"Still, this is all a guess."

"I know someone we might talk to," Cissie said tentatively. "Someone who might know something."

"I just put the kettle on. Would you like a nice cup of tea?"

Harry Barker, the retired head accountant of the MacMillan circuit, looked like a bookkeeper. Spectacles covered his worn-out, watery blue eyes. He was white haired and stooped from years of hunching over a desk. This was what a retired architect would also look like, Layton imagined, after decades spent bending over a draughting table.

Barker's second-floor flat in Bloomsbury was homey and, for a life-long bachelor, very neatly kept. Prints and paintings of seascapes covered the dark-green walls; the furniture on which Cissie and Layton sat was plush, stuffed leather.

"Good to see you again, Cissie," said Barker as he brought the tea service into the parlor.

"Reminds me of the old days, Harry. Do you miss the theatre?"

"No, all that's behind me now. Besides, I worked in the front office. I could have been adding numbers in a steel mill. No magic of the theatre for me."

"Frank here paints the cloths. He's very artistic," said Cissie proudly, taking a cup of tea from Barker.

"Oh, do you, Frank? That's grand. I always wished I was artistic, but alas." Barker sighed. "I was born with a head for numbers and naught else."

Cissie and the old man chatted and reminisced; Layton listened, sipping his tea and eating his biscuits. Barker, who seemed genuinely pleased to have visitors in his retirement, told them enthusiastically of his trips to the Royal Albert Hall and the British Museum. He'd even been to the Tower of London for the first time in his life.

As they spoke, a calico cat wandered in and jumped into Barker's lap, curling up in a ball for a nap. As he stroked his pet, Barker inquired after people he'd worked with, including Clifton and Glenn. Cissie skillfully steered the conversation toward the front office, commenting about pay scales for actors and the cost of printing bills.

"Things have gotten expensive as hell, Harry, but the circuit is doing well. Wasn't always like that, eh?"

"That's the God's own truth. I remember when we didn't have enough coal to heat the Bedford Variety. The customers about froze to death," said Barker, chuckling. "Almost went under. No one would give us credit."

"No one?"

Barker set down his cup and smiled at Cissie.

"We've known each other for more than twenty years, Cis. I remember your first day as a secretary. You were a bright young thing; everyone could see that."

"You're ever so kind, Harry," Cissie said, covering his hand with hers and smiling up at him. "You always were."

"So, between two old friends, what's your game, girl?"

For a man in his seventies, Layton thought, Barker's mind was sharp as a twenty-five-year-old's. He didn't miss a thing.

"Who helped us out, Harry, when no one would give us tuppence?" Cissie asked matter-of-factly.

"Let's just say it was a rather unconventional lender. He gave the circuit what the Yanks call a 'bridge loan.' "

"Hugh Rice?"

The old man smiled, set down his tea cup, and gently shooed the calico cat away. Standing, he walked over to his parlor window and stared down at the street.

"Never met him, thank goodness, but it was an act of God he died that night. A miracle. He was bleeding us dry with those interest rates. We were under his bloody thumb. And if we were ever late on a payment, well . . ." Barker shook his head. "Remember when Mr. Clifton was convalescing, Cissie? That broken leg wasn't from a carriage accident."

27

Electric trams were another new invention that had occurred during Layton's holiday in Mulcaster. Loaded with riders and their sides plastered with advertisements hawking Lipton Tea and Gordon's Gin, they now crisscrossed all of London, especially in the West End. It was an ingenious invention, thought Layton, in how it replaced teams of horses, making the city streets a much cleaner place. The hems of ladies' dresses wouldn't be dragged in so much shit. Just two iron rails set in the street and an overhead electrical wire. Everything today was electric. What progress in the world! They'd even invented a wireless telegraphy; an Italian named Marconi could send words through thin air. Still, in Layton's opinion, the aeroplane was the most amazing invention.

Layton and Daniel Harker watched the trams squeal by as they walked home from

watching the first show at the London Alhambra. Once in a while, Layton went to
one of the circuit's other theatres to see
what their cloths looked like. The ones he
saw tonight were damn good, he thought.
When Layton was an architect, he always
believed in giving praise where deserved,
unlike a lot of architects who always de-
graded a competitor's work. He'd invited
Daniel to come along.

"Do you have time for a pint, Danny?"

"That would be a bit of all right. I don't
have to be back until eleven," replied Daniel. On their one night off per week, servants
had a strict curfew.

"There's a place off Piccadilly that's never
crowded." Layton pointed in the direction
with his arm.

Most people who meet up after a long
absence say they will stay in touch from
then on but never do. But Layton had met
Daniel for a drink every two weeks since he
found out about Shirley Finney. He eagerly
looked forward to their meetings because of
their Dorset friendship, but they still had
dual purpose — Layton wanted more information about Clifton, but he had to probe
for it with surgical skill without arousing
suspicion.

After chatting about tonight's performances for a while, Layton tried to ease in a question.

"Bloody small world isn't it, you and me working for the same bloke."

" 'Tis, Sir John being our boss," said Daniel with that wide smile of his.

Although the separations between social classes in England were as solid as steel boiler plate, there was one fissure. The lady maids and valets who personally attended their mistresses and masters were of the servant class but often formed close bonds with their superiors that almost bordered on friendship. "Don't get too familiar with servants" was what Edwina always crowed. But Layton knew his ex-wife had grown very close to her personal maid, Valerie. They exchanged the closest confidences like old school chums. Layton had often come into Edwina's dressing room while they were chattering away like magpies, and they went silent at his presence. Maybe Daniel had a similar relationship with Clifton and knew some secrets.

"Talk about a small world, mate, I think I had some clients who knew Sir John . . . Ted Hardy, I believe was one of them."

Daniel furrowed his brow. "No, don't recall that name."

Layton had to tread carefully, in case Daniel remembered the names on the list that he'd shown him at their first meeting.

"There was another fellow . . . Mmm . . . Rice, yes, a Hugh Rice."

Daniel crinkled his brow and started to shake his head, then broke into a smile.

"Hold on . . . Yes, I do . . . remember that name," said Daniel with a chuckle. "Every time that fellow rang up, Sir John told the staff to say he was not at home. He even came to the house in Devon and was turned away."

"Really? I . . . remember Rice saying he had a good enough voice to go onstage," exclaimed Layton. "Maybe he wanted Sir John to hear him sing."

"Oh, yes, you'd be bloody amazed, Doug, to know how many people pester Sir John about getting into the music hall. Once, a Turkish chap came up to him in a restaurant and began juggling cricket balls."

"But you recall Rice?"

"Yes, because he came to Devon right before Sir John broke his leg in the carriage accident. I'm sure of it."

Along the curb at Shaftesbury, a group of people waited for the next tram to pull up, four deep, like they were watching a parade. Layton and Daniel had to squeeze through them to get across the street. Worming their way to the front, he and Daniel got separated. At the curbstone, Layton saw the tram rumbling toward its stop, its steel wheels giving off an ear-piercing squeal and the power rods connected to the overhead wires throwing off showers of sparks into the damp night air. Layton looked up at the tiny, yellowish specks of light and smiled. It reminded of the shooting stars he'd seen in the night sky over the countryside of Dorset near his home in Puddletown. It had been a mesmerizing sight to him as a boy. He turned to tell Daniel, but he wasn't there. Directly behind him, he thought he heard someone say "Fuckin' gobshite," and suddenly, he was falling forward into the street.

As he fell, he looked up and saw a terrified look in the eyes of the tram's motorman, just a few feet away. When he slammed down onto the wet cobblestones of the street, there was a deafening screech of metal, then complete silence.

When Layton opened his eyes, he was looking at the undercarriage of the tram. It looked like a maze of steel beams. The acrid smell of burning metal shot up his nostrils, making his eyes water. There was shouting and great commotion all around him, and hands grabbed at his overcoat and began to drag him out from under the tram. Layton was flat on his back. Above him was a great circle of faces of every description that stared and shouted at him.

"Jesus, Mary, and Joseph, is he still alive?" shouted a voice.

"Poor bugger."

"Did the wheels cut off his legs?"

"He looks in one piece, thank God," screeched an elderly lady.

"I bet he's sozzled."

Daniel's face now appeared above his.

"Christ, Doug, it's a bloody miracle you're still alive," Daniel cried out. "I lost track of you in the crowd."

The motorman in his uniform was now directly above him, shaking him by the shoulders. He was joined by the conductor.

"Tell me you're still alive, mate. I'll lose me job if you ain't," pleaded the motorman. When he saw Layton was all right, he breathed a sigh of relief, then turned cross. "You're a right Charlie, falling flat on your face and stopping me tram. Damn you, I've got a schedule to keep." The conductor also looked mad.

"Leave the man alone," shouted Daniel. "Can't you see it was an accident?"

The onlookers now pulled Layton to his feet. A woman in a boa handed him his spectacles. They steadied him as he got his bearings.

"Feel better, mate?"

"That was a damn close call."

A bobby in a cape bulled his way through the crowd.

"What's all this now?" he shouted.

"Man fell in front of the Number 11 to St. Pancras."

The officer eyed Layton up and down. "Aren't sozzled, are ya?"

"No, sir, I must have lost my balance. I'm sorry for all the hubbub," said Layton in a contrite tone of voice.

"Well, if you're not injured, off you go then," commanded the bobby. "Get back on the curb, all of you!"

The motorman and conductor climbed back onto the tram, and the passengers crammed on behind. Daniel guided a trembling Layton across Piccadilly, then leaned him against the doorway of a fish and chips shop. Layton calmed down and examined himself to see if he had torn his greatcoat or his trousers. He winced, an excruciating pain radiating from the middle of his back.

"Crikey, Frank, you didn't lose your balance," exclaimed Cissie as she lifted the back of his shirt up. "There's a welt the size of a bloody potato. Like someone rammed a rod in your back to *push* you in front of the tram!"

28

"Where the hell do you think you're going, you little brat?"

Ronald jumped back, shocked. The old man sat directly inside the stage door, in a tiny room with a low counter at its front. In all the time Ronald had watched people go in and out of the Queen's, he'd never seen him. Now, fear coursed through his body. He tried to speak, but no words came out.

The stage doorman took his pipe out of his mouth and started jabbing the air with it as he spoke. His teeth were a horror to Ronald: crooked and yellow-colored like an animal's.

"If you want to see the actors, wait in the alley like the rest of 'em, boy. Now on your bike, and don't let me catch your arse in here again," he snarled.

Ronald didn't need to be told twice. He bolted down the alley. But after twenty yards, he stopped and looked back. The doorman hadn't chased after him. Slowly, he walked back toward the stage door and leaned against the brick wall directly across from it. When a group of five adults approached, Ronald trailed behind them.

They stopped in front of the old man, who began passing out keys.

"When am I going to get a better dressing room?" groused a skinny man with greasy hair and a hawk-like nose.

"When you get your name in bigger type on the bill," answered the old man.

"And more talent," said another, which made the others laugh uproariously.

With the crowd blocking him from view, Ronald snuck past and down the interior corridor. He was a bit confused; this part of the theatre was very different from what he'd seen when he and his nanny had attended the show. It was very plain and reminded him of the downstairs where the servants worked in his home in London and his grandfather's house in the country.

With his back to the wall, he slunk down the narrow, winding brick corridor. So far, there was no one else around. Far off in the distance, he heard the plinking of a piano.

Up ahead, two men turned a bend in the hall. Ronald ducked into a doorway, which was partially open. The men passed without noticing him. Inside the room, he could hear a woman's voice giving someone a rollicking.

"You bloody nancy boy, you get eight minutes for your turn, not a second more or less. Last night, you went over by twenty seconds telling that extra joke! I'll have your guts for garters if you pull that again."

The man she was berating tried to answer, but the woman cut him off.

"Don't argue with me, Cyril."

"I wouldn't dream of arguing with you, Cissie. I'm just explaining why I'm right."

Straining to hear more, Ronald leaned too far forward and bumped the door. To his horror, it swung open. Inside, he saw a woman standing next to two men in dresses, the sight of which really bewildered him.

"What is it, lad? Do you have a delivery?" asked the woman in a stern voice.

Tongue-tied, Ronald nodded his head.

"Then don't just stand there like a dolt. Who's it for?"

"Layton" was the only word he could think of at the moment.

"Dearie, there's no one here by that name," said one of the men.

The woman was about to say something more. But then she stopped and looked down at the frightened little boy.

"Leave the poor child alone, Cissie," the other man said. "He looks as though he's about to piss himself."

"Shut your gob, Cyril," the woman said.

"Here, sweetie." The man in the dress gestured Ronald forward, holding out a battered chocolate box. "Have a caramel crème from your old Auntie Cyril."

"Yes, she'll be your *fairy* godmother," smirked the other man.

Ronald politely took the candy and mumbled a thank-you. The woman drew near and examined him carefully; as she did, her scowl melted into a smile.

"Come along, lad. I think I can help you." She took Ronald gently by the shoulder and eased him out into the corridor. But as she left the room, she twisted her body and shouted, "Remember what I told you, you daft poof!"

In the corridor, she said, "My name is Cissie. What do they call you?"

"Ronald," said the boy, trying to sound confident.

"Ever been in a variety theatre?"

He looked up at her, smiled, and nodded.

"Lovely. But I'll wager you've never been backstage before!"

They had reached the stage, where the Randolphs, Football & Fun on Unicycles, were rehearsing. Eight men on unicycles played football, with four to a team, including the goalie. They moved the ball expertly, bumping it off the wheels of the unicycles like regular football players on a pitch.

Ronald's eyes widened. It was more like a real match than an act; each side was intent on winning. They watched for five or so minutes, and then Cissie gestured at one of the cyclists. He rode up to them, panting slightly.

"Freddie, take my mate Ronald for a whirl," she commanded and lifted the boy up under his armpits, handing him to the man.

Freddie perched Ronald on his shoulders as if the boy weighed no more than a feather and took off across the stage. Ronald squealed with delight as the unicycle made wide circles around the football game. Finally, Cissie waved them over and took Ronald off the cyclist's shoulders.

"Let's have our tea," she said. Taking Ronald by the hand, she led him through the door into the auditorium and up the side aisle to the stalls bar. There, she nodded to the barman, who disappeared into a rear room and emerged a few minutes later with tea.

"Milk and sugar?" Cissie asked.

"Yes, please," Ronald said politely.

Cissie pushed a plate of lemon bars and biscuits toward him, but the boy lifted the plate, offering her first pick.

"You have ever so nice manners, Ronald," said Cissie, pouring his tea.

"My mother said manners show a man is well-bred."

"And she's absolutely right."

As they took their tea, Cissie asked Ronald the usual questions: how was school; what was his favorite food; did he prefer football or cricket? At last, she looked at the little watch pinned to her shirtwaist.

"Well, I think it's time. Come with me, young man."

Cissie led Ronald to a huge room behind the stage. Two men were there, painting pictures on enormous canvases. One was doing a forest scene; the other, a full moon over the ocean. Cissie called out to the man painting the forest, "I have a delivery for you now that you're back from lunch."

The man turned and smiled. Then a puzzled look came over him.

Slowly, he put his long paintbrush aside and wiped his hands with a rag. He walked forward, his puzzled look giving way to one of astonishment. Reaching Ronald, he stooped down on his knees, so his eyes were in line with the boy's.

"Ronnie, it's so good to see you," Layton whispered, his eyes welling with tears. "You're so grown-up! But I still recognized you."

Layton reached out to grasp his son's shoulders, then pulled him forward and hugged him fiercely. He held the embrace for over a minute, savoring every second. He hadn't dared believe this could ever happen. He had thought his son lost forever. All those years of hoping to reunite, and it actually came true. Still on his knees, Layton leaned back and looked the boy straight into his clear-as-crystal blue eyes. He looked so much like Edwina.

"Father, I rode atop a unicycle, and we played football. It was most thrilling!" Ronald was so excited that the words emerged as a near-shout.

"I'm glad you liked the Randolphs, Ronnie. Audiences love them too."

"Can I stay backstage with you, to see the acts close-up? I especially love the animal acts."

"Why, of course," Layton said enthusiastically.

"I'd like to see the acrobats too." Ronald was practically vibrating with excitement.

"And you shall."

Cissie stroked the boy's sandy-colored hair. "You chaps have a lot of catching up to do. I'll see you later."

She made to leave, but before she could go, Layton looked up at her and mouthed a silent *thank you.* Then he turned back to his son and asked, "Your mother doesn't know you're here, does she?"

"No, but Nanny Hawkins does. She helped me find you," Ronald said in a low, conspiratorial tone.

"Nanny's a spiffing person."

"I'm supposed to be at the park now with Cedric Hardwicke, but he covers for me — two bob each time."

"I'll be sure to reimburse you. I'm so glad you're here, Ronnie. We have so much to talk about. You must tell me every single detail about yourself. And don't leave a single thing out." Again, Layton bent forward and took Ronald in his arms. He felt as if his body could not contain the enormity of his joy; his heart was going to burst right out of his rib cage.

"Father, are you an artist in the theatre here?"

"Yes, I paint the pictures you see behind the performers," Layton said, waving his arm toward the cloth he'd been working on.

"I say," Ronald said, blinking in amazement. "You're talented."

Countless times, Layton had wondered what his son was like now. Was he still the amiable, outgoing boy he'd shared story time with? Meeting the boy in person, he was not disappointed. As the grandson of Lord Litton, Ronald would of course have been taught manners; politeness was the way of English gentlemen. He would have been learning to shoot, to ride and play cricket — the thought made Layton's throat catch. All these were things he had imagined teaching his son.

But he could plainly see that the boy had an innate basic kindness that exceeded mere manners. That pleased him. Layton had wanted to guide his son into becoming a good person with the set of values he had learned from his own dad growing up in Dorset, not in Mayfair. During his elaborate masquerade among the upper classes, he'd always felt that he'd been better brought up than those who were supposed to be his betters. He was amazed to find so many shallow, selfish people in the smart set. Rarely did he meet a good, decent human being. Daniel Harker was a better man than ten toffs put together.

In his absence, Edwina had no doubt left

the child-rearing to her father, just as she had left mothering to Nanny Hawkins. She had always cared for her son in the way of society ladies: small doses of affection, given intermittently. In the upper-class world, the needs and desires of parents came first.

Layton knew his son was probably on holiday from his boarding school; this was why he'd had time to seek out his absent father. He wasn't surprised that Nanny had set him on her search. Like all nannies, she was the true mother of his son.

A boy should know his father, he thought, looking down at Ronald. Even though he was a convicted murderer.

"Where do you go to school?" he asked.

"Stansbury. When I'm thirteen, I'll go to Eton."

"I'm sure your grandfather will insist on it," Layton said, forcing a smile. "Now, what time do you have to be back this afternoon?"

"By four thirty."

"I'll walk you back to Hyde Park, and we can talk. Then you can come visit me again."

"Tomorrow?" Ronald asked eagerly.

"Yes, indeed. Tomorrow won't be soon enough for me," Layton said with a laugh. "When you come to the stage door, ask Simon for Frank Owen and he'll come get me. A confused look came over Ronald's face. Layton had known that, sooner or later, this question would arise.

"Everyone in the variety theatre has a stage name, Ronnie. Raymondo the Great was born Gus Cobb. And my pretend name is Frank Owen."

Ronnie nodded, satisfied.

To Layton's delight, there was no awkwardness or long spans of silence on the walk to the park. They chatted as though they had seen each other only the day before. Both asked questions of the other and took genuine interest in the answers. Ronald was most interested in his father's life in the music hall and in such matters as whether the Great Cosmo really swallowed razor blades.

"I'll see you tomorrow, Ronnie. And here's ten bob for Cedric's kind cooperation."

All too soon, Layton waved goodbye, waiting and watching his son disappear into the park. He knew he wouldn't be able to sleep in his anticipation of tomorrow.

29

Because Layton had wanted a particular shade of purple to paint heather on a cloth for Wee Geordie, the Scottish Prankster, he had to go to a warehouse off Waterloo Road across the River Thames to fetch it. Wee Geordie was anything but wee; he was the size of a building and was one of the very few Scottish comics to do well on the West End. Maybe it was because his native accent wasn't so thick that the audience couldn't understand what he saying. Layton liked the giant comedian and wanted to do something special that would remind Geordie of the Scottish Highlands from whence he came.

Layton sat at a window seat on the Number 7 motor omnibus as it crawled along the street. With the paint can resting on his lap, he watched the hectic world of London pass by. When he saw some boys about Ronnie's age on the sidewalk, he smiled brightly. This week, he was supposed to take Ronnie to the London Zoo, something he had never done before. There were scores of other things he wanted to do with his son — go to a cricket match in the spring, take him to the seaside resort of Bournemouth, a circus.

On the sidewalk was an old man holding the hand of a six-year-old as they looked at a display in a store window. Seeing the two set Layton to thinking about his father. They say that all parents want grandchildren to spoil and fawn over. He wondered if behind that stern visage, his father harbored the same wishes. His late mother certainly had, good-naturedly badgering his older brothers to produce some grandkids for her. Raymond, being a professional soldier, thought it cruel to be away from a family for months or even years, so he never married. Roger thought children a bloody noisy nuisance. Layton pondered whether his brother would like Ronnie and change his tune. But maybe he wasn't the marrying type and preferred the string of strumpets he had in Dorset. The sight of the boy and old man gave Layton an idea to drop his father a line informing that he had a grandson he may want to meet, but he quickly decided against it. Maybe in the future, when things were more settled in his life.

With a low groan, a man plopped wearily down in the empty aisle seat next to Layton. As passengers normally did, each flashed a quick sidelong glance at the other. Layton felt a flicker of recognition — *I know that fellow!* He could tell that the other man was feeling the same. Simultaneously, they ever so slightly turned their heads toward each other, which confirmed the identification. Then both twisted their bodies sideways to face each other squarely.

"Douglas Layton, you bollocks-eating turd," said the rotund man in surprise, a shock of pure-white hair topping his head.

If an old friend said something like that, it would be an affectionate jest, but this was said with pure maliciousness. Alec Shaw of Shaw Construction Ltd., the builder on the Britannia Theatre. Shaw's watery blue eyes were focused on Layton's like lighthouse beams. Layton remained silent and turned to looked straight ahead at the back of the head of a man with oily brown hair sitting in the seat in front of him.

"I was really hoping that you'd be murdered in Mulcaster, but here you are, sitting next to me on the Number 7 bus. No justice in this bloody world."

By nature, Shaw was an unpleasant, blustery man who came from the north of England near Manchester. Layton remembered that fact because Shaw would often start a sentence with "where I come from in Manchester," explaining how tough he was and how he didn't abide any foolishness. He never tired of telling anyone of his humble beginnings — "I rose from the scum of the gutter" — and how he created one of England's biggest construction firms from nothing — "just three quid in me pocket." Like all insecure men, Layton had discovered in life, the more the insecurity, the more the boasting of their wealth and success. Shaw would never stop bragging about his possessions: a new carriage, a second home by the sea, a racehorse. The minute Layton had met Shaw at the start of the Britannia project, he had disliked him but tried to get along. Shaw had hated Layton on first sight, he could tell. There wasn't even time for a personality clash to arise, so Layton had assumed it was because he was an architect, and Shaw, like most builders, disliked architects. But Shaw was different; he had an almost pathological hatred of architects. "Why do we need these poofs? I could build the whole bloody thing myself, and it would look better than his design," Shaw had thundered frequently.

During his articling with John Hicks in Dorchester, Layton first learned of the traditional fissures between builder and architect. The architect does the design for the client but does not actually construct the building. A builder is hired to do that. Like the lion and the hyena, Hicks once told him, the architect and builder are natural enemies. With a laugh, Hicks would say that the architect is the lion, an artist, and the builder is a hyena intent on a profit. Most builders hated to be bossed around by architects, and Shaw especially resented it.

"You piece of shite, you only got *five* years — because Lord Litton was your father-in-law," Shaw said in disgust.

Layton remained silent and kept staring straight ahead.

"You fuckin' ruined me on the Britannia. Did you know that, you shite?"

From the beginning, the Britannia project had blown up into a state of total war with Shaw. As a matter of business, a builder would give the architect client a firm price based on the architect's drawings. But in this case, Shaw hadn't read Layton's detailed drawings properly, and he had seriously underbid the job, even boasting he might bring the job under that price. The owners' representative, the late Basil

Dearden, had been delighted. But beginning with the building of the foundation, Shaw realized his mistake. The foundation was a complex bit of engineering, because the theatre had to span over an underground spring used in the days when London was a Roman town. Shaw tried to blame Layton for an oversight in the foundation drawings, but Layton proved him wrong. Then Shaw tried to cut corners on the construction of the foundation, and Layton, with Basil Dearden's approval, made him rip it out, do it again, and eat the cost of the work. This set the pattern for the entire job, in which Shaw constantly blamed Layton for mistakes, trying to raise the project cost to make up for his low price. Shaw continued to try to cut corners, so Layton and Dearden would force him to redo the work without a price adjustment in his favor. The brick and stonework, the ornate windows, the roof, the interior plaster and woodwork all had to be corrected at his expense. This enraged the builder, but he was bound by the contract and couldn't walk away.

Shaw would constantly try to change the design to something less expensive, such as saying the simplified detailing on the plasterwork looked so much better than Layton's design, and he shouldn't have to change it. The London County Council had strict building codes about theatres, which Shaw tried to sidestep because of cost. Items as small as the upholstered seating became a problem, with Shaw trying to substitute a cheaper, inferior-quality seat. "Someone's bum won't know the difference," he had growled. Even on the legitimate change orders Layton would initiate, Shaw would try to charge three times what they were actually worth.

The odd thing was that Shaw did first-rate work! Layton had admired it in other buildings Shaw had constructed. Layton wanted that kind of quality in the Britannia. And in the end, he got it. The paradox was that though the theatre was Layton's downfall, the workmanship was beautiful.

"I used to travel up this road driven by a team of the finest horses you could buy. Now, I'm using the Number 7 bus. And you're to blame, Layton."

"Don't blame me for your blunder on the Britannia," replied Layton, still staring straight ahead.

"Hah, you're one to talk about a blunder, mate. Fourteen dead people."

Layton flinched a bit.

"You shit, you made me redo that whole entire plaster domed ceiling. Do you know what that cost me?"

"No, I had no idea about your business finances. That wasn't my concern."

"And that foundation! I went bloody broke and lost my company by the time I finished your job. Me and my family lost everything."

"Maybe you should learn to read architectural drawings. Or don't people from Manchester do that sort of thing?"

"I was in the courtroom when they sentenced you. I was mad as hell when they didn't hang you. Bloody architects, always building monuments to themselves. They should hang all of 'em."

"You'll be glad to know that I'm no longer practicing architecture. And I'm extremely sorry about your company, Shaw. I remember you saying that you had started from nothing."

Shaw glared at Layton, trying to figure out if he was making fun of him.

"I'm doin' house renovations now. *Me,* who used to put up office buildings and banks. I live in Southwark now. *Me,* who used to live in South Kensington with *servants.*"

"My stop is coming up. Jolly good to see you again, Shaw," said Layton in a hurried voice as he slid past Shaw into the aisle.

"Fuckin' gobshite," Shaw muttered under his breath.

Layton fled out of the bus onto the sidewalk. He had gotten off two stops before he was supposed to. Holding his paint can against his stomach, he walked in step with the river of people in Piccadilly Circus, then he went over to the doorway of a newsagent and stood there, shaking. The word *gobshite* kept echoing through his mind like a thunderbolt. He knew where he had heard that word before. The tram accident.

Meeting Shaw on the bus opened a floodgate of bad memories. The scenes of the constant battle with Shaw replayed in his head. Yes, he remembered, many times during the project, Shaw, his face beet red, had cursed him for sending him to the poorhouse, and he had said he'd get even with him. Layton brushed off the abuse and the threats of a blowhard.

But now he realized that Shaw had been in the perfect position to exact revenge — by bringing down the balcony. The builder had the knowledge to bring it off and, more importantly, direct construction access to the structural steel frame. He had just said he wanted Layton to be hanged for murder! And the Britannia job *had* ruined Shaw, a proud man who had fallen down the ladder of success. Did he hate Layton that much to do such a terrible thing? He also may have wanted to get even with Basil Dearden and the circuit for siding with the architect, making him redo all the work with no compensation. He could ruin both Layton's *and* the circuit's reputation at the same time. Then Layton remembered Cissie telling him how Basil was found dead in his house. His mind began to race.

Layton started walking toward the theatre. His brain was spinning around like a toy top, trying to fathom Shaw as the murderer. It was entirely possible. *But Shaw hadn't gotten the revenge he truly wanted from the disaster — that's why he pushed him under the tram.*

30

"Hold, throw."

Ronald leveled the spear, strode forward, and made a pretend throw.

"Right as ninepence," exclaimed Mangogo.

Layton, who was backstage watching the tutorial, couldn't help smiling.

"Did you see that, Father? And in exchange for cricket lessons, Mangogo is going to show me how to use a bow and arrow!" Ronald squealed.

Mangogo had been fascinated by the baby elephants playing cricket and wanted to learn. If an elephant could play England's national game, so could he.

"Mbuti ripping good with bow," Mangogo said, nodding affirmatively.

Cissie approached, put an arm around Layton's waist, and pulled him close. "Ronnie will be the only boy at Eton who'll know how to hunt like a Pygmy," she said.

"It'll certainly make him stand out in the admissions process to Oxford," Layton agreed, grinning.

"Mangogo can write him a letter of reference."

"Pygmies don't write," Layton said, teasing now. In a passable imitation of Professor Evans's voice, he added, "They communicate only orally and by song."

"Well, he can bloody well write a reference song, go to Oxford, and sing it to them," Cissie said, laughing.

They watched Mangogo follow Ronald down the stage right steps to the stalls.

"Your boy loves being with you," Cissie said softly.

"It's being backstage, I think," Layton said. "It's a magical world for a boy."

"Bollocks. He's happy finally meeting his dad. A boy needs a father."

"I could get into a lot of trouble for seeing him like this," Layton said. "If Lord Litton found out, he'd have me behind bars." In England, an ex-wife could legally keep her children from their father, particularly if the man was a convicted felon.

"After what that bloody cow did to you? To hell with her," Cissie exclaimed.

"He'll be going back to school soon," Layton said.

Cissie raised one eyebrow. "That school of his is in Essex. Plenty of trains go there. We'll figure something out."

Layton smiled at Cissie and drew her closer against his body. She had told him that she enjoyed the surreptitious nature of these rendezvous. The secrecy gave her a thrill of excitement.

Ronald could only visit the Queen's Palace on the afternoons when he was meant to be playing in Hyde Park. The theatre was just minutes away, making it easy for Ronald to slip off. Layton had thought he would never risk a place like Mulcaster again. But for Ronald? The choice was easy. Seeing the joy on his son's face gave him a pleasure unlike any other. He would continue to see Ronald as much as he could.

In the afternoons, certain acts rehearsed onstage. Ronald was allowed to sit in the front row of the stalls and watch: a personal command performance. Today, with Mangogo sitting next to him, the boy was entirely transported. Luigi had just finished his rehearsal. He tossed Mangogo one of the bricks he had been juggling.

From stage right, a voice called out, "Next!"

Two stagehands carried a long table with a heavy wood top and metal legs onto stage.

As they stood there waiting by the table, Dainty Amy came out stage right, smiling and waving at Mangogo and Ronald. She was wearing a white shirtwaist and a long, charcoal-gray skirt.

"Come on out, lads," she yelled behind her.

Three stagehands sauntered onto the stage. Their expressions said they didn't want to be there.

"Everybody take a seat like I showed you before. Be sure to crowd together in the center."

All five stagehands sat on the table with their legs dangling over the edge.

"Sit your bums in the center of the table," commanded Amy, her arms crossed, her shoe tapping impatiently on the hardwood floor of the stage. As she strode toward the table, she stopped and called out to Mangogo and Ronald.

"You boys come on up here too. The more the merrier."

Mangogo and Ronald exchanged puzzled expressions but did as they were told, scampering up the side steps to the stage.

"Go sit in the laps of these blokes."

They both hopped up, to the displeasure of two of the men.

"Here we go, lads. Hold tight!"

Amy ducked under the table, spread her legs, and bent her knees. With her back flat against the underside of the wood table top and hands grasping the edges, she drew in a deep breath, then, with her back, thrust the table six inches off the floor.

"One, two, three, four, and five," she called out before setting the table back down on the floor.

"Mangogo bloody amazed," the Pygmy yelled out with joy, waving his spear.

Ronald hopped off the table and counted the men, making a mental calculation.

"That's fifty-seven stone — eight hundred pounds you lifted," the boy exclaimed. "Plus me and Mangogo."

"Are we finished here?" grumbled one of the hands.

"Off you go," replied Amy. "I'll ask for five volunteers from the audience tonight, and they can be fatter than these blokes. The men always want to show me up, but the bastards never do," she said with a look of great satisfaction.

Layton appeared stage right and motioned for Ronald to come backstage. His visit was over; he had to get back to Hyde Park. Though the boy's heart sank visibly, he did as he was told, waving a sad goodbye to Mangogo. Backstage, he bid farewell to Cissie and the other performers. Cyril gave him a bag of toffee sweets and a kiss on the cheek.

"It's been a crackin' day, Father," Ronald said. His eyes were bright and joyful, like two little miniature suns, and they made Layton feel aglow inside.

On the way to the stage door, a beautiful blond stopped them.

"This must be Ronald," she said. "I'm Helen."

"It's a great pleasure to make your acquaintance," Ronald said, shaking her hand and bowing.

"He's a good-looking chappie and already a proper gentleman, Frank," Helen said, smiling at them both.

"She's so pretty," the boy remarked as they walked down the alley.

"That's Helen McCoy, the Piccadilly Lilly. She's just started her career, and already she's a sensation. 'Daddy's Little Girl' is her signature song. Cissie says she's going to be a great star, that she's got a once-in-a-lifetime voice."

"You and Cissie are sweet on each other, aren't you?"

The directness of the question shocked and amused Layton in equal measure. His son didn't beat around the bush. He liked that.

"Right you are, lad," he said. "Cissie's a spiffing girl."

"Father, why do they all call you Frank Owen when you're Douglas Layton?"

Layton had known that, sooner or later, this question would arise. "Grandfather Charles once said that actors have pretend names so they don't disgrace their families."

Layton burst out laughing. "Lord Litton is right. For many people, the theatre is an evil place. Decent people don't dare be part of it."

"I don't think that at all! It's a wonderful world of make-believe and fun. You're so lucky to be a part of it."

They had reached Hyde Park Corner, where they always parted ways. Layton stopped and smiled down at his son.

"You're absolutely right, Ronnie. I'm very lucky indeed."

31

Layton loved running his hands over the bolts of cloth at the tailors on Savile Row. Flannels, woolens, linens — each had its own sensation, and each was wonderful.

Before the long years of blue woolen uniforms in Mulcaster, Layton had taken great care in his dress. Clothes were an essential part of upper-class life, and dressing well was a crucial part of his charade, of pretending to be a trueborn gentleman.

In some circles, ladies made as many as six changes per day. Before 1:00 p.m., men could not be seen in anything but morning dress — a tailcoat, waistcoat, top hat, gloves, and striped trousers. Evening meant an array of tweed suits, Norfolk jackets, summer linen suits, and white-tie dress. Sporting events like shooting, bicycling, or foxhunting had specific wardrobes. Woe to the man who defied the conventions of dress in England!

After working steadily for nine months and not spending all his funds on drink, Layton had extra money in his pocket. Nor had Archie Guest drained his coffers; it had been weeks since he'd seen the man, and Layton thought that Reggie Ash must have done quite a job convincing him to leave well enough alone. It was a relief; forty quid a month would have crushed him.

With Ronald back in his life, Layton had decided that the first thing he would buy when he had the funds was a new tailor-made shirt. He didn't want to look tatty for his son, and no new, ready-made item from Harrods would do.

The West End was a shopping mecca for London's well-to-do, with shops on Bond, Regent, and Oxford Streets, Piccadilly, Knightsbridge, and Westbourne Grove. Ladies reveled in all-day shopping trips; the attendant tearooms and women's clubs allowed the fashionable set to dine in public without a male escort.

As for the gents, Savile Row, in Mayfair in central London, had been the province of men's tailoring since the late nineteenth century. There, one of the many tailors would take a gentleman's measurements and create new sets of clothes for him each year, adjusting slightly to favor new fashions

— or the customer's expanding girth.

In making his selection, Layton avoided his favorite tailor, Henry Poole, for fear of being discovered. He chose another reputable shop on nearby Regent Street and ordered one new shirt of Egyptian cotton so soft to the touch, it was like stroking a lamb. Layton also purchased two snow-white detachable collars with new collar studs.

After placing his order, he lingered, looking at the great variety of fabric bolts on display. A wistful smile crossed his face; the air of relaxed luxury reminded him of better days, when he lived a life of comfort and privilege, when his bespoke shirts and suits were laid out daily by his valet, Gerald.

When Layton exited the shop onto Regent Street, he realized there was another customer directly behind him. Instinct told him to beware. He kept his head down and quickened his pace, a habit he'd mastered since leaving Mulcaster.

"Douglas Layton?" whispered a voice just inches from his ear.

His first instinct was to walk rapidly away. But it was not to be.

"Douglas Layton!" the voice called, more loudly now.

Despair rose up inside Layton. Shaw had

recognized him and now someone else. What bad luck! The young man who had hailed him was in his early thirties and of medium height, with a full beard and mustache. *Thomas Phipps,* Layton's memory whispered, an architect and colleague from the Royal Institute of British Architects. *Ex*-colleague. Layton had been expelled for life from the RIBA.

"It *is* you," said Phipps. He sounded bewildered, like he was seeing a ghost.

"Hello, Tom," Layton said, striving to sound casual. "You're looking well."

Phipps was. He'd been a rising young talent when Layton was sent away and had just started his own firm. They'd competed for projects then; Layton blinked, surprised at the memory. It seemed a million years ago. But Phipps had impressed him. A design of a university building he'd done had been published to great acclaim in *The Builder,* a professional architectural magazine.

"I was in the shop here, and I thought it was you, Douglas."

"Yes, I needed some new shirts," said Layton in a matter-of-fact tone.

The awkward silence between them seemed to stretch on for a century. At last, Phipps said in a hushed voice, "We all thought you'd been treated most unfairly, you know. Everyone blaming you for the accident — bloody bad business, that."

Standing now in front of Phipps, Layton wished he could shrink down to the size of an ant and crawl into a crack in the pavement. The embarrassment was unbearable.

"No one in RIBA condemned you, Douglas." Phipps's voice was low and urgent. "We knew something like that could happen to any of us."

"They said I brought disgrace on British architects," Layton said faintly. "That's why I was booted out of the RIBA."

"They had to do that. The public line, you know."

"The fact is, Phipps, I'm no longer an architect and never will be."

Phipps bowed his head, as if in shared embarrassment. "From the looks of it," he said haltingly, "you've taken a new identity and started a new life. Good for you."

"I'm Frank Owen now," Layton said, nodding. "I have a new career too — so long as no one knows of my past."

Phipps rested his hand gently on Layton's shoulder. "I won't tell a soul, Douglas."

"And how has your practice been going?"

"Just ripping," Phipps said. He seemed relieved to speak of happier matters. "The central library in Leeds, a hotel on the Strand, a new estate for the Earl of Rutland, the Eagle Life insurance headquarters in Glasgow, All Saints Church, a new building for the Admiralty in Westminster . . ." He trailed off, as if afraid to seem a braggart.

"That's marvelous, Tom. We all knew you had a great talent."

"Well, thank you, Douglas . . . but it's also luck in getting the commissions. But you know all that," he said sheepishly.

"Architecture is a business as well as an art. No clients, no art."

"That's the bloody truth. Say, Douglas, it's almost noon. What say I buy you lunch? I'd love to get your advice on a project I've got coming up."

Layton fought down a surge of panic. He didn't want to reconnect with anyone from the past, and the desperation of that desire almost blinded him to the present moment. But then he looked at Phipps and reconsidered. Seeing him, he felt like a lonely expatriate, longing for company, meeting a fellow countryman in a dusty bar on the outskirts of civilization. He hadn't talked to another architect in years. On top of the grief from the disaster and losing Edwina and Ronnie was the shame of being shunned by his profession, men who had once admired and liked him. He felt like a dishonored army officer, standing before the entire garrison as the commanding officer ripped the medals and epaulets off his uniform and broke his sword in half. Though Layton now knew the truth about the disaster, the disgrace still seemed unbearable.

"Yes, that's very decent of you," he said in a halting voice.

"Splendid."

Phipps took him to an out-of-the-way restaurant on Cavendish Place, north of Oxford Circus. He seemed to understand Layton's need for anonymity. Over pints and shepherd's pie, they talked endlessly about architecture — new stylistic developments; the new prominent players, besides Phipps; what big projects were on the horizon. Phipps praised some of Layton's past projects, particularly his Law Courts building, and asked his advice on a new office building he'd been contracted for on Earls Court Road. For a short time, Layton was an architect again, and the boon to his self-worth was wonderful.

The afternoon passed and the drink flowed freely, as did Layton's words.

"I loved being an architect, Tom. What a bloody good feeling it was to see the drawing turn into a real building," he slurred.

"You were a great architect, Douglas."

"Maybe I will be again." Phipps seemed puzzled by this remark. Layton looked straight into his eyes and said more forcefully, "It wasn't me that caused that accident. Someone else did. On purpose."

The second the words had come tumbling out of his mouth, Layton regretted saying anything. But then he felt heaps better. Telling another architect that he wasn't a murderer and an embarrassment to the profession . . . In that moment, it felt like everything.

Phipps looked down at his pint as if embarrassed. The architect thought he was drunk and talking nonsense, Layton realized.

"My assistant, Peter Browne, was part of it." He spoke more urgently and clearly now. "Reville, the structural engineer, was in on it too. Someone paid them to tamper with the structure. And they've been murdered, to silence them forever."

Phipps sat back, wide-eyed. "Are you absolutely sure, Douglas? What proof do you have? Have you taken your story to the police?"

"I'm not ready yet," Layton said, "but I'm working on it."

"Can I help you in any way?" Phipps

asked in a hushed, urgent voice. "You can't let them get away with it. They killed all those people — and they destroyed your life!"

"Yes, Tom," he said slowly. "I could use your help."

32

For two weeks, the Gazelles, a troupe of acrobats in gold and scarlet, had filled the Queen's Palace stage with flying bodies. Though they were great applause getters, the stagehands hated them.

The Gazelles were the only act to use the bridges, two sections of the stage floor that could be raised and lowered to create spectacular visual effects. Because the bridges were labor intensive, they were used mainly at Christmastime, when the theatres staged big pantomime pageants. Now, to the delight of the audience, the troupe had choreographed a routine in which they leapt and somersaulted from one bridge to the other while the bridges continuously rose and fell. It was an exciting change from bouncing around on a flat stage floor.

But the bridges were operated with huge, geared wooden drums, located under the stage and turned by hand crank — something the crew was loathe to do. It was one thing to raise them once during a turn; to do it over and over for eight minutes was exhausting. The Gazelles had to "sweeten" the crew with beer money to work the drums for their twelve weekly performances. And now, for Thursday night's show, Stewart Caves, one of the stagehands that was to operate the bridges, hadn't shown up.

He was probably drunk somewhere in Piccadilly, Layton told Cissie, who was standing stage right and was angry.

"Caves has made a total bollocks of the act, that clot!"

Cissie ran the performances with the accuracy of a Swiss watch and absolutely hated when things were at sixes and sevens. The Gazelles were the third act on the top half of the bill, and time was running out to find a replacement.

"*I* will stand in for old Caves," said Layton with a smile.

"Then pull your finger out, me boy. Your reward will be a Guinness tonight — and *maybe* a slap and a tickle later on if you do a good job of it."

Since joining the variety theatre, he had grown ever more fascinated with the technical workings. The architect in him wanted to understand how everything worked, from flying the cloths to lighting the stage with the new electric spotlights and working the traps in the understage.

Five minutes before the Gazelles were due on, Layton walked down the black metal spiral stair to the understage. The other operator, Alfie Elkins, was at the stage right crank, out of view. The band room and the orchestra pit were directly beside the understage, and Layton could hear the music as if he were in the front row of the stalls.

When the snappy, fast-paced intro for the Gazelles began, he placed his hands on the wooden handle and began to crank the drum. Like a watch gear, the drum was shaped like a wheel, with heavy wooden spoke teeth around its circumference. These teeth turned another wheel, connected by a shaft to the ram that lifted the bridge. Once the bridge was raised to full height, Layton lowered it by cranking in the other direction.

Directly above him, he heard and felt the continuous thumping of the acrobats.

But in the noise and the chaos, Layton didn't hear someone come up from behind.

Two hands grabbed the sides of his head and squeezed with enormous force, like the clamps of a vise. The pain was so intense that Layton thought his eyes would pop out of their sockets. He let go of the crank and tried to cry out but found himself paralyzed from the neck down; he couldn't raise his arms to defend himself. His vision blurred and swam; his head was jerked in the direction of the still-spinning spokes.

They blurred before Layton's eyes, and he knew what was about to happen. In a fraction of a second, he had to make a decision: give up and have his head squashed like a watermelon, or save himself, no matter the cost. In the end, it was easy. He grabbed the crank and held on, winning himself a precious few seconds. On instinct, he yanked off his right boot and lunged forward, jamming it into the gears and bringing the wheel to a halt. With a muffled curse, his assailant rammed his head against the edge of the wheel and let go. Layton dropped to the floor like a stone.

He woke up facedown on the wooden floor. Leo, one of the Gazelles, swam into his vision, screaming and cursing.

"You stupid bastard, you screwed up the whole act! You threw off our timing. We crashed into each other like ten pins! Why'd you stop cranking?"

The pain in Layton's skull radiated down to his feet and back up like an electrical current. The strain was too much, and

Layton curled up in a ball, holding his head, trying to gather his wits about him. The entire Gazelle troupe had arrived now, and they were cursing him up and down. Henry Wilding, the stage manager, joined them.

"Frank, what the hell happened? Are you sick, man?" he yelled.

"Bollocks, he's sick!" screamed Ralph, another Gazelle. "I did a triple somersault right smack into the stage floor. Almost broke me goddamn neck!"

Grabbing on to the wheel, Layton pulled himself up to face the angry mob. Leo was poking him in the chest, screaming at the top of his lungs, his face beet red. Layton could feel saliva spraying him in the face as the man raged.

"The whole house was laughing their bleedin' heads off at us. We're pros, god-dammit! We can't be laughed off stage. I'll see you in court, Owen."

Standing was too much. Layton knelt down on the wood plank floor, clutching his head in agony.

33

Tom Phipps sat in the armchair in Cissie's sitting room, smoking his pipe and looking at the list of the Britannia victims. He reminded Layton of Sherlock Holmes in his study on Baker Street.

"The bloke who tried to kill you must be a stagehand," he said gravely. "I'd wager he knew someone on this list."

"Or he could have slipped into the theatre to come after you," Cissie said tentatively.

It had taken all Layton's nerve to tell Cissie he'd revealed their secret to Phipps. To ease her fears, he exaggerated their relationship, claiming Phipps as a friend rather than a professional acquaintance. Still, he'd feared her anger. But to his surprise, Cissie welcomed the news. An architect, she told him, could aid them in understanding what had happened. He was one more person who might help get to the truth.

"That's unlikely. The attacker would have

had to get backstage undetected last night, follow Douglas down to the understage, and wait for the opportunity to kill him," Phipps said.

"You're right. Whereas someone working there already might have known that I had to operate the bridge for Caves, that I'd be by myself next to the drum," Layton said.

Phipps had turned back to the list of the dead, which he waved in the air between them. "We have four names checked off here that are linked to the ownership in some way — Finney, the pregnant servant; Hardy, the homosexual blackmailer; Reverend Blair, the molester; and Rice, the extortionist. Then there's Mr. Mapes, the child of that woman who accosted you outside the prison, and another child. Six names left — Sir John Richardson, Sybil Treadwell, Trevor Stanton, Jocelyn Shipway, Ronnie Cass, and James Croyden."

"Which Cissie and I checked and found no connections to Clifton or Glenn."

"Except for James Croyden," interrupted Cissie. "That was Sunny Samuels's real name."

"You never told me that," exclaimed Layton.

"Sunny Samuels the comedian? Why, I loved his act! Yes, now I remember he died in the collapse. What a shame to lose such a funny bloke," said Phipps. He furrowed his brow. "He's certainly connected to the owners, but there was no reason for Clifton and Glenn to murder Sunny. He was a top-of-the-bill star for them, wasn't he?" asked Phipps in a puzzled tone.

"About six months before the accident, Sunny jumped from the Hall circuit to ours along with a few other big names," said Cissie.

"Like Liverpool stealing the best players from Manchester City," replied Phipps with a smile.

"You're right on there, mate," answered Cissie. "That's how the theatre game works."

"He was probably there by chance — like Cissie's husband," interjected Layton.

"And then there's Shaw," added Phipps. "He was once the top builder in London, then his business went under because of the Britannia job, and he never recovered."

Layton had been so troubled by meeting Shaw that he couldn't help telling Cissie and Phipps what happened on the bus — and the tram.

"I agree with Douglas. Shaw probably knew that he had seriously underpriced the work, and it destroyed his company. He blamed Douglas and may have wanted to destroy him and the circuit."

"A man'd be mad as a hatter to do something like that," hissed Cissie.

"Shaw lost everything — especially his pride," replied Layton. "His success was the most important thing in the world to him."

"He was hoping Douglas would hang for murder or, like he said, die in prison," added Phipps solemnly. "When that didn't happen, he tried to push him under the tram."

"There's one thing we've overlooked in all this," Layton said suddenly.

Cissie and Phipps exchanged glances. "What?" Cissie asked.

"Why was Peter Browne a part of this?"

"For money. It had to be a great deal of money," said Phipps. "The same for Reville."

"Or he was being blackmailed," said Cissie.

Layton shook his head. "It's a monstrous evil thing to do, even for money. I knew Browne; he was a first-rate architect, came from Sir Edwin Lutyens's office. There *has* to be more to it."

"People'll do anything for enough lolly, Frank," added Cissie.

The room went silent. Layton walked over

to the window, placing both his hands on the thick wooden frame and looking down into the dark street. A chap in a bowler with his hands shoved in the pockets of his mac hurried by. He probably forgot to tell his wife he would be late from the office, and she had overcooked the roast, waiting for his arrival.

Layton then did an about-face from the window.

"You know, maybe if I talk to Browne's wife, Alice," he announced, "I may find out more information on Clifton and Glenn. She may know something about all this. Peter could have talked to his wife about them."

"Or Shaw," added Cissie. She was coming to believe that Alec Shaw was the prime suspect.

"That's a topping idea," exclaimed Phipps as he refilled his pipe. "She could have overheard something."

Layton didn't like the image of himself, standing on Alice Browne's front stoop in Brompton, banging on the door and pleading with her to talk to him. So he gambled and used the telephone. It was risky; she could hang up on him all too easily.

The telephone rang for a bit. At last, a

soft, feminine voice answered.

"Alice, this is Douglas Layton."

He heard a gasp on the other end of the line, then silence. At last, Mrs. Browne began to sob.

"Mr. Layton, I haven't seen my Peter in more than four years. One evening, he went out, and he . . . he never came back. Vanished into thin air. The police said he was a missing person, that he just ran off. Maybe with another woman."

Layton looked at the wedding band in his right hand and grimaced. He could almost see the poor woman standing there, tears in her eyes, holding the telephone receiver to her ear. It was one thing to know a loved one was dead. To have a person just disappear, without ever knowing what happened — it must be hell.

"I'm sorry," he said lamely. "I was very fond of him. Such a talented fellow. He was my right-hand man."

"He was quite fond of you as well, Mr. Layton. He liked you far better than Sir Edwin."

That made Layton smile. A popular saying in the architecture world held that the more famous an architect was, the worse he was as a boss. Sir Edwin Lutyens was Britain's most renowned architect.

"I'd like to come talk to you, Alice. Maybe tonight?"

"Well . . . not tonight. I'm going out with my cousin, Cynthia. Tomorrow morning? What did you want to talk about?"

"About Peter. After the accident, how did he act? Did he say anything?"

"Oh, Mr. Layton, he was ever so upset about what happened at the Britannia. He was never himself after that. A different man entirely."

"What do you mean?" Layton asked.

"Always angry and upset. He never could get a good night's sleep but was always rolling about in bed, sweating as though he had a fever. Nothing I'd do would put him right. He felt terrible when you were sent away to prison. After your firm went under, he went to work for Mr. Stratton's office, but he couldn't keep his mind on his work. He decided to go out on his own and do small projects."

"Did he have any financial problems?" Layton hated to press a woman who was clearly still grieving, but he forced himself onward.

"Oh no, Mr. Layton. You paid him a handsome salary, and Peter was very grateful. His practice was beginning to prosper at the time he vanished."

"He was worth at least double what I paid him. He was a good chap. Did you have any children?"

"No," Mrs. Browne said faintly. "I lost the baby right after Peter disappeared."

Layton's heart sank to his knees, and his will all but failed him. He couldn't continue this over the telephone. It was too cruel.

"I'll never forget the day he disappeared, Mr. Layton," Mrs. Browne was saying. "Peter was so excited — he was getting his first big commission. He said he had to meet the new client somewhere in the West End, and he'd be back late."

"And he never told you the name of the client?"

"No, Mr. Layton."

"Alice, I'll see you at nine tomorrow morning."

Layton spent the twenty-minute walk to Brompton in agony. Should he tell Alice about Peter? Though he was desperate to ease her misery, he couldn't risk revealing the location of his body or the circumstances of his murder. Again and again, his fingers brushed the ring in his suit pocket. He couldn't give it to Alice without a thousand questions. But then, he had questions of his own. There must have been some evil involved in Peter's decision to sabotage the Britannia. The terrible betrayal of it hurt Layton deeply; he realized his fingers had tightened into a fist around the ring.

By the time he reached Ovington Street, the world was enveloped in a morning pea-soup fog, which restricted visibility to less than ten feet. The electric streetlamps were like dim candlelights, barely visible.

In years past, Layton had been to Peter's house several times for tea, a common ritual between important employee and employer. The brick-and-stone terrace houses were all identical, and Layton walked slowly by the stoops until he found Number 22.

Except for a hansom cab slowly clip-clopping up the street, no one was about. Layton made his way up the stone steps. Above him, the lights in the house were on. He tapped the brass doorknocker, but there was no response. Alice was likely making her way down from the upper floor or up from the kitchen in the basement, Layton told himself. But after five more minutes of knocking, he realized she had gone out — or had second thoughts about talking to him. It was strange; on the telephone, Alice hadn't been at all reticent about Peter or her situation.

A creeping dread was twisting knots in

Layton's stomach. He tried the door, but it was locked. The basement stair went under the entry stoop, however; looking through the windows into the lighted kitchen downstairs, Layton saw no one. Usually a servant or housekeeper would be about, but then, perhaps Alice couldn't afford one anymore.

He tried the door. To his surprise, it was unlocked. He entered slowly, calling out, "Alice?" Still, there was no response. The knots in his stomach drew tighter; he took the stairs to the entry hall two at a time, calling out Alice's name repeatedly. When he found no trace of her downstairs, he stood at the foot of the main stair and shouted her name up. Still no answer. Nor was there any sign of her on the second floor, in the bedrooms or study. It was only when he stuck his head into the small servant's room in the attic that he noticed the shadow cast by the spread of light from the hall.

With a groan, Layton snapped on the light switch. There, hanging from a rafter, was Alice Browne. A wooden chair lay toppled beneath her, a cord knotted around her neck. Layton approached slowly and reached up to touch her dark-green dress. She had worn her best for his visit. His eyes moved up to rest on Alice's face, on her bright-blue eyes, staring vacantly out into space.

Layton's head dropped, and he let out a moan. Why had this happened? Alice had been a pretty, happy girl. Peter had been talented; their future had looked so bright.

In a flush of panic, Layton wondered if his call had precipitated Alice's death. Had she been teetering on the edge of hopelessness, and had he pushed her over the line? He looked up at her again, closed his eyes at the wash of fresh pain.

What calamity had brought this on? What had forced Peter to do such a thing?

Layton left, leaving the light on, and went to the study. Alice hadn't changed a thing; it was still a masculine refuge, with a rolltop desk and chair and comfortable sitting room furniture facing the fireplace. Once, he had sat here with Peter, drinking brandy, smoking, and talking about architecture. It was all they'd ever talked about. He actually didn't know much about Peter, Layton thought, surveying the man's handsome possessions. Had he been conservative or liberal? Was he for women's suffrage or home rule for Ireland? Layton had never asked. Their passion for architecture was their bond.

He went to the desk and raised the lid.

Again, Alice had left everything in place. The good wife, keeping things neat for her husband's return. To the law, Layton thought, Peter was a missing person, one of thousands of husbands who had abandoned their wives and disappeared without a trace. To Alice, he'd been away on an extended business trip, yearning to come back to her.

Forcing his mind to the task at hand, Layton began examining the papers stuffed into the desk's many pigeonhole compartments. An assortment of old bills: the tailor, the coal delivery, his wife's dresses. Taking his time, Layton worked his way from the left side of the desk to the right. Nothing caught his attention. The side drawers were also fruitless — all but the bottom right-hand drawer, which was locked. Layton took a letter opener and jammed it into the tiny keyhole, jiggling it until he heard a click.

Inside were notebooks and loose leafs of papers pertaining to financial matters. A black leather appointment book was shoved toward the back; Layton fished it out. The last entry said only *Shaw at 8 p.m.* The entries for the weeks before were mostly short jottings: *see Cantwell 6 p.m.; Shaw 2 p.m.; Rhys-Jones lunch; Shaw at 10 p.m.* There were some appointments that just had the letter *S* with a time.

Unsure what help it would be, Layton shoved the appointment book in his mackintosh pocket. Before he pulled the rolltop down, he took one more look at the desk. In the center, flanked by pigeonholes, was a small drawer that he'd missed on his first search. Dumping its contents on the desk, he examined the drawer, turning it over and over. Taped to its bottom was a wad of hundred-pound notes.

Leaving the money in place, Layton slid the drawer back in place and left. As he walked hurriedly down the street, a depression as heavy as the sulfur-laden morning fog blanketed him. It felt like it would knock him to the pavement. Had his telephone call put Alice over the edge of despair, and she killed herself? In all this misfortune, the woman had lost a husband *and* a baby. Layton knew that nothing could be worse than losing a child. He immediately thought of Ronnie; the image of that void in his life sickened him. Alice had given up on life because she had no hope. He knew the feeling from his thwarted attempts at suicide in Mulcaster. Layton slowed his pace and came to a halt. But did she kill herself because she knew the truth about Peter and didn't want to betray him?

At a call box in Bayswater, he placed an

anonymous call to the police, informing them that there was a dead woman on the third floor of 22 Ovington.

34

Layton felt as if the entire world were crashing down about him. He had to clear his mind. He had to forget his troubles and Alice Browne's suicide — even for twenty minutes.

One of his favorite acts, the Nine Hindustanis, were on soon. That might do the trick. The performers, all Englishmen made up with sepia to look Indian, balanced on huge red-and-yellow rubber balls and bounced from one another's shoulders. Layton loved the group. And though it was his usual custom, watching a performance from the wings wasn't as enjoyable as watching it from the front of the house. No, he thought, frowning. That wasn't quite true. In the wings, one could witness all the intimacy and turmoil of the theatre: performers taking a last-minute sip of gin to fend off the collywobbles; playfully insulting an act that was coming off; pinching a girl on the bum as she was about to go on. It was familial, cozy. But being at a right angle to the performers on the stage was awkward, and one missed a lot of the performance. Truly, the audience had the best view.

And so, in the interests of distraction, Layton went up to one of the walls flanking the proscenium arch, where a peephole had been installed. Instead of sticking your head out from the side of the arch, into full view of the audience, all you had to do was peer through a lens, which gave a 180-degree view of the house. There was one on the opposite wall too. Performers liked to see the size of the night's audience or whether their friend was sitting in the free seats they'd given them in the stalls.

Luigi, the singing juggler, had gotten himself in a real muddle once, Layton remembered, smiling in spite of himself. He'd seen his wife, who automatically got free passes, sitting just two seats away from his current lover!

Tonight, the house was packed as usual. At the very right, Layton noticed, one of the boxes at the dress circle — or first balcony level — was empty. These private compartments, with their cushioned, high-backed chairs, were where the wealthy or politically powerful sat to watch a show.

They were the best seats in the theatre.

Percy, the Incomparable Dancing Bear, was onstage, twirling and swaying to the patriotic march "The British Grenadiers," played by a three-piece brass ensemble behind him. Soon, it would be the Nine Hindustanis' turn.

Layton walked down a short flight of steps to the pass door, between the auditorium and the backstage area. Normally, only the stage manager and the theatre manager were allowed to use this door, but Cissie had given him permission.

The door let him out stage right of the orchestra pit, and Layton snuck unnoticed along the side aisle wall, past the stalls, to the dress circle. The boxes had private corridors, set off at the end of the horseshoe-shaped dress circle hallway. And guarding the door to that hallway was Deidre, an usherette.

Just a few years ago, it would have been unthinkable to hire a girl to be an usher. Deidre was dressed in a man's navy-blue military uniform, with scarlet piping and rows of gold braid across her ample chest. When she saw Layton, her expression of dead boredom shifted to one of delight. She opened the hall door with a white-gloved hand and followed Layton inside.

"Well, this is ever so nice a surprise, Frank," she cooed.

"Thought I'd sneak up here and catch the show since no one's in Box B. You won't tell, will you, luv?"

"I'd never tell on a good-lookin' bloke like you, Frankie," Deidre said, running her hand up his arm.

Layton looked down at her in surprise. Cissie liked to tease him about the usherettes; she claimed some of the girls had taken a fancy to him. He'd thought her daft. Apparently not.

"You and me should pop out to the pub and have a friendly drink after the show," Deidre was saying in a silky voice. "Buy me a shandy or two."

"That's a topping idea, Deidre. One night, we'll do that," Layton said impatiently. The Nine Hindustanis would be up soon.

But Deidre was persistent. She edged closer, until her face, which was rather pretty, was just a few inches from his chest.

"You're such a proper gentleman, Frank. Remember when you picked up all the programs I dropped?"

"Why . . . yes," Layton said, trying to place the incident. She had backed him right up against the plaster wall. He put his palms out to brace himself. "You're a handsome lass, Deidre, and you can be sure we'll go out for that shandy sometime soon," he stuttered.

"I'm going to hold you to it, Frankie." To his relief, Deidre drew back then and left, giving him a flirtatious wave over her shoulder.

Layton didn't move from the wall until she was gone. As he was about to start down the corridor to the box, he stopped, looked at both palms, and placed them on his cheeks.

They were warm, very warm. Almost hot. It was as though he'd placed his hands over a stove. Layton's first thought was that Deidre's advances had sent his body temperature shooting up, but no . . . He turned and placed his hands against the wall. Instead of the normal, cool feel of plaster, heat radiated through him.

Stunned, Layton ran his hand from the bottom of the wall up as high as he could reach. Terror left his knees weak and watery. In the stud cavity, a fire was raging. A wire must have shorted out. Layton got on his knees and put his nose to the wooden baseboard; he smelled acrid smoke. Back on his feet, he looked at the ceiling. The cavity would act like a chimney, drawing the fire up to the roof directly above the auditorium. Once it got into the wood and steel framing, it would spread like a forest fire.

Layton bolted down the dress circle aisle, past a surprised Deidre, and back to the pass door. But now he remembered: one could go out the door, but not in, a precaution meant to keep the public from getting backstage. Desperate times called for desperate measures. At the edge of the orchestra pit, Layton ran up the little side steps onto the stage — the Nine Hindustanis were just beginning their turn — and ran into the wings.

"Wilding, lower the fire curtain! There's an electrical fire on the south wall," he yelled to the stage manager.

Without missing a beat, Wilding ordered the stagehands to lower the sheet-metal fire curtain, located directly behind the proscenium arch. He walked calmly onto the stage, stopping the acrobats in midtumble, faced the crowd, and smiled.

"Ladies and gentlemen, there have been some technical difficulties with tonight's performance. Please exit the auditorium now. For your inconvenience, you will be given a full refund, plus a free pass to a future performance."

As he finished his announcement, the

curtain came down behind him. A collective groan swept through the theatre, but everyone rose from their seats and began to shuffle out in an orderly manner. Wilding ordered the orchestra conductor to play the regular exit music, as they would at the end of any show. Obediently, the band cranked out a jaunty John Philip Sousa march, "The Washington Post."

In the meantime, Layton had rung up the London County fire commission from the stage manager's desk. The performers knew something was amiss and had gathered in the wings, looks of confusion covering their faces.

"Everyone out the stage door to the alley, please," ordered Layton in a polite but firm tone.

"Yes, do as you're told," Wilding yelled, as if he were commanding dull-witted schoolchildren.

In the alley behind the theatre, an incongruous crowd assembled. They all milled about: a magician and his assistants, dressed in the golden finery of Arabs; acrobats in orange, skintight leotards; a female singer in a lavish white satin gown; a pack of collies; five Pygmies; comics in absurd suits; and a man holding a dummy dressed in white tails.

Layton and Wilding had made their way

to the grand entrance foyer when the fire trucks clanged up. The fire commander, in his red helmet, ran up, demanding to know the fire's location. He and four of his men followed Layton down to the first-floor wall, below the boxes. After Layton pointed to the approximate location, the firemen began to chop away at the ornate plaster wall with axes. Smoke and yellow-orange flames gushed forth from the hole.

Two of the other firemen had run into the auditorium, dragging a canvas fire hose behind them, and hooked it to a wall valve that connected to the public water supply in the street. They poured water into the cavity. The commander ordered the men to chop away the walls directly above them, on the second floor, to get to the fire in its entirety.

In twenty minutes' time, the fire was out. Luckily, the men had contained it within one cavity and prevented its reaching the roof. Pieces of wet plaster and wood lath covered the ground.

Thank God, Layton thought, staring at the char and scorch marks, that the fire had been concealed behind the wall. If smoke had billowed out into the auditorium, it would have set off a panic and a stampede to the doors.

Wilding went out into the alley and brought everyone in.

"We're still going to get paid for tonight?" someone bellowed.

"Read your contract, you clot," yelled Cissie, who had just arrived. "This is an act of God, and you don't get tuppence."

"Shut your gobs, get dressed, and go home. You'll be told when to come back," snarled Wilding.

An explosion of cursing and grumbling erupted. As the crew and performers shuffled back in, Cyril and Neville spotted Layton, standing by the stage manager's desk. They approached and hugged him fiercely.

"Good show, Frank, damn good show," shouted Neville. Everyone gathered then and began shaking Layton's hand and pounding him on the back.

"He's a hero. Three cheers for Frank!" yelled Wilding.

Cissie threw her arms around Layton and kissed his cheek. Mangogo shook his hand like a proper Englishman, then let out a shrill yell — likely Pygmy praise for bravery, Layton thought.

"Let me stand you a Guinness, Frank. It'd be an honor," said Luigi.

"I'll buy you a drink too," added the

Incredible Paul Cinquevalli. "As many drinks as you want."

Though Layton was embarrassed by the attention, he had to admit that he felt good inside, happy and elated. Most of the artistes and crew had left, but a few hung back, talking to a middle-aged man in a gray tweed suit by the stair to the fly gallery.

As Layton watched, Florrie Robins, the singer, turned and pointed . . . to him. The man gave her a nod and walked over.

"Good evening, Mr. Owen. Jack Pennington of the *Daily Mail.* Just a few questions about tonight's fire."

Layton froze. Before he could retreat into the shadows, the reporter pounced, asking him what he did in the theatre and how he'd discovered the fire. For discretion's sake, he omitted Deidre's role in the matter. If she hadn't pressed her affections on him, the Queen's Palace might have been engulfed in flames! He further downplayed the discovery as pure accident: he'd bent to tie his shoe and smelled a whiff of smoke.

The reporter scribbled busily in a little leather-bound notebook, then said curtly, "Well, thank you for your time, Mr. Owen," and strode off. Unlike the artistes, Pennington didn't seem at all impressed with Layton.

As he left, another stranger approached Layton and Cissie. This one was a short, plump man, bald as a coot.

"Hullo there. I'm supposed take a snap of Frank Owen," the man said, holding up his Kodak camera.

Layton flashed a look of panic at Cissie. She smiled.

"Hold on, mate, while I fetch him." Cissie ducked into the scene shop and, out of earshot of the photographer, shouted, "Joe Clayton, you pillock, get your arse over here."

Clayton was busy setting cans of paint on a shelf. He looked up, confused.

"There's a fellow in the wings from Fleet Street. He's doing a story on the people who work in variety theatres, and he needs a snap of a good-lookin' backstage bloke. You'll get a whole quid for doing it."

Clayton stared at her in wonderment. "You're pulling me plonker. My face ain't worth a farthing."

"No, mate. Management selected *you*. Look, here's the lolly."

Clayton's look of puzzlement turned instantly to joy, his mind clearly calculating how many pints of Guinness he could get for the quid in Cissie's hand.

■ ■ ■ ■

"May I congratulate the hero?"

"You may."

Cissie draped her naked body over Layton's and gave him a long, passionate kiss, which he returned in kind. Sighing, she laid her head on his chest and enfolded him in her arms, pressing tightly against him.

Layton loved lying in bed with Cissie, her body warm against his skin. Her sandy-blond hair splayed out against his chest; he adored the smell of it, the silky feel. Like all Englishwomen, by day, Cissie wore her hair pinned up. When she undid the tight knots and let its long, golden weight come tumbling down, the erotic charge that shot through Layton took his breath away.

"That was some quick thinking tonight," Cissie said. "And don't tell me it was something any Englishman would do. Most would have pissed their pants and panicked."

She had taken the words from Layton's mouth. He replayed the night's events; though it had all happened so suddenly, he was pleased with what he'd done.

"Why the Cheshire Cat grin?" Cissie asked.

"Because I'm happy, and I'm cuddling the girl I love," said Layton. He kissed her on the forehead. "I adore you, Mrs. Mapes."

Cissie propped herself up on her elbow and looked into Layton's eyes.

"And I love you," she said. "With all my heart."

"Then please marry me, Mrs. Mapes."

Layton felt elated, as if he were rising up off the bed and floating to the ceiling, like one of those new German dirigibles that had been invented. The sensation was incredible. Instead of hydrogen levitating him, it was pure joy and happiness. Layton had never thought that love would return to his life again, and he had stoically accepted that as fact. But two miracles had occurred: he had found his son — and fallen in love again.

"I'll make you happy the rest of your life. I swear to you I will," Layton said softly, looking her square in her beautiful eyes.

"I'd put a shilling to a pound you will, and I accept. Yes, I'll marry you, Mr. Frank Douglas Owen Layton."

"No matter what comes of this bad business?" Layton said quietly.

"No matter what. I'm yours, ducks."

"If the truth comes out, you'll be Mrs. Douglas Layton. If not, Mrs. Frank Owen."

"Either name's jolly good for me. But in the end, my last name will be Layton, because we'll bring the bastards who wronged you to justice. It'll all come out in the wash, luv. You'll see." Cissie looked up at Layton, her eyes wide and earnest. "You've got me and Sherlock Phipps on the case."

"You're a practical girl, Cissie. You know that wishing for something doesn't necessarily make it true. Suppose we can't prove I was framed?"

The minute the words were out, Layton regretted them. He hadn't wanted to muck up such a special moment.

Cissie just propped herself up on both arms and smiled.

"You're right, life can be shite, and evil often isn't punished. But, luv, you and me are together for life." With that, she settled down next to Layton and pulled the thick blanket over them. They drifted off to sleep, wrapped in each other's arms.

And the following evening, Joe Clayton's face appeared next to a short piece in the *Daily Mail* about Frank Owen's wonderful bravery during the Queen's Palace fire.

35

It was almost noon, and Cissie hadn't made it to work yet. Though she'd never met Alice Browne, somehow, she had found the news of her death deeply unsettling. Cissie couldn't get the poor woman out of her mind. Layton's description of her eyes staring out into space got to her. But she had to get back, she told herself sternly. Today was Monday, and every Monday afternoon, in her office at the MacMillan circuit's flagship venue, His Majesty's Empire on St. Martin's Lane, she gave critiques to nervous agents. When she suggested an act be tightened or a gag thrown out, it had the power of a papal bull, and she was instantly obeyed.

As the tobacconist gave the change for her purchases of cigarettes, the bell on the front door of the shop rang. In strode Nigel Stockton, the head of the Hall Syndicate, MacMillan's chief rival.

Cissie smiled. She had no intention of trying to avoid him.

"Good day to you, Nigel. Haven't seen you in a million bloody years."

"Hello, Cissie," replied the tall man in a terse voice.

Cissie always had the impression that the man's face was carved from granite like those statues in the museums.

Cissie, who possessed a professional mean streak, desired to continue the conversation when it was apparent that Stockton didn't wish to do so.

"I see that attendance has been down for you, Nigel. In fact, it's been down for the past five years or so."

"We've been holding our own."

"Must be bloody hard to do without any top stars. Oh . . . hold on, *we* have all the top stars. Jimmy Conway signed with us last week. Didn't he have a long-term contract with the Hall Syndicate at one time?"

Cissie could see that the blood vessels in Nigel's temples were throbbing.

"The circuit has a wealth of talent to draw on," replied Stockton.

When a theatre circuit lost big-name performers, it had to depend on second-rate specialty acts and singers. Since everyone in the world wanted to perform onstage, the circuit had no trouble filling the bill with acts, but audiences knew they weren't up to snuff. The ventriloquists always moved their lips, and the jugglers often dropped things.

"Why, of course, you still have Martini's Birds. Amazing what you can train pigeons to do — and they never shit onstage. Is that Egyptian dwarf-tossing act still with you? They're a spiffin' lot."

Hall still made money, because the variety theatre was so popular in Great Britain, but made nowhere near the money MacMillan made, which was a big sore point with its investors. As Cissie expected, Stockton lost his composure.

"Listen, you bloody bitch, we discovered and nurtured all that talent, then you stole them right from under us. You wouldn't know a talented performer if he came down from the sky and bit you on your fat arse."

Instead of launching a rebuttal, Cissie did something far more effective — she started laughing uncontrollably in Stockton's face. People in the tobacconist shop looked at her with astonishment. She couldn't stop laughing, which enraged Stockton, a man who usually commanded great respect.

"Damn you, woman. You're lucky you weren't with your no-talent husband that night. You would have gotten yours, m'girl."

That comment stopped Cissie's laughter dead. She stared at Stockton.

"Samuels and the rest of those turncoats got what they deserved," snarled Stockton. "Your circuit *should* have gone under."

Cissie ran out of the tobacconist's shop, all the way to her office. People on the street stopped to watch her bolt by. Out of breath by the time she reached the Metro, she had to sit on the gold-carpeted stairs in the grand foyer to compose herself. As her lungs huffed and puffed, she lit a cigarette to calm herself down.

She remembered an incident some years ago when Stockton had come unannounced to see Clifton and Glenn. It came right after Sunny Samuels, Hall's most popular performer, and Dainty Amy came on board. Those were two *big* fishes MacMillan had landed. Lots of jealousy. Nigel Stockton had lost a packet. He was mad — mad as hell. One day, out of the blue, Stockton had come storming into the head office, screaming his head off. He and Clifton and Glenn went into Clifton's office, and all hell broke loose. The shouting continued for over an hour. Stockton walked out, swearing he'd get even with them. He slammed the door so hard, the glass shattered.

Cissie trudged up to her office. Connected directly to it was a big storage room stuffed full of filing cabinets and open shelving. Cissie wanted to book a specialty act, the Cambridge Brothers, Fun on a Billiards Table, for the MacMillan Empire. To complete the deal, she needed to know how big their names had been on another theatre's bill. These bills, forty-by-sixty-inch broadsheets posted throughout London, were a show's main means of publicity. The typography and position of an act on the bill were deeply important to the artistes, as they established backstage status and determined who got the best dressing rooms. Cissie had weathered many a fight over lettering size, with artistes even whipping out rulers to prove a point, and positioning, with the top spot and that directly below it being most desirable.

Flipping through the broadsheets, she came across Sunny's name at the top of the bill in the biggest letters. Losing him that night was a crushing blow for Clifton and Glenn, who had paid big money to steal him. They had been lucky the other top performers who'd been given complimentary tickets, like Dainty Amy, Kitty Rayburn, or Queenie Laurence, didn't show up that opening night. Many more stars than

Sunny would have been dead. Stockton's tirade echoed in Cissie's ears. "The circuit *should* have gone under." Stockton had been wishing that had happened to MacMillan. She could hear the anguish in his angry voice.

"Stockton may have wanted to get back at Clifton and Glenn by killing our top stars that night and making people afraid to attend MacMillan theatres," Cissie explained excitedly to Phipps and Layton, sitting in Layton's room. "He could have conspired with Browne and Reville to destroy MacMillan's talent sitting there that opening night. He bloody well had a motive to do such a thing."

"You did *pillage* the Hall Syndicate," said Phipps. "It wasn't just Sunny."

"I suppose we did. Look, this is a cut-throat business. That's the way things are done. You make the opposition's stars *and* their agents feel like they're being underpaid and underappreciated, and then you steal 'em."

"How badly did your little coup hurt the Hall Syndicate?" Phipps asked. "They didn't go bankrupt, did they?"

"No, but losing Sunny and Amy made it look like they weren't a number one chain anymore. Lots of artistes jumped ship after that. The Johnson Collies, a big dog act, the Four Armattos, Clive and Clive, the comics . . . Really buggered 'em sideways."

Phipps started pacing the carpet. A seemingly unconscious habit, Layton thought. He did it whenever he was pondering, again reminding Layton of Sherlock Holmes and he as Dr. Watson.

"You said that Peter's appointment book had entries with the name Shaw?" Phipps said. "May I see it?"

Layton nodded and retrieved the book from the bedroom nightstand. Phipps sat once more and read carefully through it, dog-earing some pages as he went.

"There are appointments with the name Shaw," said Phipps. "From then on, the appointments don't list a name, just the letter *S*. Some of them are after working hours. Here are two with Reville."

"*S* could be for Shaw — or Stockton," interjected Cissie.

"Shaw could have caused the collapse," said Layton. He was beginning to believe it was Shaw who had the biggest motive for revenge.

"Both faced financial ruin and wanted revenge," added Phipps.

Cissie opened her mouth again to speak

but was cut off by Phipps, who drew out his pocket watch and gave a muffled curse. Rising to his feet, he handed the appointment book back to Layton.

"You'll have to excuse me," he said. "I've a building committee meeting about the new Imperial Hospital in Chelsea — I damn near forgot. The Prince of Wales is on the board; he'll be attending. But as soon as I can, I'll be back."

36

Ronald cut through White Horse Street to the corner of Piccadilly and turned east. At every block, something caught his interest. He stopped to peer into storefront windows, to watch a man chalking Big Ben on the sidewalk, to speak to a blind and begging Boer War veteran. On Shaftesbury Avenue, he examined the theatre bills along the way. At a sweets vendor cart, he counted out coins for a bar of Cadbury chocolate.

"Keep following with the motor, Bolton."

"Yes, Lady Edwina."

Odd to see her son in such a setting, Edwina Layton thought. Off by himself, strolling along as he pleased . . . It annoyed and fascinated her at the same time.

Edwina was a busy woman; her weeks were full. So full that she barely had time for Ronald. Today, for instance, she was preparing for Lady Alstyne's ball. She had purchased a special gown for the occasion from Paquin, which she knew would greatly please her husband-to-be, Lord Percival. Her son was far from her mind; in fact, she had no idea where Ronald was supposed to be this afternoon. Nanny took care of all that. If her chauffeur hadn't turned down Park Lane, she never would have seen — or thought of — her son. Ever more intrigued, Edwina leaned closer to the window.

The carriage and motor traffic was crawling along. Given all the stops he took and the forest-green jacket and shorts he wore, it was easy to keep the boy in sight.

Following Ronald felt like a kind of lark to Edwina. Whatever was he up to? Perhaps he was going to a store to buy himself something or maybe a special place he wanted to eat. *No.* She shook her head. Her son had never been to a restaurant in his life.

She stuck her head and elegant feathered hat out the window of the motor, her eyes glued to her son. He was headed for the West End. Might he be going to the theatre in secret? How little she knew about Ronald, she thought. Sometimes, he seemed as inscrutable as a Chinaman, his facial expressions giving nothing away.

"He's on Shaftesbury, m'lady," the chauffeur said.

"Keep following, but at a distance. We'll run our little fox to ground yet."

On Shaftesbury and Rupert, alongside a music hall, two men and a woman stopped to say hello to Ronald, as though they were old friends. Soon after, a man in a derby patted him affectionately on the head. A look of great consternation contorted Lady Edwina's lovely, high-cheekboned face. Nanny had warned Ronald never to talk to strangers.

But then, these people didn't seem like strangers.

Ronald abruptly turned left into an alley behind a theatre.

"Speed up, Bolton," Edwina commanded.

The motor drew up alongside the alley as the boy sprinted down it. Alarmed, Edwina got out and followed. She watched as her son leapt like a gazelle into the arms of a tall man by the stage door, who swung him around and hugged him. Ronald was giggling; she saw the innocent joy on his face. After a moment, the man set him down, and the boy offered him a piece of Cadbury. Edwina rushed forward, ready to intervene, but stopped in her tracks.

The thin, clean-shaven man looked vaguely familiar. He had spectacles and chestnut-colored hair, and yet . . .

The boy and the man were about to open the metal stage door. Edwina moved closer, some twenty feet away. Ronald disappeared into the building, but as the man was about to follow, his eyes locked with Edwina's. An expression of surprise, then hatred and loathing came over him, which had the effect of a punch to Edwina's nose. She recoiled. He stared at her for five seconds more, then smiled and slammed the stage door defiantly behind him.

As people streamed by her on both sides, Edwina stood there in complete shock. *Douglas!*

Edwina turned and shuffled back to the motor. She was baffled, angry, and about to burst into a flood of tears. By going through that stage door, it was as if Ronald had crossed the River Styx and lost himself to her.

Settling back against the rolled leather seat, Edwina looked up at the theatre, taking in the glories of its ornate stonework. From where she sat, she could see the bill listing the performers on the sidewall. She half expected to see Layton, her ex-husband, appearing as a conjurer.

For she now knew the truth: her ex-husband was back in London. She would never ever forget Douglas's expression. It had said defiantly *This is* my *son. Try to take him away from me!*

After all this time, she had never expected him to appear again. He'd been meant to vanish from her life forever, in punishment for the unbearable humiliation he'd brought upon the family. Surprising, really, how quickly the shame had erased her love for Douglas. Edwina had — she believed — once been in love with him. But maybe, she thought, staring at the theatre lights, she'd never truly loved him in the first place.

In a way, she had married Douglas to annoy her father. Edwina had always been intimidated by her father and always did what he demanded. Douglas was quite a good-looking chap and a brilliant architect to boot, but he wasn't the ideal selection. In her world, a real gentleman was not supposed to work for a living. The tribal customs in upper-class British society believed that marriages weren't supposed to be based on love but on the right social connections to titled men of means, to increase the wealth and bloodlines of the families. But Edwina had learned in her husband hunting that rank did not equal mettle. Many suitors from the aristocracy and gentry were weak in will and nature, while Douglas was the direct opposite, and that was what she really liked about him. But she knew rebellion toward her father played a part in the decision as well.

Lord Litton had raged about the Britannia accident for months, shocked and horrified that a member of *his* family was a convicted murderer. He forbade Edwina from seeing him, not even allowing her to explain to Douglas that she was divorcing him. Ronald would be told he died in a boating accident. Litton's continued fury had mentally battered Edwina; she shuddered at the memory. Any remaining love for her husband had died then; she was glad he was in Mulcaster, out of sight and out of mind. The truth was that she didn't care what happened to him. She wanted to get on with her life and maintain her position in society by marrying the Earl of Gainsford.

As a girl, her mother had taught her to ignore bad things. Eventually, they would go away. But now a bad thing was back, and she had to face it.

And why the devil was Douglas in a music hall of all places?

Edwina didn't ask herself why Ronald was there. The answer was obvious: Nanny Hawkins. She'd been a child of privilege too, and her nanny had been her real mother, just as Mrs. Hawkins was Ronald's.

Nanny liked Douglas and thought him a caring father, which Edwina knew was true. Douglas had been a wonderful father to Ronald, probably better than she was a mother. She had applied the mothering skills that her mother had used in her childhood, which were based on the notion that children were an annoying fact of life one left to the nanny's attention.

Stroking her ostrich-feathered boa, she stared at the back of Bolton's head, her mind replaying the memory of Ronald's face as his father swooped him up in his arms.

"Drive on, Bolton," she said at last. "Lady Alstyne awaits."

"Yes, m'lady."

Back at her father's house in Mayfair, she passed Nanny Hawkins on the great mahogany stair.

"Afternoon, m'lady," said Mrs. Hawkins with a slight bow of the head.

Edwina stripped her gloves from her hands in silence. Then, about five steps past Mrs. Hawkins, she turned and said, "Nanny, I think a boy *does* need his father."

"I'm glad you understand, m'lady," said Mrs. Hawkins with another small and graceful bow.

37

December had once been Layton's least favorite month. Every one of the five Christmases he'd spent in prison had depressed him severely. Fond memories of holidays at Edwina's family estate in Kent with the tall tree in the three-story entry hall, of watching Ronald rip the wrapping off his gifts and shout with excitement, became a punishment.

In Mulcaster, he'd been surprised by the many inmates who made Christmas a special time. They'd get their mates little things — a pack of fags, a deck of cards, a bar of soap. Gifts that were taken for granted on the outside had a special significance in prison.

Now, at last, Christmas would be special again. Ronald was back in his life, and this would be his first Christmas with Cissie. He couldn't wait to give them their gifts. Layton had kept an open ear the last few weeks, hoping to find both of them the perfect gifts they really wanted for Christmas. Most of the presents he'd exchanged in the past with his family were tokens, a scarf or a tie, nothing that meant anything. Edwina had come close once, bless her heart, buying him a volume on Bernini's architecture. But it was the Palladio book he'd wanted. So he had wound up buying it for himself.

Despite Layton's resolve to be cheerful, the winter fog made Decembers in London hard. The usual fog was bad enough: raw, dark, damp, and dismal. But the winter variety came with a numbing cold that deadened the limbs, like soaking one's bones in an ice-cold bath.

Hands thrust deep in his pockets, chin tucked into his scarf, Layton pushed on, back to his digs in Bayswater. The night fog robbed London of its shape and form. The street was enveloped in a murky gloom; the buildings he passed oozed dampness, and the street seemed slippery with slime. One could barely see two feet ahead. Pedestrians would emerge from the gloom in front of him, then disappear just as suddenly, vanishing in the mist like phantoms.

In the last week, conditions had gotten so bad that an army of "linkboys" had taken to the streets in force; these chaps held torches or lanterns and for sixpence would light the way through the fog. Layton had already passed two of them, leading groups, pointing their lights down to avoid the puddles in the gutters. Many had thought that with the invention of gas and later electric street lighting, there would be no need for link-boys. But the fogs at night were so intense that even streetlamps were no help.

Layton was walking west now, alongside Hyde Park, which was enshrouded in fog, not a tree to be seen. He pulled the collar of his greatcoat more tightly around his neck, but still he was chilled to the bone. He couldn't wait to be home before the fire, a cup of cocoa warming his hands.

As he walked, he tried to sort matters out, but things had become muddled.

With the discovery of what Hugh Rice was doing to them, Clifton and Glenn seemed likely to be the murderers. Even though the balcony failure had scared away customers for a short while, getting Rice off their backs was worth the pain in the long run. From his prison years and his more recent run-ins with Archie Guest, Layton knew that once the underworld got its hooks into you, it never let go. Rice was the person that had to go. Maybe unbeknownst to each other, the owners also arranged for some other troublesome people in their lives to be eliminated that night.

But the builder, Alec Shaw, could also have easily orchestrated the collapse. He was the one who actually built the balcony. His hatred of Layton, for whom he blamed his financial ruin, was almost insanely intense, maybe putting him over the edge to do such a heinous act. His desire for revenge must have been all-consuming.

Now Stockton, the rival theatre circuit owner, came into the picture. Cissie insisted his hatred of Clifton and Glenn could have driven him to conspire with Peter and Reville to bring down the balcony. After losing so much talent that he'd discovered to MacMillan, he wanted revenge. His plan would have been twofold, to embarrass the circuit on an opening night and to try to kill the turncoat performers.

Layton turned right on Leinster Terrace, now just ten minutes from home, the question still beating at his mind. Who was the murderer — Clifton and Glenn, Shaw, or Stockton?

Carriages and motors loomed out of the mist, appearing in an instant and vanishing just as swiftly. As Layton stepped off the curb, he was so lost in thought that a motor appeared out of nowhere and came close to running him over.

When he got back to his digs, he rushed up the stairs, because he couldn't wait to get in front of the fire. He felt as though he were entombed in a block of ice. While he was unlocking the door, he began taking off his wet greatcoat, since he was in such a hurry to warm up. As he swung the door open, his foot stepped on something. He looked down to see an envelope. Mail that came for the lodgers was routinely shoved under their door. But Layton had never received any mail until this moment. He stood there staring down at the envelope like it was a one-hundred-pound note he had come across in the street. Layton pondered — who would send him a letter? A performer and friend who had moved on to another theatre? Or maybe his father or brother? That was highly unlikely. Then it came to him — Edwina. She had seen him in the alley with Ronald that day. She was writing to tell him that she was glad he was out of prison and could see Ronald anytime he wished. Yes, that was it! With a big smile on his face, he closed the door, snatched up the envelope, and eagerly tore it open.

YOU WILL DIE FOR WHAT YOU DID, said the unsigned letter.

38

"You know there are graphologists — people who can match a person's handwriting," said Phipps, holding the death threat in the air.

"Tom, please hide that note." Layton didn't like the fact that Phipps was waving the note around at the theatre.

To Phipps's delight, Layton had taken him to the backstage of the Queen's while the show was going on. Layton could tell that the architect was thrilled to see the show from this vantage point, with all the hustle and bustle of the show's operation. He was fascinated by the sight of the performers waiting for their turn and the stagehands raising cloths and moving props. He insisted on bringing the note with him in the hopes of coming across anything with similar handwriting. He even began asking the performers for their autographs to find a link. He looked about for notes that stagehands may have written. On the rear brick wall of the backstage was a chalkboard marked with daily instructions, and he examined it for similarities.

Layton saw no hope in all that. The note was deliberately done in crude, oversize block letters. It would be impossible to trace, but he liked Phipps too much to throw cold water on his idea.

At the moment, Phipps wasn't interested in handwriting analysis. With a smile stretched ear to ear, he was standing next to Layton, watching the act that was on the stage. An attractive middle-aged woman stood near them with a stopwatch in her hand.

"Every morning, me mum would get up at six, eat her breakfast, and go to work. Then me brother Tom would get up and go. At half past six, me brother Charlie would go to work. Then at seven, me dad would get up. By that time, I had the bed all to meself." A ripple of tittering arose from the audience.

Ally Bransby, Master of Mirth, had two minutes to go in his turn. From the stage, he glanced at his wife, Sybil, who waited in the wings with a stopwatch. Layton knew that she was calculating the length of the applause after each joke, a common way of honing timing and choosing the best material.

"You know, they're making all these ladies' hats with bird feathers all over 'em. Now they're making a new kind of hat with a live pigeon on top. If you don't pay the bill, the hat flies back to the shop."

That one got a big laugh, especially from Phipps in the wings, and Ally glowed with satisfaction. He took his call and skipped off the stage, Sybil right behind him.

"Damn you," she was hissing. "I told you that bed joke was bollocks. It was as funny as a dog turd. And you paid ten bob for that one. That's money down the bog!"

Ally grimaced and slunk away. The minute his makeup was off, Layton thought, he was off to the Prince of York to hide from Sybil until the second show.

"Bloody fool," Sybil screamed after him. To Layton, she said playfully, "Can you write jokes — in addition to your other artistic talents, Frank?" She reached up, playfully rubbing the underside of Layton's chin as though he were a cat. When Cissie appeared behind them, Sybil quickly lowered her hand.

"On your bike, girl," Cissie said grimly. "And tell that husband of yours that if he doesn't get funnier, he'll be playing the Alhambra — the one in the middle of Australia."

The orchestra was playing "College Life," a march that was all the rage in Britain. The audience was caught up, clapping along to the lively tune.

Out from stage left came Helen McCoy, the Piccadilly Lilly. The crowd roared. She lifted her dress to expose her pretty ankles and two-stepped expertly across the stage. The crowd, especially the men, exploded with joy. The orchestra repeated the tune, as they sometimes did when the audience seemed particularly enchanted.

Finally, the song ended. Helen waited patiently for the applause to die down before beginning her first song, "I Want What I Want When I Want It."

By this time, Layton had seen many acts come and go. Very few performers were able to forge a truly special bond between themselves and the audience. Helen was one who could. There was definitely an electric wire connecting her and the audience. As she piped up her energy, the house in turn piped up theirs. And her voice was lovely, dulcet and clear, never straining for notes, and always full of emotion.

Halfway through "I'm Trying to Find a Sweetheart," shouting erupted from the rear

of the theatre's main level. Variety performers were accustomed to disruptions from
drunks and hecklers, and at first, Helen
ignored the noise. But the shouting increased, and the audience began to rumble
angrily. Who dared interrupt the beautiful
young singer?

Along the side aisle of the stalls came a
bald man in his sixties, wearing evening
dress and a top hat. Some men rose from
their seats and tried to grab him, but he
bulled by until he reached the orchestra pit.

"You get the hell down from there this
minute, Gladys!" he shouted.

Helen stopped singing and stared at the
man in disbelief.

"You're the daughter of the Earl of Suttonfield. No child of mine will disgrace our
name by going onstage!"

The entire auditorium erupted in anger.
People were booing and hissing the old
man. Men from the stalls and a male usher
caught hold of the Earl of Suttonfield and
tried to drag him away, but it took six men
to make him move — barely. His face beet
red, saliva spraying from his mouth with
every shout, the earl kept screaming at
Helen, who stood paralyzed on the stage.

"You're a tart," he shouted. "Parading
your ankles in front of this trash!"

This classist remark further incensed the crowd, especially those in the gallery. A small group began making their way down to the main level, determined to beat the hell out of the earl.

"You're a disgrace to our family!" he ranted on. "William the Conqueror himself granted us our lands!"

"Shove off, slaphead!"

"You toffee-nosed twit, get the hell out of here!"

Wilding, the stage manager, sprinted down the side stair to the stalls to join the melee. Layton, Cissie, the crew, and the artistes all came right out onto the stage to watch.

"If you don't come down from there," the earl screamed, "you'll never set foot in Suttonfield again! Do you hear me? You're Lady Gladys Suttonfield! You have a title to uphold! Who the hell do you think will marry a music hall singer? You'll be a social leper, my girl!"

At last, the gang of men had the earl under control. They dragged him, kicking and screaming, to the door of the theatre and flung him out into the gutter on Shaftesbury Avenue. Thirty seconds later, the earl was back in the theatre, shouting at the top of his lungs, and had to be thrown out again.

Helen still stood, dumbfounded, on the stage, her arms hanging limp at her sides. Unsure what else to do, she turned to leave. But the audience cried out for her to continue.

"Give us a song, Helen."

"Don't mind what that horse's arse said, even if he is your dad!"

"Sing, girl, sing. Sing, girl, sing. Sing, girl, sing," chanted the crowd.

From the wings, Cissie smiled at the singer and motioned her to go back on. Helen did an about-face. At the center of the stage, she smiled brightly and bowed to the crowd. The orchestra struck up "Is Everybody Happy," and she belted the song out proudly, the audience joining in on all the choruses.

When Helen finished, the crowd jumped to their feet and cheered like crazy.

When she walked past Layton in the wings, he caught her attention.

"Helen, meet my friend Tom Phipps. He's the best architect in Great Britain."

"How do you do, Mr. Phipps."

"You have a magnificent voice, Miss McCoy. May I have the pleasure of your autograph?"

39

"Be *brutal,* Frank. Be *brutal.* Tell me what you really think."

Neither in his days as a famed architect nor his days as a disgraced prisoner would Douglas Layton have dreamed he'd find himself in Harrods, helping two men shop for dresses. But here he was.

"I prefer the red-and-blue frock, Cyril," Layton said in a grave tone.

A look of disappointment washed over Cyril's face.

"Ha! Thought he'd fancy the lavender one, you cow," crowed Neville.

"You told me to be brutally honest, Cyril," Layton said.

"But when someone says that, they don't really mean it, luv." Cyril sounded very hurt indeed.

"Then don't pay me any mind. If your gut says the lavender, then you must buy it," Layton said.

Instantly, the smile returned to Cyril's face. "Thank you, dearie. I'll go with the lavender."

"What do you think of this number, Frank? With a boa?"

"I never liked you in yellow, Neville."

"Ha! Take that, you old queen," shouted Cyril with glee.

Eddington & Freddington had become big West End favorites, which meant an increase in wages and an upgrade to the act's wardrobe. Artistes had to pay for their own costumes and props, be they an acrobat's tights or a magician's turban. It could be an expensive investment; some acts played long past their time, simply because they had to recoup the cost of their wardrobes.

"Try the red one with fur trim. I think the Duchess of Shelbourne has a similar outfit," Layton said now. As they'd dragged him here, he might as well give them the benefit of his experience. Edwina had been one of the most fashionably dressed women in London; with what she'd spent on clothes, one could have built an office building.

Layton smiled privately to himself. Edwina wouldn't have been caught dead in Harrods — so common.

"You have to tell us what Ronnie would like

for Christmas, Frank," said Neville as he poured tea. The three men had paused for refreshments at the Harrods tearoom.

"Yes, what would the nipper like? Soldiers, books, a new cricket bat?" Cyril asked, dipping a scone in honey.

"You fellows have been much too generous already," Layton said firmly. In truth, Ronnie couldn't take the duo's gifts home, or he would risk questions. Even with Edwina's tacit permission, the risk was too great. The presents Cyril and Neville had given Ronald were stored away in Layton's digs.

"Nonsense. We're his aunties, don't you know?"

"Well, something small then," Layton said, smiling.

"Here's a good one I heard," cackled Cyril. "How do you make an Englishman laugh on Monday?"

"Tell him a joke on Friday night!" Neville crowed. The table erupted in laughter.

"I have a joke you can use," said Layton.

"Go on, luv. We adore free jokes," Cyril said eagerly.

"A Scotsman comes home early and finds his wife in bed with another bloke. He gets his gun and points it at the man's head, and his wife bursts out laughing. So the Scotsman says, 'What are you laughing at? You're next.' "

Cyril and Neville screeched so with laughter that every woman in the tearoom turned to look disapprovingly at them.

"That's wonderful, Frank," said Neville, dabbing at his eyes. "You know, when we met you, we thought, 'What a handsome, gentlemanly chap he is.' We both wanted to get inside your knickers. We didn't know you had a ripping sense of humor too."

"His knickers are out of bounds," Cyril said sternly. "Except for Cissie Mapes."

"Here's to a man in love," said Neville, rolling his eyes up at the ceiling.

Layton was laughing too, so hard that he struggled to swallow his tea.

This had happened many times when he'd gone out with the boys to pubs and restaurants. Like time spent with Mangogo, the joy of his life at the variety theatre seemed impossibly powerful, able to shoo away even the darkest of specters.

Layton had had such a fun afternoon at Harrods, but walking home, it couldn't make him forget that someone was dead set on killing him. Several times, especially when he stopped to cross the street, Layton looked around to make sure Shaw wasn't behind him. But his attacker could be any one of these hundreds of men on the street alongside him. Every stranger was an enemy.

40

It was Sunday morning, and Layton had the Queen's Palace entirely to himself. All the variety theatres were closed on Sundays — not because the performers or syndicate owners were religious, but because of the stern opposition they faced from Britain's clergy, be they Church of England, the Roman Catholic Church, or worst of all, the Presbyterians. No laughing on the Sabbath, much less looking at scantily clad girls.

Instead, Sundays were a day of travel. All across Britain, hundreds of artistes donned their best clothes, packed up their big wardrobe trunks, and boarded trains to their next engagement. They'd begun to travel in such numbers that they'd formed a trade association, winning reduced fares and luggage fees from the railways.

On Sunday mornings in the West End, one could hear the church bells off in the distance, beckoning their congregants. It always reminded Layton of his childhood in Dorset, when his father led his brood on foot to the C of E church in Stinsford. He wasn't a religious man at all but insisted on the family going to Sunday services. The most vivid memory was how loud and terribly off-key their father sang the hymns, causing Layton and his two brothers to almost burst at the seams to try to contain their laughter. Being the proper wife, his mother never chastised her husband for singing like a hinge. Like her children, she loved and admired Thomas Layton as a kind and patient man, even though his voice was an utter embarrassment.

The peace and quiet of a long Sunday by himself at the Queen's Palace was just what Layton needed. He wanted to touch up a cloth he'd done the day before. The celestial scene he'd painted showed a dark-blue sky filled with stars and planets; he wasn't yet satisfied with Jupiter, on the left side. After he corrected its proportions, he would meet Cissie outside the theatre for tea at Miss MacIntosh's on Shaftesbury, a Sunday ritual he'd come to cherish.

The cloth had already been flown up to the grid in the fly tower, which meant Layton had to climb the very tall black metal ladder to the gallery and lower it using the fly ropes. But it was worth it, he thought. He'd come to take fierce pride in his scenic painting; at heart, he was a creative person, and the passion he poured into his cloths had replaced architecture, which fate had stolen from him.

A cloth was raised by three rope lines: a long, a center, and a short, all of which were tied off to a cleat on the railing of the fly gallery. Layton worked at a knot in the heavy hemp rope.

He had just untied it when someone from behind grabbed his throat and began to crush the hell out of it. Though he tried to scream, only a pained gargling sound emerged. His face turned purple; he flayed his arms wildly, to no effect.

Just as he was about to pass out, his assailant released the chokehold, grabbed his left arm, and twisted it up behind his back. Layton groaned in pain — then groaned again as he realized the center rope he had just untied was being wrapped around his neck. He felt the painful rub of the scratchy hemp against his skin as something was thrust into his pants pocket.

Those same powerful hands grabbed him, lifted him over the railing.

"You should have hanged for murdering my sister, Jocelyn! Now I'm the hangman," screamed a voice directly behind him. "And they say three's a charm."

Thirty feet below, the wooden stage swam before Layton's terrified eyes.

"Frank didn't murder Jocelyn Shipway! I swear to it," a familiar voice screamed up at them. "Someone else did! They murdered them all that night. My husband too! But he didn't do it. I'm telling you the God's own truth, luv!"

Layton's body jerked back like a rag doll's. Looking down, he saw Cissie, standing on the stage. He twisted his head and saw, to his amazement, a pretty, petite girl in a maroon dress. It was Amy Silborne, the strongwoman. She lurched forward, grabbing his belt and bending him over the rail, the rope still tight around his neck.

"I gave my ticket to Jocelyn. She died instead of me."

Cissie dropped to her knees, sobbing. "Please, Amy, don't. Let me explain."

For what seemed an eternity, Amy stood, debating whether or not to hurl Layton over the rail to his death. Finally, she pulled her hand from his belt and unwound the rope. He collapsed on the floor of the fly gallery, his chest heaving like an asthmatic's.

"I'm very sorry, Frank, for having tried to

kill you . . . three times."

"Three?"

"The shooting party at the Duke of Denton's estate. I felt terrible the beater got hit, but thank God he recovered."

Upon hearing this news, Layton automatically raised his hand to where the shot grazed his hair.

"My world was destroyed when my sister died. We grew up together in my uncle's family, who didn't give a damn about us. Jocelyn and I looked out for each other. I was lucky as hell to be a success onstage so I could take care of her. She was all the family I had. I was mad with anger that weekend when I discovered who you really were, after the king made that remark. Insane and bent on revenge. I wasn't able to stop myself. You had to die." Amy sounded sincerely contrite.

Layton shook his head, amazed. Despite having seen her act many times, he couldn't believe the delicate girl standing before him had such incredible strength. To almost squash his head like a melon, to crush his windpipe as if it were made of cardboard!

After twenty minutes of explanation, Amy had been convinced of Layton's innocence. Now she wanted to kill either Clifton,

Glenn, Shaw, or Stockton. Whoever was the killer.

"Every single day, I say to myself, 'I can't believe she's gone.'" Amy started crying.

Cissie put her arms around her little shoulders. "I say the same thing about my Johnnie, luv — almost every bloody day."

"When we find out who the murderer is, Frank . . . I mean, Douglas," Amy said, sniffling, "I'll take care of him." She held up both hands, slightly curling her fingers.

Layton didn't think it was the time to argue for handing the killer over to the police. In silence, the three of them shuffled toward the exit.

Out in the alley, Layton placed his hand on Amy's shoulder. "We'll find out who did it, Amy. We won't stop until we find him."

As he and Cissie watched Amy trudge sadly off, Layton felt in his pocket for the piece of crumpled paper she'd stuffed there. It read:

I couldn't live with the guilt any longer.
Douglas Layton

The handwriting was a quite refined cursive, very neatly done in ink, like one was taught in grammar school.

"Amy," Layton called out. "This wasn't

the fourth time? After pushing me into the street?"

"Why, no, Frank. I never did a thing like that!"

41

"Champagne Charlie is my name
Champagne drinking is my game
Good for any game at night my boys
Good for any game at night my boys
For Champagne Charlie is my name
Good for any game at night my boys
Who'll come and join me in a spree?"

Dressed as a down-on-his-luck aristocrat in a tatty white shirt and tails and a smashed top hat, Timmy Donovan had the Friday night house in his pocket.

"Now help me out with this ditty," he shouted, and the audience happily joined in on the next chorus of "Champagne Charlie." The customers *always* joined in the choruses of songs; it was a variety theatre tradition.

Songs about getting drunk were allowed but never any even hinting about sex. Cissie kept an eagle eye out for performers, especially comics, whose material was too suggestive and policed them rigorously.

It surprised Layton that a woman so passionate in bed could be so puritanical in business. Last month, Cissie had actually ordered the stage manager at the Walham Green Empire to drop the curtain on a comic who had made an obscene gesture at his crotch. She'd cursed him up and down and had all the possessions from his dressing room thrown into the alley — with the comic sent tumbling after them.

For his part, Layton was enjoying Timmy's turn. He and Mangogo stood in the wings, stage left. The cold London weather had been hard on the Pygmies; the MacMillan circuit had had to provide them with coats. Sizing proved difficult; Mangogo's greatcoat, which he wore inside because of the theatre's cold draughts, almost touched the floor.

Two stagehands carrying a crate bustled past; Layton moved out of their way and found himself next to the prompt corner. On the desk was a newspaper a crew member had left behind, and a headline at the bottom of the front page caught Layton's eye.

GRUESOME DISCOVERY AT BUILDING
SITE IN KING'S CROSS

He started to scan the first paragraph, then snatched up the paper and ran to the scene shop. In privacy, he read:

Two days ago, workmen on the construction site of the Hall Syndicate's new Victory Hippodrome Theatre made a horrific discovery. Brickmasons noticed three human fingers protruding through the cement in a section of newly poured footing. Police ordered the men to break up the footing and discovered the naked body of a man, approximately sixty years old with a ginger mustache, embedded in the cement. The man had a large bruise on his forehead.

The body has been identified as that of Edward Beverly of Lambeth, a worker at the Cook Foundries in Wapping. His wife, Mabel, had come to Metropolitan Police headquarters to report her husband missing and made the identification.

Police are making inquiries. All information is welcome.

The next morning, Layton found himself on Reardon Street, gazing at the massive brick buildings that housed the Cook Foundries, the mill that had supplied the Britannia's steel.

Taking a deep breath, he walked through

the wide iron gate into the rear yard. The workers were busy loading metalwork into wagons and paid Layton no attention. They likely thought he was a reporter, Layton guessed, looking for information on the murder of their coworker.

In his days as an architect, Layton had visited such places to inspect ornamental metalwork before it was installed on his buildings. In the yard were stacks of finished work ready to be shipped: metal fencing, steel beams and girders, iron doors, and window gratings. Out of habit, Layton examined the goods, which were of the best quality and workmanship. He could always tell the quality by looking closely at the metal's grain. Good quality iron was smooth and tight, with no pitting or voids.

A wide opening at the rear of the building led to a massive three-story fabrication plant, whose furnaces and forges were going full tilt. Layton strolled inside, acting as though he owned the place, and passed slowly by the equipment. On this damp, miserable December morning, the place was hot as an inferno. Crucibles and furnaces boiled furiously; the red-and-yellow molten steel and iron would be poured into molds or cooled and hammered, making scores of machine parts, tools, sheet iron, and boilerplate. On Layton's first visit to a foundry in Dorchester as a young architect working for John Hicks, he'd thought it the perfect image of hell.

Like all fabrication plants, this one was dirty and cluttered, with piles of raw bar stock and plate metal scattered all about. A layer of thick, gray soot covered everything, including the cups on the table where workers took tea breaks. Imagine the lungs of these men, Layton thought, coated with years of dust like a coal miner's.

As he walked past a long table filled with tools and wooden crates, a crate of rivets stopped him in his tracks. Picking one from the pile, Layton stared at it in amazement, as if he'd found a legendary South African diamond on the sidewalk. He rubbed his fingers over the rounded head, feeling its slightly rough texture, then slid them along the smooth, cylindrical shaft.

Rivets were the primary means of fastening steel, a new construction material that had come into wide use just before Layton went to prison. A metalworker would use iron tongs to place a red-hot rivet in a predrilled hole; by hammering the end of the shaft, he could create a new head and tightly fasten down the metal plate. Rivets were excellent for carrying loads perpendicular

412

to their shaft, or shear loads, which made them ideal for bridge and building construction.

But, Layton knew, a chain was only as strong as its weakest link. He threw the rivet up in the air and caught it again. And as it spun end over end, he realized what had happened.

Rivets had been used in the steel cantilever beams of the Britannia's balconies. They had spliced together two sections of beams in Section C of the dress circle, sitting directly on the great, curved girder that stretched from wall to wall. Extending out sixteen feet from the girder were the cantilevered balcony beams, with concrete steps to attach the seating. It was this section of balcony that had snapped off, breaking as easily as a breadstick, killing and maiming the people in the stalls below. The rivets at that point on the girder, Layton thought, his fist closing tight around the one in his hand, must have failed because of poor-quality metal.

It reminded Layton of a great oak in a field near his home in Puddletown. The tree was huge, its thick, long boughs radiating out from its enormous trunk. As a boy, Layton thought it the strongest thing on earth. So he was shocked one day, walking back from the village, to see a massive bough lying at its foot. Puzzled, he'd examined the end of the branch, where it had snapped, and found it rotten at its core. The bough that had looked so mighty and solid was basically hollow, and its own dead weight had brought it down.

The rivets in the Britannia balcony had been the same — so strong-looking on the outside, but weak at the core.

Outside, rain had begun to beat down, hammering the dirt in the yard so hard that puddles formed almost immediately. The men retreated indoors.

"Rainin' stair rods out there, eh, guv?"

Layton turned to face a workman with a bulbous red nose and a mop of stringy gray hair.

"Good morning," he said, holding up the rivet. "Everybody was so busy that I decided to have a look around on my own. I'm looking for someone to do foundry work — rivets. Like these."

"Aye, guv, you've come to the right place, but at a bad time. One of our mates has passed on." The speaker doffed his cap and pressed it to his chest as he spoke.

"So sorry to hear that, old chap. Was he a rivet maker?"

"Aye, that was our Eddie's specialty, but

he could make anything," the man said. "Good with any kind of metal. Twenty-one years I worked with him, and never did I meet a finer man. His rivets was of the finest quality. He was like a bloomin' scientist; could make any kind of cast iron, steel, you name it, guv."

Layton nodded. Metallurgy was a complex science, in which the chemical composition of iron was altered with carbon to make it stronger — or weaker. Ferrous alloys like cast iron had high carbon content; wrought iron's was low. Steel contained carbon, but if the proportions were lowered even slightly, the steel quality would become inferior and lose its ability to withstand applied forces.

Metallurgy was as much art as science. One could manipulate metal as much as one wanted to get the desired result. In the case of the Britannia, that result had been a structural failure.

"Thank you for your time, sir," Layton said, his voice hollow. "You've been most helpful. Again, I'm dreadfully sorry for your loss."

"Thanks, guv. He loved his job," said the worker, a sad expression on his sagging, weather-beaten face. "Never pulled a sickie in all my years here."

In the foundry yard, the rain had slowed to a drizzle. Layton walked in a daze, the rivet still in his hand. He'd said that this was all a giant puzzle. Well, slowly, the pieces were fitting together.

It was apparent now that the bad rivets had been installed at the splice point on the girder. And Browne and Reville . . . or Shaw could have made sure that happened at the building site, Layton thought. For a great deal of money — or because he was being blackmailed — Beverly could have altered the rivets.

After five years, like Peter, Beverly must have been so guilt-ridden that he was ready to confess. Or he might have had no con-science at all but had approached the murderer for more hush money. Either way, he'd wound up in the footing.

Was it time to approach Scotland Yard? No. Layton shook his head. Despite all his labors, he still had no real proof of the murderer's identity. He himself couldn't figure out which one it was. All had mo-tives. And if he played his cards too early, the police could have him committed to Broadmoor — Britain's lunatic asylum for criminals.

42

"This is magnificent."

Layton and Phipps stood in the rotunda of the almost completed Royal Physicians Hall. Above them soared four stories of balconies, topped by a ribbed dome. Each rib was done in gold leaf gilt; between were murals depicting milestones in medical history. Workmen were busy setting the green-and-white marble floor and staining the oak arches and columns that framed the entry foyer.

What a tremendous feeling, to watch a design on paper transformed into a real building! Layton had almost forgotten the rush. Strange. For almost ten years, he had seen design after design built. Each gave him the confidence to do something better, bolder. How could he have lost sight of that experience?

Beside him, Phipps gazed up at the dome, a pleased expression on his face. Layton didn't fault him; he'd have been proud to design such a place. This was the first of his buildings Phipps had shown him; he realized now how talented his friend really was. To be so young and such an important British architect! From what he'd told Layton, he had built hospitals, men's clubs, a corn exchange, banks, and country estates.

A feeling of sadness came over Layton like a cold draught. He would never design anything again.

"Thank you, Doug," said Phipps, giving a slight bow. "A compliment from you means a lot to me."

"The way you detailed the directors' conference chamber was topping. And that fireplace is stunning."

All architects lapped up compliments like a cat at a saucer of milk. Phipps beamed at Layton and said, "I'm on a run of luck. Not all my buildings are as fancy as this. I'm doing an electric power plant in Manchester right now."

They continued to stroll through the building with Phipps occasionally stopping to give instruction to a worker. Back in the grand entry foyer, he turned to Layton.

"You're right about Beverly," he said. "He probably tampered with the rivets at the cantilever splice, and he wanted more money to keep quiet. So he got the snuff, poor bugger. Buried alive in cement." Phipps gave a tiny shudder of disgust. "Terrible way to go."

"But who murdered him?" Layton said. "I can't make it out."

"The more I go over it, the more I put my money on Clifton and Glenn. To both of them, Rice was the biggest threat. And they had other scores to settle too."

"But then again," Layton countered, "Shaw hated me so much, he wanted to frame me for murder of all those people. He could have easily set up the collapse. His name was in Peter's appointment book too. And Stockton wanted to destroy the chain, to put them out of business. It was his bad luck that most of the top stars didn't show up that night."

"True," Phipps said. "But a man has to be full of hate to do something like that to a rival." He shook his head. "Whoever it is, we need *proof.*"

43

The cheering was almost deafening. As Helen McCoy, now atop the bill at the Queen's Palace, took her bows, every single person in the house was on his or her feet.

Helen scanned the stalls below, then, to everyone's amazement, walked down the little side stairs at the end of the stage, went to a boy in the first row, and gave him a kiss on the cheek. Ronald Layton flushed red like a beet.

"Ronnie," Helen said sweetly, "you come backstage to my dressing room. I have some Cadbury for you."

"Oh yes, Helen! Thank you," Ronald cried.

Nanny Hawkins smiled and put her hand on his shoulder. Some of the nearby audience members looked jealous; others patted him on the back joyfully — he'd been kissed by the Piccadilly Lilly and thus turned into a talisman. Ronald felt very grown-up. To be paid attention by adults! It was a wondrous thing. In his world, children were invisible.

Helen skipped up the stairs and gave another wave before disappearing into the wings. Her dressing room, which she shared with no one, was filled with flowers of every description. So brilliant were the colors that she might have been in the Royal Botanic Gardens in Kew.

Mildred, her former lady's maid from Suttonfield and now personal assistant, helped her out of her feathery white satin gown and carefully removed the tiara from her chestnut-brown hair. Helen had been offered ten pounds for a lock of that hair but had indignantly refused the gentleman.

"Your ladyship, will you be wanting your black gown for tonight's party?"

Helen had given up her efforts to get Mildred to call her by her first name. It wasn't proper, Mildred always said firmly, and she wouldn't do it. Now, to Helen's dismay, other variety hall performers were calling her "your ladyship" too.

"No, I'll have the lavender gown, please, Mildred," Helen said, applying a blob of Pond's Extract to her cheek. As she wiped away her makeup, she asked, "Do you think 'I Would Like to Marry You' came off well tonight, Mildred?"

"It's not my favorite song, but you sang it in a very sweet way, m'lady. I'd perhaps add in another one, though."

Mildred never hesitated to give her frank opinion of her mistress's performances. Helen liked that. A singer needed one person to be honest with them, instead of kissing their bum, like a lot of performers' so-called friends.

" 'Goodbye, Sweetheart, Goodbye'?" she offered, raising an eyebrow.

"Now, that's the ticket, m'lady."

Having finished her toilette, Helen and Mildred made their way down the corridor toward the stage door. Ahead, a familiar female voice was lifted in outrage.

"You bloody shite, if you ever plant applauders in the house again, you'll never set foot on a stage in England, Ireland, Scotland, or anywhere else on God's green earth."

Cissie and the stage manager, Wilding, had Clive St. Clair, the Superb Card Trickster, backed up against the corridor wall.

"I'd never do such a thing," wailed St. Clair.

"Bollocks. No one's cheered that loudly for your act in years. I know a plant when I see one, my boy," said Wilding.

Helen and Mildred exchanged a significant glance. Sometimes, when an act's popularity faded, the performer would pay people to cheer extra loudly — usually a quid, plus admission. Six paid applauders clapping and cheering could lead the rest of the audience to join in.

The trick worked the other way too, Helen knew. Some performers would pay people to heckle competing acts in other theatres to drive them out of business. All the Queen's Palace artistes knew that Bimba Bamba, the magician, had arranged for plants to boo his rival, Voldor, at the Majestic in Islington.

"Remember, mate, you've been warned," growled Cissie. But her expression turned from hateful to happy when she spied Helen. "Hello there, luv. I've wonderful news. We want you to move over to the Metro."

Helen could hardly contain her joy; she beamed enormously at Cissie and squeezed Mildred's hand. The Metropolitan Royal Theatre off Leicester Square, the circuit's flagship theatre, could seat almost four thousand. Playing there was every performer's dream. In less than six months as a professional, she had made it.

And to think, she thought wryly, she owed

it all to Lionel Glenn's wife, who'd forced her husband to attend a society recital, raising money for Boer War veterans. Helen — or Gladys, as she was then known — had volunteered to do a song, and Glenn had almost fallen off his chair when he heard her beautiful soprano voice singing "The Boy I Love Is Up in the Gallery." By dogged persistence, over the course of a year, he'd persuaded her to go onstage.

"Oh, Mrs. Mapes, when do I start?"

"The first of next month, ducks. We'll talk about the details later," said Cissie and turned her attention back to St. Clair, who was still cringing against the wall.

Outside the stage door, as usual, many gentlemen in evening dress were milling about. When they saw Helen, they all started talking at once.

"Miss McCoy, would you do me the honor of supper tonight?"

"Miss McCoy, my carriage is at your disposal."

Laughing sweetly, Helen started to explain about her evening engagement. But she stopped abruptly; beyond the circle of men was a figure, standing in the shadows of the alley: an elegantly dressed woman, with a veil covering her face.

Helen stormed through her ring of admirers, straight toward the figure.

"Mother, what are you doing here?" she gasped.

Without lifting her veil, the woman replied, "Gladys, my dear, please stop this at once and come home to Suttonfield. Your poor father will take you back, I swear it."

Helen lifted the veil and looked into the cornflower-blue eyes she had inherited.

"Mother, I've made my decision. I want a career on the stage. I'm good at what I do, and I'm proud of my talent. I'm not chucking it all for the sake of the family name."

"You must come home," her mother said, clutching desperately at the lapels of her daughter's coat. "Your father rages every minute about the disgrace you've brought upon us. He's gone crazy, I fear."

"He'll recover in time, Mother. There are worse things that can happen," Helen said airily. "It's not like I had a child out of wedlock with a servant."

"Never even think of such a thing," shrieked her mother.

"Mother, you should come one night and hear me sing," Helen said earnestly, pressing her cheek against her mother's. "I would ever so much like that."

A horrified look came over her mother's face. "Your father would kill me dead with his pheasant shotgun if I ever set foot in a place like this."

"It's a theatre, Mother, not a knocking shop."

"The theatre is the Haymarket for Shakespeare with Beerbohm Tree, not people in bowlers and red-check suits singing lewd songs."

Helen smiled but held firm. "I've made up my mind, Mother. We should have tea sometime. For now, I must go."

And with that, the Piccadilly Lily walked down the alley to her carriage, leaving her mother, a forlorn little figure in the circle of dim light thrown off by the light pole.

44

"Mr. Owen?"

Layton cringed. He didn't need to turn to know it was the reporter from the *Daily Mail.* He'd half expected to hear from him after Joe Clayton's photo appeared in the paper, not his, but nothing had come of it.

But he was wrong. A stocky, broad-shouldered figure stood about six feet away, in the dim light of the alley behind the Queen's Palace. Stunned, Layton didn't speak for a few seconds. Then he stuttered out, "Hello, Dad."

His father stepped forward. Layton looked behind him to see if his brother was there too but saw no one else.

"Hello, Doug. I 'ad to come to London on business, an' I thought I'd go to the variety, see them scenes you paint. The one of the Albert Hall behind Mendel, the Blind Pianist, was damn good. Too bad Mendel couldn't see it. He is blind, isn't he?"

"Blind as a bat," Layton said, smiling. "But he's the Paderewski of the music halls."

It was late; the second show had ended, and the artistes and crew were exiting the stage door. Layton extended his hand to his father, and they shook heartily.

"Let's take a walk," he said. "It's a beautiful night. Not much fog."

They walked down Whitcomb Street toward Trafalgar Square. For a few minutes, there was silence. Then Layton's father cleared his throat and said, "I'm glad you got on with yer life, Doug. Yer a good lad. You deserve to be happy."

"Thanks, Dad. I'm trying to work everything out. It's not easy to forget that night. It'll haunt me all my life."

"It was an accident, Doug, an accident. They shouldn't have sent ya to prison for it, shouldn't've ruined your life. You should know, yer brother says hello," Thomas Layton added awkwardly.

Layton chuckled. He knew his brother; he would never send his good wishes. "If it wasn't for Roger," he said, "I wouldn't be here. He set me on my new path in life."

"You shouldn't mind your brother," his father said. "He was always jealous of your success. When you went to prison, he felt you got yer comeuppance for rising above your station."

"Yes, I could tell that night," Layton said. "When I returned home."

"You must be making good wages in the theatre. Hope you're not pissing away that lolly on drink and tarts. A lot of temptations here in London," Thomas Layton said, looking suspiciously about.

"I know I was sozzled most of the time when I came back to Puddletown," Layton said awkwardly. "The drink made me forget all the bad things. But I have control of it now."

"That's the ticket, lad."

They strolled through Trafalgar Square, which was entirely deserted, and on to the Victoria Embankment. As they walked, Layton realized that other than hunting, this was the first time in his life that he'd taken a walk with his father. It was quite pleasurable. Rather than parent and child, they felt almost like friends in a way.

"That scene behind that Irish singer looked a lot like Cannon Field in Dorset."

Layton smiled and looked at his father.

"You're absolutely right. It is Cannon Field. Did you recognize the two big trees?" At his father's nod, he added, "Whenever I do a country scene, I paint something from my memory of those Dorset days: Thorn-combe Wood, Snail Creep, Bulbarrow Hill. I remember them all."

"You and yer brothers knew every square inch of that countryside," said Thomas Layton, a tinge of pride in his gravelly voice.

"It was a wonderful boyhood. When I was in my cell in Mulcaster, I'd try to transport myself back, imagine that I was free to wander through the downs like I used to. I became good at putting my mind in another time and place. I'd do the same with the house I built in Surrey. It was like I was there, walking through the rooms."

They reached the Embankment, stood, and watched the Thames flow silently by. To the right and left, a few people milled about in the distance. At this time of night, it was a place for lonely people and illicit lovers, for embracing in the shadows beyond the thrown glow of the streetlights.

"Roger was right," Layton said abruptly. "I was a bloody shit pretending to be someone I wasn't. To turn my back on family and my roots like that . . . What happened was almost like a punishment for what I did."

Thomas Layton turned to his son and looked him square in the face.

"No, lad," he said quietly. "Ya did nothin'

wrong. You wanted to better yourself. And in this country, that's bloody impossible to do. There's always some bastard putting ya in yer place. You beat all that, became one of the empire's best architects. You'd've gotten a knighthood."

"I was a fake."

"Bollocks." Now his father's voice was fierce. "If you had told them who you really were, the son of a stonemason from a Dorset cottage, they'd've thrown yer arse down the ladder in a heartbeat. I don't blame or hate ya for what ya did. It's what ya have to do in this bloody country. *And ya made it.* With yer talent, ya made it."

Layton had never seen his father so emotional before. But now a fire burned in his eyes, and his body trembled with the force of his words.

"When I articled you to Hicks, I wanted ya to become a success. I'd've been embarrassed of where I come from too, in your shoes." Still facing his son, Thomas Layton placed a hand on his shoulder. "Remember when you invited me to that library opening in Bournemouth? I didn't come because I didn't want to embarrass you. But a few weeks later, I went to that library, and I walked around inside, and I said to meself, 'Blimey, my boy did this!' For a hundred years, people will be using that library. I was proud of you, lad. As proud as I was of Raymond, winning them medals."

Layton bent his head. The love in his father's voice threatened to overwhelm him.

In silence, the two men went back to gazing at the river. After a few minutes, as if by mutual agreement, they turned and walked toward Piccadilly Circus.

At Haymarket, Thomas Layton said, "I'll be off in the mornin', but I'm glad I found ya. Take care of yourself, Doug."

Layton watched the old man walk slowly away. And in spite of himself, he called out, "Dad, can you stay until tomorrow afternoon? I want you to meet my son — your grandson."

45

In the evenings, at work in the scene shop, Layton could hear the sounds of the performances coming from the auditorium behind him. Though the singing was muffled, the melody was distinct, and it brought a smile to his face as he worked.

He was just starting a cloth for Ian O'Toole, Quick-Change Artiste, who portrayed all the characters in *Oliver Twist* from Oliver to Bill Sikes by performing lightning-fast costume changes. He would play Fagin, then dart behind a screen onstage and in five seconds emerge from the other side in a totally different costume and makeup of another character. An amazing act, he even did Nancy.

Cissie had come to keep him company as he worked — and to discuss the murders. They spoke cautiously, in low tones, looking about every once in a while to see if anyone was there who might overhear.

"Maybe, but Phipps is right in saying that Clifton and Glenn's biggest enemy was Rice," Layton said, adding painted detail to the arched mirror of a dressing table.

"But to murder Sunny Samuels too? And they'd have killed Amy, if she and her sister hadn't swapped tickets."

Layton shrugged his shoulders. "Maybe the partners thought they wouldn't show up. The rest of the performers didn't. It could have been plain bad luck, like your Johnnie. Or maybe . . ." He paused, considering. "That was the cost of eliminating Rice. Like you said, stars come and go. In time, even a novelty act like Amy could be replaced. I've only been here a short time, and already I've seen it happen to Bert Quist. You know, the whip-cracker? He doesn't get the applause he used to."

"Well, his drinking has a lot to do with that," said Cissie in a scolding tone. "He snapped off the tip of his assistant's nose."

Layton smiled. Almost all artistes drank. Some could hold their liquor; some could not.

"But I can't get Shaw out of my mind. He's . . ." Layton's brush stopped mid-stroke; he stepped back from the canvas cloth and looked around, confused, as if searching for a buzzing fly. "Do you hear

434

that music?"

Cissie blinked, puzzled. "Why, yes, I . . ."

But before she could finish her sentence, Layton dropped his brush and sprinted from the room. Baffled, Cissie hurried after him and joined Layton in the wings. On-stage, prancing about and clapping his hands, was Jimmy Doyle, the top of the bill.

"I was outside a lunatic asylum one day,
      busy picking up stones
When along came a lunatic and said to me,
      'Good morning, Mr. Jones;
Oh, how much a week do you get for doing
      that?'
'Thirty bob,' I cried."

The audience was singing and stomping their feet in unison. The stamping was thunderous; it practically drowned out the lyrics. Layton could feel the vibration of the stage under his feet.

He watched until the song was over. Doyle took his bow and skipped off stage, brushing Layton's sleeve as he passed.

"That . . . song," Layton said quietly. "I remember where I first heard it — the Britannia's opening night. I was having a drink in the stalls lounge. *Jimmy Doyle was on-stage when the balcony fell.* Top of the bill,

435

next to last act."

"What does that mean?" Cissie asked, drawing closer and plucking at his sleeve.

"The balcony didn't collapse when the audience filled the seats. But whoever planned this knew that there was a chance their weight alone might not be enough to sunder the rivets. So they used resonance."

"Resonance?" Cissie said, blinking.

"A force, rhythmically applied to a structure, in the same period as the structure. That force is said to be in resonance."

"And what the bloody hell does that mean?"

"A period," Layton said patiently, "is the time a structure takes to complete a full back and forth oscillation. If the applied force is steady, lasts long enough, and *matches* the timing of that oscillation, it can collapse the structure — that's resonance. In this case, by stamping their feet during Doyle's song, the audience fell into exact rhythm with the oscillations of the balcony cantilever. *That's what brought the balcony down.*"

"Crikey!" Cissie said, shaking her head. "Aren't you a clever boots!"

"There's an old story about an infantry company of Prussian soldiers goose-stepping across a wooden bridge. Their marching cadence accidentally fell into rhythm with the oscillations of the bridge, which collapsed. The whole company wound up in the river."

Had Browne and Reville thought this up? Layton wondered. Both had the engineering knowledge about resonance.

But there was more to it. For the plan to work, Jimmy Doyle *had* to be on the bill. He'd been booked intentionally. And when the word *book* came to mind, Layton could think of only one person.

He stopped and stared down into Cissie's eyes.

"You booked Doyle for that night, didn't you?" he said in a quiet, calm voice.

"I don't exactly remember," Cissie said. "It was over five years ago, mind. But who else would have?"

Her eyes were clear and open; her voice did not tremble. Was she part of the conspiracy or not? Being in prison taught a man to expect the worst in life, and Layton couldn't control his freewheeling suspicions. Had someone *told* Cissie to book Doyle? Or maybe she'd wanted her husband dead all along.

Ashamed, Layton squeezed his eyes shut, forcing the thought from his mind. He was in love with Cissie, he reminded himself.

Aside from his reunion with Ronald, she was the best thing to happen to him since he'd left Mulcaster. His first real Christmas in five years was less than a month away; the thought of having someone to share it with made him happy, despite all else that had gone wrong, and he was a bastard to think ill of her for even a second.

Cissie looked worried now. He smiled at her and said, "I have to find out how Doyle got on the bill that night. Was it just a coincidence, or did Clifton and Glenn tell you specifically to book him?"

Cissie nodded; she understood. Gently, she caressed his cheek and said, "Come on, luv. Let's go to my office and check the files. You're a lucky man — I never throw anything out."

46

"The year is 1900, *D* for Doyle," Cissie said briskly.

And again, Layton thanked his lucky stars that she was such an efficient business-woman.

With twenty-four theatres putting on twice-nightly shows six days a week, the chain's contract department was huge. Gray metal filing cabinets lined the storage room on all sides. Another row of cabinets, stacked on top of this lower level, was accessible by rolling ladder. Each drawer held artistes' contracts, arranged alphabetically and by year. Cissie scurried up the ladder like a mountain goat and pulled out a folder. The bigger the star, the fatter the folder, and Doyle's was thick.

She flipped quickly through the folder, and her face fell. "No, not here, but . . ." A thought hit her, and she brightened. "Hello, now I remember! Hold on a bit, luv."

Handing Layton Doyle's file, Cissie moved the ladder across the room and climbed back up to retrieve another. She fanned herself with it as she descended.

"Whew, I'll need a nice cup of tea after all this. This is Tommy Towers's contract. He was supposed to top the bill that night."

"The Most Beautiful Man in the World," Layton said, nodding. The name was ironic; performers like Towers sold themselves with catchphrases or physical gimmicks. In Towers's case, he wasn't beautiful but uglier than a dog's arse. His looks — or lack of them — were a constant joke. Such reverse acts did brisk business; May Mason, who called herself the World's Greatest Soprano, was a current sensation. Her gimmick, of course, was that she sang like a screeching baboon.

"He got hurt, and we had to replace him. Look." Cissie handed Layton a yellowing telegram from Towers's file.

FELL ON ME HEAD STOP HARDEST PART OF ME BODY BUT BROKE ME LEG STOP CAN'T GO ON STOP TOMMY

"He even got us that doctor's certificate we ask for. But look at this now." Cissie pulled another telegram from Doyle's file:

HEARD TOWERS OUT STOP DOYLE
AVAILABLE STOP

It was signed by Jack Langham, Doyle's agent.

Layton examined the telegrams, which had been sent from two different London post offices. The posted time of Towers's message was 9:05 a.m. Langham's was 9:45.

"The agent's message was sent only forty minutes after the one Towers sent off," Layton said, tapping the yellowed slips of paper.

Cissie laughed. "Bad news travels fast in the theatre world, Frank. One bloke's misfortune is another's opportunity."

"Y'know, I don't recall I was that plastered, but I still went down hard. Like a bloody football, bouncing off every one of them bleedin' tube station steps. Hard cement, y'know. Was laid up on my arse for a fort-night."

Layton and Cissie sat on either side of Tommy Towers as he put on his makeup. He was playing the Brixton Hippodrome; though he had a dressing room to himself, it was low and dingy. Plaster peeled off the yellowing walls, and the old upholstered chairs were filled with tatty-looking hangers-on.

Such men and women surrounded the variety theatre's biggest stars, stroking egos and kissing arse for the privilege of being near the famous and wealthy. In exchange for their adulation, the star bought them drinks, meals, and gifts of clothes and jewelry. Attractive girls, Layton had noticed, were especially effective at extracting money. The more beautiful the woman and the uglier the man, the more largess flowed. If he'd been a "civilian," the two girls hanging all over Tommy wouldn't have come within a mile of him. But if he knew that, he certainly didn't seem to care.

"I hobbled around on crutches for two months," Tommy was saying. "Looked like Long John Silver."

Drinks were flowing freely, and his followers laughed like hell at this line. A drunken, balding man in a rumpled suit bellowed, "You should have got a green parrot for your shoulder!" and held up a tumbler of gin, as if toasting Tommy's comment.

"But, you know, it helped the act," Tommy said, not minding the interruption. "Gave me a lot of new material. I was a cripple on top of being so 'beautiful.' " He winked.

A beautiful blond in a black, low-cut gown

bent down, kissed his cheek, and gave his pickle nose a playful yank. "You're a 'and-some bloke to me, Tommy darling," she crooned.

A sharp rap sounded on the dressing room door, and a freckled callboy stuck his head through. "Five minutes, Tommy," he said with a big smile.

"Thank you, Phil," Tommy shouted back, mussing his salt-and-pepper hair.

"So you just fell down the steps? No one bumped you?" Cissie said, edging the blond girl out of the way with her hip.

"Come to think of it, there may have been someone behind me. But I'm afeard I can't remember, Cissie me girl." Tommy rose and shrugged on his signature green-striped jacket, which had been hanging on his chair.

"Did you tell Jimmy Doyle's agent you were hurt?" Layton asked. "Jack Langham, his name was."

Tommy gave Layton a look of pure disgust. "Why would I tell that no-talent bastard's agent anything at all?"

"At first, it seemed a wonderful bit of luck when that ugly shit broke his leg," Jack Langham said. He sighed gravely. "But then look what happened."

Langham's office, like that of all London's

theatrical agents, comprised just two spaces: the waiting room, in which desperate would-be artistes sat for hours on hard wooden chairs, hoping to win a meeting; and the agent's office. Cissie and Layton were in the latter, across from Langham, a lanky fellow who'd once played the straight man in a comedy duo. Many agents, Cissie told Layton on their way to the meeting, were former performers who preferred collecting ten percent of their clients' earnings to suffering out the grind of show business. With a roster of big stars, they could make out very well indeed.

"Top of the bill on opening night in a brand-new theatre?" Langham shook his head, remembering. "It's a performer's dream. I was bowled over when you wired me, Cissie."

"But . . . you wired me," Cissie said, puzzled.

Langham blinked back at her, just as confused. "I never sent you a wire, girl. You wired *me.*"

47

"He's a fine, smart boy, Doug."

Ronald was scampering joyfully across Hyde Park, in hot pursuit of a cricket ball. Layton and his father sat on a nearby cast-iron park bench, watching him romp. When he was sure the boy was out of earshot, Thomas Layton turned to his son and smiled.

"Your mother always wished for a grandchild. I'm glad I could meet the lad."

His father's light-gray eyes, Layton realized, were welling with tears. He blinked, shocked anew by these open displays of emotion. But then, how much grief had his father suffered in the past five years? One dead son, another son in prison. To sit now in the crisp London air, watching his grandson play . . . Layton could only imagine the feeling.

For his part, Ronald had been overjoyed at the prospect of meeting his other grandfather. But being the proper little gentleman he was, he hadn't jabbered on about himself; he'd asked Thomas Layton polite questions — what was Dorset like; what had Layton been like as a boy; and other such matters. With each story he told, Thomas Layton's face grew more animated, flushed with color and joy. At the end of the conversation, Ronald had exclaimed, "You're nothing at all like Grandfather Charles!" to Layton's great amusement.

Now that it was turning twilight, the electric lamps in the park flickered on.

"That Cissie is a corker," Thomas Layton said abruptly. "A blind man could see how much she loves ya. She'll make you a damn good wife."

Layton smiled, knowing the joy in his eyes matched his father's. Thomas Layton was the first to know of Cissie and Layton's marriage plans. And just like Ronald, Cissie seemed to breathe new life into the old man.

With the coming of darkness, it was time to bid goodbye to Ronald. They waved and watched the boy spring off confidently into the gloaming. Layton felt a twinging at his heart; he wasn't ready for his father to leave.

"Why don't we have supper before you catch your train?" he suggested.

"Don't have much of an appetite these

days, I'm afraid, but what about a nice cup of tea in Paddington? I have time."

The restaurant was busy, full of commuters having a quick meal before they boarded their trains. Layton and his father found a table by the great window wall, which enclosed the shop and allowed customers to look out on the station concourse. People rushed by — mothers dragging children; businessmen in homburgs going home to the suburbs. Father and son drank their tea in silence amid the cacophony of the restaurant.

"I'm dyin'," Thomas said at last, muttering the words as if he were talking to the tile floor.

"Did you say you'd prefer dining?" Layton said, turning his full attention back to his father.

Thomas lifted his head and looked straight at his son. "I said I'm dying."

Layton's biscuit slipped from his fingers and fell to the floor, breaking in two.

"What? How do you know you're . . . You can't be! You're not dying."

"I'm done for, Doug." He shook his head. If he had seemed impossibly joyful in the park, now he looked unbearably weary. "I'm not in the city for business. I'd seen a doctor in Dorchester. We're friendly-like. Well, he wanted to send me to a specialist in London. Told him I couldn't afford it, but the doc said he'd see me as a courtesy." He hunched forward, stirring his tea, staring down into the depths of the cup. "Both of 'em said the same thing: I'm done for. Cancer eatin' out my innards."

"How long did they give you?" asked Layton, his voice quavering.

"Maybe a few months — or I could keel over dead right here."

"Does Roger know?"

"No, I was waiting to hear from the London doctor. At least Roger can build me a spiffing casket." He forced a laugh and took a long sip of tea.

Across the table, Layton buried his face in his hands. Tears threatened to overcome him; he fought them back.

His father's face fell, and he stretched his arms out toward his son. "Look at me hands, Doug. Look!" Thomas insisted. "I've laid many a brick and piece of stone with these here hands. All first-rate work, and I'm bloody proud of it. I got nothin' to complain of." He could tell his son wasn't convinced, so he pressed onward.

"My boy, I have a son who was the best architect in England, a son who was one of the bravest soldiers in the empire, and a son who's the best woodworker, bar none. And now I know I've the finest grandson a man could wish for. Bloody hell, boy, don't feel sorry for me!"

Layton smiled wanly. Memories of his mother's death swamped him — how robust and healthy she'd been; how completely she'd fallen apart. In just a month, she was gone. His father looked healthy and solid; finishing his tea, he set the cup down with steady hands. How could he face his loss? Layton felt like running out of the teashop, out of Paddington, out of London, and out of England. Of running until he dropped, until he felt no more of the pain that had just ripped through his body like a shotgun blast.

"I have to see a man about a horse," his father said bluntly. "That's how I knew somethin' was wrong, son. I was pissin' blood all the time. When I get back, let's have another cup of tea, what d'you say?"

Layton stared down into his teacup. It was now or never. God had forced his hand.

"There's something I have to tell you," he said in a clear, steady voice.

"Well, be quick about it. I've got to go."

"I didn't kill all those people," Layton said. The words felt strange in his mouth.

"Of course you didn't. It was a bloody accident, Doug, and ya shouldn't have gone to prison for it."

"But it wasn't an accident."

Thomas Layton's expression was one of sheer bewilderment. "But that's daft. No one would do such an evil thing. No one," he said in a hushed voice, making sure no one would overhear.

After perhaps twenty seconds of deafening silence, Thomas nodded and settled back into his chair. "You never lied to me as a boy," he said simply. "So I know you're not lying to me now. Tell me everything, from the beginning."

48

"Oy, here's a whole bob," cried Winnie, holding up the coin as if it were Captain Kidd's treasure box.

Joan, Winnie, and Connie were the charwomen who cleaned the Metropolitan Royal after each night's final performance. The three old women were always on the lookout for any loose coins that might have fallen from the audience members' pockets. The stalls yielded the biggest bounty; the gallery, up in the clouds where the poor bastards sat, the smallest. Management told them to turn in any money they found, but they never did. The crones were paid a pittance and felt their findings were a kind of tip from God.

Jewelry was another matter, of course. If any of the women found a diamond earring or gold chain, they turned it in. If you tried to sell such goods at a pawnshop, they said, the coppers would be down on you faster than shit through a goose.

The best thing about the job was that the women had the place to themselves. As the MacMillan circuit's flagship theatre, the Metropolitan Royal was extra posh, with a beautiful barrel-vaulted plaster ceiling, velvet seats, and all sorts of sculptures. All the lights burned fully, including the grand chandelier, so the charwomen could better see the dirt. For a few hours, the grand theatre was their private palace. They swept under the seats, ran the Bissell carpet cleaner across the carpets, and dusted everything in sight.

And all the while, they had a right good chin-wag. The immense size of the auditorium meant they had to shout a bit, but it was very pleasurable gossip: stories of the performers; who was shagging who; all the events of the day, like that fuss about the war between Russia and Japan; and what Queen Alexandra was wearing. She set the fashion in London, even for women who couldn't afford a handkerchief, let alone a feather boa.

"Bloody hell, my bleedin' knees are killing me," moaned Winnie.

"Did ya rub that oil of cat tongue on 'em, like I told you?" demanded Connie.

Winnie shook her head, working her

broom under a seat in row G.

"So you know my Tommy — can talk the hind legs off a donkey. Well, Fred gets up from the table and raps him on the 'ead with a wooden spoon and tells him to shut his gob! Says he can't stand the sound of his voice no more. And then Tommy throws 'is spotted dick I made him all special like on top of Fred's 'ead," Joan lamented.

"Well, that takes the biscuit," Winnie said, sighing.

"That's terrible, Joanie! You slogged your guts out making that spotted dick." Connie sounded outraged. "Bloody men!"

"I was at the Queen's last week to see Helen McCoy," said Winnie, finishing up row G and moving on to F.

"Oh, she's loverly," Connie said. She was using the Bissell on the stairs, which the girls loved. The new invention made carpet cleaning a thousand times easier.

"And she's an earl's daughter," Winnie said approvingly. "Up on the stage and all. She don't think she's so high-and-mighty, not like most of those toffee-nosed blokes."

"Aye, I wager many a fellow wants to slip her a length," Joan said and chuckled.

"She's a smart one with her career. Won't find herself in the pudding club like most stage tarts." Connie's pride was such that

Helen might have been her own daughter.

"Did you see them cute little Africans?" Winnie shouted, rustling around under a seat. "They're bloody amazing, straight out of the jungle."

"My little Eddie's seen 'em four times," said Joan.

The three women worked quickly and efficiently, moving forward toward the orchestra pit. Connie was at row A now, the very first row of the stalls. Above were the boxes, the most prestigious seats in the house. The ones in the Metro were even fancier than most: bow-fronted boxes with intricate plaster detailing, framed by colossal columns that carried a semicircular arch. Within it, two pedestals held freestanding, full-scale sculptures. A painted landscape in a lunette hung between them. The seats were real chairs rather than fixed seating.

Connie's eyes drifted up to the box at the right of the stage and froze.

There, in one of the chairs toward the rear of the box, a man in evening dress stared out onto the empty stage.

"Take a look at that, will ya," Connie hissed, gesturing wildly at the box.

"Hush your yowling. It's none of our affair. If some rich old fool wants to hang about, let 'im."

454

"We'll be for it if we bother him," Joan said and went back to her cleaning.

They continued their work, gabbing away, and moved up to do the second level. Winnie always did the boxes stage left. She pulled the curtain of the first box aside and saw that the toff was still sitting there.

"Excuse me, guv. I just have to clean around ya, and then I'll be outta yer way, sir," she said with forced cheer.

The man did not move.

Winnie sighed and gamely swept under his chair — and noticed something red and sticky on the end of her broomstick. A chill raced down Winnie's spine. Her scream brought the others running as fast as their decrepit legs could carry them.

"Crikey, that's Mr. Glenn," Joan yelled. "One of the owners!"

Up close, they could see that Glenn was slumped in the chair, his dark-gray eyes wide and staring. The enormous puddle of blood beneath him seeped slowly across the ground. While the two other charwomen cringed at the rear of the box, Joan circled the man and peered at the back of his neck. Blood dribbled from a tiny hole at the base of his skull.

" 'e's snuffed it!" screamed Winnie.

The force of her scream seemed to nudge

the body; it keeled over onto the floor, prompting more screams, till the theatre rang with terror.

49

"The coroner says an ice pick severed the spinal cord between the base of the skull and the first vertebrae," Layton read.

Cissie, Phipps, and his father — Thomas Layton had extended his trip upon hearing the full story of the Britannia disaster from his son — had gathered in Layton's digs.

"Glenn *wasn't* in on the balcony collapse and found out," Phipps announced incredulously. "And Clifton did him in."

"So Clifton's our murderer," exclaimed Cissie with glee.

Layton shook his head. He didn't know what to think. Up until now, he'd come to believe that Shaw orchestrated the accident. Did he murder Glenn because he was an owner?

"This has gone far enough. You must go to Scotland Yard, Doug," his father pleaded. "Now!" Amid the force of his emotion, he began coughing violently.

"There's handkerchiefs in the top dresser drawer, Dad," Layton said gently.

His father's face flushed with embarrassment; he shuffled to the dresser, rummaged through it, and pulled out a cloth to wipe the thin trace of blood from his lips. Cissie smiled at him sympathetically and poured him another cup of tea.

"He's right, Doug," Phipps said gently. "It's time to go to the police. You must tell them about the two skeletons — and everything else we've discovered."

The first man to start laughing was the fat, bald one in the corner.

"He's a right Charlie, eh?" he chortled.

"Aye, this bloke's not batting on a full wicket," said another, who was standing by the window.

Inspector Jenkins had his head bent and was smiling down at the blotter paper on his desk. Layton could tell he agreed with his officers. In what was definitely a gesture of impatience, he tapped the end of his fountain pen on his desk and said briskly, "Mr. Layton, your story is preposterous. Of course, given the horrible outcome of the Britannia disaster, it is natural you would seek to place the blame elsewhere."

"But he's telling you the truth, man,"

Thomas Layton entreated.

"And I can understand," Inspector Jenkins said, looking sympathetically at the old man, "why, as his father, you would want to believe him. But your son was convicted of manslaughter by a jury. They heard the evidence."

"Not *this* evidence," Phipps cried, rising from his chair in front of the inspector's desk.

Jenkins frowned; Phipps saw his expression of disapproval and resumed his seat.

Layton, sitting between his father and Phipps, just looked down at the dark-stained wood floor. Jenkins clearly felt this was all a colossal waste of time. His tone reminded Layton of a teacher trying to reason with a dimwitted pupil.

"You have no solid proof that the owners of the circuit, Sir Clifton and the late Mr. Glenn, conspired to murder Hugh Rice so as to eliminate their debt to him. Nor do you have proof that they murdered all these other persons at the same time." The inspector shook his head, scoffing. "A vicar, a servant girl . . . It's absurd."

"Don't forget Alec Shaw, the builder of the Britannia," added Thomas Layton, who realized by saying that he'd made a bigger fool of himself.

The fat man smirked at the officer by the window, and both started chuckling.

"And you've not one shred of evidence that Alec Shaw is responsible," shot back Jenkins.

"So many killers to choose from, mate. *Which* one is it?" asked the fat policeman, grinning from ear to ear.

"*You're* responsible for the deaths and injuries of all those people, Mr. Layton," Jenkins said with careful emphasis. "I know you didn't mean to do it, but you must bear the responsibility, no matter how heavy the burden."

"Aye, I'd've killed myself by now," said the officer by the window.

"That's enough, Sergeant," snapped Jenkins, darting his eyes at Layton's father.

"You have to look into this," Phipps said, forcing his voice to be calm and level.

"Please," said Thomas Layton in an almost pleading tone.

Seeing the agony in the old man's eyes, Jenkins held his temper. "I'm sorry, sir. But I've still no ironclad proof to take to the Crown."

"Sir Edgar Montague, the head of Scotland Yard, would think us bloomin' loonies for even suggesting such a thing," said the fat policeman.

"I know it all seems total fantasy to you," Layton said wearily. He trailed off, seeing the blank, hard faces before him.

"Or perhaps *you* murdered Glenn, Layton, to get back at him for this frame-up," said the fat man thoughtfully.

"What about the skeletons?" Phipps said.

"I'll not be wasting my time busting through any walls or ceilings," snapped the inspector. When Phipps tried to protest, he held up a hand, signaling that the meeting was at an end.

Thoroughly defeated, Layton, his father, and Phipps left the New Scotland Yard building in silence and walked to the Thames to watch the river traffic flowing by. Barges, tugs, and high-masted cargo vessels churned past in a steady stream. It was cold, and a fog was settling in.

Layton heaved a great sigh and leaned against the wall, looking back at the police headquarters building — its great corner turrets, the red brickwork with white stone stripes that swept around the building. Odd, he thought. Even in his worst moments, an architect's first instinct is to examine any building that catches his interest.

He turned to his father. "Well, Dad, I made a dog's breakfast out of that. The police thought me mad as a hatter. They'll likely start watching me now."

"No, Doug. It's just that it's such a bloody incredible crime. No one can believe it," Thomas Layton said. He sounded exhausted and deeply worn.

"We can't give up."

Phipps put his arm around Thomas's shoulders. "We're *not* going to give up."

Layton smiled appreciatively at his colleague.

"I must go to Bristol for a few days, to see about the new city hall. But when I get back, I can help, Doug," Phipps said.

"Of course. But please, Tom," Layton cautioned. "Don't let the hash I'm in interfere with your practice. You've been jolly good about everything."

Phipps smiled and nodded, then took his leave, walking briskly east along the Embankment.

Thomas Layton stared out at the Thames, watching the gray waters lap and roll. He shook his head and said, "Suppose we never get the evidence, Doug? Those shits will get off scot-free. I can't bear that. They deserve to die for what they've done to ya."

"Don't worry, Dad," Layton said. He sighed. "After all I've been through, I have to believe that justice will win out in the end. Though at the moment, I can't think how."

Inspector Jenkins stood at his window, watching the three men leave. "Poor bugger," he said and turned to face his two men, Willoughby and Perkins. "It's amazing what people will say to escape their guilt."

The two detectives nodded their heads and smiled at their boss.

"So, lads, let's deal with our latest muddle."

Even in the hall outside the interrogation room, they could hear the loud carrying-on inside. The minute Jenkins turned the brass doorknob, the shouting halted.

Two gentlemen in morning dress sat on one side of the long oak table.

"Good morning, my lord. Good morning, Sir Edmond," said Jenkins.

The Earl of Suttonfield rose from his seat, his fists clenched.

"This is an outrage, sir! I am the Earl of Suttonfield."

"Please, my lord, sit down and let me deal with this," Sir Edmond Stevens, his barrister, whispered.

Reluctantly, the earl sat. Jenkins took a seat across from him and folded his hands carefully on the table.

"You didn't happen to be at the Metropolitan Royal Theatre the night before last, my lord?"

"I'd never set foot in such a place," the earl blustered.

"But you did go to the Queen's Palace of Varieties, where you shouted at your daughter to come down off the stage."

The earl sat back and crossed his arms over his chest. "That was a family matter," he said huffily. "None of your affair."

"And it was Lionel Glenn who persuaded your daughter to go on the stage?"

There was a brief silence, and then Stevens leapt into action. "Inspector, are you insinuating that my client had something to do with this murder? That's absurd."

"You bore Glenn a grudge for luring your daughter into the variety hall. He gave her the opportunity, made her a great star."

The earl maintained his stony silence, but at his side, Stevens rose from his chair. "The earl was nowhere near the Metropolitan that night. We're finished here, Inspector," he announced.

"Is the earl's household in the city or the country missing an ice pick?"

Another deafening silence.

"Very well. Thank you for your time, gentlemen," Jenkins said. The two men made for the door; just as they had reached it, he said quietly, "My lord? Are you missing a cuff stud?"

He held up a square stud — a tiny diamond edged by a silver Greek key motif.

"My men found this in the hallway, outside Glenn's box."

"No, Inspector, I am not," huffed the earl.

With that, they left, and Jenkins sat on the edge of the table with a sigh.

"What's our next move, Inspector?" asked Perkins, the fat police officer.

"There is no next move. The Earl of Suttonfield murdered Lionel Glenn because he convinced Lady Gladys to go on the stage. I'm absolutely sure of it. But this is the end of the road, lads."

At his men's baffled glances, Jenkins explained, "First, there's no real evidence other than this cuff stud. And if the Crown did charge the earl with murder, an earl can be tried only by a jury of his peers — those in the House of Lords. And they'd acquit him even if he were guilty; I've no doubt of that. The toffs would agree that Glenn *deserved to be murdered* for putting his daughter in the music hall and bringing disgrace on the family."

50

Layton sat in the high-backed, upholstered chair before the coal fire in his little sitting room. Battered by his experience at Scotland Yard, he decided to start fresh, reconstructing the crime, making sure there was nothing he'd overlooked.

In his days as an architect, he'd examined a set of drawings a dozen times to ensure they contained no errors. And he would always discover a mistake that had been staring him straight in the face all along.

He pulled out his list of the dead and, with his fountain pen, drew lines that linked all the victims to their possible murderers, whom he listed on the right-hand side of the paper.

Denys Blair, 78 _____	Glenn
Ronald Cass, 52	
James Croyden, 37 _____	Stockton
Robert Davidson, 12	
Shirley Finney, 19 _____	Clifton
Daphne Foster, 46	
Ted Hardy, 44 _____	Clifton
John Mapes, 41	
Isabel Massey, 14	
Hugh Rice, 53 _____	Clifton and Glenn
Sir John Richardson, 54	
Jocelyn Shipway, 31 _____	Stockton
Trevor Stanton, 42	
Sibyl Treadwell, 36	

A line connected Shirley Finney and Ted Hardy to Clifton; Denys Blair to Glenn; Hugh Rice to both Clifton and Glenn. Sunny Samuels and Amy's sister were joined to Nigel Stockton with a line. Then there were the people like John Mapes, the two children, and five unconnected adults who were seemingly in the wrong place at the wrong time. No one on the list was linked to Alec Shaw. Only Layton was connected to him. He knew he had to look elsewhere to find some proof of Shaw's guilt. The builder, he now believed, was the murderer.

Layton stared into the glowing fire. But before going in that direction, was he absolutely sure there were no connections to the other adults? Had he missed anything? He went back to the other names — Ronnie Cass, Daphne Foster, Sir John Richardson, Sybil Treadwell, and Trevor Stanton — deciding to check one last time for some kind of link.

Layton's hand stopped in midair as he reached his hand into Cissie's crate of newspaper clippings next to the chair. He didn't want to see the lurid headlines, hysterical articles, and gruesome photos of the disaster again. They would bring back the memories that ate painfully through him.

The article with background information on the victims was on top; wincing, he snatched it up. He picked a name at random. Under "Trevor Stanton" was just one sentence: "Mr. Stanton was a barrister associated with the Inns of Court and the son of the late Gerald Stanton of Devonshire Shipping Ltd. and Mary Weems Stanton, Bolton Street, Mayfair."

Finding Mrs. Stanton's address in the London phone directory took an instant. While looking at his father peacefully asleep in his bed, Layton tiptoed to the closet and changed into a suit and bowler. He threaded his way through the streets to Mayfair. It was late morning; the winter fog wasn't as thick as usual, and the sun was struggling to break through.

At the handsome stone house, he stood at the foot of the stoop for a few seconds, then took a deep breath and banged the brass door knocker. A housemaid barely out of her teens answered the door with a bright smile. Even though he had no appointment, he knew his dress and manner would compel her to grant him entry.

"Mr. Donald Hampton, Esquire, to see Mrs. Stanton, please."

Without hesitation, the maid ushered him into the morning room and went to announce his arrival. Less than five minutes later, Mrs. Stanton, a well-groomed matron in her seventies, entered and offered a long, thin-fingered hand in greeting.

"How can I can I help you, Mr. Hampton?" she said in a kind, quiet voice.

"I'm just back from South Africa," Layton said, bowing his head. "And one of my very first tasks in London was to come offer condolences for your son."

"How kind of you, Mr. Hampton. You knew my son from the legal world, I presume?"

"Yes," Layton said. By this time, the lies

came almost without thought. "From the time I practiced at Lincoln's Inn Fields. We weren't close friends, more professional colleagues. He was a brilliant legal mind, Mrs. Stanton."

"Trevor loved the law." Mrs. Stanton shook her head, and he saw a shadow of sorrow pass across her features. "His father wanted him to enter into the family shipping business, of course. But Trevor always knew his own mind." She gestured Layton to sit and perched on a chair across from him. "Losing him like that . . . It was quite a shock, as you can imagine. I'm glad his father wasn't alive to experience it."

"It's terrible to lose a child," Layton said quietly.

"Time has lessened the pain, but you know, Mr. Hampton, sometimes I still cry myself to sleep when I think of the loss." She gave Layton a wan smile. "I remember when I first saw him stand in court in his wig and robes. We were all so proud."

They chatted for a time, but the sinking feeling in Layton's gut told him their conversation would lead nowhere. Harsh regret filled him; he should not have come and made the old woman feel so sad. It was like what he'd done to Ted Hardy's mother.

"Thank you for your time, Mrs. Stanton.

You've been most gracious."

When Layton stood to take his leave, Mrs. Stanton rang for the maid to let him out. He stood in silence by a mahogany writing desk whose top was strewn with greeting cards and open envelopes. She must have just celebrated her birthday. About a minute later, the maid appeared.

"Vivian, please show Mr. Hampton out."

Mrs. Stanton walked into the entry hall alongside him. Layton paused before a huge painting opposite the grand staircase.

"How beautiful," he said reverently.

"It's by John Singer Sargent. A group portrait of the men in our family. Trevor, my late husband, his brother, and the nephews. Done almost twenty years ago now."

Several well-dressed males of all different ages had been painted sitting on a sofa or standing behind it; they were posed in the same room where Layton had just been received.

"Magnificent," he repeated. "Look at the shadows on the sides of their faces — he's perfectly captured the natural light from the windows. And the fluid brushwork."

Sargent was one of Layton's favorite painters. Edwina had favored him too, had even hoped to commission a portrait of their

471

family, but nothing had come of it. Probably because Sargent was an American, Layton thought, and Lord Litton would have no one but a bred-to-the-bone Englishman.

As he walked back to his digs, the wonderful painting refused to leave his mind. Perhaps it was all the cloths he'd done, Layton thought absently, that made him admire Sargent's artistry even more. Then a confused look came over his face.

51

Readying for his evening's work was an agony. It was five in the afternoon; Layton had to be leaving. Normally, this was his favorite time of day; he looked forward going to the theatre, but now . . .

At the moment, Thomas Layton was sleeping soundly. Still agitated by their reception at Scotland Yard, his father had had a bad night, coughing up blood and wheezing like a bellows. Only Bayer Heroin, the cough suppressant Layton had fetched from the chemist, had stopped his spasms and enabled him to rest. Layton nodded at the little bottle of German-made medicine on the dresser; he'd have to get more for his father to take back to Dorset. Layton stood by the bed, looking down at his father. An overwhelming sense of sadness and dread threatened to overwhelm him, like a freezing-cold ocean wave knocking one down into the surf.

But he had to go. He'd told Cissie he was working late, that he had to finish two cloths for next week and would see her at breakfast at their digs. She had started house hunting for them and had a place in Kensington she wanted to show him.

With a heavy heart, he adjusted the blanket over his father's shoulders and left.

It was going on three in the morning, and Layton was working on a cloth for Cliff & Kean, Comedy Artistes. He'd painted two huge caricatures of their heads, floating in a blue sky; the sun behind them had a smiling face, as though it were laughing at their jokes. It seemed silly to Layton, but that's what the artistes wanted, and he never argued with specific wishes for a cloth.

He laid in the black outlines of the sun's face and began infilling them with bright yellow. He began dabbing some orange over small areas of the yellow to avoid a flat impression.

"I heard you paid a visit to my aunt," a jolly voice called out behind him. "A very grand lady, isn't she?"

The voice didn't startle him. He'd been expecting it tonight. Layton put the paintbrush down on the cart and turned. "I know you did it," he answered. Though he was scared to death, his voice carried clear and strong, with nary a waver.

"I knew you did the minute I heard my aunt had a visitor who said he knew my late cousin," Tom Phipps said. He was leaning casually against the door of the scene shop, hands thrust in his pockets.

"That was a wonderful portrait Sargent did of your family," Layton said. "I envy you, old boy. You haven't changed much in all these years."

"Yes," Phipps drawled. "I've been blessed with a youthful countenance. But your brain . . ." He gave a low whistle. "Puts mine to shame. You're a clever dick, indeed. Once you found those bodies, it wasn't long before you had the whole tangle figured out." He paused, then added, "Except exactly who did it, of course."

"You didn't just happen to be at that tailor shop, did you?"

Phipps smirked. "No, old man. I use Henry Poole."

Layton gave a knowing nod; Poole was the finest tailor in London.

"I had been in Nottingham on business and decided to check on my handiwork in the wall of the Grand gallery. You're a damn fine plasterer, I must say. When I met your father and discovered your working-class roots, I realized who taught you the craft so well. My skills in that field weren't as nearly good as yours, though I admit I was in a bit of a hurry. But your plasterwork was just the teeniest bit darker and hadn't completely hardened. Only an architect would pick that up, of course, just like you picked up on the bulge in the wall. I didn't bother to check on Browne's body at the Queen's. I knew the jig was up, so right then and there, I began following you."

"Why didn't you kill me and stick me in a wall?" he asked.

"Had to find out who you'd told your theory to first. Had you gone straight to Scotland Yard? I couldn't take the risk."

"You saw how they received my theory. They thought I was balmy."

"Yes, our police force is none too intelligent and hardly fond of creative thinking." Phipps was still smiling. He'd been smiling all the time they'd been talking, and that fixed grin sent a shudder down Layton's spine. "But it could have been worse for you, old boy. If you'd persuaded them to go to the cupola of the Queen's, well . . . I took the precaution of removing poor Browne's bones."

Layton chuckled. "I really would have

looked like a horse's arse, and a mad one at that."

Phipps took a cigarette out of a gold case, sparked up, and exhaled a thin stream of smoke. "But do you know *why* I did it, Doug?"

"To kill your cousin Trevor," Layton said simply. "To get his inheritance, the shipping company fortune. I bet you provided him the ticket."

"Oh, that's only part of it," Phipps said. He'd begun to walk steadily toward Layton, but the other man held his ground. "But more than that, I wanted to destroy *you*, old chap."

Layton's brow furrowed — and then he began to laugh. "That's bloody absurd!"

"You're a damn good architect, Doug, but I'm a far better one. Remember when you won the competition for the Royal Post Office? Back in '99?"

"Yes," said Layton. The puzzled look on his face was genuine now. Phipps's whole murderous scheme had been aimed at him?

"My design was far superior to yours. I saw both, and I know. But because of your wife's family influence, you got the commission. Lord Litton's close friend, Sir Herbert Pryor, ran the Royal Mail, and he steered the work your way. I'd lost two buildings to you before: the Corn Exchange and the Colonial Affairs Office. Both prestigious, both projects you got that I should have won. I just couldn't stand by and let it keep happening." Phipps's lip twisted in disgust. "I needed that building — I *wanted* that building."

"You're having me on. I don't believe a word of it," Layton said incredulously.

"You should," Phipps shot back. "You stood in my way, Doug. The construction of the post office was postponed for over a year because Parliament wouldn't appropriate the funds. In that time, I resolved to ruin you."

"And you certainly succeeded," Layton breathed.

"When you were sent away, the government awarded the post office project to the second-place finisher: me. They weren't going to use a murderer's design. And that commission was the catalyst. My career skyrocketed."

"You give 'ambition' a completely new definition, old boy," Layton said, inching closer to the paint cart, where he had hidden a knife. All those afternoons they'd spent together, trying to unravel the mystery . . . and all the time, it had been a ruse. His head spun; he fought to stay calm.

"To be ambitious, one has to be a bit unscrupulous."

Layton laughed. "And you've given the word 'unscrupulous' a whole new meaning."

"*I'm* England's best architect," said Phipps with quiet pride. "Better than Lutyens even."

Layton crossed his arms against his chest and smiled. "You might be, but you're also an incredibly evil man and mad as a hatter to boot," he said. "But as an architect, I really am impressed by your ingenuity. It wasn't just the inferior rivets, but the way you brought the balcony down with Doyle's song. You have a keen sense of engineering for an architect."

"That was a last-minute decision." Though they were discussing murder, not architecture, Phipps still seemed to bask in Layton's praise. "I was afraid the loaded balcony wouldn't give, so I put Tommy Towers out of action and substituted Doyle."

"Brilliant," Layton said, shaking his head.

"But you're absolutely right on one count: I killed Trevor to get my inheritance too. An architect makes a healthy wage, but he doesn't become rich. You of all people should know that. If all those people were to die, why not add another to the list, put some money in my pocket?" Phipps shrugged and added casually, "Besides, I never liked him. Such a pompous ass. But then, I suppose all barristers are."

"As the male cousin, you were next in line for the inheritance."

"That's the way of English inheritance law, thank God," replied Phipps with a big grin.

"Well," Layton said, staring at his former friend, "you achieved everything you wanted. You destroyed my life and career and won yourself riches and professional success."

"As you know all too well, being an architect means getting bossed about by the rich. Now I have a hundred thousand quid in the bank. It's a wonderful feeling to be on an equal footing."

"Now *you're* getting ideas above your station."

Phipps laughed. "That's interesting coming from you, a Dorset country lad a thousand miles above his station."

"Yes," Layton said baldly. "I was a fraud. I admit it. But I never killed to move up the ladder."

"Some marry to move up," Phipps said with a silky shrug. "Some kill."

"So Clifton, Glenn, Shaw, and Stockton had nothing to do with this," Layton said.

"Not a thing, old boy. Pure coincidence about those others, I'm afraid. But let's be fair: some of those chaps had it coming, like Rice and that poof, Hardy. World's a better place without them."

Layton smiled at Phipps. "You know, Tom, I'm a bit of a graphologist. Interested in handwriting analysis. You have one of the most distinguished architectural lettering styles I've ever seen in my whole career. So much so that I matched those *S*s in the fake appointment book you planted in Peter's desk with the one on the envelope of the greeting card you'd sent your aunt, Mrs. Stanton," said Layton. "Along with the painting, that sealed your guilt."

"An architect's sharp eye," replied Phipps with genuine admiration.

With tiny, barely noticeable steps, Layton had reached the paint cart. Idly, he picked up a jar of paint and turned it back and forth in his hands.

"You had some nerve," Layton said coolly. "Hiding the bodies in plain sight, so to speak."

"Oh, not really. Construction sites are most convenient places to hide bodies, if you have the architectural know-how. You could have done the same thing."

"I suppose Beverly tried to blackmail you

about the rivets?" Layton cocked an eyebrow.

"He did indeed, so that blackguard needed to be taught a lesson," Phipps said airily. "I was a bit careless about his final resting place."

"*You* made it look like Browne's wife hanged herself," Layton said.

"I regretted that, but she might have been a problem. I couldn't take the risk. Peter, you see, wasn't actually in on the collapse, but he suspected Reville. After the accident, he began asking lots of questions about the structural design . . . Most inconvenient. I pretended to be a prospective client to lure him to the West End, where they were finishing up the Queen's. I didn't want to kill the poor thing when I snuffed Peter, so I let her live. Then you started poking around, and I had no choice. What if his wife had known something? Put yourself in my position, old man."

"I can't," Layton said flatly. Alice's pretty, innocent face flashed before his eyes — shadowed by the horrible, swollen face of her corpse. "I can't imagine doing that."

Phipps just shrugged his shoulders. "In a way, you're responsible for the poor woman's death."

Layton set down the jar of paint.

"You know the really unfair thing about this whole affair?" Phipps was pacing back and forth now like Sherlock Holmes, just as he'd done in Layton's digs, only he'd turned out to be the evil Moriarty. "I most enjoyed your friendship, Doug. You're witty, charming, and you've a ripping sense of humor. I still burst out laughing whenever I recall some of your jokes, especially the one about the whore and the Irishman. We had many a good architectural talk too. 'Tis the God's own truth: I'm going to be very sorry for having to kill you."

"And I wager tuppence to a pound," said Layton, keeping his hand on the cart, "that after you kill me, you're going to kill Cissie too."

"Of course, of course." Phipps waved his hand casually. "She knows too much — and she's hardly one to keep quiet. When you both disappear, people will assume you've eloped. Very romantic indeed. I plan to send the theatre postcards from Blackpool, where you'll be honeymooning, as the Americans say."

With the utmost care, Layton placed his hand on the knife on the cart. The jars of paint in front of it blocked Phipps's view of it. He stared into Phipps's face and thought how fascinating it was that such incredible evil could reside in the handsome exterior of such a truly talented man.

"And to prove I'm not a total shit, I won't kill your father. He's a topping fellow, plus he probably has just a few weeks to live."

Layton blinked at this last remark, and in the next instant, there was a revolver in Phipps's hand. This late at night, no one would hear the shot. Layton picked up the knife from the cart. He wasn't scared in the least, he realized. In fact, a surge of energy had shot through his body, electrifying his limbs.

Phipps smiled, began to raise his gun — and froze suddenly, in mid-motion. His eyes bulged; his face drained of color; his mouth gaped.

Layton's gaze moved down the man's face to his throat and the protruding, blackish-looking shape where Phipps's Adam's apple should be. Blood trickled down his neck. With the gun still clenched in his hand, Tom Phipps fell face forward onto the floor, landing with a dull thump. Extending from the back of his neck was a familiar long, brown-colored stick.

Layton heard the clomp of footsteps and looked up to see Mangogo, in his greatcoat and hobnail winter boots. Instead of his usual toothy smile, the Pygmy was frowning. He grabbed hold of the spear lodged in Phipps's neck and yanked it out, muttering, "Bloody rotter."

52

"You may kiss the bride."

Layton leaned forward and kissed Cissie gently. As his lips touched hers, cheers and applause filled the Queen's Palace auditorium.

The newlyweds and the vicar stood in the aisle in front of the stalls, which were filled with close friends and relatives. Helen McCoy was the maid of honor; Mangogo, the best man; Ronald Layton, the ring bearer; and Cyril and Neville, in matching frocks, were the bridesmaids, flanking Cissie and Layton. Sir John Clifton — who, in the end, owed Layton a great deal — had given the bride away.

Cissie had insisted on a Christmas wedding at the Queen's Palace. "Everybody gets married in a church or registry office," she'd told Layton fiercely. "No one gets married in a palace like this. Let's do it up right, luv."

Now, with his arm around Cissie's waist, Layton raised his hand and called out, "Please, join us at our new home for a Christmas Day celebration."

"On your bikes, you Champagne Charlies," Cissie cried to resounding cheers.

The house orchestra in the pit struck up a wedding march. Layton's father, still healthy enough to attend; his brother; Cissie's mother, who'd worried her daughter would never marry again, and sister, Daisy; Nanny Hawkins, Reggie Ash, Daniel Harker, Wilding the stage manager, Tommy Donovan, Luigi, and the MacMillan circuit's many other artistes applauded the couple as they raced up the center aisle. When they reached the grand entry foyer, Simon Blaine, the stage doorman, greeted them and flung open the double doors.

How much had changed in a year since he walked into the Grand back in Nottingham! Layton thought, almost overwhelmed with joy. He remembered how terrified he'd been — to be back in a music hall, to be recognized as the Butcher of the West End. After five years in prison, he'd thought his life was over. All that seemed to await him was a bottle.

But from the instant he'd stepped foot into this fascinating make-believe world, his life had been transformed. Reuniting with his son, finding a wife, discovering an old friend, making the oddest of new friends, and — most importantly — clearing his name. The impossible had happened. He'd gotten his life back. He was Douglas Layton again, and he was happy.

At the curb, a shiny, forest-green Oldsmobile awaited. Before Layton and Cissie boarded the motor, the wedding party posed for photos in front of the theatre's ornate wood-and-glass doors. Then, per London custom, bystanders on the street cheered as the newlyweds drove off.

The Christmas tree in the bay window of the new house in Kensington looked splendid. Instead of real candles, the new miniature electric lights were fastened to its branches, along with wooden angels and a very jolly ornament of Father Christmas to top it off. In the fireplace, the traditional Yule log burned merrily. People stood about the large parlor, drinking glasses of champagne, brandy, eggnog, rum, and stout, talking and laughing. His brother, Roger, was having a chat with Cyril and Neville. Mangogo, in a formal cutaway jacket, was laughing with Reggie Ash. And Ronnie was darting around, showing everyone his new cricket bat.

Because the wedding ceremony had taken place on Christmas morning, Layton's family had opened their gifts the night before. Seeing his son tear open his gifts again — it was a wonderful feeling. And Cissie's joy had almost equaled the boy's when she opened Layton's gift: a real ostrich feather boa. She'd actually shrieked with delight.

Layton had bought her a matching hat adorned with pure-white ostrich feathers; she'd put on both and preened about the parlor for her mother and sister, saying she felt like a real society lady — all fur coat and no knickers.

For his part, Cissie had surprised him with a real Pathé cinematograph projector, along with a dozen reels of film. When it came to Christmas gifts, Layton realized, if someone truly loved you, they listened carefully in the months before the holiday to find out what one really coveted. How different from the Christmases of his old life!

While the guests had their drinks, Cissie, dressed in a dark-blue gown with scarlet trim, circulated, showing off her new wedding ring.

Smiling brightly, Layton approached Nanny Hawkins. He gave her a warm hug and said, "Nanny, thank you so much for convincing Lady Edwina to allow Ronnie to come."

"Oh, Mr. Layton, you won't believe it! Lady Edwina finally stood up to Lord Litton and said Ronnie could see his father *anytime.* I'm so proud of her, I am. And what could His Lordship say? When it turned out you weren't responsible for that awful accident, he hadn't a leg to stand on." Nanny gave Layton a mischievous smile. "But you know, Lady Edwina would have let the boy see you even if your name *hadn't* been cleared. She knows a boy needs a father."

It was worth it, Layton thought jubilantly. Clearing his name had been difficult, convincing Inspector Jenkins and Scotland Yard to believe his fantastic story about Phipps wanting to destroy a rival architect. But after exhuming Reville's body from the Grand, finding a fingertip bone of Browne's that Phipps had overlooked, explaining what had happened to Beverly, the rivet fabricator, and Alice Browne, and revealing the truth about Trevor Stanton's inheritance, Jenkins and Sir Edgar Montague had slowly come around.

In the end, it was Phipps's attempt on Layton's life that night at the Queen's that sealed matters. For there was a witness:

Mangogo. Between his still imperfect English and Professor Evans, who translated the harder descriptive phrases, the police got the whole story. At first, Scotland Yard tried to dismiss him entirely as an ignorant savage, but the Pygmy was a British subject — and a huge West End variety hall star. His evidence had to be admitted. At last, after enormous public pressure and Scotland Yard's recommendation, the Crown's prosecutor, Sir John Chichester, grudgingly announced that Layton had been exonerated and would be granted an official pardon.

In a matter of days, the true story of the Britannia disaster was a sensation all over the empire, and Mangogo became a national hero. He had saved the life of his dear English friend and restored his good name. Crowds descended upon the Queen's Palace in a virtual avalanche to see Professor Evans & His Pygmies. When Mangogo came onstage, the audience went wild and wouldn't stop cheering. Cissie, forever beholden to the African for saving Layton's life, was also delighted at the big business he brought in and moved him to the larger Metro theatre for an unprecedented twenty-minute turn. There was even talk of a tour in the United States and Canada.

The *Daily Mail,* which had once branded Layton the Butcher of the West End, now praised his courage and perseverance (though they never printed an apology). Layton had shown a true Englishman's backbone in standing up to the shame and cruelty of his unjust incarceration in Mulcaster. The public admired him, and while they had first demanded he be hanged, they now pestered the Crown to award him damages for wrongful imprisonment. The *Telegraph* insisted that Layton be given a royal commission as restitution. The press demanded that the Royal Institute of British Architects reinstate him, which they did, issuing a formal apology and damning Phipps as a monster despite his talent. When it was revealed that Layton was the one who had actually discovered the fire inside the wall of the Queen's, the public admiration increased tenfold.

Soon, Layton began receiving offers of commissions again. Society friends who had deserted him reappeared, as though nothing had ever happened. Dinner invitations, the truest sign of British social acceptance, began to pour in. Former architect colleagues, such as Derrick Phelps-Jones and Sidney Montfort, greeted Layton in the street as if he'd been on holiday in Scotland.

A man appeared at the door of Layton and Cissie's new house with a message from Layton's men's club, the Carlton: Layton had been reinstated, and his dues were waived for a year. But nobody mentioned his imprisonment or said how sorry they were that such a terrible thing had happened to him.

In a way, Layton wasn't surprised. As a rule, British society people ignored distasteful things. The reactions of the friends Layton cared about most, the men and women of the variety theatre, was what mattered to him. He had worried they would hate him for his deception. The Butcher of the West End working alongside them, pretending to be Frank Owen? Would they feel angry and betrayed?

But he needn't have worried. From the stage doorman up to the theatre manager, all were happy for him. They admired his pluck and smarts. And most of all, the artistes and stagehands liked the fact that a gentleman had become one of them. His hard work and talent for painting the cloths had placed him in high esteem; Layton was considered a good bloke who liked a laugh and a pint. He was already a hero to them because he had saved the theatre from burning down. More selfishly, they all secretly hoped a decent man like him could some-how expose a softer side of Cissie, making life easier for everyone. (Layton would have laughed at such a notion.)

If his variety friends were angry about anything, it was that they had to learn to call him Douglas instead of Frank.

"Couldn't we just keep calling you Frank, ducks? I hate to learn new things," complained Neville. "Just go to court and have your name legally changed to Owen."

The party was in full swing when Cissie made her announcement.

"All right, you all," she shouted. "If you're not too sozzled, let's eat!"

She pulled apart the sliding doors that separated the parlor from the dining room, revealing a long table set with blue-and-white bone china and piled with platters of food. An "ooh" went up from the gathered guests, much like the awed cries of a theatre audience when an acrobat did a difficult trick. But they paused a moment before entering to let Layton and Cissie precede them into the room.

"Are you ready for our Christmas feast, Mrs. Layton?" Layton asked, quirking an eyebrow at his wife.

"Lead the way, Mr. Layton," said Cissie, taking her husband's arm.

A lavish midday meal of roast goose with currants, roast beef, Yorkshire pudding, and brussels sprouts followed. Next to each plate was a Christmas cracker, a paper-covered tube whose end tabs, when pulled, produced a loud crack. Inside was a paper hat and a slip of paper printed with a riddle. Each person read his or hers out, to the glee of the crowd.

"What happens to a yellow hat when it's thrown into the Red Sea?" Layton cried.

"Turn red," shouted Mangogo.

"Gets wet," shouted Ronnie — the correct answer.

Wilding, the manager, who was seated next to Layton, leaned over and said, "I suppose I must put an advert in the papers for a new scenic artist after the New Year? Shame to lose you, old chap."

"Oh, that won't be necessary," Layton said. "In fact, I wanted to talk to you about a new design for the Christmas pantomime."

Pantomimes were the silly musicals, always based on fairy tales, that Brits liked to watch during the holiday season. This one was modeled after "Jack and the Beanstalk," and Layton had a splendid idea for a cloth done at a dramatic perspective: looking up from the bottom of the beanstalk as it extended into the sky.

Wilding's eyes glittered with delight. He took his fork and tapped his champagne glass, sending out a ringing tone into the room. When all eyes were on him, he rose from his seat to make a toast.

"To Douglas Layton, the new head of the scene shop at the Queen's."

It took the guests a fraction of a second to understand the significance of his words. Then everyone, including Cissie, stood to toast Layton. At last, he was truly one of them.

After the truth about the Britannia disaster emerged, Layton had discovered he had no desire to return to architecture — no matter how many new commissions came in. The variety theatre's fascinating, wonderful world of artifice and illusion had won him over entirely. He *wanted* to stay, to be with his new wife in the midst of a dazzling array of entertainments. The singers, comics, acrobats, jugglers, and animal acts gave him so much pleasure. Of course, the artistes were often vain, stupid, vulgar drunks, but they were still more interesting than the boring toffs with whom he'd once spent his days. Though most — with the notable exception of Helen McCoy — had come from the gutter, they were in general better human beings than people who'd been born with all life's advantages.

Besides, in the variety theatre, he no longer had to pretend to be someone he wasn't, to hide behind an invented facade of upper-class gentility. The pressure of being found out was gone; the shame of being a fraud had vanished. He could be a lad from a cottage on Cherry Lane in Dorset once more. He had no regrets. He had found a new life.

Joanie, their cook, came into the dining room, carrying the plum pudding, which she had topped with brandy and set aflame. Everyone cheered.

But as they dug in, a knock sounded at the door.

"Who the hell could that be?" Cissie asked, shouting to be heard above the din.

"I'll see," Layton said, rising from the table.

There on the stoop stood Mrs. Massey, the woman who'd been waiting for him the day of his release from Mulcaster.

"Happy Christmas, Mr. Layton," she said in a halting voice. "I brought you a blood pudding for Christmas, and . . . I . . ." She bent her head contritely. "I wanted to apologize for how I behaved."

Layton smiled. "Nonsense. Only one of

the rocks you threw that day hit me. And it didn't hurt."

The woman furrowed her brow. "No, I meant for pushing ya in front of the tram . . . and sending ya . . . that death letter."

Layton's face clouded over with puzzlement, then he smiled and extended his hand to her.

"Come in, Mrs. Massey," he said. "Come and join us."

ACKNOWLEDGMENTS

Again, I'd like to thank Susan Ginsburg, my literary agent, and Shana Drehs, my editor at Sourcebooks, for their guidance. They're making me a better writer.

ABOUT THE AUTHOR

An architect by profession, **Charles Belfoure** has published several architectural histories, including co-authoring *The Baltimore Rowhouse.* He is a James Marston Fitch Foundation Fellow and has received a grant from the Graham Foundation for research on the architecture of American banks. A graduate of the Pratt Institute and Columbia University, he taught at Pratt as well as Goucher College in Baltimore, Maryland. His area of specialty is historic preservation. He has been a freelance writer for the *Baltimore Sun* and the *New York Times* and is the author of the *New York Times* bestseller *The Paris Architect* as well as *House of Thieves.* Connect with him on Facebook at facebook.com/CharlesBelfoure Author.